John P. McAfee

MW00930113

Printed in the United States of America

Second Edition, March 2014

www.johnpmcafee.com

ISBN-10: 0896723860

ISBN-13: 978-0896723863

1

On Rims of Empty Moons

By

John P. McAfee

Dedicated to:
Duncan Creech a baby who knew love and that was enough.

About the Author

Born in Clovis, New Mexico in 1947, John grew up with his brother on large ranches in West Texas: Ft. Davis, Alpine, and Van Horn. He led a Huck Finn life and was probably the only kid who had an antelope named Governor for a pet. It slept with him every night until it got too large and aggressive and sent to Yellowstone National Park for breeding stock. His father was a ranch foreman and spent much of his life working ranches for absentee owners. His mother was a professional politician in Santa Fe, New Mexico where he spent many summers fishing the Pecos River and attending the Santa Fe Opera. He was educated through high school and junior college at New Mexico Military Institute, and was commissioned as second lieutenant in the Infantry. He served with the 8th Special Forces Group in South America (Ft. Gulick, CZ) and 5th Special Forces Group in Vietnam. He has a BA in English from University of Texas-El Paso and an MA in Education Administration from Western Carolina University, Cullowhee, North Carolina. He is married to the whimsical artist, Elizabeth McAfee, and they have a son, John Lewis McAfee, who along with his wife, Amy, work in the U.S.Citizenship and Immigration Services for Homeland Security. After a long career in teaching, coaching, and administration, He is now a full-time writer.

On Rims of Empty Moons

Part I

"No person who's enthusiastic about wire cutting has anything to fear from fences".
-Winfield McBride, 1875

Texas Sunlight

I remembered the West
as a place where years
turned in the sky and the sun
rolled, a burning wheel
winding the seasons,
spooling my dreams.
I traveled East
and heard War waiting
with death-rattle whispers,
scratched raw under black nights.
I discovered All turns
one way: Truth sharpens
Yucca stakes sitting alone
on rims of empty moons.

Johnny McBride

Bullish on America

My brother was tightening a "suicide knot," one that can't be untied, inside my upturned left palm with a hand-braided hemp rope. Normally, this wouldn't cause suicide. But when that upturned palm is resting on the back of a two-thousand-pound-registered Brangus – half-Brahma, half-Angus – bull – the color of oxygen-rich blood, suicide is a distinct possibility.

"How do I get off, Mac?" I asked, trying to keep the hysteria out of my fourteen-year-old voice, sweat from my face staining the bull's back the deeper red of a torn artery.

"You don't," he said.

I watched in horror as he yanked the knot tighter.

He glanced up at me. "The knot will hold you up long enough for the eight-second ride. We've only got a few days before the rodeo in Van Horn. Got to get you in shape. The Eberhards ain't going to win everything this year."

Van Horn. I was going to die for one traffic light where three roads met, one railroad track, one high school, Chuey's Drive Inn, two truck stops, six motels, and ten gasoline stations. Without the rodeo the town would wither from lack of entertainment: entertainment like watching bats fly out of the Western Auto store on Main Street, or driving to Chuey's for a chili hamburger, then, racing to Lomax's Texaco station at the other end of the town as the chili raced on through you. The chili was known regionally as "the Van Horn two-stop."

Pull out the old encyclopedia and look up "Outback, Australian."

Read the description and fix it in your mind. Take two major highways: U.S. 90 winding up from Del Rio and Interstate 10 coming west from San Antonio; add a paved cow trail traveling south from Carlsbad, New Mexico; and have them all meet in the middle of that picture of the outback.

Where all those roads meet put that one stoplight, motels, etc., and the ten gas stations, all with neon or hand-written signs that say, "Last Chance for the Next Hundred Miles," which was a lie – it was at least one-hundred-and-fifty – but each gas station also had a wrecker for towing, which, for an exorbitant fee, would pick up the stranded travelers and deposit them at the motel owned by the gas station owner.

Think of Van Horn as a landlocked Key West, using fake lights to lure ships onto sandbars in the night, so that while some of the locals were helping people off one side of the sinking ship, others would be taking their belongings out the other side. The ships passing Van Horn were cars, the ocean was the deceptive distances of the Texas desert, and while Van Horn didn't take the belongings from travelers' cars, they did take the green from the car owners' wallets.

The money from those wallets built nice brick homes along the right side of I-10. Those who worked for the nice home owners lived along the left side of I-10 in adobe shacks. Those of us who did not live in town existed on huge tracts of land called ranches that surrounded Van Horn and made up Culberson County. Between the ranches and the town lay Van Horn's attempts at expansion: a failed golf course, now an eighteen-hold sand pit; a screenless drive-in movie whose screen had been carried away by a small sandstorm, and – near our ranch – a small ghost town called Lobo. All the expansion stopped for the same reason expansion stops at the edge of all outbacks: no water.

The lack of water was ironic, considering the whole area was once the bottom of a sea. It had been ocean long enough to make a reef that began at one of the highest points in Texas, El Capitan Peak. From the peak northward, the Great Permian Reef, a mountain range composed of petrified crustaceans, stood like jagged moon peaks. And in the middle of the reef, sat the deepest cave in the United States, Carlsbad Caverns, capturing rainwater that dripped downward through the crustaceans, forever searching for the center of the earth.

South of Van Horn lay Mexico's Sierra Madre, former home to the Apache, who were driven out by Mexican farmers now settled along the Rio Grande. A bad move, since the farming towns west of Van Horn – Sierra Blanca, Fort Hancock, Ysleta, and, at the sharp tip of Texas, El Paso with its sister city, Juarez, across the border in Mexico – began making greater and greater demands on the river, leaving the poor farmers to scratch out a meager existence on a pittance of water.

The dead ocean creatures made the area east of Van Horn as good as East of Eden. Crane, Rankin, Odessa, and Midland sat on top of some of America's richest oil fields. Thus, two thousand miles in any direction, great exciting things were happening. But what was happening in Van Horn was the rodeo, and what was happening on our ranch was that my brother was tying me to a bull.

Mac gave that little insane chuckle he'd developed last year after the football game between the Van Horn Eagles and the Rankin Hornets, in which he'd taken a lick from Carl "Black Death" Smathers, who went on to greater fame the next year in the Texas State Penal System.

Rankin had won 56-0, a close game for Van Horn. There were only fourteen players – scratch that – fourteen *males* stupid enough to play football for our rural high school. That number usually dropped when Rankin came to town. Van Horn would hold its collective breath while counting the number of players gathered before the opening kickoff. If the count was at least eleven, the town's pride would be salvaged, even though our team would always be destroyed.

Rankin was Cibola, one of the mythical Seven Cities of Gold, to Van Horn. Located a hundred and ten miles due east of town, in the middle of the largest oil field, the Permian Basin, Rankin's school district was flush with money, as were the parents within that school district, who worked the oil fields. Their paychecks were steady, and those checks helped establish credit. Hence, they no longer had to depend on the weather to cooperate for raising cattle or crops. In contrast, we, the residents of Van Horn, still lived at the mercy of a vengeful Rain God, and watched yearly as animals and crops grew and prospered or withered and died. *Steady income* was a contradiction in terms to ranchers in our area.

Rankin came into town in a parade of shiny new Hornet buses filled with players and coaches dressed in the latest football gear, and band members with gleaming black-and-gold costumes and bright silver instruments that glittered under the stadium lights.

Waiting for them would be the valiant few, dressed in their ten-year-old gray-and-red "Van Horn Eagles" uniforms. Some of the men in the stands could even point with pride to a particular tear in a jersey.

"Member when that happened? That sumbich was comin' at me and..."

The Rankin buses would be followed by their new pickups gleaming with chrome, and filled with men blaring their horns and willing to bet on the outcome of their sons' athletic prowess. Over the years, Van Horn had evolved its own unique saying when congratulating someone on a recent success:

"You're on the road to Rankin now!"

Think of Van Horn as a wart on the hind end of Texas Big Bend country. All we had were stickers, thorns, and desert. Even our animals had developed stickers and thorns: the horned toad, the scorpion, the desert wasp. Everything seemed to just develop mean – everything but our football team.

And me.

I watched in terror as my brother picked up a large strap from the ground, its buckle making a clinking sound against the side of the pen.

"Mac, the old man hasn't even run a fertility check on this bull yet," I said. "Won't that flank strap do something to its tender parts?"

My brother ignored me and hollered over to his best friend, Harold Don Borden who looked like and was the same color as a big blue heron.

"H. D.! Throw me that stick over there."

Harold Don picked up the stick and came flapping over like the cancerous stork he was. I hated him at the moment. It had been his idea for me to practice in the first place. His Adam's apple looked like a fish struggling to go down, or maybe up. As Van Horn's slowest linebacker, H. D. had taken an unusual number of licks from "Black Death" the same night as my brother, so maybe I was lucky my brother was just a little off, not a full fence post short like Harold Don.

Mac, who'd inherited all of the good qualities of the McBrides – apelike arms, long body, dull wit – was going to use the stick to hand the flank strap under the bull to Harold Don on the other side of the chute so he could cinch it tight around the bull's flanks to make it angry.

A bovine jockstrap.

Size small.

"See, if I rode the bull," said my brother, who had disappeared beneath the beast as he hooked the belt to the stick and handed it to Harold Don underneath, "and got hurt, you couldn't possibly pick me up and get me to the hospital."

H. D. handed the flank strap back to my brother over the rump of the animal. I followed the complete route of the belt with morbid fascination, much like a firing squad victim watches the loading of his executioners' guns. Mac fed the end of the belt through the buckle, and began to tighten the cinch under the belly of the bull by placing his foot against the side of the animal

14

and jerking the strap hard. The animal went straight up and
came down so hard my teeth clacked together.

Through my tongue. The blood blended well with the
maddened bull's coat.

"You see," my brother explained, as he strained to get
the strap one hole tighter, "if I broke my leg or my back, I couldn't
help Dad, and you know how much he depends on me."

I waited for him to carry out the logic a little further: if my
leg or my back broke, Dad would still be in trouble, because he
needed me, too. But deep in my heart I knew I couldn't expect
such a conclusion. I wouldn't even be missed.

Mac's answer was the sound of the belt tightening one
more notch.

"Mac, the bull cost a lot of money. If there is even a
scratch on him when Dad gets back, he'll make us breed with the
cows."

My brother glanced up quickly. "Leave the blonde milk
cow alone."

I tried another attempt at reason. "Why don't you just let
me practice on the cows?"

My brother stared hard at me.

"To ride, Mac," I said, "not to...."

"Oh." He seemed relieved and shook his head. "Hell,
Johnny, you don't weigh as much as a gob of spit. I doubt if the
bull even knows you're on him."

The bull rolled a white eyeball back at me and gave a
low warning bellow. He knew. As I tugged on the knot just to
see if I could get my hand out, there was an uneven motion
beneath me, a promise of tremendous energy just waiting to
stomp the little bug now tightly stuck to the bull – thanks to a
crazy brother and his crazier friend.

I gave one last look around as Harold Don and Mac tried
to figure out how to get two thousand pounds of bellowing-bull-
with-roped-testicles to back down the narrow chute, now blocked
with a steel pipe, which was slowly bending. I'm sure it wasn't
bent when they drove the bull into the narrow holding pen and
shoved the steel pipe behind him to hold him in the chute.

I was thinking: Why did the old man have to leave? Dad
was never around when you really needed him.

"Tell you what, H. D., you whack him over the ass with
the rope, and when he jumps forward, I'll jerk the pipe out."

I could hear H. D. shuffling below, following Mac's
orders.

15

"No problem, Mac," said H.D. spitting out a brown hawker, "But how we gonna' get him to back out?"

"We'll run around front and whack him in the face. He'll back our or lose an eye!"

"Good eyedea." H.D. punctuated his stupid pun with strange gibbering sounds that to him sounded like sophisticated laughter. It fit the nightmare shaping up around me.

The whole time they worked on the bull, I kept thinking this was a lot of trouble to win a small cash prize for bull riding at "Frontier Days," the annual event dreamed up by Lion's Club of Van Horn to kill of excess fourteen-year-old boys like myself the first of each May. Many of the Lions sat on the school board and were aware of the strain on the school district's budget.

I contented myself with the comforting thoughts that the Lion's Club had at least built a rodeo arena with two chutes at one end. I wished for such a chute now.

If it had been a regular rodeo chute, there would have been a large gate opening out into a large arena filled with six or seven inches of nice, soft dirt.

If it had been a rodeo chute.

Instead, the six-foot-tall cedar posts that lined the holding pen looked like sharp toothpicks that shuddered as the bull slammed against them trying to put a gate where it was supposed to be, but wasn't. The massive weight pinioned my legs against the splintery wood, holding me on top in case I had second thoughts.

Which I had.

Second. Third. Fourth.

Usually, the holding pen was where we would drive our sheep during lambing season. We would hold them in the large corral, which was on my right where my brother and Harold Don wanted me and the bull to go. There was a smell of death in the holding pen, which didn't help. A lot of sheep had gone to that great mutton farm in the sky from here.

The idea was to back the bull down the chute to a small opening where three posts had fallen down, and ease the angry animal backwards through the opening, and out into the hard-packed corral, which was littered with deworming cans, broken bottles, one large ominous-looking hitching-post standing in the middle, and, to complete the picture, all the aforementioned stickers, thorns, and stingers.

At the far end of the corral waited a cement water trough full of green, scummy water.

I don't think I had noticed it before.

It hadn't seemed important before.

It hadn't had the potential to kill me before.

The bull gave a loud, sad moan as Harold Don whacked it with the rope to make it move forward so Mac could jerk the pipe out.

Houston, countdown had begun.

As the animal lurched forward, it crashed into the metal gate, which during gentler times, could be pulled upward, allowing sheep to be driven forward, one by one, into a concrete pit filled with creosote and blowfly poison mixed into about six feet of water. The sheep would jump in, get a bath, and jump out. Once the creosote smell got into the concrete of the pool and on the ground, it stayed there forever.

What does creosote smell like?

Find the nearest railroad.

Go to the first wooden crosstie.

Stick your nose on it.

(Watch for trains while doing this.)

That's creosote.

On the other side of the pit we would wait, grabbing the young rams and cutting off their balls, which we threw over the cedar posts to dry, thus explaining the permanent colony of flies in the pen, some of whose scouts were now crawling on my hand.

Unless Dad was there. In that case, the flies got zip.

We stacked the balls neatly in a pile that he would gather and fry for us that night. He'd dip those little suckers in egg and roll them in flour, popping them into the old iron skillet. Eating sheep balls was the old man's idea of fine food.

What did they taste like? Think of a very, very tough chicken gizzard. A chewable tennis ball. A sweet-tasting sponge.

We ate them with smiles when Dad was watching.

Which ought to say something about the family.

We were not emotionally scarred as children. We were just aware of the darker side of possibilities: *one slip-up and someone eats your balls.* It was the unwritten motto on our family crest.

Lifting my tear-starred eyes beyond the holding pen and the large corral, I could see our old adobe house with its rusty tin roof. My eyes were tearing because the bull had pawed up some of the corral's dirt, and the resulting dust haze was irritating them.

"Got it!" my brother said, the sound of a metal pipe sliding across the sides of the chute telling me one part of the mad plan had succeeded.

"Let 'er rip, Mac!" Harold Don shouted, still popping the bull on the ass with the rope like a guy screwing around in the locker room with a wet towel.

I did not have time to contemplate the awesome implications of that statement because Mac, already around front, began slapping the bull in the face with his end of the rope.

Houston, phase two. Clear the tower area, please.

The bull began backing out of the chute. From on top it resembled a large ocean liner leaving its berth, gaining speed as it nears the narrow harbor gate, just as the waves begin to surge.

I was going to be seasick.

I don't think I lost my balance when the bull burst out into the littered corral, splintering a wider gate for its massive bulk. But it was hard to tell.

I remember slamming into the side of the small opening with my head or my butt – that was hard to tell, too – but the sound of cedar posts snapping told me the opening would be larger next time I went through it.

If there was a next time.

I remember seeing Harold Don fly over my head which confused me, since he seemed to still be standing on the earth as he flew by. That was before I realized I was the one upside down on the bull, Harold Don being still right side up. I would have waved, but my hand was slowly elongating under the weight of my body jouncing against the side of the bull. I threw a leg toward the top of the animal, desperate to hook something with my spurs, hopefully the heart or the jugular vein.

Somehow, I slammed back to a proper perspective from on top and experienced the true magnitude of an eight on the Richter scale. The world was whipping up and down except for that cement trough at the far end of the corral.

It was standing still, yet coming closer.

I began to untie the knot.

Which normally couldn't be done.

Normally.

It can be done when adrenaline is mainlining through your bloodstream, through your ear lobes, your nostrils, and any way it can get to the muscles.

18

And I was lucky to get the knot untied.
Ripped apart.
With no broken finger nails.
Torn off, yes, but not broken.
One other of the dark possibilities I was about to discover was that luck is relative.
I was lucky to get the knot untied.
I was not lucky enough to avoid the trough.
I wasn't even lucky enough to hit the green, scummy water.
Oddly enough, the last thought I had as I did a two-and-one-half gainer into the cement of the trough was of Sarah Eberhard. The thought didn't stay long.
And yes, everything went black.

Brotherly Love

I wish I could say that when I came to I was in my brother's arms, looking up into his terribly worried face, drenched by his tears of brotherly concern.

I wish I could say that.

However, this is what I heard:

"Damn it, Mac," – it was Harold Don talking – "you can't bury him this close to the house. The dogs will dig him up or somebody will smell him. Then, we'll be in *real* trouble."

At least my brother's voice *sounded* worried: "H. D., the old man will notice him gone at least sometime during the week. What will I tell him then?"

"Tell him he joined the army."

There was a moment's pause as my brother tried to find the flaw in H. D.'s suggestion.

"Won't work. He's only fourteen."

I heard someone pick up a shovel and begin scooping dirt. I couldn't understand why I could just hear these things and not see them, since my eyes were open.

There are times when even a little brother needs to speak out.

I sat straight up, brushed something which flapped in front of my eyes back over my head where it belonged, looked at my brother, and said, "I'm alive, butthole! Get me to a doctor!"

And promptly passed out again when I realized that a good portion of my scalp was trying to quit its job of covering the skull and had again flapped in front of my eyes.

Sarah was still there in the darkness. She had always been in my thoughts, so it wasn't surprising to find her in the scrambled wires of a damaged brain. We swirled together in the fog. I knew Sarah wouldn't let me die.

She had been there since we first met on horseback at the age of ten. She on her side of the fence and I on mine. Aware of me first, she halted her horse as I rode towards her. I tried to intimidate her by giving a McBride stare, but soon lowered my eyes. There wasn't a lot of beauty in my life so when it came along, it was hard to look at.

Even at ten, she was a beauty. There was dignity and confidence in the way Sarah sat a saddle. Her legs, already much longer than mine, guided the horse with skill. Her hands, softer than mine, held the reins with a firmness that spoke of quiet control. Her gaze, directed at me, was framed by strawberry blonde hair that belonged to the desert sun. Her smile, growing wider at my discomfort in discovering a sudden inability to say anything, devastated me.

I tried to ride by her on my side of the fence, but she turned her horse and followed along, keeping pace, saying nothing. Surprisingly, I liked that. Silence was common and familiar on a ranch. The sad-sweet smell of catclaw blossoms dotted the air, and Sarah would always belong with that scent in my mind. If I had missed her, would my life have been different; the scars, visible and invisible, as numerous? But everything is of thorns, stickers, and stings in the desert, even love.

Over the next three years, we met almost daily. Together, we learned to find the Apache *tinajas* – small, rock cisterns filled with scarce rainwater. We discovered narrow canyons that led to the *tinajas* and pretended we were Lipan Apaches spying on the water below for the first time. Like all children, we kept our secret explorations to ourselves, rediscovering the secret haunts of the Apache and Mexican children who came before us.

Lying on our stomachs above the small pools, we watched the desert animals come to drink: comic ringtails, nervous roadrunners, noisy javelinas, cautious mule deer, and once, just once, a proud mountain lion.

For four years, we learned the desert's moods together. We laughed quietly, watching a dung beetle – Sarah called them "doodlebugs" – struggling with a round ball torn from the droppings of our horses, trying to get it into a too-small hole. Near one *tinaja* we saw a life and death struggle between a tarantula and a tarantula wasp, as the wasp fought to lay her eggs in the living tarantula. When the eggs hatched, they'd have fresh spider ready to eat. Sometimes there was no smile to the desert.

When we grew away from childhood to more distant stirrings, we didn't smile as often.

On Sarah's fourteenth birthday, we sat near our favorite *tinaja* on a rock etched with Indian pictographs and, more recently, with our names, also.

"It doesn't seem fair," Sarah said. "Why does one thing have to suffer so another can live?"

She had rolled over on her back, cupping her hands behind her head, her beautiful hair flowing and rich in the sun. It was one of the finest things I knew in my life. Her friendship was the other. Over the years since our first meeting, her body had grown to fit the long slender legs that always seemed to be her trademark.

But there radiated now a hidden warmth in her, hot as the desert sun. The heat caused even longer silences between us, as if she was waiting for me to add just the right words to the heat-filled moments. It was like trying to put together one of those big jigsaw puzzles without the picture on the box to help.

"Have you ever seen horses make love?" she asked lazily one day.

"Sure," I answered, "it happens all the time."

"You ever notice how the mare, when the stud gets off of her, stands there quivering?"

"Yeah?" I answered, tossing a rock into the *tinaja*, uncomfortable but not sure why.

She rolled over on the rock and looked at me. "Why is that? Does she sometimes quiver at night, weeks later, still feeling the power of what happened?"

"Hell, I don't know, Sarah. Why are you asking me?"

She reached out and touched me on my arm. I almost jumped off the rock at her touch.

"Sometimes at night, I think about doing things horses do."

I tried to change the subject. "See that hills, the one beyond our house?"

She looked at me for a moment, then turned to look from our perch down towards the valley where our ranch house was. Just beyond it was a small rocky knob of a hill.

"Yes. What about it?" Her voice sounded heavy, different.

"You can pick up arrowheads and cavalry shell casings all over it."

"Really?"

"Some soldiers from Fort Davis were looking for Apaches and were riding down there in the valley. The Apaches saw them and attacked."

She looked around. "Maybe they saw them from here."

"Maybe," I answered, "anyway, they were pretty mad."

"Why was that?"

"We took away their land. So they attacked. The soldiers chose to defend that hill. They did a pretty good job of it until the water began to run out.

"The Apaches sat out of rifle range, sending runners, probably to where we are now, for water."

"For the soldiers?"

"For themselves. The soldiers went crazy 'cause they had no water."

"They probably missed their women, too," Sarah rolled lazily to her side, and our legs touched. I desperately wished she would stay off that subject.

"They say you could hear the soldiers scream for water until they went crazy." My voice sounded strained, my throat as dry as the soldiers'.

"Did they all die of thirst?" Her hand brushed mine.

"Some shot themselves or their fellow soldiers. My brother and I found a piece of skull up there once with a bullet hole in it. He's got it in his room. Wanna see it?"

"Your brother is weird."

"Don't remind me."

She moved closer. "Sure. I'll go into your brother's bedroom with you. If he's not there."

I stood up, my thoughts darting as crazily as the startled wasps that flew away from the *tinaja*.

My voice blurted out something, anything, to give me time to find out why my heart was racing so much.

"At night, when the wind blows, I've heard the soldiers scream."

Sarah shivered, holding her hand up, so I could pull her up beside me.

"Let's go down there and spend the night." She kissed me. "You can protect me from the ghosts."

Hell, yes, I could.

We went down there, and I snuck some cold milk and fresh biscuits from the house while Sarah waited for me with the horses. Later, we sat alone on the hill, chewing the biscuits in the gathering darkness, and I was glad for her close warmth. The desert is always cold at night, but I was sweating from the effort of putting the jigsaw puzzle of me and Sarah together.

"What was that?" Sarah clung tighter to me.

It was the bleat of a terror-stricken animal. For a moment I thought the sound had come from me.

"Probably a rabbit getting caught by a coyote," I told her, pulling her tighter to me. She softened in my arms.

The scream came again. She stiffened in my arms. So much for first encounters. I turned my head.

24

"It sounds like it's over by Tudisishnhagoitsaye."

Sarah laughed. "You mean your springs – 'Where Buffalo Shit.' You McBrides are the only ones who call it by the old Indian name. Van Horn has called it Where Buffalo Shit for as long as I can remember."

I gritted my teeth. "That's not what the Apache name means. That's why my family uses the correct Apache term." It was a sore subject, rarely brought up around Dad.

I could feel her smile in the darkness. "C'mon, tell me. What does the name mean, really?"

"Black water, odor-rising, and smelt above." I mumbled, feeling my face burn. I was grateful for the darkness.

The screams came again, silencing her laughter.

"Come on," I said, pulling her to her feet, "that could be a calf or a lamb trapped in the mud."

"What if we fall in?" Sarah followed me reluctantly.

"We'll smell the damn place before we get to the mud," I said over my shoulder, "just watch your step!"

"Is that why it got that name, because it stinks so bad?"

"Yes," I lied, knowing the real reason was that drinking the water gave *all* animals the squirts. The water was so bad not even the dying soldiers tried to get to it. At least no bodies were found between the hill and Tudisishn. I didn't know about the Apaches.

The rotten-egg smell hit us both at the same time. No, not even the Apaches would drink that water.

"I think I'm going to vomit," said Sarah. "Smells like fresh crap to me."

"Yeah, it smells pretty bad tonight."

Sarah grabbed my arm and pointed. "Look out there in the mud."

There in the darkness, barely visible, was an antelope trapped in the deep mud that surrounded the stinking water. There was something struggling near her rear haunches.

Sarah's grip tightened on my arm. "She's having a baby. It's trying to get out of her!"

The mother quit struggling until the baby came out. Trying to follow the instinct of all mothers to clean their young, she turned to lick the little one. Her legs made small sucking sounds as she would lift one out trying to reach back, only to have the others sink deeper. We watched as she sank to her belly, while the baby, still trapped by the afterbirth, lay on top of the mud, shivering. The mother wanted to reach the bloody sack, but turning her head to lick, only succeeded in making her body sink deeper. Soon her head could not turn back. It lay at a right angle to her body, her nostrils snorting against the mud as she gazed at her baby, unable to get to it, trapped as much by her instinct as the mud.

Imminent death made her panic. She screamed and began a frenzied attempt to crawl from the mud, bent only on survival. The head whipped back and forth, plowing a muddy furrow.

Sarah punched my arm. "Do something."

I stared at the sinking animal. "What?"

"Get the baby. Please get the baby." She whispered, "I'll love you forever if you'll just get the baby."

Giving Sarah my boots, I began wading towards the little antelope, feeling the mud ooze between my toes and grip my feet. Fifty yards. Twenty-five. Ten. The rotten smell lived permanently in my nose. Five. Surprisingly, the mud was warm, not cold. Something crunched beneath my feet, throwing me off balance. I put my hand in the slime to push myself back up, but almost succeeded in trapping one arm. I began to struggle in earnest watching the head of the mother in front of me slowly disappear.

Four yards. I stretched to reach the little fawn, now staggering to its feet. Three. As I reached to touch the little animal, I went too far. Suddenly, the mud was to my waist, and I had a sticky-wet baby antelope in my arms. The flickering ears, all that was left of the mother, slowly sank in front of me.

"Johnny! Don't let go of the baby!" Sarah's scream matched that of the dead mother.

She had nothing to worry about. The little body was keeping the rest of me from going under.

"Flatten out." Her voice sounded lower.

It spoke again. "Listen, you little SOB, if you think I'm coming out there to get you, you're crazy!"

Definitely lower.

"I'll sink!" My voice sounded as weak as the bleating of the little fawn in my arms.

"You'll die if you don't flatten out." It was the voice of a man. My Dad had come looking for me!

"Johnny, do what Daddy says."

Well, someone's dad had.

Hide Eberhard had organized a search party for his daughter. She wouldn't have to tell him about us spending the night on the little hill behind our house. Now he knew. For a moment I was glad to be sinking. Hide was a big, barrel-chested man of German ancestry with a mixture of Viking anger and the Alamo deep in his blood – a terrible combination when aroused. My being with his daughter in the middle of the night could possibly irritate him some.

Survival took over. I flattened out on my back and quit sinking, the baby antelope content to rest on my chest. Something oozed into my ear. I couldn't let go of the fawn to dig it out.

"Now what?" I was not ashamed to scream the question.

"Swim towards me." Rolling over, I began to make swimming motions with one arm, holding the dripping antelope in the other, and was surprised to find myself slowly moving back to where Sarah, her father, and a couple of ranch hands stood with lanterns in their hands, the light illuminating the little bugs between me and them, a few animal skeletons, and something large, gray, slimy, and slithering between them.

I didn't want to see what was in the "swimming pool" with me.

"Turn those lights away!"

The lights went out and I struggled back to shore. I stood there, smelling of rotten eggs, the oozing mud making gross plopping noises at my feet. The little antelope stirred in my arms nuzzling for food. Hide held the lamp up so he could see me.

"God, what a mess. We tried to get your old man, but he was too drunk to wake up. We came on our own."

"Thanks, Mr. Eberhard."

"I ought to kick your McBride butt for almost killing my daughter!"

"Daddy!"

"Hell, honey, you could have fallen in!"

"But…" She shrugged her shoulders at me. "Can I at least have the antelope?"

"Happy Birthday," I said and handed her the antelope.

"Sure, darling. That animal is the least Johnny here can do for almost getting you hurt. Now, take the antelope and get in the pickup. I need to talk to this young man for a moment."

Hide put a hand on my shoulder and gripped hard to keep me from running.

He was no dummy.

When she reached the truck, he turned his large frame towards me. "If I ever hear of you getting together with her again, I'll throw you back in that mud myself, and, while I'm at it, your brother and your murdering father, too!"

Well, I agreed with two of his three choices.

It wasn't a long ride home that night – actually, I walked since my horse wouldn't let get close to it – but I don't know what stunk worse – me or the thought of never seeing Sarah again.

In the evenings that followed, I'd saddle my horse, ride to the fence separating our two worlds, and wait until it got too dark to see. I didn't know what I would say if she had shown up. But the thought of seeing her seemed to make my life bearable. Without her, I felt the emptiness around me.

The only other time I felt that way was when Mama died.

Helping Your Neighbor

Now would be a good time to tell the story behind the Eberhards and the McBrides. It'll make it easier to understand why Sarah and I were forbidden to be friends.

It began with Colonel Sam Colby, a tall, handsome Georgia banker, who had the good sense to fight for the North, because, he reasoned, anyone stupid enough to start a war with all the steel and iron factories located in the enemy's territory didn't deserve his time and loyalty.

He looked at the railroad tracks in his home state of Georgia and asked his neighbors, "Where do these things go?"

"North," they replied.

"What for?" he asked.

"To bring steel, guns, wheels, ammunition, and more tracks so the trains can expand westward," they explained patiently.

"And you want to fight these people?" he snickered.

"The honor of the South, suh, is at stake!" said his neighbors, shaking their fists in anger as he loaded up his family into a wagon specially built for him in Pennsylvania, its wheels made to fit on railroad tracks, and recently shipped to him on the very railroad where his neighbors now stood watching his retreating form.

"You people have lost your minds," were the last words they could hear as he disappeared north, his slaves pumping on the iron handles to take the wagon north to their freedom.

After the war – as he had helped destroy the economy of his own state and, by association, his own neighbors – it would have been difficult to return and begin again. They would have noticed the wealth he had accumulated; for in the meantime, he had made a lot of Yankee dollars.

His ex-neighbors used their Confederate money for toilet paper.

So Sam Colby came West looking for good rangeland, and found it near the western edge of the Davis Mountains, north of the Big Bend in Texas, at a place called Needle Peak.

Needle Peak was a large volcanic plug sticking straight up into the sky, all alone, abandoned by its volcano, which had long since been eroded by the violent winds of the desert. Little hints, such as hot springs, reminded the Indians of the terrible giant who lay wounded beneath the plug shaped like a spear point. It was a holy place to them. From any vantage point in the valley, the Apaches could see the giant spearhead stuck into the earth's heart by an angry spirit.

Like most Indian holy places, it was desired by the white man, specifically, in this case, by Sam Colby. Because it jutted so high into the sky, the mountain caught the rare moisture from the sparse clouds that dotted the West Texas horizon, small white umbrellas stretching into the dry, tawny distance, their shadows bringing but a moment's respite from the relentless heat. Only Needle Peak had running water fed by springs, and good grama grasses for cattle.

Colonel Sam was pragmatic enough to beat his rivals to Needle Peak first, and tough enough to kill the Indians who were already there. He was fresh from the Civil War, so killing was natural. He wrote about what he'd found, and former soldiers of his acquaintance followed. The soldiers followed because Sam Colby had a knack for making money. A man could get fat off the crumbs Colby let fall from his table.

Hearing the rumors of where Colby had settled, one Georgia neighbor followed, too. That neighbor was Winfield Roy McBride, a dirt farmer content with his hardscrabble lot until the Civil War rescued him and made him a sniper for Jeb Stuart's small band of Southern guerrillas. After the war, Winfield ended up in jail for robbing the neighborhood bank. But Winfield was no Jesse James; the bank he robbed held only Confederate dollars.

Always ones to hold a grudge, Colby's southern neighbors pitched in and hired my ancestor to ride out to Texas and kill Colby. They considered it a bargain to achieve two goals with one payment: they got rid of McBride by sending him after Colby. Fifteen dollars in silver was a bargain price. As a goodwill gesture in parting, they let McBride keep the bank's Confederate dollars, which was a boon to him, since he suffered from chronic diarrhea.

Halfway out of Georgia, riding a horse much slower than Colby's, Winfield used up his neighbors' silver drinking and whoring, and found himself destitute and the job unfinished.

"Hell," he said to himself, "I'm so deep into this pond, it's as hard to go back and ask for more money from people who don't have any and might be a little mad I haven't fulfilled my contract, as it is to go on and starve."

Fortunately, he met a few fellow travelers, who made the mistake of trusting him at cards, and after taking their money and eating their food, he was soon feeling better. Spirits lifted, he continued on his way to kill the traitorous Colonel Colby.

Meanwhile, Sam Colby knew what he had. He dammed up the streams and made a series of small lakes – stock tanks – which kept his cattle and horses healthy during droughts, but caused the few buffalo, antelope, and mule deer that dotted the valley below Needle Peak to die gradually of thirst, since their streams no longer ran with any regularity.

The clans of Apaches that lived in the shadow of Needle Peak watched the buffalo leave and felt their bellies growl.

"That asshole," they said to each other (this is loosely translated), "we're going to kick butt."

And they tried. From fifty yards on in, the Apache is the deadliest fighter on earth. Unfortunately, a .44 caliber Henry has an effective range of over a hundred yards, and, with it, even the dumbest cowboy on earth could create havoc with the best laid plans of Apache attack.

The Apaches called the .44 Henry the "Spirit Rifle," since it often settled for them the question: "Is there life after death?"

There was only one other area in the Van Horn basin, which is what the valley surrounding Needle Peak was called, that had permanent water – the place called Tudisishnhagoitsaye. Drinking the water affected the buffalo in such a way as to give the place its name, and the constant replenishing of dried buffalo chips, which the Apaches used as fuel for their fires, made the area an important stop for the Lipan and Mescaleros traveling to their winter hunting grounds in the Sierra Madre, fifty miles due south of the popular watering hole.

Because it never rained at Tudisishn, where the water came from was a mystery to the Apache. The basin was southwest of Needle Peak and downhill, so it was probably some ancient volcanic fissure that, like a Roman aqueduct, funneled water from under Needle Peak to Tudisishn.

The Apache legend claimed that the water was really the blood from the earth's body pierced by a giant's spear, Needle Peak. The legend also said that it would be at this water where the end of the world would be decided by two men, one Apache, the other a white man, fighting over the last water on earth. Both men would die, and then each would reborn as his enemy, the Apache as a white man and vice versa. It was the only way either could ultimately understand the other, the legend concluded.

Tudisishn was also the first fresh water spring weary travelers came upon after crossing the Rio Grande from Mexico, a distance of about fifty miles. The taste of the water prepared them for the *Jornada del Muerto*, the Dead Man's Journey, that awaited them. For many it was their last taste of water, rotten as it was.

Even Colby wasn't crazy enough to try to chase away the Apaches who camped and used the sump hole. There were too many of them. But Winfield Roy McBride, sniper extraordinaire, who had finally made it to West Texas and was extremely thirsty, had a plan.

He needed water to drink before he killed Colby.

Tudisishn had water.

He was going to get a drink.

Picking off one Indian a day from the mountains overlooking the valley, and arranging to leave proof that someone from Sam Colby's outfit had done the shooting – a stolen hat, an old branding iron – my ancestor was able to direct the Indians' wrath towards Colby while gradually laying claim to Tudisishn. The Apaches swore clan revenge on his ranch and stock, a promise all males within the clan of the dead person were bound to honor. Soon, since there were many deaths, there were many clans swearing revenge against Colby.

Naturally, there was some concern and hard feelings on Colby's part. It was like killing wasps. Just when one Apache nest would dry up, more would come swarming. For a long time Colby couldn't figure out what was going on. There were plenty of Indian holy places, and he'd only taken one. Why should the Apaches pick on just him?

Then, some of his cowboys, while checking some butchered cattle, which they assumed were killed and eaten by hungry Apaches, found a dead Indian. The hole in him didn't say ".44 caliber Henry," the weapon of choice of most cowboys in the area. Instead, it said ".51 caliber Baker," the weapon of choice of Civil War snipers. Only one man had been seen with a Baker in the area: that new guy, the one who stayed up in the hills…Winfield Roy McBride. Colby swore his own clan revenge.

Unfortunately, it was too late for Colby to stop McBride. Apache mothers didn't raise fools. If some idiot waned Tudisishn that bad, the Apaches knew of other springs deeper south in the Sierra Madre. They left, and McBride settled in, picking up a squat, half-Lipan, half-Mexican woman named Angry She Throws Sticks, left behind in the Apaches' haste to leave. He

32

would later conclude it was a masterful stroke of revenge on the Lipans' part. He did, however, shorten her name to Angie. They had one child.

She was as mean as he was, a tough companion and a tougher cook, but she knew the country and its ways. What she stirred in him probably wasn't love, but as close as he was ever going to get to it. What he stirred in her, she never said.

Winfield still planned to kill Colby, but he decided he'd make him sweat a little first. Besides, he could bide his time now that he had enough drinking water to survive.

In clan retaliation Colby sent cowboys to kill McBride. But good cowboys were hard to find, and, when his work force started to disappear, one cowboy sniped down at a time, Colby opted to let McBride have his dirty little lake.

The Colonel was a patient man and could afford to wait for the opportunity to kill McBride. While he waited, his cattle prospered under the shadow of Needle Peak and, with the profits, he began buying the land around McBride's spread. In a way, his hatred of Winfield was what enabled Colonel Sam to become an even greater success.

Once he'd surrounded McBride's small spread, Colby began to string barbed wire. But as his herds grew, so did McBride's. The ability to steal horses and cattle was greatly admired among the Apaches, and no doubt Angie had plenty of reason to be proud of Winfield on that score.

Many times an irate mob, stirred by Colby's accurate accusations of rustling, had ridden towards Tudisishn with the express notion of hanging McBride, if a tree could be found within a hundred-or-so-mile radius. (Stoning would have been a better alternative. Rocks were plentiful in West Texas.)

But sniper fire caused the angry mob to lose interest, one mob member at a time. Those remaining alive decided it was better to just let old man Colby handle his own damn problems. An armed sniper hidden in the surrounding mountains just made the task of hanging McBride much too hard.

Undaunted, Colby continued encircling the McBride land with barbed wire. Crouching there in the evening as the sun went down, he chuckled to his men as they finished the day's wire stapling. "I feel like a warden, and McBride is my prisoner, watching his prison being built around him."

The men said nothing.

They were too busy scanning the surrounding hills for the warning puff of smoke from a rifle.

It was hard to find good wire men. The hazards of stringing wire that close to McBride had resulted in large holes where some lungs used to be. Still, men were desperate for work after the Civil War, and the job of fencing McBride in was done.

And undone.

Several times a year.

The fact that undoing the fencing coincided with McBride's quarterly trips into Van Horn for supplies and a week's drunk was not lost on Colonel Colby. But when Colby went to Sheriff Skinner, who'd once been Colby's foreman, demanding that something be done about it, he was told, "I wouldn't mess with that man if he was Eve and I was Adam!"

Skinner had strung wire for Colby.

And was missing an arm to show for it.

So Colonel Colby bought stronger wire, McBride bought stronger wire cutters, and the game continued escalating until the sudden "blue norther" of Christmas, nineteen-ought-five, which brought a truce between the two of them.

They died.

Frozen, more specifically.

They were found within thirty yards of each other. Colonel Colby had a bale of wire in one hand and a hammer in the other. McBride had a pair of wire cutters and the old .51 caliber Baker in his hands.

Colby bequeathed four-hundred-and-ninety-seven thousand acres to his son, John Nathan Colby, Jr.

Winfield Roy McBride passed on Tudisishnhagoitsaye and his .51 caliber Baker to Winfield Roy McBride-Angry She Throws Sticks, Jr., my grandfather. We never did know what happened to Great-Grandma Angie. She dropped out of the picture after the last Apache raid into Culbertson County. Family legend had her following tracks of the stolen cattle into Mexico, never to return. Truth was she saw her chance to leave Winfield Roy Sr. and took it.

John Nathan Colby, Jr., tall, thin, and arrogant, did everything he could to see the McBride bloodline didn't stretch any further. He made sure Colby money found its way into the political process of Culbertson County, the little Texas county about the size of Massachusetts, where Van Horn, Needle Peak, and Tudisishn were located.

Naturally, that meant trouble for Winfield McBride, Jr. He was always being stopped on the highway for driving infractions by the local constabularies, former employees of old man Colby. He didn't have a license to drive, but he always said Van Horn had no right to tell him to get one. This small difference of viewpoint had resulted in several arrests.

But Granddad was a resourceful man. With a shrewd eye for horses, he began raising good pack horses and horses bred for distance and strength. And he rode them to town instead of driving, a distance of about thirty miles, one way. He had inherited his dad's old wire cutters and used them well.

"Can't arrest me for riding a horse to town too fast," he'd yell to anyone who wanted to know.

This next part I'm definite about, since we had the old *Life* magazines wrapped up in Saran Wrap and, every now and then, usually on special days, we'd get them out and read them aloud. *Life* had written a human interest story on Granddad, complete with pictures of this "cowboy throwback," as the caption under the photograph so aptly put it. We always giggled at the part about how he was the only man in the United States with two arrests for riding a horse drunk.

"Hard to carry a case of beer home on horseback, so I was just making the load lighter," he was quoted as saying.

Life did not quote what Granddad said about the Colby-backed sheriff who arrested him the two times for DUI – the same sheriff who is still missing and presumed dead. Dad always frowned when he read that part of the article.

The article did mention how famous our horses were. The endurance-class horses Granddaddy developed were in high demand. Since he was the only one who dared steal horses from the Mexicans and cross them with the thoroughbreds and quarter horses he stole from Colby, he had the market cornered.

Unfortunately, much of our breeding stock would wander back to Colby land, stepping over wire that had been cut during Granddad's drunken forays into town, and Colby, never missing a chance to increase his ever-growing fortune, would use our Mexican studs to impregnate his mares, thus increasing the value of Colby horses.

At least the rivalry gave us another family holiday. Some people celebrate the Fourth of July and Christmas.

Naturally, as Americans, we celebrated those, too.

We also celebrated "McBride Wire Day," the day when a young male in the family was finally strong enough to cut Colby wire with a pair of wire cutters without any help. It was a rite of passage into McBride's manhood. The same wire cutters pried from old Winfield McBride's frozen hand were always used. The oldest in the family always kept them well-oiled. There were repeated investigations of Colby wire being cut, but some secrets are always passed along in a family.

When World War Two broke out, John Nathan Colby, Jr. immediately volunteered, but was told by the draft board, which he handpicked and financed, that he would be more valuable here raising cattle for our boys "over there."

"Darn shame. I really wanted to go," said John Nathan as he shook hands with each of the draft board members, whose sons also were exempt. Each board member found a small memento of Colby's gratitude in their palms after shaking.

Seeing a chance to finally make some money, Granddad Winfield bid on a contract to sell pack horses to the Army supply depot located east of Van Horn in a small town called Marfa. The contract was awarded to him and things began to look up.

So did my grandfather.

Things tended to fall on McBrides whenever they felt fortunate.

Three months into the war, the army mechanized. The Marfa army base became an air base, and horses were no longer needed except as practice targets.

Two months later, my grandfather was drafted. Some said at John Nathan's request; others said it was to get a McBride shooting at other nationalities instead of Americans. Whichever way it was, he left my father in charge of the ranch at sixteen. With no one to tell him otherwise, Dad married an Irish beautician in Van Horn named Helen O'Connell when he was eighteen. She was twenty-seven. By the time he was twenty-seven, my brother, Mac, and me, had come along.

Between the births of the newest McBrides, Granddad, who I never knew except by reputation and the article in *Life* magazine, was killed on some island called Iwo Jima. He had been stringing concertina wire on a defensive perimeter when he was attacked by a Japanese patrol. Some of his buddies wrote Dad said after the ammunition ran out, Granddad had gone down using his wire cutters like a club.

"He was a natural wire cutter and a fine killer," his commanding officer had written in a letter home, which he sent along with a statement of past due charges from the NCO Club at his last posting. "He just seemed at home cutting Jap wire."

The night the commanding officer's letter arrived, people around Van Horn said you could hear the pinging of Colby wire being cut until daybreak. We found Dad the next morning, staring at the sunrise, hands in his pockets, not trying to stop the tears. It was the first of two times I ever saw him cry.

He changed after that. He began beating us, my brother and me. Since there were no families around with whom to compare our lot in life, we just assumed we led a normal childhood. We treated Dad like you would a horse when you're shoeing him: we stayed out of his way when he was kicking.

One of the few things that cheered him up, besides beating his children, was the news of John Nathan Colby, Jr.'s death.

Colby died in bed after giving Hide Eberhard and his only child, Barbara Anne, his blessing. She was already pregnant, so it was like shutting the barn door after the cows had gotten out. Hide came from an ancient stock of well-hung Germans, the current edition of which owned the only grocery store in Van Horn.

According to town gossip, Old Man Colby's last words, whispered in Hide's ear, were:

"Hide, you're a sonofabitch for getting Barbara Anne pregnant. How you did it, I don't know, since I've had her watched like a hawk. Don't know how you got around all my eyes in town, but you did. It shows you're devious, so I die leaving my ranch in good hands."

"What did he say, Hide?" asked Barbara Anne with tear-filled eyes.

"That he loved us all," said Hide, smiling benevolently down on his beloved meal ticket.

Hide's parents were never married, but lived together so long, they had been awarded the license in the town's eyes. Hide's dad worked him hard and taught him the value of a dollar. His mother taught him the dollars would never be his. Her constant arguments with his Dad over finances only made Hide's determination to achieve riches that much stronger. Fortunately for him, the only asset Hide had – the one that was genetic – came to the attention of Barbara Anne at about the same time it came to the attention of several other women in Van Horn. Being as competitive as her father, Barbara got Hide to marry her first.

Actually, he improved the Colby breed. He was well liked, civic-minded, and extremely kind to most folks. He was the kind of man who could make you smile as he cheated you out of your family savings, usually in the name of progress. He would draw others in on his schemes, sharing his successes, and making sure blame fell on others for his few failures. For example, he set up the Van Horn Christmas Disadvantaged Toddler Program, which had Santa Claus distribute packages to the more unfortunate Mexican and white children in the town, including the McBride brothers, naturally.

In school each year, just before the Christmas holidays, we used to be trotted as a group to the gymnasium where we were supposed to run gleefully to our individual "squares," marked with Santa tape and rip into the packages. Mac and I stood there, refusing to run. We wouldn't even walk to our packages. Dad had told us what he'd do to us if we ever came home with a toy bought by Hide Eberhard.

Maybe it was the packaging itself that dampened our enthusiasm.

It was always personalized Christmas paper, with cows, and horses, and the Colby/Eberhard brand covering every package.

Advertising.

There was obviously no Santa Claus.

Just Hide Eberhard.

We would be paddled by the embarrassed school principal, told we were ungrateful white trash, and sent back to our classrooms to wait.

But eventually the McBrides did get a good Christmas present.

Oil was found.

Naturally, it was found on Colby/Eberhard land – God is pretty consistent in his jokes – but the shortest shot from the oil fields to the highway linking Van Horn to Marfa to San Antonio to the Houston refineries was right across McBride land. Otherwise, you had to go around the whole mountain range on the Eberhard side of the valley adding about fifty miles of road to the trip.

God also is consistent with the little twists on his jokes that keep them fresh. Hide Eberhard asked for access rights.

Dad said, "No."

Under Eberhard pressure, the county tax man tried to reevaluate our property taxes upwards to force a foreclosure.

Didn't work. The state tax assessor took a look at Tudisishn and decreased our taxes by twenty percent.

The county then tried to condemn the land, but a state judge said the land should have been condemned when we settled there back in the 1800s.

"They've survived there three generations," he said in his ruling, "that's got to be worth something."

So Hide Eberhard agreed to build a road across McBride land and pay a monthly fee for the privilege of using the road he'd just paid to have built.

It was one of the few things that ever made Dad smile.

When we were little, the oil trucks would roar by late at night scaring our brother and me. We'd go crying to Dad, and he'd beat the hell out of us.

"Listen, you little turds," he'd say, "that ain't a monster out there. That noise you hear is money."

I've been scared of money ever since.

A Religious Experience

My idea of heaven would be a beautiful woman stroking my injured forehead with a cool washcloth.

When I opened my eyes, Barbara Anne Eberhard was stroking my forehead with a cool washcloth.

Did the Eberhards own heaven, too?

Dazed, I looked around and saw more things in one bedroom than in my whole house. I was dead. That was the only explanation. Otherwise, what was I doing in the Eberhard mansion? Dad always said it would be over his dead body before a McBride would visit an Eberhard, and I already knew Hide felt the same way. I looked about anxiously for him.

I started mumbling the Lord's Prayer – what I could remember of it: "Our Father, who something in Heaven, something, something else…"

"Settle down." Barbara Anne's voice was soothing. "You're not dead. Your brother brought you here because we have a phone that works."

She was right about that. Ours was a crank-type that only worked during thunderstorms. At least it rang every time lightning hit the wires. My brother was the only one stupid enough to answer.

Barbara Anne continued working on my forehead. It felt great.

"I made Hide fly you to Alpine, and Doctor Coates stitched your head. He asked that you stay in bed a week until the swelling around the stitches goes down. So you've been with us for two days now."

"What about Dad?" I asked.

"I talked to him on the phone and just told him you needed a woman's touch and that was all there was to it."

Barbara Anne's hand on my forehead focused my attention on her. She took the washcloth and dipped it into a little rose water basin next to the bed. I watched that beautiful hand with its manicured red nails squeeze the excess water out of the cloth.

Pure sex.

My fantasy was short-lived.

"If his family had any money, he'd stay in the damn hospital where he belongs!"

The girl in the doorway was a harder, thinner version of her mother.

Her short, light brown, nearly blonde, hair tried hard to bring out beauty in her face. Kay Eberhard was almost pretty, but something in her eyes was as hard as concrete. She was barefoot and sipping a Dr. Pepper, which is what all eighteen-year-old girls in Texas did for enjoyment. She was the best athlete Van Horn ever produced, holding all the basketball scoring records. Kay had gotten a scholarship to Southern Methodist University in Dallas, but immediately lost it by trying to seduce her female coach and the Dean of Men. She was kinky like that.

I tried to look behind her to see if Sarah was there.

Kay's voice snapped me back to reality.

"Mother! I asked you a question. What the hell is a McBride doing here?"

Barbara Anne placed the washcloth gently on my forehead.

"Now, Kay, the McBrides are our neighbors. This is the Christian thing to do."

I watched her lean over me to straighten the quilt I had pulled tightly around my neck. I felt the considerable weight of her chest when she did this. I pulled the covers tighter around my neck as my erection began to show, something that had started earlier this year with uncomfortable and embarrassing regularity. I was beginning to understand the puzzle Sarah wanted me to finish there on the hill where the soldiers died.

Despite the erection, or, because of it, I loved all Christians at that moment.

"Mother. It's not safe to be alone with a McBride if you're a woman!"

I closed my eyes and waited.

Kay was going to repeat something I had heard many times before.

I wished I could close my ears, too.

But Van Horn would just force them open again to pour in the cruel gossip that always springs up in little towns when one of life's unexplainable tragedies happens to one of its citizens. They nurture the incident, feed it, water it, and each year it bears more fruit to make their dull lives more interesting.

Barbara Anne took the washcloth from my head, folded it, and placed it on the table.

"Kay, what happened at the McBrides' is over and done. Don't open old wounds. If you can't act like a lady, then leave."

"Hell, I did that a year ago. I'm just back because you asked me to."

Barbara Anne frowned at her daughter and shook her head. Since she was a tall lady, I had to tilt my head back to see everything. That movement hurt and I gave a little groan.

"See? You've upset him. Let's go outside and straighten some things out about how we treat our guests in our home."

"Can't we at least lock the door?" Kay whispered as she followed Barbara Anne out the door.

"We haven't finished our conversation, young lady!"

Kay slammed the door behind her. I could hear their muffled voices rise and fall in argument as I lay back on the cool pillows. I didn't have to hear what they were saying to know what they were talking about. I'd heard the tale from the whole town since I was six.

That was when my mother died.

I closed my eyes and tried to picture my mother. Strange how, since her death, she had become an ache, spiraling down across my ribcage, a constant pain with nowhere to go. I keep seeing her cleaning the house, washing the dishes, cooking on the stove, and playing domino games – all in a wedding dress.

Maybe that's because I saw her floating face down in the water tank just below our windmill wearing a wedding dress. The only other time I had seen her in a dress was during that family trip to the beach at Padre Island, off the coast of Corpus Christi.

I remembered the trip because my brother tried to drown me by telling me you could breathe underwater in the ocean.

"It's the salt," he said. "Trust me."

It was the wedding dress that kept my father from being convicted of murder. His story had been that he had returned from a buying trip and found her floating in the old steel tank, with me standing on the edge of the tank holding her wedding veil, crying. My brother must have seen something because Dad found him wandering in the pasture, screaming. He kept that up for a week, I know. I could hear him in the barn where Dad locked him up so we could sleep.

The cops questioned Mac, but he couldn't tell them what he saw. He wouldn't even talk. He'd just keel over in a dead faint when pressed about that day. Six-year-olds like me don't faint. We just can't make sense of what's in the memories.

We should have been in school at the time, but for some reason Mom kept us out that day. The prosecuting attorney speculated in court that she didn't want to be alone for fear of her life.

Dad's attorney argued she was nuttier than a fruitcake.

"Why else," said Attorney Sanderson, "would she be running around in broad daylight in a damned wedding dress? Is that any way a ranching woman should act?"

That was the point that cleared Dad.

"How," some of the Van Horn jury members argued, "would a crusty old cowboy like McBride know how to dress a woman properly in a wedding dress? Is that normal for a cowboy to know how to dress a woman?"

"What the hell is normal for a McBride?" someone retorted, and their deliberations deteriorated into a laughing BS session.

"They were too poor to afford a bathing suit!"

"She was trying to use the only washing machine the McBrides ever owned and decided to do her bath and her washing at the same time! You know how Irish women are."

After the laughter, the conversation turned serious again:

"So, do you think one of the kids might have killed her?"

"No, they're too young. Couldn't lift the body into the tank. The old man – he's the only one mean enough."

"But the way she was dressed..."

"McBride is poor and mean, but he's not dumb."

"Wonder what really happened?"

"She did have a temper. Wasn't she committed once?"

"She disappeared for awhile, that's for sure."

"Came back, though."

"That was a mistake. Now she's dead."

In the end they walked out with a hung jury.

As I grew older, I understood the silences that greeted my brother and me when we went into Red's Barber Shop for our monthly haircuts. It was church-quiet when we came in, nothing could be heard except Red's clippers and the flipping pages of the old coverless magazines. I could feel their eyes on me and my brother, questioning, evaluating. I'd bury myself in a magazine, pretending to read it. My brother would stare back at the men until they dropped their eyes.

We had our trial every time we were in town.

People sold us horse and sheep feed in a way that said: "guilty."

They handed us our letters at the post office in a way that said: "guilty."

Even our grades in school came back: "guilty."

Had she ever been committed? I didn't know. But Mac and me busted a lot of noses in school trying to deny that fact, if she ever had been. Soon, they left us alone, but branded "guilty" for life.

Neither of us said anything about mother's screaming fits. They were normal to me. She never hit anybody; she just threw things. A lot of things. Maybe she was raging at her life, trapped in a rural society that was quickly dying, though not fast enough to save her.

There weren't a lot of memories left over from when I was six.

Two to be exact.

Memory one was of her tall, thin form standing in the middle of our small living room, which was dominated by an old oil heated made from a fifty-gallon drum turned sideways and mounted on a pair of rusted angle irons, shovel in her hand, scooping up dirt from the latest desert sandstorm that had filtered into the room through the holes insects made in the adobe.

She would cry a little, brush stringy brown hair from a face strained with sweat and tears, and have me sweep the dirt onto the shovel. Then she'd carry the shovelful of dirt out the front door and pitch it into the yard, all the while crying.

"It doesn't matter," she said as we spent the day and night cleaning. "It'll just be like this again tomorrow. We're carrying sand to the beach!"

My brother and Dad were out riding the pastures, and since I was too small to help them, the task of helping Mom fell to me. I could help her with the sand, but not with her sorrow. I knew something was wrong, but I didn't know who to blame for her tears: God who brought the sandstorms; Dad for staying in this desert hell; or my brother and me for tying her here with our love.

It didn't matter. There was plenty of guilt to go around.

Memory two was just as sharp. It's early morning, and she's in the kitchen. I always wondered why anyone would get up while it was still dark to cook for a sleeping family. Hearing the old icebox open and the clink of the crock jar full of fresh cow's milk as she took it from the coolness to use in her cooking.

The cracking of eggs.

Remembering what came next.

"Sonofabitch!" I would hear her say.

Then, silence.

Another cracking of egg shells.

"You damn sonsabitches!" Banging of a skillet on the stove.

More cracking of eggs.

"Go to hell, you rotten bastards!"

I rolled hurriedly off my bed and looked out the window just in time to see a black iron skillet go sailing through the air and out the back door with three helpless eggs hovering half in and half out of the pan like little birds blown from their nest.

The skillet skidded across the ground and came to rest against the cedar posts that surrounded our backyard. Then I heard the angry footsteps of a woman out of control, thundering through the house as she stalked into the bedroom she and my father shared next to mine. My Dad wasn't the only one full of violence.

"Damn it, Winfield! You can cook your own damned breakfast!" she said to the sleeping form of my father, and she stalked out again, slamming the door.

I peeked in to see if the slamming woke my father, who was hovering at least a foot off the bed and whose considerable bulk was beginning to respond to gravity, coming down hard on complaining springs. I heard him sit on the side of the bed, rolling his morning cigarette, contemplating the true meaning of marriage and breakfast.

He called to me softly, "Johnny, get up and go get the damn skillet. Your mother lost it."

He never said, "she threw it"; just, "she lost it."

I got the skillet, brought it back, and here's the odd thing: following the outburst, she cooked breakfast like nothing ever happened. I'm not saying everything was sweetness and light, but we got fed.

The years my parents had been married were building to a climax, of breaking one too many eggs, or sweeping one too many shovelfuls of dirt; years building towards that one day when she changed her clothes, remembering a time when she felt happy, and walked down to the nearby stock tank to jump in, or when Dad's wrath built towards his own solution.

Did she look around at the desert? Did she listen to cicadas in the mesquite bushes one last time? Did she hear the mourning doves singing their sad refrain as a funeral dirge? Did

46

she dive down as deep as the water tank would let her and deliberately breathe deep? Was her suicide a sincere form of self-criticism because she couldn't cook a perfect egg? Did she break those eggs wishing they were our heads?

Or did my father get away with murder?

I would know the truth before I died.

It was a promise made by a six-year-old. That's one that is never forgotten. The heavens sealed my promise with a two-day slow rain.

My brother and I cried the night of her death, he out in the barn, and me alone in our silent and empty bedroom. Together, we cried down the skies. When I could stop, I lay awake trying to hear Dad cry. The silence from his bedroom chilled me like a tomb.

The second night I crawled into the barn through a hole in the side to hold my brother, trying to console him and to get away from the emptiness in the house.

I told him to listen to the rain. "Even God is crying. It's okay. It's okay."

Sometimes my mind throws her memory at me like a mesquite branch broken in a high wind.

I missed my Mama.

A Nightmare

I must have fallen asleep there in that sweet-smelling bed, dreaming my usual dream of a woman in white silently floating on a dark lake, because I awoke at the party in the dream where she is waving to me and I try to jump into the water, but can't, because I'm only six and don't know how to swim or what to do with the wedding veil in my hands. Something is always there, holding me back, preventing me from jumping in.

There is a sense of sadness, too, for there is no rope to throw to her and the veil is too short.

My eyes open.

It was dark in the Eberhard mansion, but someone was in my room. Now, I'm not afraid of ghosts, but the dream about the woman in white seemed relevant to the whispering sounds of light cloth rubbing against itself. A nightgown sound.

"Who's there?" I said.

No answer.

I lay there in partial fear and partial sexual excitement. If it was my mother's ghost, she was going to get me for being in the Eberhard mansion. If it was Sarah, I hoped she was going to get me for another reason. I had my part of the puzzle now.

A hand clamped over my mouth.

Hot words whispered in my ear, "Shut up! You want to wake up the whole house?"

Ah, romance.

The hand wasn't wet so it wasn't the ghost of my mama. It smelled clean and fresh, but it was as rough as a dried piece of leather.

I couldn't believe Sarah had developed dishpan hands in two years.

I panicked for a moment thinking it was Dad coming to kill me for sleeping with the enemy. But I dropped that thought when the other hand slid down the sheets until it found my growing anticipation. There was a giggle. The thought of Dad giggling did not seem to fit.

Since I'm more sensitive down there, I could tell the hands were definitely made from industrial strength sandpaper.

"Who?" I whispered, confused.

"Shhh." The hand slid further and cupped me. I put my arms around her feeling her hair. It was short, tight, not like Sarah's long silky tresses. Who in the hell...?

The hand squeezed and I was racked with pain. I kicked hard, pushing her away.

"Christ, Kay," I whispered. "What the hell do you think you're doing? My brother will kill me if he knew you were in here."

I wasn't the only one attracted to Eberhard women.

"Your brother would kill you. Your dad would kill you. My whole family would kill you. So best be quiet while I check you out, unless you want me to scream and have them line up."

A female raping a man might be uncommon, but with Kay, it was a distinct possibility.

"My stitches, Kay," I said earnestly. "They could come loose at any time. I'll be here for awhile. Give me a chance to heal."

"No."

Later, I heard her slide off the bed and back into the darkness of the room.

"Apparently, all men are equal. I thought you McBrides would be different." She sounded disappointed.

I lay there grateful and scared at the same time. I had the complete puzzle now. I owed Kay that much. The door closed, and I heaved a sigh of relief, only to have it catch in my throat as I thought of my brother.

He had often told me of his secret desire for Kay. If he only knew what I knew now. I remembered the stitches and how they got there. Maybe I wouldn't tell him. The stitches had occurred when he was in a good mood. God knows what Mac would do if he got mad.

Somehow, Kay fit the criteria for a possible mate set forth in my brother's twisted genetic code. A representational side view of Kay would be a broom standing in a corner with a couple of knots. But, to my brother, she was an object of lust. Maybe he felt he would be a better athlete if he got close to her.

She could play basketball better than anyone else in high school, male or female. She held the all-time scoring record for a single game and a single season for the Eagles, and had led the girls to the state championship trophy – really, the only trophy – Van Horn ever won. The trophy now sat forlorn in a case with several empty but ever-hopeful, shelves in the middle of the hall next to the principal's office.

My brother was the only man for Kay.

No local guy – thanks to Mac who never dated – would go out with her, because they were either afraid of Mac, or because they were jealous of Kay. Every young man in Van Horn had lost a girlfriend to her. Since Mac never had a girlfriend to lose, h e was the only unprejudiced male left in town.

"You know what's surprising?" he said lovingly as he pounded on my head after I'd discovered his secret passion and threatened to tell Dad. "Around her, I swear, I always think of the ocean."

Lying in the Eberhard bed, I realized why Kay, despite her affection for her own kind, bothered with me. The McBrides were forbidden fruit. It was her way of sticking it to her old man. I admired her for that.

But those hands of Kay could rub a man raw. They were as calloused as any man's. I had a strawberry in a place not normally noted for raw skin. I took some ointment off my head and rubbed down there.

My first sexual adventure brought to mind Sarah's questions about when horses make love. But even in my inexperience, I knew that Kay damn sure wouldn't quiver.

Maybe horses just have more fun.

Can't Go Home Again

By the morning before Van Horn Frontier Days, the stitches were healing into a constant itch; the sheets were stiff in places where the results of ointment-rubbing had taken their toll; and I was out of ointment. My stay here had played out.

Barbara Anne frowned at the oft-squeezed tube. "The doctor said this would last for at least a month or two."

"Pervert," said Kay, smiling, from the doorway, again sipping on a Dr. Pepper.

I ignored Kay and watched Mrs. Eberhard. There was an irritation to her movements, a remoteness to her kindness. McBrides were sensitive about wearing out their welcome. Their lives often depended on that sensitivity. Call it an inherited trait. It was time to get out.

"I'm feeling much better," I said, smiling at Barbara Anne. "Maybe we could call my brother to come get me?"

"We're taking you back tonight." Hide was standing beside Kay.

I looked at him, then back to Barbara Anne. "Mr. Eberhard, I don't think it's a good idea to go on our property, especially with me..."

Hide threw back his head and laughed. "The gratitude of your old man blows me away."

"You don't know how true that could be, Hide," I said nervously under my breath.

He brushed my concern away with a wave of his hand. "My boy, we're taking you to 42 Night at Hovey. We'll return you there."

My heart froze. All the ranching families met once a month on the second Saturday to play dominoes in various teams at the little railroad spur of Hovey. Not really a town, it consisted of holding corrals for sheep and cattle waiting for the train and an authentic clapboard one-room schoolhouse. The corrals were no longer used since trucks now drove to each ranch to pick up the animals, but the families still kept up the schoolhouse for the dominoes.

The adults would draw or pick partners and have brackets. Losers played the winners, and the winners were gradually winnowed out until the night's champion team remained, which, more times than not, was my father and brother.

They were the best. No other couples could beat them. The two had played together ever since Mama died, Mac taking her place, and they simply never lost. Rather than grow discouraged, all the families kept coming to try and beat them. The pioneer spirit was still alive in Hovey on "42 Nights." Hide tried to change rules many times, sometimes playing straight dominoes, other times "Moon." But it didn't matter. Dad and Mac always won. It drove Hide crazy, deepening the hatred between the families. Drunk or sober, the McBrides could beat him and Barbara Anne at dominoes any time, any place.

Once Hide placed a board as a blind between them to keep Team McBride from giving any visual cues. It only made the losses worse. The others needed to cheat just to hang in there with Dad and Mac.

We weren't good at a lot of things as children, but we were the child prodigies of Texas dominoes. Mac and I learned early. We had to play Dad for our wages. (I think on the day I was hurt by the bull I had already owed him my paychecks into my thirty-third birthday.) We would sit in the dirty living room and play on an old Montgomery Ward card table held together by tape. Under a single light bulb we learned to count tricks, follow playing patterns, remember who had what, and keep Dad preoccupied with the game rather than the bottle. The better we were at playing, the more we challenged him, the less he drank.

Since there were three of us after Mama died, I didn't get to play much at Hovey unless somebody from the other ranching families didn't show. Most of the time I'd catch the insects that flew around the one light outside the schoolhouse and scare the girls with my catches. I didn't like to play games, at least not adult games.

"Why there, Hide?" The image it brought to mind was that of a Berlin spy exchange on a cold, damp bridge over foggy water, and it just didn't fit in West Texas.

"Safer, Johnny, simply safer. Lots of witnesses. Sheriff Snyder and his family will be there as my guests. Just seems right somehow."

The thought of the whole ranching community seeing me handed back to the "enemy" seemed to give Hide a great deal of pleasure. He gave a little chuckle and walked away. He didn't care one bit what would happen to me after Dad got me home. If only Sarah could come by, maybe she would have some insight.

The strange thing about my stay at the Eberhards was that I hadn't seen Sarah once. The hurt I felt from her absence was worse than that of the stitches. Did she know I was there? I didn't dare ask about her, so I kept silent. Still, why hadn't she come by? I had spent the days in bed straining to hear her voice somewhere in the other rooms, the beautiful free laughter, the soft, sensitive tones when she was serious. What had gone wrong?

The last words I did hear leaving the house were Barbara Anne's and Kay's arguing about who would clean the sheets.

"Just burn the damn things! I don't want to sleep on anything a McBride has slept on," shouted Kay, stomping off. I waited to hear Sarah's voice. Nothing.

Barbara Anne shut the door to Hide's Cadillac and I rode in the back seat feeling the velvet plushness, thinking about that Frog Prince in the story, and wondering if such a spell could be reversed. Could the Prince accept being a toad in the pond again when the castle grew weary of him?

When we arrived in Hovey, all the families were outside waiting for the swap. Word got around fast on party lines. The scene was strangely quiet, with only a few muted hellos to the Eberhards when they arrived. Soon, an old truck could be heard shifting down the dirt road towards where we stood. The families seemed to huddle into tighter formation, much like some animals do when wolves are hunting them. In the fading twilight, I could see the red, rusty old Dodge Power Wagon coming across the valley, its motor screaming like some wild desert witch.

The Dodge was the only vehicle we had, and, since Dad treated it like he would a horse, it went places horses went. No, that isn't right. He had taken it to places horses knew better than to go. As a result, it had an interesting shimmy that would shake out the fillings in your teeth at forty-five miles per hour; when it hit sixty-five, however, the truck would run smooth again, so Mac and Dad drove constantly at a terrifying rate. I just assumed that was the normal pace for driving on ranch roads.

The Power Wagon leapt the cattle guard, touched down briefly next to the Hovey corrals, skidded to a halt just in front of the crowd, scattering gravel right up on the tin roof of the old schoolhouse. Some of the women went inside.

Mac stepped out. Bad sign. Dad never missed 42 Night at Hovey. He pitched his old football helmet to me. The sun was completely down and I shivered in the early darkness, but not from cold.

"What's the helmet for?" I asked, cleaning some mud out of its ear hole.

"Brakes are bad on the truck again. It'll protect your head while we're headed home."

Since when had Mac ever used brakes?

"Can I drive?" I asked.

Mac shook his head. "It'll take too long. Dad's waiting. One of the windmills is busted, and it's your turn to help him fix it."

He turned to Hide. "Dad said thanks for helping."

Hide stuck out his hand. Mac looked at it.

"You ungrateful son of a..."

"Hide! Remember there are women here." Barbara Anne made a show of giving me a hug in front of everyone. There were a few muffled laughs at Hide's discomfort. My brother just turned red under the single light, now on, over the door of the schoolhouse.

"Tell your Dad," Hide boomed, "we'll miss him tonight. I feel damn lucky. When he sobers up, tell him he's welcome back here any time. We'll be sure to drain the water troughs, in case he brings a date."

With the laughter pushing me towards my brother like a wave, we climbed back into the truck. I pulled on the old helmet, tilting it back to keep it from falling over my eyes.

The trip was rough, mainly because of the little dips in the road, which are called "spreaders" because that's what they do to the water when it rains. In theory the water would spread over the pastures and create more grass. What usually happened was the spreaders washed out, eroding a crack in the fragile soil that quickly turned into an axle-and-head-busting Grand Canyon.

Since bridges didn't fare well against flash floods, roads were built down into these eroded canyons and up the other side. After a violent storm, the only thing ranchers could do was wait until the rushing waters in the arroyos subsided and the road was passable again. All trucks in West Texas carried spare tires, two or three shovels, a crowbar for working heavy boulders away from the middle of the road, and a pickax for rebuilding washouts. After all, if you wanted to get home, you might have to repair the road.

Question: What holds the rain when it falls in the desert?
Answer: Nothing.

Each raindrop merges with the next, and a raging torrent several miles away soon spills into the dry arroyos to become a brown wall of water, sweeping all before it, including stalled pickups and ranchers trying frantically to remove boulders from the road where their only truck is stuck. It's embarrassing at one's funeral to have old cowboys snickering when the preacher talks about how one drowned in the middle of the desert.

Fortunately, it hadn't rained in the past two weeks while I had been at the Eberhards. No big surprise there. It hadn't rained all year. Even the cactus looked thirsty.

I glanced at Mac as we drove home. The helmet, failing to twist with me, blocked one eye, so I saw the inside of the helmet and part of my brother's face through the face mask. I was wondering whether or not to ask him again to let me drive.

He had been letting me drive for the last three years. Mac had gotten his license at fourteen because in Texas there is a hardship clause for children of ranchers who live where the distances are too great to make busing feasible. In some school districts children would get up at five in the morning for a two-hour bus ride to the nearest town, and wouldn't get back home until six in the evening.

We were further away from civilization than that.

Now that my fifteenth birthday was fast approaching, I wanted to get as much driving time as possible before taking the test.

Mac was touchy when it came to my driving. Maybe I shouldn't have blackmailed him into teaching me how to drive by threatening to let the old man read his poems of unrequited love to Kay, carelessly left in the glove compartment of the pickup, where I found and read them. Realizing the value of the poems, I buried them on the ranch and offered to trade their hidden location for driving lessons.

The initial beating my brother gave me was not sufficient enough to jar loose the location of the poems, so he had to teach me how to drive. I would sit in his lap and shift the gears while he worked the clutch and the accelerator. This continued until the end of school and the return of the letters. My driving time had been limited since then.

I decided to start a conversation to soften him up so he'd let me drive. Besides, he had been silent since leaving Hovey. The laughter had hurt him, and when he bottled up like that, he reminded me of the old man.

"Mac," I said, "how come Dad doesn't like me?"

He glanced over at me as he shifted down a gear. "He thinks you're crazy."

"Well, I ain't," I said defensively.

"Yeah? Then how come you never used to sleep in the house when we left you alone?"

"That's because when you and Dad went on horseback working the ranch, you'd leave me alone for two or three days! That was hard for a six-year-old to take. I needed someone to hold me."

Mac's face strained at the image. "Dad? Holding you? You mean, with tenderness and care? Besides, we left you enough beans, cornbread, and milk to tide you over."

I had to admit the foot was adequate to keep me alive. But Mom supplied more than cornbread to me.

Mac laughed out loud at a sudden memory.

"When we came back from working, we'd find you underneath the feed trough asleep."

"So? It was a good place to sleep." My heart beat rapidly.

"He'd kick you awake and ask you what the hell you were doing under there."

"And?"

"And you said it was to keep the monsters from eating you."

"Yeah, well, you ever try staying alone in the pitch black emptiness of our house when you were a little kid? It ain't easy. I heard all kinds of things in the night."

Mac looked at me. "But why hide out in the corrals underneath the feed trough?"

"Two reasons: if I saw any monsters coming across the open corral, I had a better chance to run; and if the monsters ate the cows and horses first, they might fill up on them before they got to me."

Mac laughed again. "There are no monsters, dummy."

"Yes, there are, Mac. Now that I'm older I just know where they live." With talk like that, perhaps my head was more scrambled than I thought.

Mac grinned sheepishly. "Hey, you're not mad at me, are you? About the bull riding?"

Was I mad at him? If it hadn't been for him, I never would have stayed at the Eberhards, never would have realized we were so poor, and never would have realized how bad I wanted out of the adobe shack we called home.

No, I wasn't mad. But I was sad, which surprised me.

Mac dodged a large pothole and promptly hit one larger.
I hung on, grateful for the helmet.

"Dad is pissed you went to the Eberhards."

"I was knocked out," I reminded my brother.

He shrugged his shoulders. "Makes no different to the
old man. You went over to the enemy."

I glanced incredulously at my brother. "You and H. D.
took me there!"

Mac nodded his head. "Yeah, but he doesn't know that.
He thinks H. D. drove you over there by himself."

I started to protest the lie but Mac held up his hand. It
belonged on the jerking steering wheel.

"How was I supposed to stay alive if he knew I took you
there?"

He had a point. After all, he had saved my life – albeit
after colluding with H. D. and the damned bull to take it in the
first place.

"I'm not going to let him hit me, Mac. Not ever again."

Mac frowned. "That lick you took on the head must have
knocked all your brains out. What are you going to do, live out in
the desert?"

"Mac, we already do."

An hour later, we pulled into the ranch and stopped at
the old broken fence that surrounded our adobe ranch house.
My home had shrunk during my stay at the Eberhards. I was
aware for the first time that the tin roof was rusty in places, the
adobe walls had chunks missing, and the yard was full of old
tires, rusty auto parts, and discarded tools.

Perhaps Dad knew this would happen when he told us to
stay away from the Eberhards. Once you know you're poor, you
resent it. As long as you're ignorant of the fact, you can be
content, if not really happy.

We walked inside listening for the old man. We tiptoed
over the cracked linoleum tile floor, the sand gritting beneath our
boots. I couldn't help but compare my home to the Eberhards'.

Seven empty beer bottles sat on the kitchen table, which
slanted crazily on its four bent legs in the small dining room. The
kitchen smelled of burnt beans and unwashed dishes. That was
usually my job, so they'd left the washing until I came home. It
showed confidence in my return.

The living room with its barrel stove, the dirty kitchen,
and the dining room, would all easily fit into the guest bedroom

59

where I'd stayed at the Eberhards. Walking back towards my bedroom, I glanced at the toilet without its tank lid and tried to imagine showing this to Sarah Eberhard.

"All this is yours, darling."

In my room I found my brother's clothes hanging in my closet and his boots on the floor. So much for mourning.

"Better breeze in your room than mine," he said, plopping himself onto my former bed. "I didn't know how long you'd be gone, so I changed rooms. Your clothes are in my closet."

Before I could protest the change of rooms, I heard my short-term future calling from somewhere between the mesquite and the sand.

"Johnny? Get your ass out here! We got to go fix the windmill."

I grabbed some clothes, fully intending to spend what was left of the night in the barn, and tried to get out of the house before Dad came roaring in. I would have made it, too, but Mac hadn't *hung* my clothes in the old closet, so I lost time digging through the large pile on the floor. My father met me at the door.

"By God!" he shouted, "when I tell you to hurry up, I mean..."

"Dad, in case you haven't noticed, it's the middle of the night."

He stared at my helmet. I anticipated the swing and stepped aside. He stumbled past, clearing my way to the door.

"Hold still damn it!" He was breathing hard, but it wasn't from exertion. He always got excited when dealing out pain.

"Why?" I noticed he hadn't shaved for a few days. Bad sign.

"So I can hit you," he said, stepping forward, catching me off-balance.

His hand banged against my helmet.

I could hear bells. Sanctuary, sanctuary...

As he shook the fist that had connected with the helmet, I stuck my hands out and pushed hard on his chest. I caught him off balance, and he fell. He sat stunned on the floor, his face a study in quickly passing emotions.

It was the first time I'd ever fought back. My breath came out in short bursts driven by an anger I could barely control. My eyes clouded because he looked older and smaller sitting on the floor in front of me. I hated myself for feeling sorry for him.

Dad stared at me. An evil grin creased his face. "The Eberhards gave you airs, boy. Well, this is where you live. Look around. I'll teach you never to go over there again."

He started to get up. I waited for his charge, fists doubled.

"It wasn't my fault I went there." My own voice sounded strange to me. "You're not going to hit me again."

He paused on his way up, and sat back on the floor.

"Ever see one of them calves that don't break the birth cord off the cow when they're born, Johnny?"

His eyes were like branding irons. "It drags her innards out till the cow dies. You remind me of one of them calves, boy. You killed your mom, and now you're pullin' my innards out, too."

It was the only thing left he could hurt me with.

I could feel something crack in my personal sky.

"She was already dead," I said defensively. "You found me crying at the edge of the tank. I didn't kill her."

Run, Henny Penny.

"Yeah? How do you know that? She probably reached for help, but you were crying so much, you couldn't help her. You never broke the cord, boy."

The sky began to fall.

He stopped and passed a calloused hand over his face. The voice changed, more tired and resigned.

"Look, it ain't personal, but every time I see you, I see Helen O'Connell, floating there in that tank. You kids drove her crazy. I ain't going to forgive that. Can't."

I stared at him across that dirty living room battlefield, swallowing back my tears. I thought about how she was always bent over scooping up the dirt from the floor, trying to ease this dirty hell that trapped all of us. I wasn't going to end up like her.

"Mac said you wanted me to help with a windmill. Let me get some sleep, and we'll get to it in the morning."

He turned and counted the bottles on the table.

"Haven't had my supper yet. Grab some shut-eye and I'll get you up when I'm ready to go. Your brother is too big to climb now. I ain't going to waste time fighting with you. We're stuck with each other, so I might as well face it. I need your help."

"I think I'll sleep in the barn in case your supper doesn't sit well with you."

He gave that grin again. "Want to know what's wrong with the windmill?"

61

"Not particularly."

"It's a top break," he grinned, following me out the door.

I stopped in the darkness. His statement explained why our fight had ended as fast as it began. Dad didn't have to fight me. It was easier to kill me fixing a top break on the windmill. It would look like an accident. Take less effort, too.

Tilting at Windmills

During May, winds would swirl the desert to a dusty hurricane. These winds would push a windmill past the breaking point. The wooden guide rod, connected to the top of the windmill by a wooden connector and to the sucker rods that disappeared a thousand feet or more into the stingy soil, would break. If the guide rod broke the connection with its sucker rods, the rods would plunge deep into the ground, plugging the well. Stock troughs, fed by the pipes from the windmill, would run dry and livestock would die of thirst.

Sucker rods are longer-than-normal broom handles with a metal female connector at one end and a metal male connector at the other, so they can be infinitely joined. In the middle of each sucker rod is a leather washer. Each sucker rod is screwed into the next one and lowered down the metal casing of the well hole to the water source. As the windmill pumps, the washers create a suction within the casing pipe, which brings water upward and out to the surface.

Or as my daddy bluntly put it. "It's like playing with yourself, son."

A sucker rod break can take weeks to fix if you have to fish for a connection with a clamp deep in the bowels of the earth. You always hope to find enough left of the wooden rod to reconnect with so you can begin pulling the broken rods out, one at a time. If you're lucky and reconnect, you still have to pull each rod to check for breaks. All the sucker rods have to be pulled, the broken ones replaced, fitted and lowered again, connected to the ones below, until all the rods are back in place.

That's easy on a well two hundred feet deep. Each sucker rod is 20 feet.

That's hard on a well two thousand feet deep. Each sucker rod is still 20 feet.

A connector break at the top between the guide rod and the metal windmill is simple by comparison. All that's needed to be done is to reconnect the wooden connector of the windmill to the guide rod.

Just one problem.

To reconnect everything, you have to climb a ladder two-thirds up the side of the windmill. Once there, you have to crawl out to the middle of the windmill on some kind of board, usually a rotten two by six. If the board doesn't break, plummeting you to your death, you straddle the unattached guide rod, fitting it with a new connector, which then has to be bolted to the stopped metallic arm jutting down from the circular portion of the windmill. That is the portion with the sharp blades that twirl in the wind – or through the repairman's head if the rusty brake chain snaps under the wind's pressure.

If the wind blows thirty miles or under that usually doesn't happen. In West Texas the wind always blows thirty miles or more when windmills need fixing.

All this has to be done while dangling over a forty-foot drop to the desert floor below, which is full of yuccas, barrel cactuses, and sharp, thorny, flesh-tearing plants, somehow always growing in profusion below windmills. The only thing standing between you and certain hideous wounds is that cracked wooden plank laid from one side of the windmill to the other; a plank that hasn't been tested since the last break, which could have been years; a plank easily dislodged if the brake gives in to the wind's insistent force, thereby knocking the hapless individual off the board to plunge to his death on the plants below, if he hasn't already been decapitated by one of the windmill blades.

If he is quick and lucky, he could grab hold of the sucker rod connector on his way down, thus stopping the fall, and ride it up and down, screaming at whoever is at the bottom – if there is anyone – to set the brake again.

Think of it as riding an anorexic merry-go-round horse on a vertical plane.

Other than that it's a simple job. Holes have to be drilled in the wooden connector and fitted over the corresponding holes in the guide rod with nuts and bolts.

Naturally, a job this dangerous falls to the youngest.
Why?

The official explanation given by a large father and a very large brother is that the youngest was also the lightest, and the wooden plank less likely to break under the lighter weight.

Personally, since I was the youngest, I had always felt it was a way to get the respect I so desperately sought from my family. My brother had had to do it before I became old enough, and I assumed my father had to do it for his father. He always seemed to be angry that my grandfather never had more than one child.

"Damned dangerous being a kid around Dad," was all my father would say.

When I was younger, it always puzzled me why my brother ate like there was no tomorrow. Now I realized, as my father and I drove towards the windmill, that Mac ate to ensure there *would* be a tomorrow.

"Watch for *la migra*," Dad said as we crossed our land.

He always had us watching for the Border Patrol on the ranch. It wasn't that they could arrest him for driving at an unsafe speed. They just had a disconcerting habit of stepping into the middle of the road to stop any vehicle that might be traveling on the ranch road and search it for illegal aliens.

Since the shimmy disappeared from the Power Wagon at sixty-five, it often proved hard to stop for anyone on our dirt roads. Consequently, there had been a few brushes with the law over our inability to stop.

Close brushes with the law.

Today, Dad had gotten it into his head that the Border Patrol men were spying on us.

"Van Horn cops still think I killed your mother, and they've asked the Border Patrol to watch me in case I try to kill you," he shouted at me over the road of the engine.

He put a hand on my shoulder. "You know I'd never do that, don't you, son?"

Through the football helmet I was still wearing, I looked at his hand, wishing it was back on the steering wheel where it belonged.

I didn't answer, just turned and looked out the window for the Border Patrol.

And I saw them. They were backing up a hill beside the road so they wouldn't be seen when they got behind the small stand of creosote bushes that grew halfway up the side.

As the Dodge Power Wagon roared by, Dad shot them the finger.

They didn't chase us.

Since there was only one ranch road, they knew we'd be back. All they had to do was wait.

The windmill was an old rust one on the side of a mountain close to the Eberhard boundary fence. Of course, all windmills were old and rusty. Most ranchers, father included, just assumed there wasn't enough moisture in the desert air to rust completely through the four load-bearing legs of the windmill.

Every now and then, though, one would collapse, killing the climber, and the accident would be routinely reported in the weekly newspaper of the little town where it occurred. Since the article always came out after the funeral, nobody read it; therefore, the event, forgotten by then, was of no concern to ranchers, who continued to send their youngest and lightest up the rickety steel ladders attached to the rusting spindly legs of windmills. Those who survived learned to climb quickly before the ladder collapsed.

My father was watching me climb with a skill born of that awareness. The drill I'd tucked into my back waistband dug into my back.

"Might want to climb a little quicker." Dad sounded unconcerned. "Some of the rungs are breaking below you there."

I scrambled faster to reach the board, not daring to stop to admire the view. I could feel and hear the metal ladder bend and twist beneath my weight, and I was grateful to reach the plank. From here, my father's bald head shone up at me like a beacon.

"Be careful," he yawned. He hadn't slept much the night before. I wondered vaguely whether he remembered, but there was no sense in reminding him.

My first step on the shaky, wooden plank was one inspired by a confidence that the old man wouldn't let me do anything which could harm me – at least permanently. Hadn't he just said on the drive out that he wouldn't hurt me, that he needed my help?

I mean, who else could he find to walk out on the plank?

With the second step on the wobbly, creaking plank, I remembered my mother and the rumors about her death, and quickly dropped to my knees. The board sagged and groaned in protest. I lay my head against the board to steady my nerves. I could hear wooden fibers popping deep within.

Not good.

Dad's voice drifted up from below. "If it breaks, jump for the rod or the side of the windmill."

"No," I said quietly to the snapping board, "I'll just hang on and spear myself on the yuccas below."

"You say something, Johnny?"

I blew the sweat out of my eyes. "No. Just straining."

Somewhere, over the mountain range, I was sure I could hear my brother's laughter, and I made a mental note to start eating larger meals.

But the board didn't break, and after a couple of terrifying hours, I almost had the job finished with the exception of the two nuts and bolts. I drilled the bolt holes through the new guide rod and the new connector.

"Dad? I need those bolts and nuts now." Silence.

"Dad?" I could hear him snoring in the truck.

"Dad!" I screamed.

He stumbled out of the truck. "Did you fall? Where are you?"

He staggered as close as he could to the mass of cactus huddled underneath the only water source for miles and peered in.

"Johnny? You in there?"

"Still up here."

"Oh. What you need?" He sounded disappointed.

"Two bolts and nuts."

"Couldn't you come down and get them?"

"Board's not too steady here, Dad."

As he climbed towards me, I hid my respect for the courage he displayed climbing the ladder to hand me the two bolts and nuts.

While he clung to the edge, waiting, I tried to fit the bolts in the holes, but the holes were too small.

"I'll go and get a larger drill bit," my father announced, yawning still, and he promptly turned and walked off the ladder.

Forty feet up in the air, he just stepped off the ladder.

I think a physical description of my father at this point would be helpful. Imagine a ten-foot bowling ball. Now squash it to six feet. That's my father: thickly muscled arms from years of wire cutting and other ranch work, a long back, and short stubby legs...which were flailing wildly the moment he fell, much like a very large bird leaving its nest for the first time. Unlike birds, which fly most of the time, Dad hit on his ass, bounced once, then again.

I don't know whether I laughed out of relief it wasn't me, from the sight of my father as a bouncing ball, or because of the fact he was still alive.

Or was he?

"Dad?" I couldn't get the image of his falling out of my mind. I tried to keep the laugh inside.

The still form lay on its stomach where it had rolled.

"Dad?" I chortled.

We were a strange family.

The laughter poured out of me. That's probably what brought my father back to life.

"That's it, you little bastard! Sit up there and laugh while your father is dying." His voice made little puffs in the dirt where he lay, face down.

From the way he held on to his behind I knew he wasn't dying, but since he hadn't gotten up off the ground to climb the ladder and jerk me off the windmill to my death, it dawned on me that he was really hurt.

Trying to control my laughter, but failing about every third rung, I climbed back down the ladder, and once on the ground, approached my father carefully, staying just out of his reach. In anger, he was quite capable of killing his only hope for help.

McBrides were never noted for thoughtful reflection.

"Are you...," I had to choke back a laugh as I carefully rolled him over, "are you okay?"

A grimace of pain crossed his face. "No, son, I'm not. I think I broke something in my butt."

He looked at me in a way that made me want to help. "I've got to depend on you to drive me into town."

My father in my debt. There truly was a God.

I felt my chest swell with pride. Maybe Dad would see me in a different light if I could get him to Van Horn.

"Don't worry, Dad. I'll save you. Mac's taught me to drive. Everything is going to be alright."

There was a groan from my father. "You wouldn't lie to your old man, would you, son?"

"It's the truth, Dad. Help me help you to the Power Wagon."

I put my hands under his arm pits and began tugging him over the rocks and thorns towards the truck.

He tried to help by pushing himself along the ground with his boots, making about three inches per try, just about the distance a slow snail would cover. He breathed heavily after each failed attempt. I was enjoying this.

And I really couldn't lift him because he was so HEAVY.

But between his pushing with his legs and my coordinated tugging, I managed to drag him on his broken butt about five feet at a time before my arms gave out, and I dropped him.

I think his screams were probably heard all the way to Old Mexico.

I timed my laughter to match the screams every time.

Finally, I got him into the bed of the pickup.

"Now, son, you will drive carefully?" he yelled as I shut the tailgate.

"Trust me, Dad."

There was a loud groan from the pickup bed as I got into the cab. I studied the console and the long stick shift. Unfortunately, I couldn't reach the pedals with my short legs, and there wasn't enough time to wait for me to grow another two inches. But a McBride is not so easily defeated. I got out of the pickup and looked around for two large stones, which were not that hard to find in the desert.

I rolled them to the truck.

From inside the bed of the truck came my father's worried voice. "What are you doing, son?"

"Oh, nothing," I said, lifting the stones inside.

There was another loud groan. Then, praying.

I stopped for a moment to listen. Until then, I hadn't thought much about my father's religion. I'd just assumed, naturally, that if he had one, it involved human sacrifice.

When I got the rocks in place, one resting on the clutch, the other on the gas pedal, I was able to reach them from where I sat at the wheel. By pressing on either stone, I could get the pedals to work. The problem was I could only press by sliding down below the steering wheel. My brother's legs had made a real difference back when I was an eleven-year-old sitting on his lap. Since I hadn't grown appreciably since then, working the pedals would be a challenge.

Still, I had to get my father to town and a doctor. He was praying louder in back. That unnerved me more than his fall.

Pushing on the clutch rock, I was able to start the truck and was surprised, when I raised up to see above the steering wheel, that we were already rolling back down the hill the Power Wagon had struggled to climb just hours before. I aimed for the road as we caromed backwards, and by turning the steering wheel in a complete circle, I even got us pointed back in the right direction.

"I didn't kill your mother!" I heard him plead. "Don't do anything rash. They'll find me eventually."

I hadn't even thought about revenge until Dad brought it up.

As we picked up speed, I was able to shift into second.

We were already moving at a good clip – the shimmy had drowned out Dad's screams – when we hit the dirt road to town. I shifted into third and fourth.

Dad's voice shifted into falsetto.

As we approached the first dip, I attempted to shift back into third to slow the speeding truck, and, in trying to do so, accidentally rolled the clutch rock away.

Thus, through a simple act, the art of dip-jumping was born.

When we came down on the other side, I glanced in the rearview mirror and saw my father levitating momentarily above the bed of the truck, then disappearing quickly out of the mirror's view.

I thought of Mom's eggs hovering out of the frying pan.

Fortunately, I couldn't hear his screams over the road of the Power Wagon's engine. I was also unaware, as we roared over the Power Wagon's engine, that the two laconic Border Patrolmen we'd seen earlier, had noticed our large dust plume approaching from the distance and in anticipation of stopping us, had parked their jeep next to the road.

I watched in horror as one *chota* - an uncomplimentary term applied to the Border Patrol locally, and meaning something like "stool pigeon" – strolled confidently out into the middle of the road and calmly held up his hand. His confidence turned to panic as he saw a driverless truck bearing down on him.

Since my little beady eyes barely cleared the dashboard, I knew he couldn't see anyone at the wheel. I heard a scream and saw a pale face leaping out of the way from my window as we shot past their jeep, and I guess my momentary thought of a third rock for the brakes was pure hindsight.

Glancing in the rearview mirror, I was startled to see the Border Patrolman kneeling in the middle of the road with his pants half-torn off, then slowly disappearing within a thick cloud of dust. That apparently explained the occasional flap of green cloth on the front bumper.

Three miles later, hearing sirens, I looked up in the rearview mirror and saw flashing lights inside the swirling dust tornado that tailgated the Power Wagon. Startled, I did the only plausible thing. I slid down and pushed on the brakes.

Hard.

With my hands.

Since there was no brake rock, it was the only way to stop.

And it worked, but the brakes locked too quickly, and I was thrown underneath the steering wheel, my body jammed between the wheel shaft and the seat.

As the truck skidded sideways, I peered through the rusty hole in the driver's door. The Border Patrol jeep's bumper and tire whipped past my porthole, barely avoiding filling it.

The jeep hit the fence and began taking out about two hundred feet of Hide Eberhard's barbed wire, which slowly wrapped itself around the jeep like a skillfully tossed calf rope. The snapping wire made little whipping sounds that reverberated over the skidding tires, my father's screams, and the curses of the men in the jeep.

Actually, I saw just one-fourth of the action since the Power Wagon had settled into a circular waltzing slide that kept pace with the wire-cocooned jeep. The other three-fourths of the time I was looking at one side of the road, the other side of the road, and the road from whence we had come.

I was still tightly wedged between the steering wheel, sitting on the brakes, unable to get back to the driver's seat. Both vehicles spun gradually to a halt.

As the dust settled, I could, by peering through the rust hole, see two shaken and badly scratched Border Patrolmen crawl out through the jeep's broken windshield. They stared for a moment at the stilled Power Wagon, then drawing their guns, rushed me.

"Come out with your hands up!" the one with the torn pants shouted. Through the door, I noticed he had a hole in his underwear. I stuck my index finger out the rusty hole to get his attention.

"Help me!" I squeaked, unable to get my breath in the confined space.

"What the hell...?" he said, stumbling backwards and firing his gun in the air.

I felt around for a rock to protect myself.

The door was jerked open.

"Drop your weapon!" the one with complete pants said, cocking his pistol.

"It's my clutch rock!" I pleaded.

"What the hell is a clutch rock?" asked the other Border Patrolman.

I was about to explain when, from the rear of the truck, came the excited voice of my father, "Kill him! Kill the little sonofabitch before he kills us all!"

Leaving Home

What happens if a family is bad luck to itself? If every throw of the rope misses? If, somehow, ancient crossings of blood lines tie the family to a patch of earth in a suicide knot, and that knot can't be untied?

After signing a few papers for the Border Patrol, and watching the ambulance drive Dad away to the El Paso hospital, I made up my mind to leave home. Fourteen was a little young to step into the world alone, but if the possibility existed that a broken-butted father would stop at nothing to ensure there would be no future time to make that choice, fourteen wasn't that young at all.

Though I tried to tell them the phone wouldn't work, the Van Horn cops insisted I try to call my brother. When that fell through, they didn't even offer to drive me home. By suppertime, I had had it and simply took the truck (clutch, gas, rocks, and all) home myself.

On the way I thought about leaving. Dad had muttered vague threats towards me as the ambulance left, and, if it was true he had a broken coccyx, whatever that was, he would have to sit on a whoopee cushion all the rest of his days, a continuous reminder of me and the windmill. It was time to leave.

Maybe I was fortunate. How many of us are aware of that moment when we say good-bye to our home forever? Most major transitions in life seem to begin with small decisions made at invisible crossroads. It isn't until later we become aware that there was a crossroad where we made the choice in the first place. Like a Dodge Power Wagon out of control, we shoot through those intersections oblivious of lives redirected.

Mac was asleep when I came in. He took the news of Dad in the hospital better than I thought he would.

"Hell, Johnny, he's going to stay so mad at you, I'll be able to get by with murder, at least for a time."

"Bad choice of words, Mac."

He nodded his head in agreement. "Since Dad won't be back for a while, we can catch the rodeo and some supper in town. It's been a hell of a day."

As Mac put on his boots, he glanced at my football helmet.

"How long you going to wear that damn thing?"

We didn't talk much on the road to Van Horn, each of us lost in our thoughts about the future. I hadn't told Mac about my decision to leave. He couldn't have stopped me whether he knew or not, but I didn't want Dad to blame him for my leaving.

"Big crowd tonight," Mac said, as we drove toward the bright lights surrounding the grounds.

The high school Future Farmers of America were manning the parking lot and tried to tell Mac where to park, but he gunned the motor, and drove through them, nearly hitting two of his classmates.

"Screw 'em," he said. He wasn't in the best of moods, thinking about Dad's return. There was a moment of panic when I thought maybe he was planning on leaving, too. I almost asked him, but didn't. He disappeared into the stands, leaving me alone by the stock pens.

The pens held most of the rodeo animals that were to be used for that night's excitement. I watched them mill around inside the pens, eating hay thrown out for them: bulls, bucking horses, steers with long horns for steer wrestling, and small calves for roping contests. They seemed content, having forgiven for the moment the human beings who screwed with their lives at rodeos, and grateful for the hay strewn about in the holding pens. It beat the hell out of a packing house. I took a deep breath, taking in the mixture of smells: manure, fresh hay, cigarette smoke from somewhere. I could also smell fresh plowed earth: a cool scent, reminding me of caves, and campfires. This was something basic.

Hopeful young cowboys with identifying numbers on the backs of their shirts were rosining their ropes and their gloves. The rosin made everything sticky, allowing the gloves to grip and hold better. Some were watching the animals, pointing out the ones that earlier in the day they'd drawn to ride. They propped their feet on the lower fence rails, eyes following the animals closely, hunting any clue to their staying atop the beast the eight violent seconds that they had to. My stitches began to ache.

There was another scent – fear maybe – and perhaps a lingering sadness that this dying ritual was all that remained of the rites of passage in an earlier, rougher America. Somewhere, from a pickup radio, Johnny Horton sang of "Whispering Pines." The song seemed to underscore something that vanished decades ago.

The leather chaps the young cowboys wore over their tight blue jeans were the colors of the rainbow. On them, for all

– and especially the judges – to see, were sewn the owners' initials in contrasting bright colors. Garish against the brown of the earth and the dried gray of the corrals, the display trumpeted the desperation of these sons-of-sons-of-cowboys snagged, like parti-colored tumbleweeds, in the fallen wire of abandoned frontiers.

I closed my eyes and listened to the spur rowels make the little *ching, ching* sounds of a lost land. I thought of the struggling animals in the mud of Tudisishn. Were we struggling just like those animals? By some flash of insight in my damaged head, I realized the sad truth of a passing way of life: this forgotten section of America was fighting a battle that was already over. The county had roared by us, and Van Horn's ranching families never even heard the train.

"Hey! Frankenstein." Sarah Eberhard's voice shook me out of my pensive mood. "Don't be sad about missing the rodeo. You can share my victory."

"Sarah!" Overjoyed, but cautious, I looked around for Hide or Barbara Anne, and not seeing them, ran to her.

I started to hug her, but she quickly picked up her saddle. The motion wasn't wasted on me. At least I could still see all of her. She was beautiful.

"Heard you were at the house." There was a distance in her voice.

"Why didn't you come see me?"

"I wasn't there. I was showing show bulls for Daddy in Houston. Didn't they tell you?"

I shook my head. She was dressed in her golden barrel-racing outfit, the rhinestones catching the golden arena lights and outshining the moon. Her blouse was tight and I could see the shape of her breasts, taut with excitement. Was it for me or the rodeo?

"Let me help you, Sarah."

"Sure. I think Daddy is over talking to the judges. Mother and Kay are arguing in the car. You can carry my saddle. I'm first out tonight. Number one."

She pointed to the number on her back. "I like the sound of that. Don't you?"

When the call came for all barrel racing contestants to report to the starting gate, I took the saddle and blanket from her and threw it over the nervous horse. I glanced again through the boards of the arena gate.

A dusty haze over the grounds gave an otherworldly quality to the night. The bulls and calves snorted their anger as they were driven from their hay in the holding corrals, down the narrow passageway that led to the numbered chutes, and into the tiny space where they awaited their riders for the night. A lot of trouble for eight seconds.

The horse laid its ears back on its head as I tied Sarah's saddle on, ensuring that the cinch strap was tight. A cool breeze blew over, sending a shiver through me. There aren't many cool breezes in this part of West Texas.

"Rain might be coming," Sarah said quietly, coming up behind. The horse shook itself, protesting the cold wind.

Sarah patted the horse and looked at me. "She wants someone to keep her warm."

Our hands met as I checked the cinch one more time. Her hand slid over mine.

"Don't ride tonight." I blurted out, surprised and not sure myself why I was pleading. "There's something wrong here. This whole night feels crazy to me."

Sarah touched my stitches. There was concern in her eyes.

"I think the cement trough did more damage to that pea-sized McBride brain than I thought. I always ride in Frontier Days. I can't back out now."

I helped her step in the saddle. The horse's ears were back, and its head didn't move as Sarah adjusted something on her outfit. My head was aching…somewhere in one of the stitches was the certainty of something bad about to happen.

"Forget it just this once, Sarah."

She ignored me, handing me two strings of leather.

I stared at them. "What are these for?"

"Tie downs. I learned the trick last year in Houston. Tie my spurs to the stirrup so they won't slip out."

I looked up at Sarah. "Tie down the spurs? How are you going to get loose if you're tied to the stirrups?"

Sarah just laughed. "Tie them down."

My hands shook as I began to wrap the pieces of leather around the spur to hold it and the boot tight in the stirrup. Sarah told me it helped prevent a sudden jolt from throwing the boot out of the stirrup, leaving the rider off-balance and out of the prize money. It was an old trick, but a hard one for the judges to catch, because the action is a violent blur once the barrel racer's gate swings open. The stitches on my head reminded me that tying a human being to an animal can be hazardous to a person's health.

"Sarah. Dad's not home. Maybe we could get out of here and go listen for ghosts again."

"No need. I met a boy in Houston. He doesn't have any ghosts and he's got a good car."

""Does he give you antelopes?" My hand touched her golden pants leg.

Tears appeared in her eyes. She took an angry swipe at them. "Know what dad did with my baby antelope? He let me feed it for two months, then barbecued it for some local politicians. He let Kay serve it to them."

She looked directly at me. "Kay gets a lot of things I wanted."

I opened the starting gate for her as the announcer called out for contestant number one. As the gate swung out, Sarah disappeared into the dirty haze, and I heard the crowd cheer each time Sarah sprinted around a barrel, her horse making popping sounds as it drove around one barrel and angled towards another. Sarah stayed tight in the saddle. She and the horse were vague shadows through the haze.

Somewhere, I heard a roll of dirty thunder.

The horse zigged again. This time Sarah zagged in the opposite direction. There was a collective moan from the crowd as the snap of a femur echoed like a gunshot in the arena. The leg had followed gravity forward as the horse turned sideways.

There are some laws not even Eberhard money can buy an exception from.

The horse burst out of the dirty fog next to the chutes and ran towards me, its nostrils flaring in anger. Sarah was bouncing behind the horse, her body linked to the saddle by one boot and spur that could not quit the stirrup.

At least one of my knots had held.

As the horse ran towards me, I could see something red and jagged poking through the golden pants. Sarah's loud scream could be heard over the arena, and it silenced the crowd. Like in a slow-motion movie, Sarah and the horse came galloping by, her boot flopping useless against the saddle, her body making little puffs of dirt every time it bounced hard against the floor of the arena.

There was blood coming out of her nose.

I climbed to the top rail of the fence, balancing there, as the horse came circling towards me, the arena guiding it directly beneath me. What I had in mind was to jump in the saddle, and somehow try to stop the horse. But I'm no Hoot Gibson, Roy Rogers, or Gene Autry.

I missed the horse.

Bouncing off the saddle, I grabbed for the leather strap that help her leg to keep from slamming my poor damaged head into the dirt. Fortunately, our combined weight broke the strap, and we rolled free of the pounding hooves.

As Sarah lay there, her leg at an odd angle to her body and the blood spreading from the gleaming gash where the bone poked through the skin, I didn't know what to do but cradle her head in my lap.

I raised myself out of the rodeo dirt just in time to see Hide Eberhard running towards us, along with several rodeo officials. I was dead meat. Why did I agree to tie the knots?

"Don't let Dad kill my horse." Sarah grabbed my hand with hers. It felt clammy and cool. Her face was the color of the fog.

I heard the announced say, "FOLKS, PLEASE CLEAR THE SOUTH SIDE OF THE ARENA TO ALLOW THE AMBULANCE IN."

Hide got to us first. "Sarah! Oh, God, Sarah. Are you okay, darling?"

Sure she was okay. She could probably use the bone poking through her leg to hold donuts, freeing her hands for something else.

Sarah reached again for my hand and squeezed tight.

Real tight. In the midst of her pain, a wild joy grew within me. We were together again, and this time, I didn't care if the whole world knew.

"Dad?" Sarah's voice was weak.

"Don't talk, little one. Where the hell is that ambulance?"

A worried judge shouted from the fence, "It's on its way, Mr. Eberhard. We're doing what we can."

"This is my daughter. By God, you better have something here double-damn quick! I'll sue this damn town for everything it's worth if she dies."

Sarah touched his arm with bloody fingers, trying to calm him.

"Dad, Johnny saved my life. If it hadn't been for him..." Her voice drifted away and her eyes closed.

Eberhard looked at me and then at the silent crowd. I felt like I had to tell him the truth. After all, I was partially responsible. Holding her hand tight, I looked Hide in the eye.

"Your family took care of me. It was the least I could do. I didn't mind risking my life to save Sarah." I said this while slowly pushing the broken leather string in the arena's dirt with my other hand.

As the ambulance arrived, we stood up to let the attendants work on Sarah. Hide held out his hand. We stood there, together, shaking hands in front of Van Horn. It was a night they would talk about forever. An Eberhard shaking the hand of a McBride.

Sarah waved weakly at her father through the window as the ambulance drove out of the arena to the polite applause of the crowd, already growing bored by the drama.

Hide walked with me out of the arena, his hand on my shoulder.

"I won't forget this, what you done here tonight. How would you like to work for me this summer? I'll pay you well."

His smile was calculating, but I wasn't worried about him throwing me into Tudisishn from here. I looked hard at him to see if he was serious.

"Better than your old man could pay you, eh?"

Hell, if he just gave me a good meal and a warm bed, it would be better than what waited for me at home.

Keeping his hand on my shoulder, Hide walked me over to one of the judges who had Sarah's horse. Taking the reins without a nod of thanks to the man, he handed the horse's reins to me.

"I need someone to work with my foreman, Jose Navarrete, on the other side of the ranch. He does a good job running the place, but is getting too old. Learn what he has to teach and I'll send you to..."

He hesitated, wanting to impress me. "...send you to New Mexico Military Institute."

I glanced quickly at Hide. Military school? Maybe he was the one with a damaged head.

I chuckled to myself. A disciplined McBride?

"I'm not joking, son. What do you say? A little work for a fine education? I keep my best quarter horses over in that section of the ranch, and it's important to me that they get broken in right. After all, our horses keep the Eberhard name before the right people."

Only after *our* horses wander into the right people's pastures, I thought to myself.

"Why a private military school, Mr. Eberhard?" I toyed with him, trying not to laugh out loud.

"Boy, you been brought up like an animal. Your Dad's taught you nothing about manners, morals, virtues. Need to learn those if you're going to be associated with my operation. Besides, you stay herein Van Horn, you'll just reinforce the bad habits you already know."

"We're putting Sarah down the road at the Rayford School for Girls in El Paso. Dropping you off in Roswell only adds a couple of hours to the drive."

He paused, frowning. I suppose it was at the prospect of my knowing where Sarah would be. Still, his pride wasn't going to let him break a very public offer.

Mac's voice came from behind me.

"Saving a Eberhard's life? When Dad gets out of the hospital, he's really going to love this."

I turned to see him walk out of the haze that still spread over the arena. The cool breeze blowing him did nothing to lift my spirits.

He tossed me my football helmet. "You're going to need this again when Dad gets back."

I turned to Hide and quickly stuck out my hand. "You've got a deal."

Hide smiled. "You won't regret this. Jose Navarrete needs the help. Someday, someone will have to take over as foreman of my ranch."

He slipped a fatherly arm over my shoulders. "And I think I just found the man, if he'll stay with me long enough."

Somewhere in the darkness, a coyote howled.

Or it might have been Roy McBride, sniper and fence-cutter, screaming in his grave, but before I could figure it out, I was sound asleep in the back of Sarah's truck as Hide drove me and her horse back to Needle Peak.

Yes, sir. I was on the road to Rankin.

Jose Navarrete

The Eberhards even gave me back my old bed with clean sheets. Barbara Anne's surprise at seeing me again had given way to gushing affection after she learned what I'd done for Sarah. Even Key hugged me when she found out what had happened.

I locked the bedroom door, just in case she wanted to squeeze more.

As I stretched out on the bed, I thought about the turns my life was taking. I now had the prospect of a good summer job, and a guaranteed education for at least a year. I could see myself being foreman as Jose Navarrete faded out of the picture. Of course, I had never met the old man.

Sarah was off in the ambulance to the El Paso hospital, which was a two-hour drive from Van Horn. It tickled me that she and Dad would pass each other in the night – one going to, the other coming from the same hospital. I could still feel her hand in mine.

Two hours to competent medical facilities was quick by Van Horn standards. The town had once had its own doctor, Dr. Skousen, but he had diagnosed himself with stomach cancer and committed suicide to avoid the inevitable, according to the note he left behind. The autopsy, however, showed he had a small ulcer, nothing else. When the news about the circumstances of his death leaked out, a lot of Van Horn patients fingered their operation scars.

Lying there, my thoughts turned to the prospect of living with Jose Navarrete, a legend around Van Horn. It was probably his reclusiveness that had fueled the stories that made him larger than life, but I knew only what I had heard.

He had come out of the border village of Ojos Calientes. He had blond hair and blue eyes set deep in a wrinkled, but strong, brown Mexican face, which made his blond hair and blue eyes stand out that much more. He was whippet-thin and full of nervous energy. Barbara Anne's father, Old Man Colby, had recognized early Jose's ability to learn. He took Jose and taught him everything he would need to succeed as a cowboy. Maybe it was the fact the kid had walked from Mexico to Needle Peak at the age of thirteen that impressed Colby.

Jose was a man who used every fiber of whatever he discovered within himself to its fullest potential. Over the years he proved he could ride, rope, brand, spot worms in a cow or calf across the pasture, gather and move a herd by himself and not lose an animal. His legend began because he liked working alone.

The other ranch hands didn't mind. He made the rest of them look bad.

The blond hair and blue eyes only added to the mystery. Some said he was the illegitimate son of old Tom Bell, who was the wealthiest rancher in the state of Chihuahua and a former outlaw from Texas. Of course, no one mentioned to Jose his resemblance to old Tom, who had killed several men during his eighty-some years.

That's why Bell settled in Mexico. Things like murder are easily accepted over there, the tradition of *la mordida* paving the way around bothersome laws. Around Van Horn on Saturday nights, Jose refused to acknowledge his Anglo background, going out of his way to underscore his Mexican heritage by beating the hell out of anyone stupid enough to question his bloodline. He steadfastly refused to speak English – a fact that kept him from being a foreman at any ranch except Hide's.

He wore an old hat that had become his trademark, a straight-brimmed army job from cavalry days. Where he had picked it up was just another curiosity about Jose. Why he continued wearing it over a lifetime of working for Colby and Hide, despite its ragged appearance and sweat-blackened crown, spoke volumes about his stubbornness.

Jose elected to break Hide's horses at the isolated section of the ranch called Barrel Springs. He enjoyed the isolation and he was too good a horseman for even Hide to argue with. Alone, with supreme confidence, and ignoring the chance of an injury killing him before help could arrive, Jose broke every horse brought to him. If he broke his own bones, they healed quietly.

"Ain't right," townspeople would gossip, "for that half-breed to stay off by himself. It's not natural."

"He is, when it comes to horses," was the general agreement.

The legend got a major boost when Hide Eberhard, shortly after taking over the ranch from Colby, invited the world's champion cowboy, a certain Grady O'Neal of Phoenix, Arizona, to his ranch to go deer hunting. Once there, the story went, Hide pretended to get drunk, and bragged about how much better Jose was than any other cowboy in the country.

Mr. O'Neal took offense at this. A small wager of fifty thousand was quickly decided upon, and the next afternoon the deer hunting party drove to Barrel Springs to meet Jose. Since the group consisted of two surgeons from Houston, a senator's son, and an oil man out of Dallas, fifty thousand *each* was not that outrageous.

Two events had been decided upon: saddle-bronc riding and roping. Jose and Mr. O'Neal would go in for the clear winner of the two events. The contest would be held in Van Horn at the rented rodeo arena, under the lights, with no fanfare or publicity. Naturally, the whole town knew about it. The town cops, eager to supplement their meager pay, would block off the road to the arena except for invited guests. The city would look the other way, grateful for a little rent money from Eberhard.

They agreed that, in the first event, each contestant must ride three of four horses to a standstill. For the second event, and without time to rest or recover from injuries, each would have to rope ten calves and ten steers. The one with the least average time and fewest misses won.

When they saw Jose with his thin body and shambling walk coming out of the old line shack at Barrel Springs, sizable side bets were placed between Hide and his hunting party over and above the fifty-thousand each. Supposedly, as the story was retold in Van Horn over the years, Jose even had a broken hand when he walked out to the pickup to accept the challenge.

According to the story, when the arena dust had settled, Grady O'Neal flew back to Arizona. Later, he had an All-Around Cowboy prize saddle he had won in Calgary sent to Jose. No letter. Just the saddle. One champion's respect for the other.

The surgeons sued Hide for fraud, trying to get back their money. They lost in the local court. The senator, whose son had been at the ranch, lost the next election because his son wouldn't pay off his bet to Hide. Mr. Eberhard had just taken the money he would have won from the son, and, by careful payoffs to selected individuals, secured a win for the senator's opponent in the election.

Jose went back into his self-imposed seclusion.

Why did Jose do it? My father said it was to prove his superiority over the white cowboy. He said Jose's talent was fueled by hatred of Americans.

"Nobody rides like he does without a reason," Dad said.

And Hide Eberhard was sending me, a fourteen-year-old kid, to sit at the feet of the master.

Lying in that soft bed at the Eberhards' mansion, my young mind explored all the possibilities that spread before me in a series of Technicolor fantasies:

- Jose and me build a raft to escape down the Mississippi, and our adventures along the shoreline illustrate the great evils of our country. We both gain our freedom at the end.
- Jose buys me a dog, which I name Shep, and that dog one day leaps between me and a rabid mountain lion, then runs back to Jose and, tugging on his sleeve, directs him to my torn body so he can save my life just in time for me to marry Sarah.
- Jose beats Hide to death for mistreating one of the horses he's trained, then rides off into the sunset with me running after him, shouting, "Jose! Jose! Come back, Jose! We love you, Jose!" With the words reverberating off the great snowcapped mountains around us.
- Jose teaches me everything about horses, and one day I become a great horse trainer for one of those fancy farms. I take a crippled colt and work with him night and day until he becomes a Triple-Crown winner. I take the money and find Jose abandoned in a nursing home, and, after thrashing the manager, I take Jose home, where he dies happy in my arms.
- I marry Sarah, inherit my family's ranch as well as the Eberhards' and rise to national prominence. Jose becomes my ranch foreman. In the end he dies in our son's arms – our son named Jose.
- My father and brother, ill and destitute, ask my forgiveness, and I come back to merge Tudisishn with Hide Eberhard's ranch and lead them into the twenty-first century as prosperous and happy enterprises.

None of that is going to happen. For me the possibility of that kind of Technicolor "happy ending" died years ago…about the time Mama died.

Wake-up Call

I sat there watching Hide butter his toast.

"Just tell him you're working for me," Hide said, stuffing his mouth. "Hell, there's enough room in the shack at Barrel Springs for the two of you."

"But, what if he doesn't want me there?" I asked, wondering if Hide was going to offer me breakfast. "I heard he likes to work alone."

Hide's face clouded over. "Jose works for me, not the other way around." Then, he smiled, taking the last piece of toast.

"Kid, everything I do is for a reason."

As I watched him wolf half the toast down, I hoped I'd discover that reason before I starved to death. I couldn't see Jose cooking breakfast for anyone, and especially not for an uninvited guest.

"Hide, I know this is a minor problem, but what about my school now? It's still early May and there's about three weeks left, including our finals, at the high school."

"Took care of it," he mumbled around a mouthful of toast. "Made a call to the school board president, Joe Lomax, this morning. You and Sarah will get credit for the rest of the year. She got her usual grades, and you got...well, you passed, anyway. Besides, working is better for you. Keeps a McBride out of trouble."

I looked at the half-chewed toast in his mouth while he laughed at his own joke.

Simple problem. Eberhard solution.

Hide pushed me the plate with that last half-a-piece-of-toast.

"Wait for one of my men at the truck. He'll take you over there. Do a good job and I'll be over to check on you in a week or two."

My heart was soaring as I chewed my meager breakfast. But my education into the extent of Hide's power and reach had just begun, and my place in that power grid lay in the toast I chewed. I just didn't realize it.

Barrel Springs was in the most remote part of the Eberhard ranching empire. Parts of it touched the border between Texas and Mexico. The name came from a spring whose precious water was caught by a huge wooden barrel made from a cottonwood tree which had formerly stood watch over the spring.

The barrel was the handiwork of an old Dutch carpenter working for Colonel Colby in the early days of the ranch, who cut down the cottonwood, turned the wood into barrel staves, then bound them together with large copper bands. He hoped his handiwork would find favor with the Colonel. After all, it was useless as a tree, wasn't it?

The poor Dutchman didn't know, however, that the local Apaches had considered the rare desert tree some kind of a god, and, upset that one of their gods was now a barrel, the Apaches immediately killed him.

Though the builder hadn't survived, the barrel had, and gave the area its name.

The springs weren't the only oddity there.

Huge boulders, piled on top of each other like some giant kid's blocks, surrounded the area and formed cool caves, whose walls had been used as stone canvases for nameless tribes long before the Apache. Their wiggles and dots had long ago ceased to communicate their importance and were now just curiosities.

How had the boulders arranged themselves that way? Professors from some of the great Texas universities had been invited by Hide Eberhard to look at the formations, and they had left, scratching their heads. Some said glaciers; others, erosion.

While the professors were there in one of the numerous caves formed by boulders on top of boulders, they found scrawled next to what appeared to be a visual record of Indians hunting, the words: "Kit Carson wz here, 1860."

Hide immediately had the area declared a protected state site and wrote it off on his taxes, although it was still off-limits to the general public.

We drove past the rocks, down into a small basin where the ranch house was located, past a crude barn, and a perfectly round corral with large fence posts and a well-used snubbing post directly in the middle. Behind the round corral were working pens for livestock and a horse pasture full of young horses. Hide's man deposited me and my worldly belongings near the front gate and drove away. He hadn't said a word to me all the way over there.

I stood looking at the house and waited nervously. When no one came out, I picked up the saddle given to me by

Hide and a suitcase full of old clothes Barbara Anne had gathered for me.

Standing at the wire gate, staring at the path leading into Jose's house, I wondered out loud, "What the hell am I doing here?"

With a heavy sigh, I opened the gate.

Jose's house was not the typical line shack of most cowboys along the border. Those usually consisted of one room with an oil stove and a bed in the corner, screenless windows with wooden shutters, and an ill-fitting door usually missing a hinge. I noticed there was a neatness and an eye for detail about this place.

It was as if Jose wanted to break every ranchers' stereotype about the Mexican cowboy. There were morning glories climbing the fence on either side of the gate. Jose had carried flat boulders from the large arroyo to the left of the house and created a pathway leading to the door.

To the right of the house was a beautiful garden with orderly rows of fresh beans and corn. Behind the garden was a windmill that had a leak in its sucker rods. Jose had dug a small ditch between the windmill and his garden. An old rubber deworming glove tacked onto the small frame of wood with a hole in it waited patiently for one finger or another to be lifted so a small stream of water could race into the individual furrows and give life to the plants. When the windmill pumped hard all the rows were watered; when it pumped slow, the watering depended upon the direction of the trickle.

In front of the simple freshly stuccoed home, which was actually adobe, desert flowers bloomed. Against the fresh white of the house, the flowers added color to the muted tones of the desert. I paused to admire his work, then carried my bag and saddle onto the screened front porch and set them on its cement floor. At the far left corner of the porch sat a dusty old army canvas cot against the inside wall of the porch. I walked past the cot and into the doorless front room. There was an old gray couch, two springs showing, with one corner propped up by a broken cinder block. To the left of the couch and in a corner was a picture of Jesus Christ set back into an old apple crate turned on its end. Two candles burned on either side of the picture.

I wondered how Jose kept the house clean of dust without a front door, then noticed the garden hose coiled neatly in one of the corners and the drain in the middle of the floor.

That explained it; he just washed off the concrete floor whenever it was necessary, which also left the concrete cool and moist.

To the right of the couch a door led into the kitchen. Framed in the door was an old man, staring out the window. He wore a pair of khakis torn in the seat, a clean white shirt with some permanent stains, gloves hanging out of his back pocket, and a pair of boots, as scuffed and brown as he was.

"Excuse me. Mr. Navarrete?" I said, knocking, and felt immediately stupid. Who else would this be? Who else lived at Barrel Springs?

Jose came to the kitchen door and stared across the living room at me. There was no surprise on his face, no questions, just a hard acceptance.

He glanced at my bags, saddle, and chaps. Crossing the living room, I stuck out my hand. He ignored it, walked past me out to the porch, picked up my things, and placed them neatly under the canvas cot.

"*Cochino*," was all he said.

Great beginning.

I began talking to him as he brushed past me and walked into the kitchen. "My name is Johnny McBride and I..."

"I don't speak English, Shorty," he said to me in perfect English, "*Dimeloo en espanol, Chapito.*"

So I had to speak Spanish to him.

Great. I hardly understood any, but I had a feeling if I expected to survive, I'd better learn more. Jose didn't speak to me the rest of the day. I fell asleep wondering if he remembered I was there.

He did.

Jose began my training early.

Real early.

Somebody was kicking my cot. I opened my eyes just enough to see the pitch blackness of the desert through the screen porch. Groaning, I turned over to escape the bad dream, and promptly found myself dumped on the floor.

Stumbling to the kitchen, I stared at a plate of fresh tomatoes, two tortillas and a piece of *asadero* cheese, which Jose shoved at me with some harsh Spanish words. My first international breakfast. But I wasn't Heidi and he sure as hell wasn't a kindly old grandfather pretending to be gruff.

He poured me a cup of coffee so thick I could have cut a piece off and sucked on it just to get it soft enough to drink. For cream, he shoved a can of Carnation evaporated milk at me. I noticed a whole shelf full of the canned milk behind him, then took a tentative sip from the tin cup. The coffee, rich and strong, woke me up. It also woke up my digestive system.

He cooked his coffee like all old cowboys did, by boiling the water, then pouring the grounds on top. After it had boiled with the grounds for the proper amount of time, he poured a cup of cold water on top of the grounds to make them sink to the bottom of the coffee pot. The strength of the coffee accounted for the sprinter's speed of my bowel movement.

Drink. Take a dump.

I found the outhouse with no problem, but I did make a mental note to wear my boots to the breakfast table. It's hard to take that morning crap while pulling cactus thorns out of your foot.

It can be done; just painful, that's all.

When I got back to the kitchen, he was gone, but the dishes were piled for someone to do. So I did them in an old ceramic sink with steel pipes that pumped in cold water. That's when I realized there was no hot water.

I had always thought the McBride home was poor.

I was wrong. *This* was poor.

As I walked back to my cot, I glanced into Jose's room, but he wasn't there. His bed was carefully made and the room was clean. I did the same to my little cot and slipped on my boots after shaking them upside down to check for night boarders. Beside the boots was an old pair of Mexican spurs left for me by Jose. Their rowels, double the size of those on American spurs, looked large and cruel. I put them on and stumbled out into the darkness.

I could hear the horses in the corrals waiting to be fed. They make a different noise when they're hungry. It's an impatient sound. Then, I heard someone pouring "cake" in an old tin trough. Cake is hard feed for horses and cows. It's shaped like small green cylinders and smells of hay. Dad used to let me chew on it when I was teething, and, as a result, I developed an unnatural craving for alfalfa. Not too many people salivate when they smell cut hay. I'm probably the only one.

When I got to the barn, Jose was putting a hundred pound sack of cake on his shoulder. As I stood there, he threw the sack over my shoulder without warning. I wished for a single light bulb to show me the way inside the one-story tin building that served as a tack and feed room. Instead, I stumbled backward in the darkness under the weight, feeling like some

Chinese coolie burdened with a large sack of rice in the dark hold of a slave ship bound for Shanghai.

I shook my head to clear my vision.

The laughing mice scurrying around on top of the feed stack didn't help.

I was in an Uncle Remus cartoon from hell.

Instead of helping me, Jose let me stagger around with the sack for a while, then adjusted it on my shoulder. It was still heavy, but now manageable. I followed him out to the trough, where he whipped out his old barlow knife and cut the strings of the sack. I stumbled clumsily behind him, feeling the sack's weight diminish as the cake poured into the trough. Not once did he offer help.

I knew better than to ask for any.

After the horses had eaten, Jose cut out the ones we would work with that day and let the others out to pasture. He drove the ones he kept into the high rounded corral, then crawled up on the high fence, and watched the horses as daylight started to do its thing.

I joined him on the fence, having no idea why we were there.

I don't know how long we stayed up there, but his eyes never left those horses, and it dawned on me that he was reading them like others read a book. I thought back to the kids at the rodeo. Here was a man who could have helped them. Still, I didn't see anything except two mares, two small geldings, and one very large black stud horse.

I watched the black as he stood off away from the others, and I swear he was studying us as hard as we were studying him.

Jose must have thought the same thing, because he pointed at the horse and said, "I call the big black one Oso, because he reminds me of a bear. It is Hide Eberhard's prize colt, now grown, which he purchased so I would train it to be a cutting horse for his daughters. He paid twenty-five thousand dollars for it."

He was silent for a moment, then added, "I think the horse is worth more than its owner."

Now, he didn't say all of this in English, but I'll translate it, so you won't have as much of a problem as I did learning the language.

The only way to learn a language is by plunging deep into its society. When you're starving and asking for food, that is a great motivator for plunging deep into the society. When you're alone a long way from civilization with a complete stranger who just might be an escaped killer from Mexico, and what apparently triggers his violence is English, you learn Spanish quickly.

"I'll break Oso different. He's too intelligent to break quickly; the others, you learn on."

Me? I looked at Jose. Wasn't he supposed to teach me? I touched my aching stitches hoping for pity, recognition, something. Jose glanced at my stitches.

"If you can break horses when you're hurt," Jose said as he climbed down from the fence, "think how much better you'll feel breaking horses when you're healthy."

Killer. I knew it.

I dreaded the job already, and it was just day one.

The first horse we worked was one of the mares, a paint. Jose knew she would be the easiest to break, but I didn't know how he knew that. After driving the nervous horse into the little round corral, he joined her in the circular pen with a coiled rope in his hand. I noticed the rope didn't have a loop at either end. How could he rope the horse with it?

But that wasn't what the rope was for. Standing next to the snubbing post in the middle of the circle, Jose threw the rope at the horse, careful to hold on to one end as it sailed through the air like a striking snake. The horse bolted and began to run around the pen.

Jose lazily coiled the rope back up as the horse ran around the small circle. Letting her run a few times in the confining circle, he suddenly threw the rope in front of her. She skidded to a halt and began running the other way. This went on for about twenty minutes.

Finally, the horse skidded to a halt and wheeled around to face Jose, who was still standing in the middle. He walked at a ninety degree angle to the horse, until he got to the corral posts, then he threw the rope toward her head.

The horse wheeled and bolted in the other direction. For a moment I thought she would come full circle and run over Jose. Instead, she skidded to a halt before hitting him. You could almost feel her shock at finding him in her path.

It was then I understood the genius of the circular corral.

The old cowboys understood that a horse's only defense, besides kicking, was running away. The circle just brought the horse back to its trainer. To a horse, that meant the trainer could run as fast as it could. After finding Jose always in front of her, the horse finally stopped, faced Jose, and stood there trembling, awaiting her fate.

Tying a quick knot in the rope, and feeding the other end of the rope through to make a lariat, Jose roped her and snubbed her to the post, holding onto the rope until she grew tired of fighting it. Finally, exhausted, the mare stood still.

Oso and the others watched us from a holding corral. They were definitely interested in what was going on.

Jose looked at me. "What are you going to ride with, your ass?"

Ashamed, I went back to the house, got my saddle and saddle blanket, and brought them back. Jose took the blanket, picked up the saddle, shook his head, and threw it over the corral into the bushes.

"Horses deserve better than that crap," he grumbled.

I didn't say anything or argue. It was Hide's saddle. At least Jose liked the saddle blanket.

He took the blanket and held it up in front of the tired horse. Her ears flicked forward in interest, then lay straight back when he began wiping her down with the blanket.

First she tried to break free. The rope held her. Then, she tried to bite him.

He popped her on the nose.

She fought the rope again.

He approached her again exactly the same way as he did the first time, but this time, she didn't try to bite. He gave her a piece of hard cake. She chewed it, eyeing him suspiciously.

"She learns quickly, gringo." Then, he frowned at me. "Can you learn that fast?"

Now I know that the great horse farms of Kentucky and Tennessee have plenty of time to break their horses. The blanket phase of breaking could take weeks, but that isn't how cowboys, especially Mexican cowboys, break horses. A Mexican-broke horse flips its front feet up when it's cantering. There is a reason for that, and Jose was about to teach me why.

Talking quietly all the while, he began wiping the trembling mare down the front legs with one hand while he reached slowly into his back pocket with the other. He took out a leather strap with a loop at one end. Reassuring the horse in low tones, he looped one end of the strap around one front ankle and tied another loop around the other.

Handcuffs.

Hoofcuffs.

Whatever.

Still talking gently to the animal, he slid the blanket slowly over her back. The horse protested by rearing backward, and when it came down with its tied front feet, immediately fell. As it shakily got to its feet, he slid the blanket over the back. The horse bucked and fell.

Again.

And again.

The fourth time, the puzzled animal stood still.

Jose continued rubbing the blanket on her back. He did this twenty times. The twenty-first time he threw the blanket and his own saddle over the horse without trying to tie the cinch.

The horse fought, fell on its face, and Jose's saddle rolled free. Soon, the horse gave up. Jose tightened the cinch.

Jose's saddle was different from any I had ever seen. Just as race car drivers have their own hand-fitted seats, Jose had his. The saddle-bow was higher and wider than normal. The fork rose straight out of the pommel then looped out on either side so the fork had a clearing for each knee between the base and where the saddle horn should be. This saddle didn't have a horn.

"A man needs to keep his nuts the older he gets," Jose informed me, "and a saddle horn can rip them off when you're breaking a horse."

He paused, as if looking into the past. "I saw it once."

I didn't ask for details.

The saddle, made by a Mexican saddler to Jose's specifications, was unique. The cantle in back was higher than usual and sloped inward, not back like normal cantles. The flanking strap was lined with sheep's wool and Jose buckled it loosely around the horse.

Next, he picked up a hackamore, which is a bitless bridle, and slid it over the horse's head, but not without protest from the horse. Continuing his stream of conversation with the horse, he slide the single-braided hackamore rein beneath the rope loop around the horse's neck, handed the rein to me, and gave a sullen nod.

With one swift motion, he slid the rope loop off the mare, jerked her head down, and motioned for me to get on.

I sighed. It was going to be a long day for me and my stitches.

I stepped in the stirrup and quickly slid into Jose's saddle. It was then I understood its unique design.

Jose let go of the hackamore and spoke softly to the horse.

From the way the little mare reacted, she didn't like what he said. He continued talking to her as he eased the strap from her forelegs.

Jose didn't know I was used to people trying to kill me. The aching around my stitches reminded me that a few weeks ago, my own brother had tried it. I took great comfort knowing I could at least jump off without having to rip apart a knot or two first.

Releasing the mare's head, Jose stepped back. That was when I discovered his saddle held me tighter than my brother's knots. As the horse pitched forward, my thighs jammed under the fork. The high pommel remained relatively level pushing against my front. When she reared back, the cantle behind me held me snug in the middle.

After five or six jumps, I rode the little paint to a stop. It wasn't that hard to do. She had expended all her energy earlier in running away from Jose, and just decided it was easier to give in, than to keep fighting Jose's system. The whole process had taken about an hour.

As she stood trembling, I looked to see if Jose had seen my magnificent ride. I trotted the mare towards him, noticing how she threw her front legs forward, always testing to see if the hoofcuffs were still down there. She would do that for the rest of her working life.

Jose wasn't even paying attention. He was circling the next horse like had done the mare. I mentally calculated the hours of work we would need to break the horses we had chosen for the day. There was one mare, and the two geldings.

I didn't fall off once that day. With Jose's saddle it was almost impossible to get thrown. Shaken to pieces, yes, but not thrown.

That night, every bone in my body hurt. I was sore in places most people aren't even aware they have. My right arm ached from trying to hold the horse's head up. I had learned by the second horse that when the head went down, it was like cocking the trigger on a loaded gun.

As I lay my body down on the old cot on the porch, too tired to eat the beans Jose cooked for supper, I couldn't imagine doing this for a living. Just before falling asleep, I thought: What kind of man could do this for over thirty years?

Coming out to the porch, Jose tossed me a bottle of horse liniment. "Try this where you hurt most."

"This is for horses," I complained.

"Their muscles are bigger than yours, and it works for them," he said, walking back in to finish his beans, canned chow-chow, and cornbread.

The next day, Jose showed me the trick of holding the single thick rein under the opposite fork and across my body, using my hip as a hitch. It compensated for my weak arms.

As the weeks went by, I began to learn, but I still didn't understand why he was teaching me. Surely he understood I would take his place when he became too old. Why did he even bother with me?

He had done nothing but give me the silent treatment and plenty of disgusted looks each day.

Yet, it was a disciplined science. I found myself looking forward to the simple breakfast in the morning, the violence of breaking the horses until midday, the siestas when the simmering heat of the desert got beyond a hundred and ten degrees, and the working of the Barrel Springs side of the ranch late into the night when the coolness of the parched land was again bearable to the cowboy and his horse.

He had shown me how to survive the harshness of the land by living within its rhythms, and by opening my eyes to my own land, he had taught me its timeless beauty.

Night and day, I spoke Spanish with Jose. Gradually, I began to love the flow of the language and how the words seemed to fit the desert around me. I had been passing places and plants with Spanish names all my life, but had never really heard their names at all: Presidio, Mesa Verde, Sierra Madres, lechuguilla, tornillos, yerba, alamo, tule, stool, and chilicote.

My skin turned browner than Jose's, a fact, it seemed to me, he resented. My boots were almost white from the constant scraping and scuffing inherent in ranch work. I avoided baths as much as possible because the cold water, pumped from deep within the ground by the windmill, was enough to shrink my balls to the size of BBs. When I got too ripe, Jose would finally force me under the windmill's pipe, and sit outside on the back steps, laughing at my discomfort.

And I must admit the water felt good on hot days.

He taught me to keep a calf between me and the calf's mother. No cow will charge through her calf. He taught me how to spot cows with worms across the pasture.

"Watch their backs, Chapito. They hunch their backs like we do when we have a stomach ache."

I was already a better cowboy than Mac or Dad, neither of whom I had heard from. It was like they didn't care I was gone.

Hide sent over a copy of a letter he'd had delivered to my family. It explained why I hadn't heard from them. The letter was from the Texas Department of Social Services and said I had been removed from the home on suspicion of abuse. Since I wasn't yet sixteen, I had been remanded to the DSS representative in Van Horn for care. Hide had been assigned as a foster parent.

I couldn't want to call him "Daddy."

One Saturday evening, I idly watched Jose taking his weekly bath. I hadn't really watched him that much before, but while he bathed, I became aware of something strange about his back. I noticed a small hole just above the left shoulder blade, and as I studied it, I realized I could see the setting sun through the hole. It went all the way through! When he turned around, I could see the spider-webbing of his skin around the hole where the bullet had come out.

We always stayed home on Sunday, both our bodies and the horses' needing the rest. Since Sunday always began with Jose praying to his apple-crated Jesus while I pulled the covers over my ears in a desperate attempt to get a little more sleep, I decided to get up tomorrow after his prayers and ask him about the hole.

Sunday Confessions

He had me sitting on a wooden crate on the front porch while he cut my hair, which had grown long and curly, covering the scar on my head.

"Listen, Chapito," he began in Spanish, trying to hold me still as he cut at a particularly stubborn knot of hair with a pair of sheep shears from the barn, "I'll tell you something about the animals you break. A horse's eyes are larger than those of any other animal except those big birds in Africa. *What do you call them in English*?"

"Ostriches," I mumbled while trying to ease a cramp out of my tired calf muscles. We had been breaking horses for the past three days. My new cuts and bruises were twice as sore as the faded stitches, which had long since been cut from my head by Jose with the same sheep shears.

"Since the horse's eyes are on the side of the head," he continued, clipping close to my ear, "they have a blind spot a short distance in front of them. The two eyes can move independently, each in a half-circle. A horse can look forward with one eye while looking back with the other. It is those things directly ahead of a horse that can spook it, not those on the side."

"That brings such comfort to me, Jose," I grimaced as he clipped away.

He continued as if he hadn't heard me, a normal enough occurrence in my conversational forays with Jose.

"It takes a horse a long time to adjust to changes in light. When you bring a horse from a covered trailed into sunlight, Chapito, allow it to adjust its eyes before mounting. It is easier than getting thrown by a nervous horse."

He paused to dab at the small amount of blood dribbling down my neck from a small barber's accident with the shears involving my ear. He didn't apologize for his sloppy work.

"Their ears are the keys to their emotions. When they flick straight forward, they are curious, something up ahead interests them. It should interest the rider, too, just in case the horse decides to bolt. When the ears are laid back, they are angry about something and are about to buck or bite. A good rider should always read his horse."

I thought of the warning Sarah's horse gave her. We both had ignored it that night. I hadn't seen her since I had arrived at Barrel Springs. From the men who brought our groceries, we learned her rehabilitation was going well.

One of the cowboys said he had heard Hide say, "Might have a little limp, but not so no man would have her."

Jose stepped back from his barbering. "Finished," he said.

"Jose," I began, feeling nervous about what I needed to say, "Why are you teaching me?" You know Hide Eberhard is going to get rid of you someday when you get too old. You know why I was sent here."

It wasn't that was I grateful for his haircuts. The damage from the shears would probably stay with me for a lifetime. But I owed him something. I guess that's why I wanted him to know that Hide Eberhard had no intention of keeping him around.

He was quiet for a long time. "What he said is true, I am getting older."

He gazed out the front porch. "I've asked myself why I take time with you. You are so stupid around horses."

The man was pure tact.

Jose gave a weary sigh. He rubbed his shoulder absentmindedly.

"You want to know where this hole in my shoulder came from, don't you?"

"Well, I haven't seen one like it before." I hoped it was a diplomatic enough statement.

"The same place my hat came from, that's where." Jose's voice seemed to vanish inside himself. "Have you ever heard of the Villistas?"

I stared at Jose. "You mean, Pancho Villa's men?"

He smiled, and his voice drifted back to another time. "Pershing chased us for weeks. Typical gringo general. He couldn't even find our horses, much less our army, in the Sierra Madre. Still, Villa sent me back to see where they were."

I looked at him incredulously and laughed. "You fought for Pancho Villa?"

He stared hard at me.

"I was just asking," I said in my most humble voice. God, I hoped he didn't think I was calling him a liar.

"I was young," there was some bitterness in his voice, "but I was the strongest rider he had, and I knew the area. I found a squad of them camped close in Ojos Calientes, the village where I was born. They had my mother and the other women in the church. The men, my brother included, were already dead in the ditches."

His voice trailed off. It was quiet on the front porch; the whole desert was listening. Even the constant drone of the locusts in the mesquite bushes seemed hushed.

"I thought I had killed them all, but one of them wasn't dead. His shot lodged in my shoulder, and he would have shot again except my aunt plunged a knife into his back. He managed to hit her once in the head with the rifle butt before dying. She was never the same afterwards.

"I've kept that man's hat ever since to remind me of what this country did to my family."

"You killed a whole squad of American soldiers?"

Jose nodded.

"How old were you?"

"Twelve." He looked at me. "It doesn't take a lot of strength to pull a trigger."

"And the shoulder?" I wasn't sure I wanted to hear this.

Jose paused and laughed. "Do you think he was ungrateful for what I had done?"

"Sure. Did he give you a medal?"

"He looked at the blood on my saddle and called me an idiot. He said Pershing's Apache scouts would find the blood and track me back to camp. He gave orders to move deeper into the mountains and the men, already bone-tired, cursed me."

A line of pain crossed Jose's brow. "He had two men hold me down while a third pushed a red-hot branding iron, its brand torn off and the end sharpened to a point, slowly through my shoulder. They pushed the bullet out my front. The heat from the iron burned the broken vessels and stopped the bleeding."

"What would have happened if they couldn't get the bleeding stopped or the bullet out?"

He shrugged. "They would have killed me and dropped my body in the mountains. I had to stay conscious to stay alive."

He looked at me. "*That* was a hard day."

I thought about the hole in his shoulder.

"Jose, why did you let me stay? You could have run me off."

He looked at me, hard. "Hide has sent others, and they did not stay. But he is clever. He sent me someone he knew I would not send back."

What was he saying?

99

"Me?" I asked stupidly.

"I teach you the horses, so you can carry on for me."

"Jose, I'll never be the rider you are."

"Of course not. That isn't what you are going to carry on for me. The day of the horseman is over; at least of my kind of horseman. No, it's something else you must do for me."

"What?"

"I had a teacher once. He taught me toughness. And courage. I am getting old enough to pass that on."

"Colby?"

"That old *pandejo* couldn't have even taught me how to fart. No, my teacher's name was Doroteo Arango. When the war ended, others still feared him. They killed him one night. We dug up his body after he was assassinated and buried. Me and four others."

"And..."

Jose's eyes looked deep into mine. Suddenly, I was not looking at an old Mexican cowboy, but at a warrior.

He grabbed my arm, leaned close to me, and said softly, holding the sharp shears he'd been cutting my hair with steady in front of my eyes.

"If you tell anyone what I am about to tell you, I'll kill you."

I looked deep in those eyes and believed him.

"We cut off his head and brought it here."

I looked around. "Here?" I stammered.

He shook his head. "His last wish was to be looking forever at the country that took everything away from him."

"Why did he hate gringos so much?" I asked, hurt at this hatred of my country that I didn't know much about.

"We rode into little Columbus, New Mexico, to show the United States that when they break their word given as men, they must answer to men. They had promised Villa help, and we needed the arms. But as we fought on, they realized he was for Mexico first, that he was not the slave of the United States. They feared a strong neighbor to the south. The men who fought with Villa fought with their hearts, and those are the most dangerous of all fighters.

"When the arms were not delivered as promised, we realized we were doomed. But we stood up anyway to die as men should."

All this talk was depressing me. I changed the subject.

"So where did you bury Doroteo's head?"

"Near Needle Peak, in the Eagle Mountains west of Van Horn. We had a glass jar handblown around the head to preserve it, and buried it in a rock crevice in the Eagles."

"So that's why you stayed with Colby and Hide? To be near the head?"

"I was the youngest. They sent me to guard it."

"The Eagles are a big mountain range, Jose."

"Arango's spirit is bigger. Every year, those of us who remember our duty, ride over on the anniversary of his death and remove the bottle from its hiding place. We drink tequila to him and tell him that Mexico still stands waiting for the next revolution."

He paused and stood up, looking out the screen door. "Last year, I was the only one to show up and drink. I think maybe the others have died. I was one of Villa's youngest soldiers."

"This Doroteo guy must have meant a lot to you, to honor him this way."

He turned towards me. "Is your word worth anything, Chapito?"

I was silent. Nobody had ever asked for my word before. Even I didn't know if it was any good or not.

"I will not be able to drink to him much longer nor see that the place is kept clean.

"Will you do that for me when the time comes? Will you give me your word you'll do it when I die?"

Time to find out if my word was worth anything. I stuck out my hand.

"If you teach me everything you know about horses. I don't have a home or family anymore. Hide said he'll send me to school, but if that doesn't work out, I've got to be able to survive."

Jose gave a tight smile and shook my hand. "A good bargain. Not only do I honor my friend, I leave what I have learned of horses with somebody who hates the gringos like I do."

"Jose," I said proudly, "I love my country and its people."

"The rich ones, too?" he asked.

"No." I couldn't see how the rich had ever helped the McBrides.

"One day, you'll hate the gringos. Take my word for it."

"I'm not a Mexican, Jose."

"You were born in the part of the country taken from my people," he growled. "Because of that, you're a Mexican. True

Mexicans love the land and they love horses, and true Mexicans are the poor ones on both sides of the Rio Grande. They are the ones tied to the land because they cannot leave."

"I'm not sure I understand, Jose." I was at least trying to be honest with the old cowboy.

He thumped my tender head with his fingers. "You will when I finish. You are poor like me. If I teach you how to beat Hide Eberhard at breaking horses, at running this ranch, he will hate you, but he'll respect you. Like he respects me. I pass on my hatred for that rich bastard through your training. I will give you something he could never buy from me. If I teach you how to love this land, you will come back to it and toast Doroteo for me."

He held out his brown hand again. I took it with one browner. I stared at my skin, thinking of my ancestor, Angry She Throws Sticks. Not much of her blood left in the McBrides' veins now. Still, enough of her left to color the skin.

"When will you show me the grave?" I didn't know whether I was more curious about drinking tequila or about seeing that head in a bottle. It was a tossup.

"Maybe never. It'll take at least the next three years for me to teach you what you need to know. Besides, we don't know each other yet. I'll tell you when you're ready. Come on. Let's get some supper."

More Lessons

Days later, as we rode along checking the fence line for damage, Jose resumed my education, but this time I heard an edge behind his voice.

"Where do we come from, Chapito?"

I brushed an interested blowfly away from my face. "Our mothers?"

"Where did Jesus go to find himself?"

"I didn't know he was lost."

He slapped my head, hard. "Stupid! The desert! It is the desert where all answers come to us. There is nothing here to distract us. Here, we come to know ourselves and God."

I was just a little miffed, and rubbed my head to let him know I was.

He pointed to the dry arroyo we were riding in.

"Who made this?"

"Well, something made it, Jose. Probably a good rain."

"It used to be an old fence line. When we broke the ground digging post holes, the process began. The water eroded the soil we broke, and this arroyo is the result."

"And you're saying...?"

"We sit on the rim of an empty moon trying to decide the best use for it. But we don't understand that the best use was decided long before we ever got there."

"What's the best use for a moon?" I asked. I was on guard – I wasn't going to be brainwashed by this crazy old man. The trouble was he kept coming at it from weird angles.

"To be a moon. To raise the feeling of loneliness in the heart. The coyote howls at the loneliness of living when he sees moons. He knows what's what moons are for.

"Chapito," he said, "I will tell you why I stay with my horses. Horses can talk to you about more interesting things than human beings. They, too, are a part of this world and have much to say. For example, my horse just told me it is going to rain today."

I looked around at the cloudless sky and smiled condescendingly. "I don't think so."

"You cook supper for a week if it does."

"And if I'm right?"

"I'll take you to toast Doroteo."

I smiled. This bet was in the bag. His horse bit at my horse's side, and I was suddenly less worried about winning the bet than about staying in the saddle.

"See Chapito?" Jose chuckled. "You called my horse a liar and hurt her feelings."

And it did rain. Not much, but enough to make me lose the bet. After eating my cooking for two days, Jose admitted he had made a bad bet, but I refused to quit cooking until he told me how his horse talked.

"I watched the nose. If the nostrils seem nervous, I know a strong wind – and rain – is coming because the horse reads the air each day. Coming rain and wind block the smells of the day and make the horse edgy. He breathes faster trying to find the normal smells that create his reality, his world.

"Reality is different for different colors of horses. I do not like to ride light-colored horses. You have to be more gentle with them than with dark ones like that Oso. Their color attracts more flies and mosquitoes. Light-skinned horses are naturally more sensitive to insects. Watch them in the corrals. They kick at the flies all the time. They are more nervous than dark horses. If they get scratched, the small insects see the blood easier. And they die quicker, too."

He laughed. "Maybe that's what is wrong with white people. Everything tries to bite them."

As the weeks passed on towards summer's end, I saw he was right about everything when it came to horses. The last lesson before summer ended involved Oso, Hide Eberhard's expensive black stud.

Though he respected horses, Jose gave them no quarter. He never used the sharp Mexican spurs with the large rowels or the quirt unless he had to.

"Just like there are stupid human beings, there are stupid horses, and sometimes you have to get their attention through pain.

"Horses, like Oso, are not the same as other horses. I sometimes think they are people trapped in a horse's body. They are not afraid like the other horses, and they want to learn. But you must earn, not demand, their respect. They are too strong mentally and physically for you. I will show you how to break Oso."

And he did.

He kept Oso in a pen by himself for two days without food or water. On the third day, he walked in with hay and held it out to the dehydrated and starved animal. The horse ate, eyeing Jose the whole time. After he fed him, Jose brought a bucket of water and let the horse drink his fill while he held the bucket.

This went on for a week. Deprivation and reward. Jose never stopped talking to the horse while in the corral. By the seventh day, Oso would perk his head up when Jose would whistle and call him by name, and while the horse ate, Jose would take a curry comb and work on the mane and the back of the animal. He didn't try the tail, he said, because a horse can kill you quickly with a hard hoof.

"Only a fool works the tail of a horse."

So he made me do it.

On the eighth day Jose pulled himself over the horse's back while currying him, resting his weight on the horse. Oso did nothing.

The horse had not exercised for eight days except for trotting around the little holding pen. On the morning of the ninth day, we saddled two horses. Jose put a hackamore with an extra-length lead rope tied to it over Oso's head, and we led him around the whole day while we checked on Hide's pastures, horses, cows, and fences.

I was happy for the break. I was a little peeved that Jose hadn't mentioned Doroteo's burial spot in the Eagles. And it suddenly dawned on me that he had yet to break one horse. The calluses on my butt said I had broken all the horses that had been broken that summer.

So far all he had done was feed and water the horses and watch me break them. Maybe Hide was right. Maybe the old man was getting so old, he couldn't do his job.

The next day, we went down to the pens in the predawn darkness and fed the horses. Jose didn't call to Oso like he usually did to signal he had Oso's food. Instead, he deliberately talked loudly to the other horses as he fed them.

Oso stuck his head over the fence and, I swear, scolded Jose for forgetting to feed him. Jose ignored him, currying the horses I had broken, pointing out to me that this horse was a little sick, or that one needed more work. All the while he did this, Oso became more frantic. Was it jealousy? It sure looked like it to me.

Finally, we went inside and got his saddle and a special bridle called a Pelham bridle, which combines a snaffle and curb bit into one with a double set of reins. One set of reins worked the curb bit for a quick stop because the pain made the horse stop; the other worked a joined bit, which was gentler to the horse. Jose called it the "pain or pleasure" bridle.

"Let Oso choose his own path," he said.

He handed the bridle and saddle to me and, taking some hay and a bucket of cake, he walked into Oso's corral and motioned me to follow him.

Me? I glanced from the saddle and bridle to the huge black horse now eating hungrily from Jose's hand. What that horse could do to me would make the former experience with the bull seem pleasurable. I followed Jose into the corral, taking wooden steps and trying to fight my fear.

Jose took his saddle from me. "Go get a bucket of water."

I did as I was told. When I returned, the saddle was on Oso. The horse seemed puzzled, but was still eating out of Jose's hand, his ears flicking rapidly forward.

My heart sank. The saddle was dwarfed by the back of that huge animal. I didn't do well on the backs of huge animals. The scar on my head began to ache.

"Something is wrong here," said the old man. His eyes searched the pen, then fell on me. They flicked back to Oso.

"Chapito, do you think you are going to ride this horse?"

I nodded my head.

Jose laughed. "The horse smells your fear. No wonder he's nervous. He thinks you're afraid of something else, so he is helping you by being vigilant. Oso does not know you cannot smell or see as good as he does. Relax, Chapito, this is my horse. You'll not have to ride him. You're not good enough, yet."

With a great relief, immediately shot through with shame, I handed Jose the bucket.

As the horse bent forward to drink from the bucket, Jose picked up the bridle and slipped it on Oso.

It was so quick and skillful a move that Oso did not understand what had just happened.

"Open the gate to the pasture, Chapito."

By the time I got to the gate, the whippet body had exploded onto the horse. Jose's hands, using the reins like an extension of his arms, jerked Oso's head around, making the horse circle tightly, his head held tight against the rider's left leg. It was a thing of beauty. Oso was stunned at the sudden turn the morning meal had taken.

I had felt that way many times with Jose, and my empathy with the horse was instant.

But Oso was not confused for long. He exploded upward, a mountain of muscle and coordination, trying to dislodge the old man from the saddle. I watched the horse go up and up.

Oso was a sunfisher, able to turn his belly up towards the sun, all four legs off the ground, and get his feet back beneath himself before landing again. It is a rare horse that has the courage and the muscle coordination to do such a thing.

Even more rare was a rider who could stick with a horse through that. A half-ton animal coming down on top of your head after jumping off a high-diving board is not a good thing. Had that been me in the saddle, I would have died of fright long before the horse returned to earth.

Like opponents at a Master's chess tournament, the two of them matched wits within the corral, jump for jump, Jose smiling the whole time. He was truly alive in the center of the maelstrom. It was a grim fight, neither side wasting breath in the struggle.

Watching them, I knew the two reasons why Jose had let me break all the other horses. The main reason was to save his body for this great fight. The other reason was so that I could appreciate the artistry of what he was doing. When I had first arrived, this ride would have meant nothing to me, but somehow, the old man, through his patient persistence, had shown me how to ride. Here, now, he was showing me the next level.

As I swung with the gate to avoid the violent pair, Oso bolted through, trying to dislodge Jose by scraping his leg on the gate's post. Jose saw it coming and calmly flicked his leg, still in the stirrup, over the horse's neck until the two of them were past the gate and out into the pasture. It was a smooth gesture, one practiced many times on many horses.

My young legs didn't have the agility to do that.

I saw nothing but fetlocks and elbows as they disappeared into the pasture.

Not wanting to miss seeing the ride of the century, I raced to saddle my own horse. Following their dust at a gallop, I still could not get closer to the two receding figures. The strength and speed of the black horse were amazing. Disappointed, I rode back to the stalls in the evening light and waited.

And waited.

The old anxiety of being left alone in the middle of nowhere began to creed into my mind. I stayed in the corrals watching for Jose or Oso until it grew dark. I was hoping one wouldn't show up without the other.

But, for some reason, I was no long scared of monsters. Here, around Jose, I knew they couldn't reach me.

I went to the house and cooked supper. Opening a can of evaporated milk to go along with the beans and cornbread, I walked out on the front porch and sipped it while staring into the dark emptiness of the desert. There was no phone, so I couldn't call for help.

With no truck, I debated saddling a horse and riding to get the Eberhards, but that would take the better part of the night. Besides, the country was dangerous enough in the daytime.

I fell asleep holding an empty evaporated milk can.

The next morning I jerked awake at the time Jose would normally dump me out of the cot. I had learned to keep an eye open for his peculiar, but consistent, wake-up call.

Checking my fear, I looked in his room, but the bed hadn't been slept in. I dressed hurriedly, and went out to the barn to feed the waiting horses. It wasn't until I saddled the little paint mare and was leading her out that I saw Jose's bridle on top of the corral posts where the battle had begun.

Approaching the corral quietly, I looked over the top in the gray of early morning, dreading what I might find. I saw Oso first, head down and his hind foot bent, a sign he was either resting or asleep. In front of Oso, Jose was curled under the saddle blanket, asleep on the ground, his head resting on his saddle.

Looking at the massive forelegs, I shuddered to think what Oso could do to Jose. There were great running scratches on Oso from the desert thorns, and I knew Jose looked the same under the blanket. Yet, neither looked defeated. The scene of sleeping horse and man was one of mutual respect and trust. Neither had lost the battle. Here in the corral was a feeling that two completely different species had communicated their worth to each other.

Rare thunder sounded in the early morning, and the smell of rain framed that picture of the perfect cowboy, etched in my mind forever.

End of the Lessons

The summer ended the way it had started. Jose dumped me out of the bed while the night was still in charge. Once again, I staggered to the kitchen, but this time it was because I was sleepy, not sore. Over the months at Barrel Springs, my body had gone from stiff and aching to tough and wiry. What baby fat I had, had been long since shaken off. I had forgotten all about New Mexico Military Institute. It had required all my attention just to survive Jose's school.

Hide had not checked on us one single time; he just kept sending over his cowboys with groceries and letters. That is to say, letters for Jose, because no one ever wrote me. Sometimes I thought about Sarah, but more often my thoughts centered around fresh food and soft drinks: Chuey's French fries, hamburgers, cold root beer, and pie. Things I never used to think twice about in the past.

Our diet that whole summer was nothing if not predictable. We ate the same thing every morning: tortillas; *asadero cheese*; fresh tomatoes, if there were any on the vine; canned tomatoes if there weren't; and coffee. Lunch was beans, cornbread, and coffee. Dinner was an occasional cottontail, dove, or quail with all of the above. If we didn't have any meat, it was back to beans and tortillas. Jose gave me the old .22 he kept behind his bedroom door and orders to kill anything that dared to both his garden. I felt he was grateful for my shooting ability, since it kept our table well supplied.

That last day, I watched him sip his coffee, lost in his morning thoughts. We hadn't seen a paper or magazine since I had arrived. There was no radio or television. Whatever civilization had connected itself to me from my limited contact with it, had long since unconnected. It could have been the 1800s instead of the 1960s.

With one major exception. The huge road of a low-flying B-52 shook the house, and Jose cursed as he spilled his coffee. For some reason their fake bombing runs came directly over Barrel Springs on their way to Ft. Bliss in El Paso, where our nation's Air Defense School was located. Those runs had gotten more frequent over the summer.

Why Barrel Springs?

Because our canyons made good terrain to practice avoiding radar.

How high off the ground were these practice runs?

Mesquite branches blew right off the trees. Those pilots could fly those giants real close to the ground. Real close.

Jose was in a bad mood that morning because he hadn't killed a B-52 the day before. I was thankful for that, knowing I'd have been the one to have to hide the mess if he had succeeded.

"I smell war, Chapito," he said over the steam from his coffee.

"You think someone declared war on us, Jose?"

"When airplanes run louder and longer in the skies, it always means the gringos are preparing for a war somewhere else."

I felt excitement. Who could we be fighting? Russia? China? Maybe that's why I hadn't heard from my brother. Maybe he'd been drafted.

"Who do you think it is, Jose?"

He shrugged his shoulders. "Doesn't make any different. When enough are killed, they become friends again."

I was glad Jose hadn't shot down the B-52 yesterday. Sure, he had a reason. It took hard work to gather Eberhard's registered Herefords. Jose and I, both dead tired, were plodding along on newly saddle-broken horses behind a string of contented, cud-chewing cows. We had been out for several long, hot hours, and were now headed for the nearest corral. I was lost in a daydream, pretending I was an old vaquero on his last trail drive.

Suddenly a B-52 whipped over the top of the canyon and bore down upon us. In no time flat, we went from pastoral bliss to chaos: animals and humans, now wide-aware and slightly frightened that an air force bomber was about to run up their asses, were completely disoriented by the screaming engines reverberating against canyon walls. The general gut reaction was to desperately try to get the hell out of the way of technology.

The horses forgot they were saddled and went berserk.

The cows, choking on their cud, scattered in at least four directions.

I curled up in a ball on the ground after my horse threw me, my hand over my balls, praying that the cows wouldn't stomp me any more than they already had in their mad stampede.

Jose was still in the saddle, forgetting the frightened horse beneath him, angrily shooting his 30-30 at the receding B-52 as it roared towards El Paso.

Luckily, he didn't hit a thing since his crazed horse spoiled his usually good aim.

I said nothing as the B-52 roared out of sight. Jose hadn't emptied his rifle, and judging from the cuss words still streaming from his mouth, I knew he was quite capable of taking it out on me with or without the rifle. So I waited.

"Chapito," Jose said in a very tired voice, "we have to go get the cows again."

At that moment I hated everything modern.

Even the tinfoil icicles.

Before the B-52s made their runs, usually preceding the run by about fifteen minutes, some higher flying aircraft, so high you couldn't see them, would drop what looked to be shredded tinfoil. The metallic shower was meant to confuse the radar surveillance system. The tinfoil would float eerily down in the desert sky, decorating canyons, mesquite trees, cactus, and cattle horns, and giving the desert an odd wintry appearance.

The temperature was well past a hundred-and-five as we were trying to regather the cows spooked by the B-52 flight, but we had weird military icicles hanging on trees on a hot day in hell. It looked a little crazy.

Jose had gotten off his horse, and was reloading his rifle and scrambling to the top of the canyon, praying that God would give him another chance to shoot down another B-52.

The sudden halt to his cursing made me turn in my saddle. One doesn't have to be quiet to stalk a B-52. On the side of the canyon, I saw him reach into a mesquite bush. Then I heard the cuss words start again, this time with even fiercer vehemence.

Curious, I left the herd and rode up to see what he'd found. It was just a bird's nest. I watched as he gently lifted the nest from the bush and held it in front of him.

It was the nest of a small gray desert bird, whose habit of catching lizards, then flying high above a cactus and dropping them onto the sharp thorns below led to its name, butcher bird. The bird did this so it could feed upon the fresh entrails of its prey, proving even birds weren't normal in the desert. Strangely, the mother bird still sat in the nest. Even though Jose held the nest in his hands, she refused to fly away.

The bird sat on her three eggs, not moving in the blazing noon sun, not even flinching when Jose touched her back. Then I saw that she had lined the inside of the nest with the radar-fooling tinfoil. Apparently, radars weren't the only things the stuff deceived.

The heat of the desert had made a frying pan of her tinfoil nest, some of which had melted so that her legs were now stuck to the bottom of the nest. Her eggs were long since boiled hard. Jose took out his knife and tried to pry her loose, but couldn't.

"This, Chapito," he said, angry tears in his eyes, as he held the nest up to me, "is why we will never survive. We're forgetting about how to live with the world." With another string of curses and damnations, he tore off the bird's head and threw the nest angrily back into the bush.

He shook his head.

"After people like you and me go, who will be left willing to work with the land? Through the animals we ride, and the land that feeds them, we at least touch something that the Indians knew from birth."

He paused for a moment, trying to articulate deep thoughts.

"Powerful men like Eberhard get further and further away from the land. They let machines work the land, creating another layer between man and the dirt. There are only a few of us left who realize we are a part of all this. Do you think those flying sons of bitches who scatter our animals need my skills with horses? Does the world they serve care what I teach you? Need what I teach you? Understand the skills you've learned? Chapito, you are nothing to them. You will never be able to fit, to belong to their world, because you will understand them, but they won't understand you."

He smiled sadly to himself. "They call me an illegal alien in your country. I'm afraid I've made you one, too."

But that had all happened yesterday.

Except for the B-52 trying to land on our breakfast table, things had quieted down today. Jose and I were just kicking back with another cup of coffee, when we both were startled at the sound of a truck pulling up to the front of the house.

"Hey! Get your lazy Meskin asses up and help me with the groceries." Hide Eberhard, with the tact of a bulldozer, had decided to pay us a call.

112

Jose continued sipping his coffee as I walked through the living room, past my cot on the front porch, and out the front door. Hide was at the back of the pickup, scraping his boot on the rear bumper.

"Lord, I don't know which smells worse," he said as I began getting the boxes of groceries out of the truck bed, "you or this crap on my boot. Don't you guys ever take a bath? You smell like dried horse sweat."

I put a heavy box of evaporated milk on my shoulder. "Our laundry facilities leave a little bit to be desired, Mr. Eberhard."

Jose appeared at the door.

"Hello, you crazy ol' Meskin!" Hide's shouted greeting grated on the desert calm. "You broke that big black horse of mine yet? Sarah is still hobbled but I want to give it to her for her birthday. It'll give her something to look forward to when she's on her feet again. I want it gentle as a kitten."

As I sat the box on our kitchen table, I heard Jose tell Hide, "No, boss, I haven't gotten around to breaking the big black yet. I think I'm too old. Perhaps Johnny can do it next year when he gets back from school."

"Damn it, Jose! What the hell am I paying you for? Did you get anything done this summer?"

I walked back outside and looked at Jose. Why would he lie to Hide? He had been riding Oso every day since breaking him, although to watch the two together, it would probably be more accurate to say that they had reached a truce.

Jose stood there by the truck, a box of groceries in his hands, looking at Hide.

"Every horse except that one is ready, boss. Maybe you would like to break him yourself?"

Hide gave an evil smile. "Hell, that explains it. You trained McBride here on the other horses. Lost a little personal time with the black, didn't you?"

Hide turned to me. "Did you learn, boy? Or did you just shoot your wad against the wind?"

I think he was going to say something else when Jose interrupted him.

"The black will be broken by November, boss. Chapito here is learning fast. Someday, he'll take my place."

"Knew you couldn't beat the hell out of a kid like you did the others I sent over here. Never figured you for a sucker about children, though."

And turning to me, he added, "I hope he won't teach you to rob me blind like most of my Meskins do. You didn't teach him that, did you, Jose?"

Jose's back was straight and stiff as he disappeared with the groceries into the house.

Hide watched him go, then said to me. "Can't trust 'em, you know. They're born to steal."

I was about to answer his stupid remarks with a defense of Jose when he turned away and said, "Get your stuff, Johnny. It's time to go to school."

Time? Where had the summer gone? I looked for Jose but he had disappeared inside. I thought of asking Hide for more time, but he was already climbing back into the pickup.

I walked back to the front porch that had served as my bedroom. From there, I could see through the living room to the kitchen sink where Jose stood, sipping a cup of coffee. Outside, the insects were coming alive in the heat. August is a month when life is always overconfident in the desert.

"I guess I'll see you next summer, Jose."

The old man turned and nodded his head. "Don't forget what I've taught you."

"I'll be sore for the first few days when I'm back, but I won't forget how to ride," I said, standing there, wondering if I ought to go shake his hand, give him a hug, or what.

He poured the remnants of the coffee into the sink.

"That wasn't what I taught you," he said under his breath as he walked past me out to the corrals.

"He'll see you next summer, Jose," Hide shouted at the retreating form. "In the meantime keep the horses you've broken in the holding pasture. I'll send a truck over in the next day or two to bring 'em for sale.

"I've brought down a good bunch of fillies from Montana to winter here. When the boys bring 'em over, turn that black loose on 'em. That'll soften him up for you."

Hide waited to see if Jose acknowledged his last words.

He didn't. He just dallied out a rope and coiled it quickly into perfect circles. Jose did it so fast even Hide shut up.

School Days

How to describe my first year at New Mexico Military Institute?

Throw away all your clothes.

Get khaki pants and shirts, pour enough starch on them to make them stand up by themselves, get in them, get out of them, get in them again, and repeat the process until you can do the whole dressing thing, including tying the tie, in about three seconds.

Now, go stand at attention against a wall.

Next, find the worst case of bad breath you can, put an adolescent voice box behind the breath, house it in something called an "Old Cadet's" body, and put it two inches from your nose.

Here is what it will say: "Youdumbcrap. Whyaren'tyourshoesshined? Whyisyourtiecrooked? Youcostthecompanydemeritsbecauseyoucouldn'tmakeadecenth ospitalcorner. Youscreweditup. Youareanidiot! That'satourSaturdayfortoomanydemerits. We'llwalkyoutillyoudrop. Youwilldoubletimeatalltimes. Youwilleatontheedgeofyourchair. Youwillnotspilladropoffoodoryouwilldopushupsuntilgettired. Gotthat?"

Got it.

I would put spaces between the words, but it wouldn't convey reality.

It was hell, and Hide Eberhard was paying for the privilege of watching me roast in it.

That first year I was introduced to many NMMI games. I discovered my body was the perfect shape to be used as a Ping-Pong ball. Our rooms all had double bunks and a shoe-shine box at the foot of the bunks. Old Cadets would whack your butt, and you had to jump back and forth over the shine box. For Ping-Pong paddles they used brooms. I learned not to laugh when the same thing happened to other new cadets, who were affectionately called "rats."

"Whatareyoulaughingat, Dumbass?" the Old Cadets would say, balancing a glass of water on my head, and telling me that if the glass fell off while I stood for an hour at attention, they would throw me out the third-story window.

I believed them. They stuffed one screw-up in his laundry bag and hung him out the window. He left the next day.

My academic education wasn't much easier. Many of the teachers were old retired soldiers who, for the first time, were able to make practical use of degrees gathered between wars. They taught us well. It was a million-dollar education crammed gleefully down your throat, nickel by nickel, by an ex-marine captain or a retired ranger colonel. Their military training had not faded one bit over the years.

Many times at night, sitting at my desk by the window during the mandatory two-hour study hall, I often speculated on what Jose would think of all this. Since my roommate, David Matuzuski, couldn't talk to me, or I to him, it was a time for reflection. Besides, we didn't have that much in common. He was from Los Angeles, and talked about a band called the Beach Boys, bragged about his surfing ability, and showed me pictures of his XKE. Since I had never seen an ocean and had no pictures of the McBride's Power Wagon, I instructed him on how to tell if a cow had worms or a mare was ready for breeding.

We didn't talk much.

The TAC officers-in-charge, actually teachers with night duty who walked the three-story-stoops during study hall, could look in the window, and make sure you were studying and not asleep or talking about girls with your roommate. If they caught you asleep or talking, there were no Saturday privileges in the town of Roswell. Instead, you marched around the quadrangle with a rifle on your shoulder. That gave you plenty of time to admire the yellow-bricks that made NMMI into a formidable castle, complete with turrets and flying flags. Living and suffering behind the castle walls, you could relate to what medieval soldiers went through.

So you spent a lot of time thinking. We couldn't tell which of us came from wealth or poverty because we all dressed the same. Jose could not have picked me out of the crowd. Yet, the arrogance of the rich could be seen in the cynical, cruel smiles of the upperclassmen. The student officers were often sons of those who had been officers at the same school twenty and thirty years before. Money followed money, and their bloodlines showed through in their confidence.

But I soon realized that money was not the exclusive reason behind promotions. Talent, hard work, and intelligent decision-making were also occasionally recognized. For those reasons I didn't expect to get very far. The hard work I could do.

The other two qualifications, though, seemed beyond me that first year.

"McBride! Quiteatingpeaswithyourknife!"

"Whatdoyoumeanyoudon'twearunderwear? Areyousomekindofprimitivechick?"

Well, yes, I was.

To keep my mind off all my screwups, I thought of Sarah. She was the only human being I could think of who didn't yell at me about something. The subject of girls was a common-enough subject at an all-male military high school and junior college, although you tried your best not to think about girls too much. If you did, and your roomie was gone, or sick, you could prop open the closet door closest to the window and masturbate, even during study hall. But more often than not you were caught by the TAX officer, whose presence you had forgotten in your sexual heat, and who would burst into your more personal fantasy, causing everything to collapse.

When caught, you had to wear a white glove for a week for all to see. The school was all too sensitive to normal male pursuits. It wasn't pleasant enduring snide comments in the classroom or at the dining tables.

Maybe Hide wouldn't have sent me to NMMI if he had known that the school and the Rayford School for Girls traded two dances with each other annually: one in October, when "rats" from NMMI were introduced to the new class at Rayford; and the other in February, when Rayford girls came to the institute for the annual Valentine's Dance on Saturday night and a breakfast in their honor Sunday morning.

Sarah Eberhard and I sat out the first event in October because I didn't know how to dance, and she still limped from the rodeo accident. All of the cadets were in their dress whites, myself included. I held her hand as we watched others spin through the colors reflecting on the gym floor. A week earlier, I had watched new cadets on that same floor, following chalk marks to learn how to waltz, using brooms as partners. I had completely trashed three brooms during that exercise.

As we watched, Sarah and I didn't talk of the desert. There was no need. It was what bound us together. There was a comfort in knowing the background of the other, in the secrets that only two shared, the same two now sitting together beneath paper stars.

After the first dance came the letters. Their emotional intensity grew as our memories of each other would play out on her scented paper and my school stationery.

Here: "McBride got another letter. I can smell it from three windows down!"

There: "Sarah, you've got another letter from NMMI."

And we would open them, devouring the feeling of first love, which is the most intense, and reading – over, between, and far beyond the lines – the honest statements from the heart; those we would never share with anyone else again, the kind that created aches deep in secret personal territories, those that only people who love for the first time dare explore.

Then, in early May, NMMI's graduation week, she earned a weekend away from Rayford, and drove up with an older girl who was dating one of the student officers at our school who would be graduating.

We walked through the quadrangle the Saturday night of graduation week, and took advantage of the privilege allowed to upperclassmen to take their dates to their room for a visit not to exceed thirty minutes. It was a privilege we had earned simply by surviving our "rat" year, and the theory behind it was that you couldn't do much in thirty minutes.

The New Mexican moon hovered silently above the quad like some Spanish *duena*, watching our every move, as we walked over the stone pavement towards my room and stopped momentarily to steal a kiss.

"Why do you have a white glove on?" she asked.

Luckily, she couldn't see me blush in the semi-darkness.

"For you the memory of you," I replied softly.

"How romantic," she smiled. "Your roommate said it was because you got caught playing with yourself."

Mental note to shove a surfboard up David's butt after Sarah left.

She kissed me again in my room. She surprised me when she stopped me from taking the glove off. I vaguely wondered what she was learning at that boarding school of hers.

"Let's see each other at the ranch," I whispered.

"Can't. Mom and I are going to Europe for the summer."

"Must be nice." I couldn't keep the bitterness out of my voice.

"If we get back in time," she said, "I'll try to sneak over, but my Dad doesn't trust Jose around his daughters."

"So, are you saying we may not see each other again till next school year?" Why had she created these flames in me, if she wasn't going to feed the fire?

"Hush." She whispered as she softly pulled me down next to her on my bed.

Two observations here: I wondered if the TAC officer would make me wear a white rabbit's outfit rather than just a glove, if he caught me doing what we were about to do now; and it's amazing what two passionate human beings can do in twenty-eight minutes.

Bus Ride

My summer camp counselor was waiting for me, still wearing his old cavalry hat. There were more horses to break and Jose's mood seemed perpetually foul. Maybe I shouldn't have told him about Sarah and me. I thought he would be happy for me.

Wrong.

"You look rich. You smell rich. You almost think rich," he said, giving me one bad horse after another as punishment.

"Where is your money, Johnny? You think a girl like her wants to stay with you if there's no money? Don't think with your dick, boy. That school has messed with your mind. What good will all those books do you when she walks out because you can't take her to places like where she and her mother are now?"

I tried to ignore him, but the horses kept hammering home his point.

He paused for a moment. "And why do you keep that white glove in front of my Jesus shrine in the living room?"

"It's blessed," I answered lamely, ignoring him as best I could, while trying to anticipate the explosion of the horse under me. "It reminds me of something good, not an evil-tempered old man."

He jerked another horse's head down. "Here, Johnny. This is what is real for you: the violence, the land, and the animal. This is what makes life worth living.

"There will come a time, and you will have to see it, when she will have to choose between power and love. The only power you have is between your legs and that goes soon enough." He spat on the ground and released the horse.

"She can find that kind of power anywhere!" he shouted.

I rode the horse with anger, raking it with my spurs. I cursed crazy Jose and this hot summer. New Mexico Military Institute held out some kind of promise to me. They would dress me in fine clothes and show me the secret of making a good living so I could support Sarah. In the future, my sweat would not dry into white rings on a filthy shirt like it was doing now.

All Jose promised was another hard day of work, but I would do my time with Jose. If I concentrated hard enough on my work, the summer would end sooner or later, and I would be back next to Sarah. Jose was just a crazy old Villista. He didn't belong anywhere anymore. Our days lapsed into long hard-working silences. There would be no more lessons from him. I knew it all – or so I thought until June fourteenth.

The day was a typical one. The thermometer read one hundred and ten degrees, as it had since ten that morning. By noon I knew the sun was on its way to killer temperatures. We broke for lunch, and the old man announced over a plate of beans and cornbread that we'd wait out the heat and work from late afternoon until darkness.

Even the siesta that Jose insisted we take to escape the sun didn't help. The adobe brick continued to absorb the heat of the day as we tried to rest on the floor to escape the radiant heat in the dried-mud walls, but the air sat on its ass inside, refusing to move.

I had broken horses all morning and had three more to go that afternoon. Blowflies the size of some of the horses I had broken buzzed the room like hungry dive bombers, homing in on my clothes and the stink of dried sweat, horse and human, that permeated them. There were no screens to hold them at bay, and Chez Johnny's seemed to be the primary attraction.

"It's going to rain, Chapito," said Jose sleepily from the next room.

"Bullshit," I answered, feeling the cool floor on my aching head, "any cloud stupid enough to show will burn up."

"The horses told me," he continued, "and you know..."

"Yeah, I know, 'the horses are never wrong.'" I tried to get comfortable, and brushed an interested ant off my arm. "Sometimes you make it sound like horses are smarter than people."

There was a long silence from the next room, and I thought he had gone to sleep, but then he answered, "They are smarter and better than people, Chapito, much better."

On cue, I felt the air beginning to stir. There was a rumble in the distance; and I was angry at the horses again. The horses kept proving they were smarter than me, at least. Bad for a teenager's ego. Downright discouraging to know you're dumber than a horse.

Magically, the flies disappeared. They always did just before a storm. Where they went to keep dry, I didn't know, but the coolness on my suffering skin, and the smell of the creosote bush, which always permeated the air before a rain, lulled me to sleep. I dreamed of Sarah and white gloves. Suddenly, Jose was there in my dream holding a saddle.

I thought it was a crash of thunder that awoke me. I opened one eye and saw a gun in my face.

It wasn't thunder that had roused me. The screen door had been ripped off its hinges.

I had seen this side of a gun before. I stared at it wondering if I was dreaming or if Jose had devised a new way to wake me up. Then, I saw the green uniformed sleeve beyond the gun. I followed the sleeve up the arm and stared at the smiling Border Patrol officer. Didn't these guys ever let go of grudges? Why, even Dad's attempted murder charge against me had been dropped for lack of evidence. Something about lost rocks.

"Haven't you forgotten about my tearing up your jeep? I was only fourteen." In my sleepy state, I spoke Spanish to him.

"Get up slowly," he said. "Hey, Frank. This Meskin is dreaming."

"They all dream about being Americans!" came the reply from Jose's room.

The hand cocked the gun in my face. I got up slowly.

"Go into the room with your friend." He motioned towards the living room.

Jose was up against the wall where another Border Patrol officer searched him carefully, which wasn't that hard to do, considering he was only wearing a pair of ratty old boxer shorts/

My new friend shoved me against the wall beside Jose.

"Don't say anything, Chapito," Jose whispered, "just let them do their job." He studied the wall as if he were reading the daily newspaper. Jose didn't seem concerned at all.

"¿Donde estan tus papeles?" he asked, spreading my legs and beginning his search. I, too, had a pair of shorts on.

He still felt my shorts.

Weirdo.

"I shoved them up my ass. You can get them if you want." For some perverse reason I had continued to speak Spanish only.

"Hey, George, this guy is a real card," the Border Patrolman said in English before hitting me in the side with a short choppy punch that doubled me to the floor.

"¿Tienes papeles?" the other one asked Jose.

"No tengo papeles ni tarjetas," Jose answered between gritted teeth. He kept trying to see if I was okay, but that was hard to do since the officer's hand had Jose's head pressed tight against the wall as he cuffed his old hands behind his back.

The *chota* picked me up. "Maybe this one is still trying to be a comedian. I'll ask him again: *¿Tienes papeles?*"

I started to answer him in English: that he had no warrant to be in the house, that he hadn't told me why he was practicing his karate on my kidneys, and that Hide Eberhard was powerful enough to sue their asses.

I glanced at Jose's resigned face and handcuffed wrists.

"*No. No tengo papeles,*" I answered.

"Damn, George, we got two wetbacks this time." He pulled my hands behind my back and slapped the cuffs on hard.

I looked over at Jose and had to laugh. He was hopping on one foot while the Border Patrolman tried to get his other leg into his pants.

My personal governmental butler jerked my handcuffed wrists up high behind my back. "Think we're stupid for handcuffing you before getting you dressed? We do it to keep you from putting a knife in our ribs. We know all about your tricks."

He yanked me into my pants, causing as much pain as he could in the process.

"You're a real joker, ain't you? We'll give you something to laugh about." He jerked me around roughly, took me outside to the green jeep, and went back inside as his partner brought out Jose. I could hear things breaking in the house and saw the old apple crate fly out the door.

Coming back outside, he threw two shirts in back of the jeep, then threw us in after the shirts.

Nice of him to cushion our fall like that.

We saw in back behind a wire screen and watched Barrel Springs fade in the distance.

They drove us to a roadblock on the other side of Van Horn. It was on I-10 going towards Sierra Blanca, a little town of about a hundred people west of Van Horn. Beyond Sierra Blanca, about seventy-five miles west, were El Paso and Juarez, its sister city across the border. The roadblock was set up for stopping cars coming from El Paso.

Here's how it worked: road markers narrowed the interstate highway to one lane, and there would be flares directing you into a small area beside a trailer. A man in a green uniform would step out of the trailer, shine a light into the car or truck if it was night, or, if it was day, lean on the door, and ask, "Are you an American?"

You were supposed to answer, "Yes."

Preferably with a Boston, New York, or Alabama accent.

If you answered it, "*Jezz, yo soy Americano,*" you would be hauled from the car or truck, asked for ID, strip-searched if you had none, and placed in a holding pen full of men, women and little children whose only crime was trying to find a job in a country where they could make enough money to buy something to eat.

There was a single-engine Piper Cub airplane alongside the interstate.

"What's that for, Jose?" I asked as we joined the others in the pen.

"*Callate, Chapo,*" he said, rubbing his wrists where the handcuffs had chafed them.

I shut up, wishing I had my handcuffs off, too. My patrolman had told those at the pen to be careful with me, so the handcuffs stayed on.

I smiled at Jose and showed him the handcuffs. He shook his head and walked away from me. My smile faded.

In an hour they backed a big gray-green bus up to the holding pen and in Spanish told everybody to line up. It was an old bus with a rounded front and wire mesh covering each window.

Some macho *chota* ran his baton over the fence, scaring the little children who had fallen asleep, and driving the rest of us back from leaning on the fence with our fingers through its wire.

"Line up!" he commanded in Spanish, pointing to an imaginary line at the entrance to the holding pen. Silently, with no protest, everyone complied. Little girls clung to their mothers in the darkness and whimpered.

Jose went first. He sat at a table with a man filling out forms.

"Jose Navarrete, Ojos Calientes."

I went second, but not by choice. They took off the handcuffs and placed me in a chair facing the same disinterested man filling out the same forms.

A night stick was placed under my chin and across my Adam's apple, and two hands gripped it from behind me. I didn't have to look to know it was my dressing butler.

"Name?"

I didn't answer. The stick tightened against my neck. It was time to get tough, but I couldn't breathe.

"Juanito Bizcocho y Buscando, de Cucarachera," I gasped.

Loosely translated, it meant, "Johnny-cake looking for a nest of cockroaches."

Well, maybe, I didn't want to get tough.

The man stopped writing. "Cucarachera, eh?"

Behind me I could hear stifled laughter.

The stick disappeared from underneath my chin, only to slam me across the head, knocking me from the chair.

"Come on, you smart ass, give the officer a town name."

I could feel a trickle of blood run down the side of my face. I glanced at Jose already on the bus, his hand held in the air cuffed to a metal bar that ran the length of the bus aisle.

Staggering to my feet, I muttered, "Ojos Calientes."

"That'll do. Next."

My cuffs were placed back on my wrists, and I was shoved on the bus, and seated next to Jose. As I sat there, my hand was also attached to the bar overhead. Feeling like an idiot, I watched the others as they were processed and placed on the bus. They all smelled of wood smoke and the sweat of fear.

An old woman reached into her pouch, cleaned off a piece of dried meat, and handed it to me with her unshackled hand.

"Juan Bizcocho," she cackled. Soon the whole bus sounded like a group of school kids trying to keep quiet about a fart circulating through the schoolroom.

This is going to sound crazy, but, right then, I felt like I belonged with these people, that they were family. Kids, old people, young pachucos, two pretty girls crying quietly, and complete families, all accused of the same crime: trying to go somewhere to gain dignity through work.

At the front of the bus, the guards seemed nervous and kept fingering their shotguns. Maybe they expected us to run off carrying the bus over our heads, since there was no chance in hell we could break the reinforced steel bars we were cuffed to.

That meat from the old lady tasted like steak. I noticed some cows lying around a water trough in the pasture directly behind the Border Patrol checkpoint. They chewed their cud in time with my chewing the meat, disinterested in the silly human scene playing out near them.

The bus started out, and we sat quietly looking out the windows through the wire mesh as we drove through the early gray of morning to the processing point in El Paso, near the Hidalgo Street Bridge. There were two more single-engine airplanes behind barbed wire at the border.

"What was the airplane for, Jose, the one at the checkpoint?"

"They hunt us with it. The plane flies over the ranches looking for groups of people coming into the United States from Mexico. When the plan spots them on the ground, it radios a jeep following in the area. While the plane circles the people like a sheep dog, the jeep makes it way to them for the arrest."

"It's hard for the women to run with their children," he added.

We were checked for any outstanding warrants, then sent across the bridge to Juarez. It was a weird feeling crossing the bridge and looking back at El Paso. The buildings there looked pretty much the same, but the jobs paid a living wage.

In Juarez there were great buildings but no jobs. From where we stood, old automobiles and trucks kept running with baling wire, cleverness, and faith, puttered by. Young kids sat on the sidewalks waiting for tourist cars to stop at the first stoplight in Mexico. When the cars stopped, the kids would outrun each other and offer to clean the tourists' car windows for a small fee. If the tourists didn't pay, they spat on the windows.

Jose motioned for me to follow him. Just on the other side, in Hidalgo Park, there was a statue of Benito Juarez. The only reason I noticed it was that a prostitute whistled at me as she leaned against old Benito's knee. From there, we caught a city bus to the Juarez bus station.

"Where are we going, Jose?" I asked.

"First, we have to go to the Bank of Juarez." He left the bus terminal and began walking rapidly towards a large building two blocks to the right of the station. I dodged a couple of shoeshine hustlers and hurried to catch up.

"Jose, don't do anything rash." Bank robbery was as much a crime in Mexico as in the United States, I reasoned.

"You think I'm going to rob it?" He laughed, guessing my thoughts. "I've got a savings account there. The money I make working for Hide translates to more pesos over here and less taxes, so I deposit my money through the mail. What do I need money for in Barrel Springs?"

He had a point.

127

I waited outside while he went up the beautiful marble steps into the bank. I half-expected to hear gunshots as the old bandit ran from the gleaming interior, but he soon returned and we walked back to the bus station. On the way he explained why he didn't protest our brutal treatment at the hands of the Border Patrol.

"I had already taken my vacation last year before Hide sent you to me. So you never knew about my 'benefits package.'"

"About what, Jose?"

"How I get my vacations. You've got to know Eberhard – that *gartijo de Dios*."

It was a term unfamiliar to me. "What's that mean?"

"It is a desert lizard so stingy with its water, it will piss on itself, then lick the moisture off with its tongue. In other words, Eberhard is a cheap bastard – too cheap to even buy me a ticket."

I must have still looked puzzled.

"He knows I need to see my family," Jose explained patiently, "so when he decides the time for my vacation, this happens."

"What happens, Jose?"

"I get a free trip to Juarez."

"Why didn't you tell me?"

He shrugged his shoulders. "I thought maybe you would be back in school before my next 'vacation.' I never know when *la migra* needs to fill a quota, but somehow Hide does."

"Who looks after the place while you're gone?"

"Hide sends someone over." Jose smiled.

"Then he won't send somebody over to feed the animals because he'll think I'm still there." I was worried about the horses.

"After *la migra* drops us off, the arresting officers deliver a citation with a fine to the rancher. The citation lists how many Mexicans are arrested in the sweep. Hide always pays in cash. The officers always leave smiling. This time, his fine will be double, their smiles wider."

The bus was rickety, burning diesel in huge puffs of black smoke, and the fumes, mixed with the untreated sewage smells of Juarez to create an ambiance within that appropriately matched the chicken crap that ran down the seat next to me. An Indian held the chicken, but, in a gesture of consideration, made sure the ass was pointed towards the aisle. Traveling in this fashion on my first foray south of the border, I made several observations: if you drive a bus in Mexico, you are under no enforceable driving laws; there are no good roads in Mexico; anybody walking, riding a bicycle, or driving a smaller vehicle than the bus, is fair game to be driven off the road or killed; and, finally, Ojos Calientes is one tine piss-ant village.

As we brushed the travel dust off ourselves, I looked around.

There was a biblical feel to the image of these dusty little adobe homes that dotted the dark hills overlooking the Rio Grande. On the other side of the river was a dirt road, and, beyond that, I could see some of the mountains that surrounded Barrel Springs. The Eagle Mountains rose tall in the distance. They looked different from the Ojos Calientes side. Somehow, they were higher, more beckoning.

We watched the bus drive away.

Jose began walking towards the small brown hills behind the town. Beyond those hills rose the great Sierra Madre mountain range, ancient home to the Apache, blue and majestic in the distance.

"Tell me, Chapito, why did you not tell them you were a gringo?"

"I was mad about what they doing to us. It wasn't right."

"Chapito, you shouldn't worry about life being fair. It's just life. It doesn't know terms like *fair*, or *unequal*."

"Jose, how do we get back?"

"Horseback."

I glanced again at the mountains in the distance on the United States side. They had suddenly moved farther back. "That must be fifty, a hundred miles!"

"Probably."

"The Border Patrol will shoot us."

"Probably."

"It's illegal!" I protested.

"Probably."

I looked around at the village as we walked through it. Many of the homes had no doors, or, here and there, an old blanket served as one. There were no screens on the windows of the adobe dwellings, and people leaned out and spoke to Jose as we passed. Our boots made little whirlwinds of dust in the dir of the road.

This was a vacation?

"How do they live like this?" I asked.

"They don't know they're poor. They have no way to make a comparison. Whether or not their garden grows is all that concerns them. It is the young ones who are bored and yearn to leave. It is a curse. Once they find out what is missing here, they never return."

I remembered how I felt returning home after my stay with the Eberhards.

"I understand about that," I answered truthfully. "How do you make money?"

"It's an old problem. We don't, but we still have to eat. That's why I'm in Texas, working. That, and guarding the head of Doroteo."

"Why don't you just stay over here and work?"

Jose gave a wry smile. "The poor over here realized a long time ago, that no matter how hard we worked, the only ones who benefitted were the landowners. So we slowed down, took our time.

"All the land in Mexico is owned by the wealthy. There is none available for us, and, without hope, we work less and less. It's a sad circle, but, without land, we cannot grow food. The food that is available we must buy. So I go where I can find money."

He motioned towards the United States. "Over there, you make more things, buy more things, sell more things; there is a constant need for money in your country. But it is a corner you are painting yourselves into. Someday, you will not be able to get out of the corner. You work harder and harder for the wrong things."

He shrugged his shoulders. "So, I work there to send money home. Here, life has a good rhythm. There is a peace here the gringos have forgotten. I like the peace. With the money Hide pays me, I can afford it with a full stomach now."

We stopped in front of an adobe home built into the side of a sandstone cliff. The windows had screens on them and there was a large wooden door covering the entrance. The roof was made out of tin, not flat adobe like the other homes in the village. On the other side of the house was a small grove of cottonwoods, which meant water, and a corral with several horses, some of which carried Hide Eberhard's brand.

Jose saw me looking at the horses and nodded.

"Eberhard told me to shoot them, that they were too old." He smiled. "They were too old for Texas, but not too old for Mexico."

130

At the door appeared two small girls, faces as brown as the adobe of the house's walls, and from their screams of recognition, I knew they belonged to Jose.

Somehow in my mind, I had created this image of a loner, someone who lived with the land and the horses. Seeing him hug his grandchildren took a little getting used to.

"Are these children from your daughter or son?"

He picked them both up at the same time, whirled them around, and gave them kisses and hugs. I had missed that in my childhood. Didn't even know it existed.

"Grandchildren?" Jose laughed. "These are my kids, Elena and Blanca." He set them down and gave me a wink.

A beautiful woman in her late thirties appeared at the door. She was smiling, wiping her hands on a dish towel. Sarah paled in comparison. I followed the dark hair as it curled over the shoulder and down the front. Having your balls pounded daily by horses tended to keep your sex drive checked. However, seeing her was making it come back quickly.

The woman radiated self-confidence like adobe radiates heat. The way she laughed when Jose picked her up and kissed her hard, ignoring the little kids dancing around the two of them, confirmed that she wasn't his daughter.

I turned away, missing Sarah.

She motioned the two of us in. The interior was simple and clean. A wood stove with two pots on the fire sat in the corner of the kitchen. The thick walls kept the heat out, and the table sat in the center, the coolest spot in the room. Bright blue curtains made from flour sacks added color to the old ceramic pots and pans stacked neatly next to the stove. The room had gathered the smells of living like a cast iron skillet keeps flavors. Jose poured us a cool glass of water from an old pottery jar.

"Are you hungry?" she said, putting a plate of beans down in front of me. "My name is Sofia, and you're...?"

"Juan Bizcocho de Cucarachera." Jose laughed.

"And where is this young colt supposed to sleep, Jose? It has been a while, and I'm not sharing my room with someone who has cockroaches in his name."

I tried to apologize for showing up uninvited, and to correct Jose about my name, but I was too afraid to lose the beans in my mouth. Jose explained everything as I ate.

Asking for a third plate of food was all I added to the conversation. I was hungry.

After we ate, Jose took me out to the horse corral located under two huge cottonwoods whose large branches hung over a moss-covered spring. Behind the corral was a continuation of the large sandstone cliff, which stood golden in the evening sun. The leaves made a rustling sound above us, and the ground beneath the trees felt cool.

"Best to put you out here, Chapo." He spread his hands, palm down. "Three plates of beans inside you could ruin what passion my wife and I might enjoy tonight."

He idly scratched his left shoulder while walking over to the corral.

"How long have you been married, Jose?" I asked, following close behind.

"She is my woman of seven years. I keep saying we'll see the priest, but Ojos Calientes isn't large enough for the Catholic Church to pay much attention to, and she refuses to go to Juarez. She has given me two beautiful children, and that is enough."

"I didn't mean to pry."

"The next thing you want to know is what a beautiful woman like her is doing with an old man like me. No?"

Hell, yes, I was curious.

"Here, I'm a rich man. Women over here are practical. They want men who can provide basics like food and housing. Sofa also loves horses."

"Does she love you?"

Jose laughed out loud. "What does love have to do with it? She is a woman who chooses to stay. That is enough for me."

I watched Jose pick some grass growing around the spring and feed it to the horses.

"Where do I sleep?"

He walked to the first cottonwood. A hammock was stretched between the two trees, tied with hand-braided ropes. He dusted off a pillow that was on the hammock and threw it to me.

"Your bed," he said.

"Jose," I put the pillow back on the hammock and sat down on its side, trying to keep my balance, "You never mentioned your family before. Why not?"

He patted the head of a curious horse who was peering at us over the corral, but didn't answer.

I probed further. "Why not bring the family to Barrel Springs with you? Hide wouldn't care."

He gave a bitter laugh. Behind us, I could hear the little girls laugh at some game they alone knew how to play.

He pointed to the girls. "And have my sweet children learn to be ashamed they are Mexican? To realize how little they have here? To think of their father as poor? Could I stand to see that every day in their eyes? They have dreams here. There, they would have nightmares."

He shook his head. "No, Chapito. There are no chains on their hearts here. They think they are free, so they are. DO you think I want to have *chotas* slam them up against the wall and ask for their papers? To see the fear in their faces? Do you think I would allow such a thing? It is better they stay here and live proud like human beings should."

After he left, I thought about what he said, lying on the hammock and looking up through the cottonwood leaves as they fluttered yellow in the sun. Later, Sofia brought me out some leftover tortillas. Her white cotton blouse was stained under the arms from the afternoon heat; it clung to her breasts like a pair of soft hands.

I couldn't even say "thank you." My mouth was that dry.

She laughed at my discomfort, and I watched her sway back towards the house.

That night, the stars stretched forever in the Mexican sky and even though I knew they were the same stars that shone on Barrel Springs, they were different somehow shining on my hammock.

I lay there and thought about the uniforms, the gleaming swords, and the arrogant pride I had learned at NMMI. I was a part of that now. I wanted to be a soldier. Honor was important to me. When I closed my eyes, I could see myself leading men into battle.

But in the middle of that dream now sat an old woman, handcuffed to a metal bar, who had given me some dusty meat on a bus, and overheard, a Piper Club hunted desperate men, women and children.

I thought about little children happy in their innocence in Mexico.

Five nights later, we saddled up and rode towards Barrel Springs under the same stars that lit the waters of the Rio Grande of Texas and Mexico, like human B-52s slipping under

the radar of night. I would miss Jose's family. It was one of the
few happy ones I'd seen.

The trails we followed were the old wax smuggler trails
of the forties and fifties. Mexican cactus wax, used to coat armor
and bullets to prevent rusting, was better and cheaper than the
wax made from U.S. bees. But wax producers persuaded the
government to impose a tax on Mexican wax, which gave rise to
the smuggling. Loads of unprocessed cactus were brought
across the border to be boiled for their wax content.

Jose was just a dark form in front of me, and my horse
simply followed the sound of rocks clattering from the hooves of
his horse. I must have fallen asleep in the saddle, because
when I awoke the Eagle Mountains were directly in front of us, a
vague gray in the predawn light. Jose still rode straight and tall.

"Jose? Are you awake? Shouldn't we be a little more to
the East?"

He turned around in the saddle and smiled. "Today, you
and I drink tequila with Doroteo Arango."

We hobbled our horses in one of the canyons and began
a slow climb. I should have been tired, but I was so proud of the
honor, I didn't feel a thing.

"Why now, Jose?"

"Two reasons:" he said, climbing like a deer ahead of
me, "You didn't tell the *chotas* you were a gringo, and you gave
them a Mexican name."

"And the second reason?"

"Today is June twentieth – the anniversary of his death."

Finally, we rested on a ledge with several fissures in the
rock behind where we sat. Jose rolled back some stones and
gingerly brought out a tattered burlap bag.

With trembling hands, he untied the piece of leather at
the top and slid the dusty burlap lovingly down the sides of a
large green glass bottle. Something brown bobbed inside the
green glass. Wisps of hair floated above the brown.

"What is it stored in?"

Jose reached inside his shirt and brought out a bottle of
Jose Cuervo. "Tequila. It was the only alcohol we had."

He raised the tequila to the head in the bottle. "*Salud,
General.*"

"Was Doroteo a general?" I asked looking at the grisly
object floating in the murky liquid.

He handed the bottle to me. "Doroteo Arango was *The*
General."

I looked at the only thing floating in the bottle and quickly took a swig. "Jose, the only general you've talked about was Pancho Villa."

"Doroteo Arango was his real name. Pancho Villa was the outlaw name he assumed after they killed his family. Now go, Chapo. I have to tell him why you are here."

As I slid back down the canyon to the horses, listening to the faraway echoing of Jose's voice against dark canyon walls, the color of dried blood in the early morning sun, I wondered briefly if Jose wasn't just a little mad.

Of course, Jose wasn't the only one just a little off-center. I had just toasted a decayed head in a bottle. I guess being born in this region made that part of your birthright.

When I reached the horses, they were watching several mule deer cross the canyon behind them. An old buck was in the rear, six does ahead of him on the narrow trail. He stopped to make sure I stopped. As I sat down next to the horses, one of the does startled a covey of quail, which in turn startled the herd of deer, and they ran over the top, disappearing down the other side. The quail flew down the canyon and settled under some bushes further down, complaining loudly about clumsy deer.

I looked across the now-empty canyon knowing a secret hummed like a heart deep in the stone. It was kind of funny. The more I knew about myself, the more I knew what was out there.

Final Year

Two years pass quickly when you're told what to do each day: when to go to school, when to go to bed, when to go back and forth at the ranch. You were not told, however, when to think of marrying your boss's daughter.

I had grown proud of my achievements at NMMI. Two years of weightlifting had turned what little body I had originally into solid muscle that could twist and turn for wrestling takedowns and reversals. Wrestling was a sport that taught you to use your anger. I had worked my way up through the weight classes, and now, at the one-hundred-and-fifty-pound weight class, I held the record for the most pins by a senior wrestler. I was respected by the new cadets. I didn't shout at them. I didn't have to.

They became instantly afraid of me when I gave them a Navarrete Villista stare. Hell, I was afraid of me when I gave them that stare. I had found a way to channel all the frustrations of cadet life and all the anger of my former life with Dad.

I suppose Dad and Mac still eked out a living on Tudisishn. That part of my life seemed so foreign to me now. Almost as foreign as those words I kept hearing: Vietnam, the draft, commissioning of cadets.

Here at NMMI, even our conversations were turning stranger.

"Hey, did you hear about Willy?"

"Willy who?"

"Byers."

"Cadet Colonel Byers? Wasn't he the battalion commander of third battalion last year? Graduated from Junior College here?"

"Yeah, that's him. He got killed in Vietnam."

"Where the hell's that?"

"Beats the hell out of me. He was an infantry platoon leader over there."

"How did he die?"

"Choked to death."

"By the enemy?"

"No. On his own dick. They tied him to a tree with wire, cut it off, stuck it in his mouth, and left him to choke to death."

"Damn."

"Yeah. He was a sorry battalion commander, anyway."

"Yeah. Stuck me a few times with demerits, too. See you after dinner."

"See you around."

I traced the outlines of the sergeant stripes on my uniform. I was a senior and a new platoon sergeant. After next week's high school graduation, I would be named first sergeant of Company K. Officers and first sergeants came from the junior college ranks.

They cut off his dick?

The reason why I have risen so fast is that I have signed for an ROTC officer's commission. Upon graduation from NMMI's junior college, I can enter the U.S. Army as a second lieutenant in the infantry. Because of this place called Vietnam, there seem to be a lot of openings for second lieutenants in the infantry.

Why the dick?

On the side of my shirt collar is the metal insignia, ROTC. The letters mean "Reserve Officers Training Corps." It reminds me of the metal bands we placed around the testicles of boy lambs. For those of us who wear the insignia, it says we are serious about soldiering. If we do a good job as first sergeants, we will be officers our last year at NMMI, maybe battalion commanders.

Lt. Byers was a battalion commander.

Without a dick.

Sarah loved my stripes and she really loved my sword. I had shown her the metal one, too, with my name on it, which I will wear as an ROTC officer. We could order it the second semester of our senior year if we were on the officers-to-be list. Whenever our commanding corps officers were away on free weekends, the first sergeants who took their place wore the belt and sword. It was beautiful and gleamed silver when I wore it with my Sam Browne belt and sword scabbard during the Sunday afternoon parades on the NMMI drill grounds. The sword spoke of war as something beautiful. I felt like a knight when I saluted the reviewing stands with it, while NMMI glimmered like a magic castle in the sun. It was my duty to show up at the parade ground every weekend. It would be my duty to show up for war if called.

His dick?

As I prepared for evening tactics, I thought about the conversation I had overheard between the two old cadets. Vietnam was why the B-52 flights had increased over Barrel

Springs. Jose had been right. We were at war. North Vietnam was our enemy. President Kennedy told us that. After he died in Dallas, a fellow Texan swore to the nation that the South Vietnamese would defend their country before one drop of American boys' blood would be spilled in Southeast Asia.

Willy Byers had been an "American Boy."

His blood had definitely been spilled.

He was committed to war after a sampan attack against an American warship had been launched in the declared territorial waters of North Vietnam. Sampan attacks always spilled a lot of blood, usually from their own sailors as they splintered the wooden canoe hulls of their vessels against the steel bows of American warships. They, too, had young soldiers like Lt. Byers. The Gulf of Tonkin, unknown to Willy, would cost him his life. He was the first from NMMI.

Even as he died, Willy, like most Americans, could not have picked out the Gulf of Tonkin on a map. Had he known of its importance to him, perhaps he would have avoided the place. But, being from Kansas, his frame of geographical reference was limited.

Every Saturday, the ROTC cadets practiced small unit tactics. Captain Sabrosky, of the NMMI faculty, would lead us in our exercises. He was a captain in the regular army, and he took his job seriously. I didn't like him, and he didn't like me, especially on night maneuvers.

He tried to drive us into the ground. Usually, all the others dropped out but me. I stayed on his heels, pretending he was just another horse to break, another fence to mend, another long day of work with that old Mexican driving me under a merciless sun. Now, thanks to Jose, I even pretended I was a Villista.

Captain Sabrosky thought he was tough, but Jose taught me to be a fanatic. Tough Sabrosky finally stopped.

"Had enough, McBride?" he breathed heavily.

"If you have, sir." I had to be careful here. He could take my commission, my first chance to ever make real money, my first job that society would regard as legitimate, my first step on a career ladder. A job that would allow me to support both Sarah and me. I just had to make it through Sabrosky.

Sabrosky's face and even his body were cruel-looking. His eyebrows peaked in the middle giving him a "Ming the Merciless" look. He knew the nickname I'd given him and hated

139

it: "Planet Mongo." Some little butt-kissing squealer told him where the name had come from.

"You think you're hot stuff, don't you?" he sneered.

"I don't know what the captain means," I answered back.

"Give me pushups, sergeant!"

"Which arm should I use, sir?"

He stood on my back when I got down in pushup position.

"You'll need both of them."

He started counting as the others caught up to us. His voice faltered at fifty. It grew silent as I approached seventy-five. He stepped off when I reached ninety.

We walked back to the trucks that would take us back to the campus. I had won, and the pain in my arms was made bearable by the knowledge that he would not challenge me again. I commanded the platoon now. I was the leader. The others had to help me back into the truck.

Later, during dinner, I sat at the company table across from two new cadets. I watched them eat between bites. They had to chew ten times before swallowing, or I'd give them a demerit. Across from me, and at the far end of the table, Captain Sabrosky was talking with the company commander. They laughed together.

Time to get even. I took the plastic table cloth that hung over the edge of the table and made a trough. Nudging the new cadet next to me, I whispered out of the corner of my mouth, "Trough Sabrosky."

Each cadet quietly continued the trough until the one next to Sabrosky, who was still engrossed in talk, completed the trough circuit.

I eased my glass of tea off the table and poured the tea in the trough, elevating the trough so the tea flowed down the plastic "ditch." Each cadet elevated his section of the trough as the tea flowed silently by.

Suddenly, Sabrosky quit talking, not believing he is wet in his crotch. He glanced down stupidly watching his lap being completely soaked. At a signal from me, the trough was dropped and we stared straight ahead, busy with our eating. He looked helplessly around, knowing no one would squeal.

Then, he smiled. That smile scared me.

After dinner the old cadets with girlfriends went to the parking lot to sit in the cars with their girls. From six-fifteen until seven, we had forty-five minutes to get hot and bothered. Sarah was there in her new car. Seniors had driving privileges at Rayford.

As I slid into the front seat, Sarah said, "I'm pregnant."

My world stopped. "What? You're what?"

She touched my face. "I'm pregnant."

I heard a Dodge Power Wagon roar through a crossroad in the back of my stunned mind. I felt my boyhood slipping away, left behind like a chrysalis, and something new emerging.

I looked at Sarah. She, too, was different. There was fear in her eyes but also, a strange hardness – determination, commitment, maybe.

We sat there in silence, knowing I would have to go in soon.

"Sarah, we have to tell your parents." It was all I could think to say.

"Will you be there beside me? Will you tell them and not run away?" She was looking at me hard.

I thought about Hide and Barbara Anne staring numbly at their daughter.

I thought about Hide and Barbara Anne doing a slow turn to me.

I thought about Hide reaching for a gun...

Something inside overcame my fear of Hide. This was a new reality we would face together. It was our baby.

"I'll be there," I said quietly with all the conviction, stupidity, and love that flows from where promises like that are made.

Sarah smiled, and her tears stained my shirt as we sat there, holding each other, until the first bell rang for study hall.

She sucked in her breath. I wanted to say something to make her sadness go away in the silence but I couldn't.

Finally, she said, "After graduation at Rayford next week, we'll drive up here."

I had visions of Hide getting out of the car with a gun.

"Why?" I asked.

"We'll tell them about the baby."

I saw Sabrosky watching us, looking at his watch, his pants still stained from dinner.

"Listen, I got to go," I said, opening the car door, hurrying to avoid the second bell. "I'll call you to make sure you got back okay."

"Johnny," she pleaded, "please stay. I need to talk this through."

"I can't," I answered helplessly, backing away, "I've got to go."

Sabrosky took another step toward me.

She bowed her head on the wheel and sobbed. As I left, I noticed Captain Sabrosky walking towards her car. I watched him tell her to roll down the window.

The final bell sounded, and I sprinted through Sally Port to my room, fearing something bad was happening, but I wasn't sure what.

Old cadets know how to beat the system. My buddies on guard duty at Sally Port, the tunnel entrance into the castle, covered for me after study hall, and I called Rayford from the guardhouse.

Sarah's roommate answered.

"Is Sarah there?"

"Johnny, what's happened?"

"What do you mean?"

"The house mother called Sarah into her room the moment she got back from seeing you. She's still in there. We can hear her crying. I've got to hang up, our dean of students just went in there, too."

I stared at the dead phone, trying to control a growing feeling of dread. The dread thing sort of got out of control later in the week after I tried to get hold of two more times. It just got worse when Sarah didn't come to graduation.

Sabrosky posted the first sergeant's list. My name was scratched off.

I hitchhiked back to Barrel Springs. I had nowhere else to go.

That Last Summer

My job was still there. So was Jose. But there was no Sarah. What about our baby? What was happening? I kept looking over my shoulder expecting to hear Hide's truck, with Barbara Anne at the wheel, bearing down on me as Hide carefully aimed a rifle out of the truck's window.

I finally told Jose about it.

He didn't say anything.

He just started watching the roads with me.

Which didn't help.

To forget the ache that seemed to hang in the hot summer breezes, I worked long and hard hours, sometimes even longer than Jose. He would stand on the porch, watching me repair the corrals or saddle-soap the leather gear in the barn. I even worked at night repairing Jose's tin roof. Even then, the heat of the roof turned my legs red. I enjoyed the pain from the heat. Anything was better than thinking about Sarah.

The days blended together into hard, sweaty work. June warmed into July and July baked into August. It was shipping time for the fall markets, and we were getting ready for roundup by riding pastures and checking on Hide's cattle. There was little time to worry about Sarah. Finally, Jose tried to speak to me while we rode horseback to the day's work.

"There is time enough when you are old to regret things, but, Chapo, you're too young to look so sad."

"I don't want to talk about it." It hurt to shut him up. I know somewhere in his toughness were answers, but I wasn't ready to hear them.

"The hardest loss is not death, Chapo. It is something dying inside of you while you still live. That's why you are so sad."

I kicked my horse into a gallop. "Damn it, Jose! Leave me alone!"

"Don't tire out the horse," he shouted after me. "It's got enough work to do without being punished by an angry young man!"

As I rode off, I could hear Jose singing a Xavier Solis song: "*Cuando calienta et sol aqui en la playa…*"

And as I asked him to do, Jose left me alone. He never brought it up again. He didn't have to. The subject came right up to me.

We were in the corral, getting ready to ride one of the pastures to look for worms in the cows when we heard the truck. Jose ignored it until it stopped at the corral.

"Howdy, boys," Hide's booming voice startled our horses, "thought you could use some real cowboy help."

I looked through the corral and saw him lead three horses, two saddled and one unsaddled, out of the horse trailed hooked to the rear end of his new GMC pickup. Sarah appeared on the opposite side and took the reins of one of the saddled horses. She would not look at me. I could not take my eyes off of her. There was so much to ask.

Jose looked at Oso. It was too late to pretend the horse wasn't broken. In his usual taciturn manner, Jose threw a stirrup over the saddle and tightened the cinch.

"Glad to see that horse is broken. You do that work, Johnny?"

Jose paused in his task. "I did it, boss. He's ready for you if you would like to ride him."

Hide studied the big horse. "No. You've got him saddled. Finish the day with him, and we'll take him back with us this afternoon."

I read the sadness in Jose's shoulders. "You going out with us, boss?"

Why had Hide brought Sarah? She made me nervous. Yet, there would be no way to be alone with her while riding the pasture.

"Brought a horse for you to try, Johnny. Bought this little while mare for Barbara Anne, but she's a little skittish. Know you can handle her, though, and shake out her kinks for my wife."

He handed me the reins and I took her over to the barn to be saddled.

Jose looked at the horse and then at me. It was a strange look.

Hide opened the gate to our corral and stepped into his saddle.

"Come on, old man. I hope you can keep your stud from killing out horses. Damn horse is only good for screwing."

Jose pretended not to hear. Picking up Oso's rear hoof and placing it on his knee, he filed the hoof away from where it had overlapped the shoe.

"Now, boys," Hide continued, "I'm giving the orders today. Any cows you see, check for the afterbirth. Make sure it's clear of the cow and that those damn blowflies haven't laid any eggs in her ass.

"If they're okay, let's take 'em down to the pens so I can get a count and brand some of them. Can't have a wetback stealing 'em, can I, Jose?"

Hide was true to form: so delicate a father around Sarah and so tactful a boss around Jose.

"If they have maggots, sprinkle deworming powder where the cow is bleeding."

Jose had taken out his knife and was cleaning under the shoe. Every time Hide would boom out an order, he'd just clean that much harder.

I watched Sarah as she got on her horse. She seemed totally cool to my presence. I had never noticed before how much she resembled Hide. Maybe she didn't until now.

"Keep your mind on your business, Chapito," Jose muttered, picking up Oso's other massive hoof. "This is not normal, his being here. Besides, we have plenty of horses here."

I felt I didn't need his reminders.

"I can saddle a horse just fine, Jose," I whispered through clenched teeth.

"Then why have you just tied your cinch ring to your flank strap?" he asked.

I glanced at the saddle and saw he was right. Angrily, I tied the cinch hard; in response to the jolt, the horse sucked in its breath. Jose was on me in an instant.

"Don't take out your problems on an animal that has plenty of its own," he hissed, jerking the leather strap from my hand and loosening the belt. "Deal with problems inside your heart; talk them out when you've cooled off. Becoming a man is hard, Chapo, but don't blame an animal for that problem."

Hide Eberhard shook out his rope, growing impatient with Jose's careful attention to me and Oso.

"Getting a little slow, Jose? Pasture ain't getting any smaller and the day ain't getting any cooler. We've got work to do, so let's get on with it."

He turned his horse and trotted out to the middle of the corral. He shook out a larger loop from his rope, and began trotting by the snubbing post – first, one side; then, the other.

"Hey, old man," Hide shouted, "I haven't lost my touch."

It was the first time I had ever seen Hide on a horse, and I had to admit that he wasn't bad. He was roping the snubbing post while loping his horse around it. I realized he was trying to impress the old man. It was something I might have tried my first summer at Barrel Springs to impress Jose.

Jose ignored him now like he did me that whole summer.

As Hide lifted his loop off the post for one more try, the big bay he was riding decided to take a crap. It raised its tail just as Hide twisted a large loop over his shoulder, preparing to rope the post again.

The loop settled neatly over the tail. Hide kicked his horse around and began to run at the post, unaware the loop now included the horse's tail.

"Hide...," I called out, "I think you'd best..."

Jose stood up and quickly tapped me across the saddle of my horse.

"Shut up, Chapito. Watch how a fool makes work for himself."

"What did you say, McBride?" said Hide galloping past us. "That I was the best?"

Hide's face was flushed as he barreled by us and jerked the loop forward.

The rope tightened quickly on the tender underside of the horse's tail.

The bay went straight up.

Hide went straight out.

Jose swung into the saddle in one quick supple movement and rode over to the prone body of Hide, who was now on the ground, cursing and covered in corral dirt.

As he rode by, he glanced down and said, "Let's go, boss. The pasture won't wait for sleeping men."

I followed Jose, glancing over my shoulder to see Sarah helping Hide up and looking towards me. As we rode down the arroyo and up the other side, we heard a very loud, "Damn!" coming from the corral.

"I think the boss is ready to go now," said Jose, chuckling to himself.

When you ride a pasture to check for animals, everyone splits up. One rider goes in the hills and drives down any cattle that may be lying in the shade of the scrub oak or the stone outcroppings higher up. The other rider rides in the flatland, picks up the animals as they wander down, and keeps them moving in front of him.

If it's a big pasture, and this one was, this process is repeated with the cowboys working in sections. Somewhere to our left, across the pasture, Sarah and Hide were doing the same thing as we were.

Jose stopped me after Hide and Sarah rode out of sight.

"It's time for you to ride Oso," he said, stepping down off the horse. "If the boss takes him this afternoon, you'll not see my horse again. Here."

He handed me the reins, and I proudly stepped into the saddle, knowing the trust Jose was now placing in my hands. He took my horse and turned her back towards the pasture.

"Let's go, Chapo. We have work to do."

Such a simple gesture. So important to me.

Jose had given me the rocky hills while he followed an old dirty road that led to a windmill and holding pens about five miles distant. As I'd been taught, I kept my eyes on the horse as it picked its way carefully through the rocks on the side of the hill.

Beyond Jose, about a mile, I could see Hide driving his cattle in the same general direction. I shielded my eyes and tried to find Sarah up in the rocks, but I couldn't see her.

The day wore on, the number of cows on the side of the ridge I had been following thinned out, and I was bored watching Jose drive the herd quietly in front of him. I could hear Hide shouting and screaming at his herd further away as they kept scattering on him.

I almost missed Sarah's horse. Oso's ears flicked forward, so I immediately became watchful. Something was just over the rise to my right. I topped out expecting to find another cow on the other side, but instead saw Sarah's horse tied to a sotol bush next to an outcropping of rocks. It was unsaddled.

I glanced down at Jose and realized he couldn't see us on this side of the mountain. Hide also was too wrapped up in what he was doing to know Sarah was gone.

I hurriedly tied Oso a little way from her horse and went looking for Sarah. She was under a deep overhang, almost a cave, that looked far into Mexico towards Jose's home. The ground was smooth and she had spread her saddle blanket out to sit on.

"I was hoping you'd see my horse. We need to talk," she said quietly.

My body was tense from hurt pride, anger, longing, but I was also curious to find why there had been no communication. I had learned from the death of my mother that it was just too devastating when love ended suddenly.

"Yeah." I could hear the anger and bitterness in my voice. "There are a few things to clear up. Things like why are you riding a horse pregnant? And why didn't you come pick me up after school? Damn right. There are some things that need talking about."

She looked at me for the first time. Her eyes were clear, they were direct, and there were no tears.

"Captain Sabrosky called Rayford. He saw me crying after you left and wouldn't let me leave until I told him what the problem was. He said he could help, that he was a friend of yours. Was he?"

"Just the opposite," I said.

"I guessed as much. Anyway, the school called Mom, and told her I was pregnant. She guessed who the father was, too." Sarah smoothed out her pants leg and stared across the desert. She took a deep breath.

She looked at my face. "There's not going to be a child, Johnny. Mom knew a doctor in Juarez, and we had the baby taken care of."

I sat there thinking of the time I got a sotol thorn in my leg from brushing against the plant while chasing down one of Hide's wilder cows. The thorn festered, then hardened in my body. It hurt all the time and I was desperate to get it out. Finally, on its own, it popped out one night at NMMI. Like that thorn, I felt our love popping loose from my heart and slipping away across the desert.

"Johnny? Say something, please. I need to hear something, anything." She stretched her body towards me into the cooling shadows of the rock.

"What do you want me to say? That I'm happy for you? Happy for us?"

I hated her calmness, and then I hated myself for letting her touch my face. Even as my body responded, my mind said, "No. Not again."

I held her in the coolness under the rock just like an Apache couple perhaps had held each other a hundred years earlier.

"Chapito!" I could hear Jose's worried shout. Sarah pulled at my arm.

Damn the old man for looking for me. I walked to the top of the hill and waved down at him. "I was up here taking a shit! Be down in a minute."

"I was only worried about my horse." He waved and turned back towards his herd.

"What's that airplane?" said Sarah, shielding her eyes and pointing off in the distance behind me. I turned and looked.

"Looks like a Border Patrol spotter plane."

I searched the area for the companion jeep and saw its dust plume at the edge of the pasture where we had begun working earlier that morning.

"There's its buddy," I said, pointing. Sarah began saddling her horse as the plane came closer.

Keeping an eye on the circling plane, we led our horses to the top of the hill, after first checking where Hide and Jose were. They were both concentrating on their herds and couldn't see the airplane or each other as it buzzed towards them from behind.

The airplane turned and dove lazily towards Jose, scattering the herds in front of him, then climbed again, making a steep bank to the left.

It made another dive, forcing Jose to lean over in his saddle.

"Isn't that plane flying too close?" she asked, her hand finding mine, passing on her fear.

I watched the plane turn for another run. "They're trying to get him off the horse so the jeep can check on his papers."

The plane banked over Hide and flew towards Jose. Hide left his cattle and began trotting across the half-mile distance between him and his long-time foreman. Hide's horse broke from a trot to a full gallop. Hide was screaming something to Jose.

The plane's engine backfired and the skittish white horse bolted.

I've always wondered if the pilot was going to pull up at the last moment, or if he meant to deliberately knock Jose out of the saddle. Either way, trying to keep the crazed horse from bucking, Jose never realized how low this third pass was. All his concentration was directed towards controlling the white horse.

Only at the last moment, when he turned it towards the plane, did he see the danger he'd placed the horse in. Using his strength and the skill of all his years as a horseman, Jose stood in his stirrups and jerked his reins down hard and to the left, bowing the horse's neck in the same direction. The white went to its knees and the plane roared by inches from the horse's head. Jose had exercised a rider's responsibility to protect his mount.

But the right wheel decapitated Jose.

Sarah and I saw his head explode long before the sound, like a melon breaking, reached us, Hide reined in his horse and slowed to an uncomprehending walk. Slowly, Jose slid from the saddle and fell next to a mesquite bush, scaring two bullbats who had been waiting there for evening. The white horse, still not completely back on its feet, neighed its hear across the valley to Sarah and me. The horse jerked sideways away from the bullbats, and Jose's boot quit the final stirrup.

The plane kept circling until the jeep drove to the scene. When I could tear my eyes away from the terrible picture below me, Sarah was gone. To my left I heard rocks tumbling down the mountain, and I saw Sarah on her horse, picking her way down the mountainside to her father.

He intercepted her before she got too close to Jose. They were joined by the men in the jeep. I watched them talk as I got on Oso and rode further along the opposite ridge, hidden from the scene. As I rode, I heard the jeep start and drive away, the plane following, its angry hum receding in the distance.

I don't remember crying, just feeling numb, waiting for an explanation of why these things happen; something to make me say, "Yes, I understand all now; so *that's* why." But silence was all I had, and the hot air blowing from the desert tomb blew over me as I topped the mountain further down, closer to the pens, and rode back to where Hide and Sarah talked to the Border Patrol.

My numbness was now transforming itself into guilt. Maybe if I hadn't been with Sarah, I could have warned Jose about the plane. Maybe the plane would have dived at me.

Maybe.

Long before I got there, I saw Sarah turn and ride back towards Barrel Springs, following the Border Patrol's jeep. Hide waited for me by his horse, next to the white horse and Jose's body.

"There's been an accident, Johnny."

"No there hasn't. There's been a murder."

Hide studied me. "Did you see it?"

"Yes."

"Sarah said she didn't see anything. She's upset so I've sent her back to the truck. Apparently, Jose tried to outrun the Border Patrol plane and the horse tripped, throwing him into some rocks and crushing his skull. They've alerted the sheriff's department and they're on their way out."

He stopped and looked at me. "When did you change horses?"

"What difference does that make? Jose would have been just as dead."

Hide looked away quickly. "Damn it to hell. Why me? You plan things..."

He stopped short, remembering me. "Jose was a good man. Just wait here until the sheriff arrived. I'll tell him what's happened. No need to mention Sarah. She doesn't need to get involved as a witness in these things. 'Sides, her mom would kill me if she knew I'd brought her horse over today. Just my luck."

"Your luck?" I exploded, "Your luck? What about Jose? What about his luck? Jose didn't try to outrun the plane, and his skull wasn't crushed by rocks. The plane killed him with its wheel."

Hide shook his head. "That's not what I saw. From where you were, it probably looked different. We need to keep our stories straight. There's no need to create any problems with the Border Patrol, now, is there? We've got an understanding because of the men I employ to work the ranch. I can't afford to make the Feds mad. Besides, they were just doing their job. I'll send the sheriff out, and, after he gets the body, you bring Oso back to the corrals and ride with the sheriff into Van Horn.

"Sarah is a little shook up. I'll take her into Van Horn for dinner. Meet you in town. And Johnny...?"

I fought to keep from letting that bastard see me cry.

Hide studied me carefully. "...That's our story; what I've told you. Let's all tell the same thing and get on home. Don't worry. It's a tragic thing, but I got a good foreman standing right here in front of me. Yes, sir. You're my foreman, now. I'll take care of everything."

Foreman. A joke of a title meaning nothing.

I waited until Hide was out of sight before I worked up enough courage to do what needed to be done. I got off my horse and sat there a long time, cradling Jose. I might have been there all night if Oso hadn't walked over and nudged me.

Gently, I picked up the body and slid it over Oso's saddle, apologizing the whole time to Jose as I tied his feet and hands to the saddle. I looked around for his cavalry hat and found it in a cholla cactus, one side of it crushed by the airplane's tire.

151

"That's just like you, Jose, making me work to get your damn hat," I said through the tears, ignoring the thorns as I stretched to get his hat.

"Hell, it's too early to take another vacation, but I guess there's no talking you out of it, is there?"

After smoothing out the hat as best I could, I tied it to my saddle horn. Swinging myself up on the white mare, I reached down and grabbed Oso's reins and rode off towards Mexico in the deepening night.

I knew a place there beneath sandstone cliffs that burned red in the sun. There was a nice spot for a grave between two cottonwoods whose golden leaves fell in the pond beside the trees. Jose would like that.

The only thing he wouldn't like was that there would be three broken hearts by his grave beneath those two trees, along with mine.

Later, much later, I heard a siren in the darkness behind me, but I didn't turn back.

The Hour of the Pharaoh

What ties us to a piece of land in this country is just as often the tragedies as the triumphs. You can't pave over tears; you can't develop wrongs into a shopping mall. There's always someone who senses the price that is really paid for the dirt they stand on.

The two little girls ran screaming to get their mother. They had been young when they saw me, the two horses, and the burden we were carrying. I had covered Jose the best I could with a piece of old tarp I curled around one of the legs of Hide's windmill. But the stain on the tarp was all they needed to see to understand what had happened.

They were older now, calling for Sofia. Behind me, silent villagers gathered, blocking my path to the river I had just crossed. Their silence was eerie. I could only go on, towards the wailing woman at the door of Jose's home. NMMI had made me read "Oedipus." Sofia's deep cries reinforced all tragedies in my experience, whether real or studied in the pages of books.

She led me inside, or I her, and listened to the story for as long as she could before her shoulders said, "Enough." She walked across the little kitchen and opened the door. The villagers still stood outside.

I heard her talking to them. It was a sad voice, one born from the earth and better at dealing with death than mine was. I breathed deeply the intense smells of this kitchen, of the wood smoke and love Jose and Sofia had shared in it.

I suddenly became aware that she was standing at the door. I hadn't heard her come back in.

"Wait for me outside, Chapito. I need to talk with the children. They are still afraid to see their father."

Some of the villagers helped me slide the body off the saddle, and a discussion followed about where to bury him. The little girls' denials seeped under the crack of the door as we cleaned Jose's saddle the best we could. Behind them, through the window, I could see Sofia slumped at the kitchen table, holding her head with her hands, her tears falling on the wooden tabletop.

Timidly, the children came out and clung to my leg, as if hoping that when they looked up, they would see their father and not his friend. I didn't look down. I kept wishing they didn't have to see what they saw, that I could protect them from the reality before them.

Sofia appeared at the door with a shovel and walked through our group over to the cottonwoods.

"We'll bury him here because the dirt is soft and the air is always cool by the little pond. He always loved it."

That was the way death was handled in Ojos Calientes. Juarez, two hundred miles to the west, was where there were morticians and priests. Who could afford a proper burial, anyhow? The cost would be more than most made in a year.

The villagers and I watched her attack the dirt until we felt ashamed. I went over, gently took the shovel away, and continued the job she had started. After a while, a young man from the village took the shovel from me; others followed his example. And so, as a village, we dug a deep good-bye to Jose.

After we finished lowering him into the grave, Sofia went over to Oso and took off the old man's saddle. She carried it back to the open grave and laid it gently on his body, as fitting a tribute as any flower arrangement. I reached down and handed it back to her.

"Keep it. It is one of a kind. So was Jose."

She handed it to me. "Then, you take it. He would want you to have it."

Sofia helped the little girls place the last two shovelfuls of dirt in the grave. Solemnly, they crossed themselves; the villagers followed their example. As the children leaned against her, crying softly, Sofia told everyone in a quiet, strong voice of the love she had for Jose, and of how he had died. Her voice never quavered, but I knew: the two girls were all that propped her up.

She asked me to say a few words. It was hard, standing there in front of those people, to even think of explaining why a country needed to hunt people down like that.

Finally, I looked at the grave and said simply, "He was my teacher and my friend."

The girls left Sofia and took the two horses to the corral, unsaddled mine, and poured them some feed. The horses dropped down in the dirt of the corral to roll the sweat off their backs, grateful for their freedom. The sound of the horses rolling in the dirt distracted the villagers' attention away from the grave. I was grateful that such a simple thing broke the tension we all felt.

As the villagers walked away, Sofia touched my arm. "Are you hungry?"

"No."

"Well, I need to cook for someone right now, and you'll have to eat it."

She turned and went back inside. I followed. While she cooked, I offered to go with her to the American consulate in Juarez. She asked me what the point would be.

"At least there should be some kind of complaint," I answered.

"No. He lived a good life with his horses." While cooking she attacked her wood stove as if it had been Hide. "I shared in his happiness, and, as a family, we must share the loss. He had nothing to do with governments, and I see no reason to change that now."

She looked out the window, towards the corral where the horses were eating contentedly. The sandstone cliff towering over the corral looked in the evening sun like some great red headstone over Jose's newly dug grave.

"He was a good man, a good father. We loved him. There is nothing more to be said. We'll keep his memory here, not on some complaint form in Juarez."

The next morning I saddled the white mare, then tied Jose's saddle clumsily behind mine. I led her over to Sofia's door and waited for Sofia to come out. She glanced at my horse and at the one left in the corral.

"You are not taking the black one?" she said.

I shook my head. "Jose put his last years in that horse. It's his legacy to give to his girls. I figure a lot of people will pay or trade to have its blood in their colts. Do you have some place you could take him for awhile? Eberhard may know where you live."

She smiled for the first time. "Gringos have been coming to Mexico looking for things for a long time. First, they looked for the Apaches, then for Pancho Villa and his men. If they couldn't find his army, then a horse should be a simple thing to hide."

She looked back at the corral where Oso seemed puzzled at our leaving him behind. His ears flicked back and forth.

"So," she said, "it is the only way. Eberhard will not miss the horse, but the money in the horse. It is right Oso should stay here."

She came then and hugged me.

"Jose was a good man. He said you would be, too, one day. He treated us well. I loved that in him." It was her turn to look away.

"What are you going to do now?" she asked finally.

"I don't know."

"Why not stay here? Work, help me with the horses. Oso will bring us good business."

"Sofia, there's nothing for me back there, but I can't let them sweep Jose's death under the rug like that. I've only loved two people in my life. Both were murdered. Someone, sometime, has got to try to see that something is done."

She looked at me for a long time. Finally, she brushed back my hair.

"No one will answer for this, Chapito. We are poor. No one answers for us."

There were tears in her eyes. "*Ten cuidado.*"

I walked the horse over to the grave and tried to decide what to do. I wanted to stay, but I wanted to see Hide's face when I returned without Oso. It was important to me.

Sofia followed and touched my arm. "*Aqui siempre tienes familia.* Come back when you can."

And I left. But I didn't go directly back to Barrel Springs. I had some business to attend to. It didn't seem as long a ride as the first time I went there with Jose. His saddle did not feel heavy though I held it on my back with one hand as I climbed. Reaching my destination, among some rocks on a little ledge in the Eagle Mountains, I hid the saddle next to the green bottle.

As I finished piling back the rocks, I dusted my hands off and looked around.

"You were damn right about the view from her, Jose. And I promise I'll come back and drink to you *and* to Doroteo."

As I stepped into the saddle and turned the horse towards Barrel Springs, I tried to formulate a plan, but all I could see in my mind's eye was Hide's face.

So much for planning.

Just above Barrel Springs, I stopped my horse, wondering why a sheriff's patrol car was at the house. Maybe Sarah had found her conscience and decided to tell what she had seen. Maybe Hide and the Border Patrol people involved had been arrested, and the sheriff needed my help to convict them and back Sarah's story. Maybe the sheriff still waited for me, since I hadn't waited for him like Hide ordered.

Touching my spurs to the horse, I trotted towards the car.

Hide and the sheriff came to the old screen door and watched me dismount. As I tied the horse to the fence gate and walked towards the door, I enjoyed watching Hide look past me for Oso. The sheriff glanced at Hide.

"At least he brought one of them back," said the sheriff.

Hide motioned for him to go out. "Better wait for us outside, Jimmy G."

"Wait a minute, sheriff," I said, "I want to report a murder."

The sheriff closed the screen door behind him, looking at me hard.

"And just who was killed?"

Jimmy Goode was chewing his omnipresent chaw. He had probably gone through a hundred acres of tobacco during his fifty-some-odd years at the public trough. Like the rings on a redwood tree, the inches for each public year circled his large beergut. He was probably the reason Justice blindfolded herself.

I glanced at Hide's face, hoping to see fear. All I saw was pure confidence. Not at all a good sign.

"Jose Navarrete was killed by a Border Patrol plane, and Hide wants to cover it up." It sounded so simple when I said it.

Hide smiled and shook his head knowingly at the sheriff.

"Told you what he'd say, sheriff. But you know how thieves are. Hell, I put him over here with a Meskin, and it looks like he turned into one."

Jimmy Goode glared at me.

"Son, if Hide Eberhard wasn't in your corner, I'd already have slapped the cuffs on you for stolen property. Now, just tell him where the other horse is, and we'll forget the whole deal."

He waddled past me to his car.

I yelled at him. "Sarah saw Jose killed, too. Ask her."

He leaned over the top of his patrol car and pointed a cue-stick finger at me.

"I talked to her. She said she saw you lead Oso out of the corrals as she drove up with her father. They were going to surprise you with a visit to help you with the ranch work while Jose was on vacation. Instead, they caught you stealing a horse."

Jimmy Goode tried to spit over the car and failed. He wiped the drool with his sleeve. "You're one damn McBride who's stolen his last animal."

Hide held the screen door open for me. "Come on in."

"He's not going to believe you about Jose," said Hide, following me into the kitchen. My throat was dry and I needed a drink. He put a piece of paper on the kitchen table. I ignored the paper until I had finished a second glass of water.

I glanced at the paper. It was the deportation notice of one Jose Navarrete, dated the day he was killed.

Hide looked out the back door. "Jose has disappeared into Mexico. That's what happened according to the records of the Border Patrol. And that is what is recorded as the truth in Van Horn."

I threw the paper at him. It fluttered harmlessly to the floor. He bent down and picked it up, folding it carefully, putting justice back into his pocket.

"And what do you get in return?" Sofia's warning was beginning to sink in. People like Hide were experts at damage control.

Hide smiled. "Well, while I had the tire on the plane repaired at the little airport at my house, we kinda' arrived at a gentleman's agreement not to check on any workers at my ranch for two or three years. The Border Patrol supervisor and I have a real good understanding."

"That's all Jose's death means to you?"

Hide slammed his hand down on the table. "That son of a bitch never respected me one bit."

"You okay in there, Hide?" Jimmy Goode's voice sounded worried.

"Don't worry." Hide shouted. "McBride and I are reaching an understanding of things."

"Reason with him as long as you need to, Hide." I could hear the fat sheriff laugh. I shivered inwardly.

"Now, Johnny, ever since the day of the pharaohs, men like me have put together deals that supply men like Jose with a job, money, and security. In return we expect loyalty and respect."

I studied Hide for the first time. I could see him now through Jose's eyes.

"You're an asshole, Hide. All Jose had to give you was his time and his skills. He didn't owe you anything else. When you didn't understand what he had to give, what you had in him, he quit respecting you. That is the covenant between the landowner and the worker. Once you break that covenant, we all lose."

158

I looked around. "This house would fit into your living room, but you're not worthy of buckling Jose's spurs. He knew your land and your horses better than you because he cared for both. You only paid the taxes. You can't buy a horse like Oso with money. You earn a horse like Oso. And you can't buy respect from a man like Jose, you earn it. That's why I'll never tell you where the horse is."

Hide smiled an evil smile. "The land and everything on it is mine. The law is clear. Now, where's that horse? We'll forget this misunderstanding."

"I killed it."

Hide laughed. "No, you didn't. Jose taught you too well. Hell, you'd kill me before you'd touch that horse."

He had a point.

I popped a can of evaporated milk and began sucking on it. "Screw you" sounds weird as a burp.

His face got red. "You ungrateful little bastard. I pay for your schooling, I give you a job away from your crazy father, and this is the payment I get?"

"You covered up Jose's murder, Hide, and you're not going to get away with it. Now, you can beat me up, but I've been beaten by the best."

Hide got himself under control, slid a chair out from the table and sat down. I think I resented him sitting at that table more than anything. It was the place where Jose and I had talked about a lot of things. To me, it was sacred ground.

So I hit him.

That old fist just traveled at McBride speed away from my body and right into his face. There is goes, I thought.

He was a big man. He fell hard. And got right back up and knocked me across the kitchen.

"Keep reasoning, Hide!" Jimmy Goode shouted.

As I struggled to get up, his boot caught me in the side, slamming my body against the adobe wall built with straw and mud. It gave way and I tumbled into the back yard.

Hide stood in the kitchen, looking through the hole.

"Hear me, kid. Hear me real good! Forget about the Institute. Forget about ever working for me again. Forget about ever coming back here."

I laughed. "What are you going to do? Have me thrown in jail? I'll be happy to testify at my trial where Oso is and when we go to get him, I'll also show them the body of one hell of a cowboy killed for nothing more than a Border Patrol quota!"

Hide took out an envelope and laid it on the table.

"Don't you think I know that?" he said. "Here, I arranged for this. I wanted to deliver it to you, personally. There are two letters in here. One is from a Captain Sabrosky at NMMI. The other one is local."

He turned to walk outside, then stopped at the door. He looked back at me as I was dusting myself off.

"Never screw with a pharaoh – or his daughter – boy; you'll end up under the pyramid. I'd kill Sarah before I let her marry a McBride or have his kid."

I thought about Sarah's antelope long ago. Any man who could barbeque his kid's pet in front of her just might be capable of anything.

"Would you kill me, just because I loved Sarah?"

Hide looked at me with empty, flat eyes.

"Like a boot stomping a bug," he said, slowly.

"Then, why haven't you?"

"What makes you think I haven't tried?"

I stared at him, not understanding.

"Even an airplane can spot a white horse."

I watched him walk out to his truck, talk to the sheriff and drive off. I stood in the kitchen listening to my future drip away in the sink.

"Hurry it up, McBride. I'm to see you off this place within an hour. I'll give your sorry ass a ride to Van Horn. I suggest you keep going from there." Jimmy Goode slammed his patrol car door, started the engine and waited.

Screw him, I thought, looking around the house. Was there anything I wanted? I glanced at the envelope. I had never gotten a letter from anyone but Sara. Who would write me locally?

In Jose's bedroom I looked for something, anything to send to the kids or Sofia. There was nothing. In the living room was the picture of Jesus inside the apple crate. After lighting a candle, I turned the picture around so that it faced the wall and walked back to the kitchen.

I didn't think Jesus needed to see what was happening down here.

The envelope was still there.

Sitting down at the table, I stared at it for a long time. With one glance around the dusty old kitchen, I sighed, and read the first letter.

The letter from NMMI was to inform me I had been kicked out for conduct unbecoming a cadet officer: I had stolen personal property from one Hide Eberhard, a horse to be exact, which Hide Eberhard had noticed missing while checking on his property at Barrel Springs. Sabrosky had signed the withdrawal form with the required witness signature provided by Hide Eberhard, attesting to the theft of Oso. The letter stated I would not be allowed to return and that my ROTC commission had been rescinded.

The second letter I didn't have to read all the way through. It began: "Greetings from the Culberson County Draft Board."

Part 2

"Shit is not a problem as long as it's moving".
- Words of wisdom from Juan Bizcocho

Inside the Stomach of the Beast

The bus was an old gray-green color and hard wire mesh on the windows. We filed into it off the plane at Cam Ranh Bay airport in the Republic of South Vietnam. Nervously, we stared out of the windows as the officer in the front announced:

"You will be taken to the processing center here at Cam Ranh Bay and assigned out to your units. Here is a list of rules and regulations to follow. You will notice the wire-mesh on the windows. This is to keep kids on mopeds and bikes from throwing grenades in the window. You are at war, gentlemen."

As his voice droned on, I noticed several water buffalo sitting in the sun around a watering hole. I had seen all this before. Another bus. Same wire over the windows. Struggling with memory, I tried to bring it all back: Jose, West Texas, breaking horses, draft board, special forces training. I looked at the jungle and the distant mountains beyond the water buffalo. It was a word far from the desert I knew: lush, green, and steaming in the hot sun.

The sound of the bus beginning its journey startled me, and I began noticing my fellow riders, all dressed in green. No women and children here, but the faces were as reminiscent of those on that bus outside of Van Horn long ago as was their helplessness to do anything about their situation. Blacks with hooded eyes looked warily out on a world far from their concrete canyons; Puerto Ricans torn from their island or from the familiar barrios in big cities around the country; boys from Tennessee and North Carolina, vaguely hoping for a tinge of Blue Ridge in all that green; Tex-Mex boys squinting in a sun familiar in its intensity, but sweating in an unfamiliar humidity that was already beginning to make us old men before our time. We could see the salt of our years drying on green sleeves.

Jose was right. *Los pobres de la tierra* were the ones who fought wars. I was never conscious of it until that bus ride to the processing center. But there wasn't time for philosophizing after the bus stopped. Everything became a confused blur: shots; brushing the teeth with some kind of special grit, supposedly to keep away cavities (maybe if you smeared it on your body, no cavities would appear there either); paperwork, paperwork, paperwork; then assignment to a smaller compound for special forces, a new label I had obtained at the

163

John F. Kennedy Center for Specialized Warfare in Fayetteville, North Carolina.

The Nha Trang compound reminded me of the fort at Fort Davis, where that patrol had been sent out to its death looking for Apaches. I looked around the hills that surrounded Nha Trang trying to pick out the little hill where I was going to die. After the two-week acclimatization, we were presented with our assignment options.

Here is how it begins: You walk into a room where an officer sits in the middle looking at your records.

"We have openings," he begins, "in CCN, CCC, and CCS. Your security clearance and schools qualify you to volunteer for one of them if you would like. Otherwise, we have several A-teams with openings, too."

I don't dare ask him why there are openings.

I stare at him, my arm aching from the shots, and the heat making me sweat. He smiles at my discomfort.

"What is CCN, CCC, or CCS?" I ask.

"I can't t tell you. That's classified. If you want to know, sign here."

I sign there.

"Go to the next room, please."

I follow the White Rabbit to the next room. It's the only way out. Another officer, slightly higher in rank, sits there.

"See this map? We do special ops into the following areas: CCN is the area to the north and slightly east of South Vietnam and includes China and Laos; CCC is Vietnam itself, and due west to include some of Laos and most of central Vietnam and Cambodia; CCS is Cambodia, the lower part of Vietnam, and occasional ops where needed. Any questions?"

Only a couple of thousand.

"Is it cooler in the north?" I ask wiping the sweat off my forehead.

He laughs. "That's classified, McBride, but you are now assigned to Command and Control North."

"What's that?"

"That's classified, too. Sign here. Go through the next door, please." He hands me some more papers and I descend deeper into special ops. There, I discover that, if I perform (and survive) 11 missions in the field, I'll receive a good assignment for the rest of my tour. Those good assignments are in different colors on a map in front of me.

After one, two, even ten missions with CCN, the colors fade. There are no good assignments in Vietnam. Besides, you won't live to get them anyway. You and your comrades become the special play toys of seriously deranged men bored with convention. They spend their time pondering questions like: Can a man be strapped to a stretcher and air-evacuated by an airplane that doesn't land, but simply grabs a balloon hooked to the stretcher as it flies by? Can hand-carried diarrhea-producing germs be poured into the drinking water of the enemy in his backyard? Can LSD be turned into a gas, placed in a grenade and thrown at the enemy? Can good people be killed by special ops people dressed like the enemy, so the surviving good people will hate the enemy for killing the good people? Can radars be fooled by humans falling through tinfoil rain, hurtling downward through eight miles of air? Does CCN make sense when it has a ninety percent attrition rate this month?

On my sixteenth mission, we try to answer the last two questions.

The colors play on the inside walls of the C-141 jet transport. In the belly of this beast, you are surrounded by a weird red glow as you and your three companions sit staring at a large canister in the middle of the floor. You stare at the canister because there are horses leading from it to the masks that cover your noses. If you were back in college in the United States, this canister could very well be a water pipe, and everybody would be having a nice buzz, getting high, sucking on the hoses. There would be the fine sound of music floating through the room, and a young woman would turn and smile a heavy-lidded smile at you, as you took another toke and touched her hair.

But you're not there.

You're here, higher than anyone in the United States.

Forty-five thousand feet higher.

The red glow is from the interior night lights of the C-141. The canister to which you are connected is full of oxygen, and you are sucking it in as if it was the greatest drug on earth, which it is. Most life is hooked on oxygen.

God is the pusher. You are the addict.

When the red color reflected on the airplane walls turns green, you will shuffle to the door and drop into war from out of the sky. The trick is to get there in one piece, which ultimately may not matter, since your mission will probably be compromised, and you'll die anyway.

If the cold doesn't kill you...

If the lack of oxygen on the way down doesn't kill you...

If you don't hit each other on the way down at speeds over a hundred miles an hour and kill each other...

And *if* your chute opens – a minor detail...

Van Horn and Jose Navarrete are a distant memory. I shiver a little bit inside my combat uniform, since I just happen to be twenty-thousand feet higher than Mount Everest, the highest point on earth, and it's always cold there. The only thing I can remember about that mountain, other than its height, is that snow stays on top all year round. The air force guys are all wearing fur parkas and look a little like Eskimos.

I smile at the idea of a missile knocking them out of the air. It's hard to hike out in a jungle wearing a fur parka. Then, I quit smiling when I figure out that I'd have to walk out with them.

I am a special forces soldier, a green beret. Once drafted by Hide's hand-picked panel, I volunteered for every school the army offered, hoping that while I was in training, the war would end. McBride luck. I ran out of schools before the U.S. ran out of Vietnam.

Rangers, airborne, special forces, psy war, and the last one, which put me where I am right now, at forty-five thousand feet, high-altitude-low-opening school, known in the army as HALO. HALO gives you a great overview of war; CCN provides the up-close-in-your-painted-face view. They go hand-in-hand; make that hand-to-hand.

Each of those schools added a year to my time-in-service. I now owe five more years to the Army on top of the two years Hide Eberhard's Van Horn draft board gave me. I haven't forgotten him. He taught me to hate. Every enemy soldier I've killed had his face.

I'll worry about the years owed later. I just want to make it through the next two days. I glance across at Jack Hampton. He and I are tight. He watches my "six" and I watch his. "Six" is Vietnam slang for three-hundred-and-sixty-degrees, but you can't say all that in the middle of combat. There isn't time. So you say, "Watch my six!" Sometimes even that takes too long.

This is our third mission along the China border. We are reacting to intelligence reports of "bright lights" being seen along the line between Red China and North Vietnam. And we're not talking UFOs here. "Bright lights" is another Vietnam slang term. There are a lot of those in any war. It stands for prisoners of war, captured pilots, those on their way to spend their captured lives in the north.

Actually, we are all prisoners of war. You and me. But nobody looks for us; we're expendable.

Tonight, however, we're looking for those who have been caught.

Hampton is a black from Alabama who swears he is a fundamentalist Christian. If he is, I shudder at the thought of a religious war in America. Hampton has muscles in places where most people don't even have places. When he reads his Bible, as he is doing right now, the book looks like a small black patch lying in blacker bear paws. If he ever asks me to be baptized, I won't dare argue. I envy Hampton's blackness. He doesn't have to put on as much camouflage paint as I do.

Hampton shifts his huge body and wakes up Tiger. Tiger is our Vietnamese local who will lead us into the area. He used to be an English professor in Hanoi. His real name is Hoang Hien, but we prefer to call him Tiger. The nickname is a joke. He isn't a tiger. He's a pussycat. He's only five-foot-four, and he is probably the only North Vietnamese turncoat who does not know karate. So we jokingly call him "Tiger." He is an Oriental Barney Fife. Tiger used to hike the areas between the Red River and Black River looking for inspiration for his poetry. Then, the communist party of Uncle Ho came to power and killed his family while Hoang watched.

He's still pissed off about it.

Maybe.

Tiger could be an agent. He could be leading us to our capture or our death.

Or he might be a double agent.

Which would mean he is still on our side but would have to lead us to our death in order to convince the North Vietnamese he is really working for them.

He'll kill us to fool them and to prove to us he's on our side.

Comforting.

Or he might be a triple-agent, which means he would let us live this time in order to prove he's one of us, so he could lead us even deeper next time on a more sensitive mission which might be more important to his real bosses.

If he can remember who they are.

Breathing pure oxygen makes you giddy sometimes.

He's taking us back there, but not to read poetry.

On the other side of Tiger is Ski. His real name is Thomas Wisenowski. He is the opposite of Hampton. While

Hampton is a mountain, Ski is a foothill. He's shorter than I am. Hampton and I trained him for this mission. It is his first. Since we have been taking heavy casualties in CCN, the commanding officers have decided to do something about it. They want to cut casualties, "compromises" is their name for it, in half. So they're only sending out the four of us rather than a normal complement of eight for this type of mission. That way, if we are all killed, by their reasoning, only half were killed. Thus cutting the attrition rate from 90 to 89.9%.

Ski is more dangerous than Tiger. With Tiger you know what to expect. He always runs away from combat. With someone new like Ski behind enemy lines, anything can happen. Like horses, people go a little crazy when saddled with combat.

The crew chief taps me on the shoulder and holds up five fingers. He can't talk to me. We have been under radio silence for the past ten minutes. There's nothing to say, anyway. The engines are too loud. I tap Hampton and hold up five fingers. He passes on the information to Ski and Tiger.

We will jump out of this fine C-141 airplane, similar to the ones that transport passengers back to the United States. But this one throws its passengers out. For a moment, after exiting, we will be hovering at forty-five thousand feet until gravity calls us, at which time we will max-track our bodies downward for seven miles vertically and seven miles horizontally, pop our chutes at a speed of somewhere between a hundred and two hundred miles per hour (hoping they won't make a huge popping sound, but they always do), and land together in the middle of a jungle.

We get to do all this in the dark.

I hear a giant roar as the engines slow, and feel the cold air rush in as the cargo door at the rear of the jet slowly opens. I'm looking at stars. They're very bright, as they well should be at this altitude. Our ears pop, and we shiver from the cold air flowing into the cargo hold.

There is a sign by the cargo doors cautioning the operator to keep the door closed during flight because something might fall out. That something is us.

We will exit simultaneously in a diamond formation, less than four feet apart from each other. As we clear the aircraft's turbulence and gain clean air, we will stabilize the diamond formation and "fly" our bodies at a forty-five degree angle through seven miles of free fall.

Two of us will fly left and right of the airplane's heading, watching the lead jumped, who will be just ahead of us and in the middle. The last one exiting will trail the formation, slightly behind and above the diamond. All of us will be watching the leader's hands and head. There are little red strobes on his wrists, pulsating red in the dark, and there is luminescent tape on his helmet. When those wrists cross or the helmet disappears, we pop our chutes. If he has passed out from lack of oxygen, we will follow those glowing strobes straight into the ground at speeds approaching two hundred miles per hour. HALO will take on a whole new meaning, then.

The crew chief taps me again and holds up three fingers. I pass it on to Jack. While he passes it on to the others, I check the pouch on my parachute harness near my ribcage. There is a green high-pressure oxygen bottle there. It's three inches in diameter and a foot long. We are told it holds enough oxygen for four minutes, or enough to keep us from blacking out before we pop our chutes.

That's a lie.

It only holds three.

You don't breathe fast and last as a HALO jumper. You stay calm, very calm. If you breathe too fast, you will black out due to lack of oxygen before reaching the right altitude to pop your parachute. If you panic and pop the chute early, you will float all the way into China, or Burma, with India not completely out of the realm of the possible. But you'll be dead from the cold or from lack of oxygen long before the parachute returns its cargo to the earth, leaving some local native farmer scratching his head at the mystery of the frozen U.S. soldier thawing out in his field.

The pouch on the left of my harness holds a combination aneroid barometer and timer. A cable runs over the left shoulder and intersects with the ripcord cable housing just above the backpack. The barometer activates the timer. Jumpers using the system set the barometer for four-thousand-five-hundred feet and the timer for ten seconds. That places the opening point at two-thousand-five-hundred feet.

That's what you do for training purposes.

But this is war.

Our barometer is set for three-thousand-five-hundred feet. Our timer is set for eleven seconds. We know our chutes will open at speeds in excess of a hundred and fifty miles an hour, making a distinctive "crack" in the air. We also know anyone with night vision goggles will have plenty of time to look up and find you, if you open at training heights. Since dead is dead, we'll take our chances at one thousand feet or lower.

The crew chief taps my shoulder for the last time and puts up one finger. We pull our hoses loose from the central oxygen bottle on the floor of the plane and snap them into the individual green bottles on our harnesses. We pull the "lollipop" on the bottles and breathe the oxygen as it flows up our hoses and into our noses.

I am a damn poet up here. If I don't clear the door in less than one minute, I'll be a dead man before hitting the ground five minutes later.

No oxygen, no life: the first rule a baby learns.

Ski drops the CWIE bag as he shuffles to the door. I pick it up. It is our combat weapons individual equipment bag, and, where we're falling, we're going to need it. I attach it to a D ring on my harness.

As I exit the door, I say a prayer in the name of Jose and his family that my chute opens. I have been sending Jose's widow and kids part of my salary each month to help them. I've also made them beneficiaries of my GI life insurance. I am staying alive to get back and see them. I am also staying alive for Hide Eberhard. I am going to kill him when I get home. It's something I've decided on, fixated upon, been haunted with, since the first mission.

I don't carry a reserve parachute. My main chute is opening so close to the ground, a reserve wouldn't have time to do me any good. It also adds useless weight. In its place, I carry useful extra ammunition. If I'm still alive when I hit the ground, the ammunition might keep me alive a little longer. As I step off the plane, it occurs to me that if I live, the next mission will probably be crazier than this one.

Our map shows the ground to be relatively level where we are jumping. That's good because our parachutes will still open at eleven second even if there is a small hill stuck up our asses at the end of ten seconds. But that's okay.

You won't feel any pain as your boot goes through your brain.

Told you I was a poet.

Delta Blues

There are two major rivers in North Vietnam. They flow out of China like two twisting coils of rope. Their names are the Black River and the Red River.

Which shows how devious the Oriental mind is.

We have landed in the Red River's delta close to the Chinese border, and as the chutes fold around us, we count our numbers. Luckily, we are all here. Jack, Hoang Hien, Ski, and I. We bury our chutes, harnesses, oxygen masks, and bags in the delta mud. Later, we'll have to fill out – in triplicate – forms that document where we left the chutes, in case anyone wants to pick them up. As I fold mine, I think it's a pity we can't use them to fly back up into the relatively safe belly of the plane, because I hate paperwork.

If we find our captured "bright light," we will call in a "jolly green," a huge Chinook helicopter from a secret base in northern Thailand. It's so secret we can fly B-52s bombers out of there night and day and nobody can hear them…except the million or so North Vietnamese spies camped outside the base's fence, who relay the message that the planes are on their way.

Along with gunships and the high air-cover of jets, the slow-moving Chinook helicopter will fly over Laos, skirt along the border between China and North Vietnam, and home in on our receivers.

If we find a captured American, we'll save him. If we find any North Vietnamese – soldier or civilian, male or female, young or old – we'll kill them. These are simple rules in staying alive. Thus, they are easy to remember. If we find Chinese, easily recognized because they're taller, better equipped, and usually travel in groups of at least a hundred thousand heavily armed soldiers – a small squad in China – we'll realize we've gone too far, and apologize.

If we end up in China, *nobody* will come get us.

That's why we watch the compass carefully as we move north. The Red River is to our right about ten miles. Intelligence has reported a camp due north in the dense jungles close to the Chinese border. The S2 intelligence "contact" suggests the North Vietnamese intend to exchange an American prisoner for some North Vietnamese smugglers captured by the Chinese.

We hope "intelligence" is intelligent enough to be right.

As my boot collects another ten pounds of delta mud, I question the intelligence of anyone staying around here and working for us. Where is he now?

I try to shake the mental image of a smiling, giant frog with a U.S. flag stamped on its forehead, humming "America the Beautiful," as it slowly rises above this muck we're walking through.

Hampton is praying again. He does that when he's nervous.

I lean forward and whisper, "Hampton?"

"Our father who art…what? Oh, my God, what?!"

"What do you mean, 'what'?" It's best not to get Hampton agitated.

"What comes after 'Our father who art'…? I keep forgetting when I'm nervous. Maybe I'm under too much stress."

"Well, damn it, whatever it is, pray quieter!"

"If you can wear that stupid cavalry hat whenever we go on one of these missions, I can pray as loud as I want to!" he whispers, miffed.

We enter the jungle, Hoang Hien, in native garb, leading the way by about twenty yards. If he encounters any locals, his presence will give us valuable time to prepare our welcome. If he encounters a booby-trap, it will give us valuable time to get away. If he is a spy, our reasoning goes, he won't want to go on a trail he knows is booby-trapped. If he is not a spy, our reasoning continues, we'll make an apology to his corpse.

The trail is faint and twists and turns in the ever-thickening jungle. Wet leaves slap at your tiger fatigues. Sweat rolls down over the camouflage paint on your face. You shouldn't have to sweat in November. Even in the desert around Van Horn things start to cool off in November. The air in the jungle is so thick, it almost sticks in your throat. Everything is wet, either from sweat or the moisture on the leaves.

Suddenly, Hoang Hien appears up the trail, running towards us.

We slip into the jungle on the left side of the trail. Hoang runs by us, giving us a thumbs-up sign as he scurries past. Past me, he halts on the trail, holds up six fingers, and slides one finger across his throat. He has just told us that an American has been found. But we have to kill six people to get him back.

Jack takes out a silencer from the CWIE bag and screws the thing into his pistol. It cuts down on the noise he will be making. But, unfortunately, it also cuts down on the range of the weapon.

We'll have to get close.

Ski takes out his knife. I take out mine. We mentally county how many Jack can kill, two, maybe three. Ski and I will get one each.

Maybe. That leaves one for someone else.

We slowly turn our heads and look at Hoang Hien. He shakes his head violently. We hand him a knife. He stares at it as if it was sticking in him. I reach over and close his hand around the handle.

He shakes his head again, and hands back the knife.

No one says a word to him. He reads our expressions. They say, "suspicion." It is peer pressure at its worst.

We move out, leaving him there. Screw him. He'll either follow or walk back to South Vietnam. I look behind and see him hurrying to catch up. I hand him the knife again. This time he takes it.

You can smell the smoke from the fire as you ease a branch past your rifle stock. You bend forward until your eyes slide past the large leaf of a strange plant, and the scene in front opens slowly to your vision.

They're around the fire. One of them is writing a letter. Another is squatting at the fire stirring a pot of rice. Two more are curled up on their mats near the fire. They look to be asleep.

That's four. Tiger said six.

Where are the other two? Hoang Hien nudges me, and with his head indicates the shadows to the left of the fire. There is one standing there, pissing out towards the dark. Hoang Hien moves his head further left, and I see someone with a beard and dressed in a gray flight suit slumped against a tree, while the sixth man feeds him from a bowl. There is nothing tender about the feeding.

Jack Hampton motions towards the fire and holds up three fingers. He has the three by the fire. Ski moves to his right. He is quick and reminds me of a coyote circling a rabbit. He's got the one peeing.

I have the one feeding the American.

I point Hoang Hien to the one stirring the large pot of rice. He stares at the man, and I can Hoang's eyes start to glisten. I don't know if he's going to cry or vomit. There isn't time to wait. I circle left and wait for the soft "pfuthung-pfuthung-

pfuthung" of gases escaping and bullets hitting bodies. It doesn't take long.

The one writing the letter looks puzzled as his pencil falls from his hand. The two on the mats stiffen, then relax for a real long sleep. The one urinating turns, knowing something is wrong, but not sure what. He takes a step towards my man, saying something, but suddenly is yanked backwards into the dark by Ski.

The soldier feeding the American drops the bowl and reaches for the rifle next to his foot. He's quick. I'm quicker. I cup his mouth with my left hand, pinching his nose with my thumb and forefinger, and jamming my right hand holding the knife just above his right hip, angling it up through the liver, kidneys, and towards the lungs. When I feel my knife hand start to get wet, I twist the knife; he sighs in my ear and his body relaxes. I wipe the mucus on the hand cupping the mouth on his shirt.

I think of Hide and smile. As he sags to the ground, I feel nothing. The American is staring at me, eyes bulging, rice dripping down his chin, the spoon hanging stupidly from his mouth. I try not to snicker, but one or two laughs escape me.

His eyes glance over my shoulder. I whirl, crouching low, my knife ready for the attack, but no one is there.

Hoang Hien has made a mess. He has stabbed the man stirring the pot in the side at the wrong angle. The knife dangles from the man's side like a banderilla from the bull's shoulder at a corrida. The knife has glanced off the ribcage and lodged there. It's a sloppy job because the man is still alive. He pushes Hoang Hien into the pot of boiling rice, which breaks his fall. The hot rice spills all over Hoang Hien, who howls his pain.

The man crawls toward his weapon. I can't cover the distance in time to save myself with my knife. I grab the rifle of my dead soldier and roll to the ground, hoping to get a shot. But it is too late. He already has the gun aimed towards me. But he can't see to aim it. His eyes are gone.

Jack has popped the top of his head off with the pistol. The soldier's hand twitches towards his trigger, then falls with the rest of the body to the ground. Jack has covered my "six."

Ski lurches out of the jungle with blood all over his face. He staggers towards us with arms stiff in front of him. We rise in horror at his injury. Just as we reach him, his face cracks into a big smile.

"I'm a zombie," he whispers loudly, then breaks into laughter when he sees our worried faces, "I'm the zombie from the jungle, here to kick your ass."

Ski's feeling a little giddy from his first kill. He continues walking around, doing his Boris Karloff imitation. We start laughing among the dead. It's what the living do.

"Damn Polack," Jack mutters as he turns back to put safety shots into each body.

Behind us I hear the pilot vomiting. I walk over to comfort him. I don't think he appreciates Ski's peculiar humor. It's an acquired taste.

"That smell..." He points toward the body of my soldier.

I squat in front of him trying to untie his ropes. The ropes are tied in suicide knots, so I cut them with my bloodied knife. The knots and smell remind me of Tudisishn. Surprisingly, I wonder about my brother and Sarah, but I quickly squelch the thoughts.

"That smell," I tell him as I cut through the ropes, "is the muscles letting go."

He looks at me blankly.

I point to a dark stain on the dead man's pants. "He's pissed and crapped in his pants."

"So have I," the pilot mutters weakly, pointing to his own dark stain.

I hear Jack sending a burst over our radio. He doesn't mention the bright light. That's classified. The jolly green will be here soon. It's a perfect mission. The first one that really succeeded just like it was planned. Those missions are rare in war.

Ski shambles over and shakes the pilot's head. He's wiping the blood off his face with a towel he found next to the guy cooking the rice.

"I am shaking hands with the man who got me the Medal of Honor." He grins broadly, pumping the pilot's limp hand.

We watch as he goes around and shakes the hands of the dead men, too. Ski is a little hyper, but he's going to fit in nicely with CCN.

What Ski has said begins to sink in. We're going to be famous. We have returned a POA. That's never been done in Vietnam. Our careers are made: rapid promotions, extra money each month for the rest of our lives, celebrities wherever we go.

I glance at the pilot's uniform. It says his name is Hawkins, Samuel, and he's a major.

"Major," I hand him some burn ointment from my first aid kit, "take care of Hoang Hien here. We'll stand watch until the chopper gets on station. And, while you're at it, put out the fire."

He takes the tube from my hand, walks over to Hoang Hien and the pot and kicks the rest of the rice and water into the fire. It's a big pot. There's plenty of rice. The fire sizzles and goes out. We're alone in the dark, but I'm smiling. I just gave an order to a major, and he's doing what I told him.

And soon, me and the boys will be shaking the President's hand. All because we killed six men without anyone getting hurt. Hoang Hien moans by the fire.

Well, almost all of us will be shaking the President's hand.

"We're on the road to Rankin now," I whisper in the darkness.

The Wrecking Ball

We can hear it hovering above us, but we can't see it. The sound of branches cracking tells us something big is falling towards us. Ski shoves the major and Hoang Hien out of the way. Jack dives for the other side of the camp. I just stand there fixated by the sounds of angels "coming for to carry me home."

A steel ball, about four feet in diameter, slams into the ground two feet from my body. Straps dangle in front of me, hanging from the huge rope attached to the steel ball. They are designed to list us towards our ride home. The rope is a lifeline to the jolly green helicopter. There isn't enough time to clear away the trees and land the big chopper, so a branch-snapping metal ball is dropped straight down through the triple-canopy jungle. The rope attached to the ball is the umbilical cord for special ops warriors.

I grab a strap and hand it to the major.

"Going up?" I say jokingly as I slip the strap under his arms and lock it in.

"Lingerie department, please." Ski steps in and grabs his strap.

"Let's get the hell out here," says Jack as he locks his strap in, "I'm hungry, and I don't want to miss church."

Jack grows silent except for his lips. He's praying. Extraction is CCN's most vulnerable time. I grab a strap and hold it for Hoang. He is having trouble putting it around himself with his burned hand. I slip it over just one shoulder.

"Hey, Jack," I say as I put down my rifle to help Hoang in, "I'll get you some rice. There was a lot in the pot."

He gives me the finger, then frowns.

"The pot....," he says, jerking his head, pointing at the overturned mess on the smoking embers. "God, I didn't see it in time."

He looks at me with death in his eyes. "Sorry, Johnny, I didn't watch our six close enough..."

Confused, I look back at the pile of rice.

There's too much of it.

Six people couldn't eat that much rice in a month.

I dive for the rifle and spray the jungle with fire, rolling away from the ball where Jack, Ski, Hoang, and Major Samuel

Hawkins now hang in their straps. They struggle like marionettes on a string, trying to get their weapons on line.

Jack tugs three times on the nylon strap. It's an emergency signal to the crew above to extract immediately. Whoever is on the ground – that's me in this case – is supposed to cut the ball loose so the evacuees can be extracted. I see what's happening, and I start to get up to run back to the ball when automatic weapons open up from the treeline. You can't hear the gunfire because of the noise of the chopper, but flashes of fire shake the jungle leaves, little zapping sounds whiz by your ears, and the dirt does crazy, tiny dances just in front of you. I dive back down to the safety of the earth. It is a costly human instinct.

Jack and the others start to lift up. He looks at me, and sees that I am pinned down. In slow motion he reaches down to cut the ball.

Hoang Hien sticks a knife through Jack's arm, and I watch Jack's face twist with pain as his arm jerks the knife away from Hoang Hien. It's not a good time to discover that either Hoang Hien is a double-agent, or else he's pissed about the rice burns. I'll never know which. Ski turns and shoots Hoang Hien through his side, but it doesn't matter. For a new guy Ski has definitely proven himself, but it still doesn't matter. All of them are jerking on the line like targets at a shooting gallery as the place erupts with tracers streaking through the night and into their bodies.

To the men on the straps, hanging lifeless, the war is over. The jolly green takes off, but the ball slams against a tree, then spins around it. Hampton is impaled on a broken tree branch, ripped neatly in half as the force of the circling chopper jerks the body to the other side of the tree. The jolly green circles above the jungle like an angry June bug tied to a string. One of Hampton's halves flaps down on the ground in front of me.

The screeching sound of the rotary blades hitting the top of the jungle canopy announces to the world the chopper is crashing. I dive deeper into the jungle as a ball of flame splinters around me and the smell of burning chopper fuel fills up the leafy night.

Two men in dark uniforms run towards me, searching the green canopy in front of where I am hiding. They are wearing pith helmets, which look stupid against the light of the burning jolly green…it's like we're caught in an old black and white jungle film: "Rama of the Jungle." But this is no movie.

Come, Bwana, we must go now.

I pop up and shoot them. They look confused as they fall, wondering why they hurt and why their legs no longer hold them. The fire acts as a shield hiding my muzzle-flash from the others, who scramble around the burning downed chopper. The noise of the helicopter and its exploding ammunition keeps my shots from being heard. I plunge deeper into the jungle until I'm swallowed by the terrible darkness.

I can't stop shaking. Jack and the others are dead. I don't panic. Like hell I don't. Even knowing a damage assessment team will be sent to search the wreckage, how will I stay alive? Some animal crashes in panic through the jungle. Was it a tiger? I hold my breath.

Stay alive. I activate my beacon. It sends out a constant pulse that will eventually be monitored by another jolly green team.

I hope.

Jack is gone. I didn't watch his "six." I pound my leg. Ski's gone. I bite through my lip to keep from screaming. Hoang Hien was a spy. A killer Barney? Jesus, what's this world coming to?

"Barney, the Thane of Fife." I hear Ski's joke.

Ski's dead. Jack's dead. The next insertion team will know quickly we were neutralized. Surely they'll count the number of dead bodies and realize one survived. They'll rescue me. The backup team will count four charred bodies plus the ones in the jolly green. I will be missed.

Then I remember the men we killed. They'll count those bodies too. I won't be missed. Nobody will know I'm gone. At least they'll find the two I killed; I comfort myself with that thought.

Then another thought – curiously, using Ski's voice – pushes itself into my brain: "They won't know who shot them. You're a damn zombie, McBride, a dead soldier walking in the jungle. Didya get much experience in the jungle where you grew up, McBride?"

I start to go back and give up. I look around in the darkness. Which way is back? I hear Ski singing in the darkness of my mind.

"Show me the way to go home, I'm tired and I want to go…"

He is joined by the giant American spy toad.
"Oh, beautiful for spacious skies…"
Hampton chimes in: "Our father who art…who art…who…"
How can anybody sleep with all that noise going on?

River Tour

Given my severely limited options, I decided to walk to Thailand and find the secret B-52 base. My plan was to talk until I found the Black River, cross it, continue heading west until I arrived in Thailand, then follow the sound of B-52s landing and taking off.

How hard can that be without a compass? One just follows the sun as it sets – if one could see the sun in a triple-canopy jungle.

I found a river, the wrong river, but a river. This one, as it turned out, flows south through North Vietnam and enters the South China Sea at Nam Dinh, just below the Haiphong harbor. Since I didn't find the Black River, by elimination, this one had to be the Red River.

Plan B: Follow it to the South China Sea, turn right when I found the ocean and walk back to South Vietnam.

Piece of cake.

I found the river quite by accident. One minute there was jungle; the next, there was air. Fortunately, the banks of the Red River aren't that high. Unfortunately, the Red River is deep and the current fast. I kick out of everything – pack, ammunition shirt, and grenades – to struggle up through the sudden finding of the river and back to the surface of the water for oxygen. There is a branch in my hand. It either broke off as I stepped into midair, or I grabbed as I plunged into the river. Either way, it floats, and I don't.

A mile down the river, I drag myself to shore, coughing up the red mud from which the river gets its name. The vines along the banks make thorny handholds as I pull myself out of the water. My teeth chatter from the shock of finding the river and the temperature of the water. Mosquitoes turn my exposed wrist black.

My backpack with food, ammo, and map pops up for a moment next to me in the water, then floats quickly away from my panicked grasp, as I try for it without letting go of the vines. It isn't the ammo I want. My rifle hasn't floated to the surface. It is lost forever. It's the map and the food that are important. The pack floats faster, and my arm can't grow that quickly. I start to let go of the vines. Despite the mosquitoes and my brain's command, my hand refuses to release the vines. My fear of drowning is stronger than my fear of getting lost. It was born years ago in a West Texas stock tank, where a woman in white died, and was reinforced by a crazy brother, who talked me into breathing salt water.

A quick mental inventory of my situation reveals the following: no food, no map, no radio, deep in North Vietnam on the Chinese border, with no chance of a rescue because any rescue team will think I've burned up with the rest of my team.

Ski's voice intrudes again. "So what's your problem?"

I think of someone more up to the task at hand: What would John Wayne do as he checks his ammo while calmly gazing at the howling Indians riding over the horizon towards him? I can see him standing up with that familiar swagger, and saying, "Boys, it's your shot whether you want to die today or tomorrow."

That image gives me courage, until another million mosquitoes, acting on tips from those that gorged on my arm earlier, arrive to feast on my ears and head.

Screw John Wayne: it's time to give up.

The question now is how to find someone to accept my surrender before the insects do a Dracula number on me and drain the last drop of blood from my body? I'll have strains of malaria not yet known to medical science if I don't get away from the damn river. Or else get back in it.

I check my wet pants and belt. The only tool I have is my Randall knife. I'm not sure what the proper uniform for surrender is, but come to the conclusion this ain't. I decide to follow the backpack downriver. I'm bound to bump into somebody. If I do, the hardest job then should be to convince them I'm really a soldier instead of a walking bite. I use my belt to tie together some branches I find lying about, hoping they'll float.

If that doesn't work, I can always slit my wrists with my knife before things get really bad.

I put a piece of my torn pants over my nose because the mosquitoes threaten to clog it up with their infinite numbers.

I mean if things get *really* bad.

I try to find the sun, but my eyelids are swollen shut from the bites.

When I say BAD, I mean worse than it already is.

My brain malaria pills went down the Red River.

The only thing comforting me is that, for a McBride, things can always get worse. My family's tradition would serve me well in rough spots like this.

Behind me, a cloud of mosquitoes fights over the only bare spot left on my back. I've got to find someone soon. I let go of the vines and the river swirls me away.

After thirty minutes of bumping against every stump hidden in the damn river, I decide to get out. My testicles just can't take the pounding. There's been a trail, well-worn, following the river. It's bound to lead somewhere. I follow it by hanging on to the shore's vegetation, floating slowly downriver, taking comfort in the thought that, if I drown, a million or so mosquitoes on my back and my face will go down with me.

In a war like this, there are no "enemy lines" you cross to surrender. Besides, my eyes are so puffy I wouldn't know if I stepped over a line or not.

This country wears on a man fast. It's strange how quickly primitive sense rise to civilized surfaces when given the opportunity. I crouch low in the jungle like some wounded tiger, and, for the first time, listen to the emotional quality of the sing-song language of the Vietnamese. Normally, I would just hear the Oriental voices, but this time I tune in to the emotional content of the language, which makes the sound rise and fall with angry intensity. Someone was getting their ass chewed. Good. It meant soldiers. They'd know what to do.

Slowly, quietly, I crawl forward along the bank, silently cursing the thorns that tear at my crotch and legs, but saving the "ouches" for later. I lift each part of my body and set it quietly in front of its counterparts, like some wild animal sneaking up on its prey. Something eats one of the cities of mosquitoes on my back. I don't want to turn around to see what it is.

As if I could see what it is through my eyes.

In the dim twilight, I barely make out a landing at the river's edge and a group of soldiers in a semicircle around a man, a woman, and a small child.

Behind the soldiers is a large sampan floating on top of the half-sunken hull of a smaller sampan, its motor still uselessly turning the propeller shaft, which is sticking ridiculously straight up in the air. The woman is dressed in white peasant pajamas. The man and his son are in black pajamas.

The angry voice is from the man, who is standing next to his son in front of the soldiers. The soldiers stand quietly behind a taller soldier, who I guess is their leader. His height says he is Chinese. He has red shoulder boards, which means he's an officer, and which also means he's dangerous to everyone around him. He even has a red star on the silly little hat he's wearing.

He is nodding gravely at whatever the angry owner of the smaller boat is saying. He turns and looks at the woman, then back to the man. The tiny woman says nothing, she just clutches her son's hand. The kid reminds me of someone. That's weird, because I don't recall ever being here before.

The large man holds up his hand. He barks a command to his soldiers. Two of them go back to the large boat and float it backwards off the little sampan. The other two pull the little sampan onto the shore and dump out the water. The owner of the damaged sampan brushes past the soldiers and examines his boat. He turns angrily back to the leader of the soldiers and opens his mouth to say something.

The large man shoots him in the head, and he falls back into his damaged sampan. Birds scream from the trees at the sudden sound of death. For a moment the sound of the gunshot hangs in the air. I don't dare breathe. Apparently, life is cheap along the Red River. I change my mind about wanting to give up to this guy.

The large man barks orders and is quickly obeyed. His is a unique leadership style that causes all to obey. Bullets in the head keep a lot of soldiers in line. The two men push the body of the sampan's owner further into the little boat and slide it into the current. The little boy runs to the water's edge and screams for his father, but the woman grabs the hysterical child's shoulders and pulls him back to her. I admire her. She hasn't screamed once. She doesn't dare. The Chinese officer is a good shot.

The large man gives orders again, and the soldiers move off downriver and, finally, into the jungle. He waits until they've gone, walks back to the woman, and stares for a long time. She doesn't look up. Her long hair hides her face. He reaches out and feels her hair.

She flinches backward; he grabs her shoulder and roughly pulls her towards him, shoving the little boy between them to the ground. He holds her with one hand and traces the outline of her breasts with the other. She struggles, and he rips her white peasant blouse open. Grabbing her hair, he jerks her head back and falls roughly on top of her, driving them both to the ground. The little boy crawls towards his mother, but the man's boot catches him in the face, shoving him backwards.

She begins to struggle as she realizes what is about to happen, making small choking sounds. He laughs. She scratches him. He raises up to slap her, and she knees him. As he rolls back, moaning in pain, she twists quickly out from beneath him and scrambles towards the river.

He is quicker. Before she can reach the safety of the water, he is on top of her, driving her down into the wet mud, pinning her dog-style while he struggles to get his pants down.

Mom's hair flows with the current away from her face. My mosquito bites do not hurt anymore. My eyes open clearly to the scene in front of me. I can't let Dad do this. Mom deserves better. Knife drawn, I rush past me, still crying on the shore, and leap upon his back, knocking Dad deeper into the tank. I begin plunging the knife over and over into his kidneys and back, all the while whispering to Mom to get back into her dress. There are two people inside me: one calm, the other enraged, plunging a knife into my father. At once, I am critical that my knife technique is as sloppy as Hoang Hien's, and I keep explaining to Mom that I'm better at killing than this.

But I keep sticking him. In the gathering darkness I can see the water around him swirling darker and darker. When I stop, it's not called the Red River just for the mud anymore. I turn back to Mom to apologize, but she stares numbly at what my hands are doing.

"I can't stop." I grin weakly, poking my knife in and out of the body like it's a piece of tough beef.

I look at me on the shoreline, hoping I can't see what I'm doing in the river, but, it's no good. I'm howling there on the shoreline, a little boy in his cowboy boots on the edge of the water tank, screaming at the man in the river doing bad things to his mom. This time, Mom doesn't die. She staggers out of the water and over to me, and turns my head slowly away from the carnage taking place in the tank.

I drop the knife because the handle has gotten so slick I can't hang on. But I'm not finished. When I bend to search in the river's mud for the knife, Dad's body rolls over and begins to inch slowly downriver. But the face that floats past me isn't Dad's. It's Hide Eberhard's face. The face of Hide Eberhard looks upward towards the North Vietnam night, a hideous smile frozen on his face.

Suddenly, I am at the tank on the ranch. I hear Mac crying in the bushes. Hide is zipping up his pants, laughing at my mother. She is dressed in her wedding dress; he thinks it's funny. An animal howl comes from the pasture, and I watch my brother run away.

As the incarnadine water swirly away, I baptize myself in the river trying to wash away the memories. I turn back to shore and wonder why Mom is pointing the officer's pistol at me. Her face melts into a frightened woman-child's. Her long hair drips onto her muddy clothes, each drop making a little clean path down towards her feet. My cowboy boots disappear from the kid's bare feet. I blink my eyes at the shifting reality. I'm not in Texas anymore.

As an apology, I start babbling to her about my childhood. She snarls and points the pistol at my head. Suddenly, a weariness enfolds me, and I sink to my knees in front of her and bow my head, almost touching the water. She stands on shore not two feet from my kneeling form.

"Go ahead and shoot, lady," my voice, ancient, dead-tired, rolls across the river.

"Anything is better than this."

No Problem

A situation develops. She can't pull the trigger because the hand holding the pistol is shaking badly. She puts the other one up and steadies the gun. I can't fight anymore. There's nothing left. Go ahead – time to clock out. Shift's over. I wait for the end.

The little boy wades out to where I kneel. He hugs my neck. I look into his face, and he's crying, trying to say something in his language. I hold him up, ignoring her snarls and her angry orders to the kid. I hug him. Hard. We're both crying. The tears won't stop for either of us. They merge with the river and float towards the ocean.

She lowers the gun and kneels on the mud of the shore, her tears joining ours. I carry the kid over to her and sit down heavily beside her, keeping the boy in my lap.

"That was for you, Mama," I whisper.

The little boy takes my hand and puts it in his mother's. He gently tugs at the pistol in her other hand until she lets go, and he throws the hated thing in the swirling water. We watch the circles expand from the spot where the pistol went in. If it hadn't been for the opposite shore, the circles might have expanded around the world.

She starts talking rapidly in Vietnamese. I look at her blankly.

"*Khong beit*," I say to her, which means "I don't understand" in Vietnamese.

She stands up, her hand still in mine, and leads me to the huge sampan the soldiers came in. She motions for me to get in. I do and she puts the little boy in after me. I don't ask where we are going; I don't care, as long as it's somewhere away from here. The soldiers could come along the trail at anytime. Maybe they know exactly how much time it takes their leader to rape a civilian. Of course, I saw their leader in action with the woman's husband. With that kind of officer, they'll probably give me a medal.

The boat swings with the current and heads downriver. She points the boat where she wants it go without starting the engine, using its long propeller like a rudder. Her eyes scan the shore for the soldiers.

She says something to the little boy, and he disappears towards the front section of the boat, which consists of a palm-thatched bimini – an open-sided shelter meant to keep sun and rain off the soldiers, with a canvas flap covering the opening facing the rear, where we sit. The kid comes back and motions for me to follow.

Inside the bimini there is ammunition, three AK-47 rifles, three sacks of rice with two black-encrusted cooking woks hanging above the sacks, two cases of Russian vodka, a case of *Nuoc Mam* fish sauce, American LRRP (long-range reconnaissance patrol) rations, probably traded for in the black market, and some muddy Chinese uniforms. This sampan was both the soldiers' home and floating PX. The boy points to the pile of uniforms.

I start to put on a muddy, smelly shirt but the little boy stops me. He motions for me to get under the pile of dirty clothes. I shake my head "no." He frowns.

"The war is over for me," I say, reaching for a bottle of vodka, "you and your mother take me to the nearest village and turn me in, you get some money for a reward, which won't make up for your old man's death, but at least it's something; and, if you remember or understand what I'm saying to you, kid, get me a cold beer and let me get some sleep."

As an afterthought, I add, "And see if they've got anything for mosquito bites."

He stares hard, trying to understand my words.

"*Khong beit,*" he says, shrugging his shoulders.

The mother's face appears at the entrance. She puts her finger to her head, acts out shooting herself, and then points to me. After an exchange of hand signs, I begin to understand.

She wants me to shoot her.

No. That's not it.

She wants me to shoot the kid.

No. That doesn't make sense, either.

Got it. She wants me to hide, not for my sake, but for hers and the kid's. They'll die if I'm found. I crawl underneath the clothes, which smell of mildew, river mud, and soldiers' sweat. I break open a package of the freeze-dried LRRP rations. The package says, "shrimp creole; add boiling water." Since there is no boiling water at the moment, I open a bottle of the Russian vodka and mix it with the sawdust of the package, which forms a paste I eat with my fingers.

My own culinary creation: Shrimp Stroganoff, I guess.

I drink long and deep from the bottle to wash the "food" down. The vodka turns on the burners in my stomach and I gag.

188

I lie there underneath dirty, stinking uniforms, forcing the vodka and shrimp sawdust to stay down. The alcohol slides into my brain and calms my stomach. My eyes close as I listen to the slap of waves against the hull.

The waves stop. I awake disoriented and take a quick inventory: large headache, and larger welts and bites that itch everywhere. Feverishly, scratching for relief, I wonder why the boat is still. I lie under the clothes and listen for voices, trying to figure out how long I slept. I look at the vodka bottle in my hand. It is empty.

Easing out from under the clothes, I stare outside from a corner of the flap. Darkness and the sounds of the jungle join me under the bimini. Nothing moves. The air is heavy with heat. Sweat runs down my face.

I creep towards the rear of the boat, keeping low, not only as a cautionary measure, but because the boat is wedged underneath branches. Where are the woman and the boy? Have they abandoned me? Have they gone to get help? Should I wait? Go?

There is something by the rudder. It is a large sack of rocks on top of some kind of clothes. I slip a hand inside the sack feeling the rocks, and they feel powdery like…like charcoal. I bring one to my nose. It is charcoal.

I lift the large bag off the clothes and try them on. The shirt is baggy and the pants tight. Suddenly, there is a sound along the trail. Slipping over the edge of the boat in my new clothes, I feel the pants split at the crotch. The cold river water pours over my testicles.

Great.

Two figures jump into the boat. In the water, I try to hide as best I can alongside the boat. When I hear the kid's voice, calling me, I haul myself back in, bare ass and all. The woman stifles a laugh. It's good to hear that.

"*Di mau Di!*" she says in an urgent whisper.

Make that five words.

From the urgency in the voice, I translate that to mean "Let's get the hell out of here."

We do.

I sit down next to her by the rudder, and she hands me a conical hat she brought with her. I put it on – and I feel like the tin woodsman. Through hand signs in the dark, she tells me she went back to her former hut/home/mansion, whatever.

Her face is smooth and hard to read. Why has she returned? She has the kid to think of. Why didn't she just go back to her village and stay there? But I know the questions little villages like hers ask. After all, I came from a little village, too.

"Where's your husband?"

"How did you get back?"

"Why does your little boy tell a different story?"

Maybe there's another scenario: "Guess what I've got in the boat?"

"What?"

"A stupid American."

"How stupid?"

"Stupid enough to let me float him down to the coast and turn him in."

"Great. Take the kid with you to keep him guessing."

"No problem. Hey, give me your hat. I'll make him wear it until I can turn him in." A whole village laughs at my expense.

Maybe the village is fearful. She has stolen a Chinese patrol sampan, and the penalty for that could be death for the whole village. She has had to leave.

The kid drags the charcoal to the front of the boat. I can hear him scrounging around. Maybe he's trying to find those AK-47s. Maybe, it's time to jump overboard. He strikes a match and tries to light the charcoal he has placed carefully inside a crude small hibachi that the soldiers used. I crawl forward, underneath the bimini flaps to get some new pants. The muddy Chinese uniform fits me loosely. Possibly, I've lost some weight over the past two days. Possibly. The old pants tear more as I exchange them for a new pair.

I pick up the torn pants, dip them gingerly into the gasoline, walk over to the kid, and sit beside him. I wrap the charcoal in the pants. We wait, letting the charcoal soak, the gasoline evaporate.

In the meantime, the kid finds a pan and pours some rice in. He starts to use the river water to boil the rice, but I stop him. I use a little vodka and add Nuoc Mam sauce. A little cooking refinement will both enlighten this family and keep dysentery at bay a while longer.

He lights the fire, rags and all, and waits for the feast by crawling up in my lap and falling asleep. I glance back at the mother to see if she minds, but she's lost in the darkness at the rear of the boat.

While we wait, it begins to rain, and the boat passes silently beneath the trees on either side of the river. The woman swings the boat to the middle, ties off the rudder, and joins me underneath the leaky canopy. As the raindrops drip off my head and beard, we watch the faint glow of the charcoal fire while listening to the rain around us. The boat is part of the river now. Periodically, she looks up and checks our position.

The river seems deserted; a lonely feeling floats with us. It reminds me of riding alone back from Jose's home that last time. I think of Sofia and the two girls. I think of this woman and child who just saved my life. Soon we will eat.

I take a swig of vodka.

It doesn't get any better than this for a McBride.

Happy Waters of Nam Dinh

It rained the whole time we were on the river. Fortunately, we had containers for the rain water. For three nights, we ate rice, drank vodka, and caught the water running off the bimini roof into every available container, from which we filled the empty vodka bottles. There were no close calls, no patrol boats, just an occasional village sleeping on the shore. Since the river was much higher, we had long since given up steering once we entered the main current. The only dicey times came when we needed to get to shore each morning before dawn, so we could hide during daylight in the jungle overhanging the riverbanks. On more than one occasion, my rope-throwing ability helped us lasso tree limbs and pull ourselves into shade-filled safety. Each time, as I coiled the rope back up, I thought about Jose, Sofia, and their two girls. Each loop of the rope seemed to circle me closer to them. My two boat companions had a lot to do with my thoughts turning back towards Mexico.

Shivering from the cooling rain, all of us huddled together for warmth: the woman on one side of me, the kid on the other side. When we huddled together a strange feeling would well up in me. It was hard to identify, but I could feel it moving across my heart and into my throat, and then my eyes would sting.

As the sun rose during the day, once we were dry, we'd move apart and try to sleep while rotating a watch. Because of the vodka, we got the mornings and nights mixed up. On the fourth day, we pulled into shore just before morning, and awoke to what we thought was just before night. Actually, we had slept through the day and some of the next night – the vodka did have that effect – so in the early morning darkness the next day, which we thought was early evening darkness, we pushed back out to the middle of the river.

It was wider now, and flowing faster from the constant rain. We didn't care. The speed of the water, the haze of the rain, the darkness, all served well our purpose: to reach the South China Sea. But this time, the haze thickened and night began to change to day. The woman whimpered at our mistake. I squinted through the fog, but couldn't see the shore. The little boy hugged his mother for comfort. There was a new smell added to the rain.

The smell was of the ocean and of leaking diesel fuel.

193

As we drifted through the dissipating fog, we looked around in horror at the giant hulls of huge cargo ships looming out of the remaining patches of fog, forming steel canyons we floated through. Curious workers pointed at us from the decks above.

Magically – well, more like black magic – the fog suddenly lifted.

Our sampan now bobbed in the middle of the Nam Dinh harbor surrounded by huge off-loading military cargo ships, military docks guarded by North Vietnamese soldiers, and large Chinese junks, all towering over our little boat.

Crap.

I crouched low as we floated between two Russian cargo ships. Someone yelled at us in Russian from one of the ships. The woman glanced at me in panic, asking me in Vietnamese what to do.

Great.

Surrounded by two languages I couldn't speak.

Soon, others were also yelling, but we floated on towards the sea wall, which opened to the South China Sea and freedom just beyond. I could see the huge hull of a Russian freighter coming through the opening, blocking it, and heading straight for us.

Crap.

The revving of powerful engines behind us, and a small cry from the woman made me turn from the oncoming tons of crushing metal to see a North Vietnamese patrol boat speeding from the docks towards us, its siren screaming.

Crap again.

So we waited for the inevitable. The bow of the speeding patrol boat cut huge waves before it. Hell, the waves alone would swamp us minutes before they reached us. But a strange thing happened. One moment there was a patrol boat streaking across the harbor towards us, siren wailing; the next, there was just the siren, still wailing, skipping across the water without the boat which had vaporized into an explosion.

I saw the water plume before I felt the concussion of the bomb. It knocked all of us to the bottom of the boat. Other sirens started wailing along the harbor, angry at the destruction of their littler cousin. I peeked over the edge of the sampan. Huge geysers of water were rising all around us with bits of people and broken ships flopping back into the water. The kid was crying and hugging the rice sacks under the bimini, and the woman was screaming and pointing at the sky. They had been through this before.

Bombs were falling from unseen B-52 bay doors and scaring the hell out of the human herd surrounding us. It had taken a lot of time to get all these human beings into their dock corrals, and those damn planes that had flown low in Texas and scattered our cattle were now trying to scatter all of us once again. Great explosions tore the warehouses at the harbor's edge into small burning rubble.

A man on shore stood naked, his clothes blown off by the concussion. He staggered away as we floated helplessly past him. The noise was deafening; there was nowhere to hide.

The woman tugged my sleeve and pointed skyward. Little parachutes floated down towards us. I thought maybe a ground missile had found its mark and the parachutes were those of pilots. But as they floated down, the parachutes didn't get any larger. Underneath each of the parachutes there was a large metal container with blinking lights.

I watched one with morbid fascination as it floated down. It swayed gently down in the bright blue sky, and I followed its lazy descent down...

between me and the iron hull of that forgotten Russian cargo ship, now trying desperately to turn back to open sea. I could see the ruse on the hull as it towered above the sampan. There was a coolness from the metal as it turned close – interesting barnacles, too – real close to our sampan. I closed my eyes at the impending collision, joining my adopted family huddled around the rice sacks.

None of us saw the little parachute put its cargo in the water directly between us and the turning ship. None of us saw the little metal computer decide which boat, ours or the Russian one, was made out of metal. None of us saw the magnetic activator float the little harbor mine towards its choice of boats.

Sampans can't fly.

But ours did.

One minute I had my eyes closed in anticipation of the collision. The next minute my eyes are still closed, but they're now underwater. Something larger than myself wants me to learn to swim. This time I will oblige. There is a definite ringing in my ears, but no recall of noise. Fighting my way to the surface, treading water, I see the sampan is there, floating – stupidly, incredibly – upright, as the front end of the freighter slides slowly into the harbor.

Frantically, I look around for the rest of my crew. The woman floats toward me, bobbing like a cork, and I swim to meet her. We've come too far to split up now. She's seen too much in the past few weeks. I'm one man who has decided to be here for her. Her smile scares me as I reach for her. I touch her arm. It upsets her balance, and her upper body flips over. There are no clothes from the waist down.

Nothing at all.

No legs, no vagina, no waist.

Just a sputtering vein or two feebly doing what they had been doing normally ten seconds before. The blood is no match for the geysers of water surrounding us.

The bombs are loud enough to cover my screams.

Where's the kid? Frantically, I look around. Nothing. There is a lull in the bombs, and, despite the ringing in my ears, I hear the little boy crying. I stop and try to home in on the sound, but the bombs, ack-ack, and dockside explosions start again. Shock begins to travel through my body, and I'm suddenly very tired, very sleepy. It would be so easy to slide beneath the waves like the Russian freighter's hull.

I swim towards the sampan, telling myself that, if I don't make it, it's not a big deal any longer. Then I see Hide Eberhard drowning my mother. My strokes strengthen, and the water parts before me, Moses McBride. My struggle now is with myself: do I want to live to confront Hide; or do I want to slip beneath the waters and confront God with all the injustice and cruelty he has created?

Hide is a little smaller than God. Less dangerous, too. I decide to live.

Reaching the sampan, I hold on to the side, too tired to pull myself up. I hear crying. The boat has found an ocean current. The tide is going out, sweeping away the mess. Holding on to the sampan's side, I float past the sinking freighter, which I can see now is loaded with artillery pieces meant to protect the harbor.

The kid's crying echoes off the inside of the ship's torn hull.

Maybe he's hanging on the other side of the sampan like me. I try to peer over the side to see if I can see his little hands on the opposite rail of the sampan but another bomb makes me cringe against the cool wood of the boat.

As the sampan slides past the now silent propellers of the crippled freighter, moving towards the sea wall and freedom,

I hear the sound of the twin Vulcan guns of an F-15 fighter jet ripping across the water.

There's only one thing to do.

I dive deep, as deep as I can, feeling the bullets zip through the water around me. My breath builds in my chest until I begin to see red behind closed eyes. Breaking the surface, I take a deep breath and open my eyes to see the sampan still within my reach. The kid is at the edge of the sampan, reaching a hand towards me, screaming. As I grab his hand, his left arm raises above the edge of the boat. It has been shot off at the elbow.

Khong beit. Crap.

Call Me Ishmael

I know how ninety-year-olds feel when they wake up in the morning because it's the way I felt once I was back in the sampan: surprised I was still alive.

That was the good news.

The bad news was the kid's arm. With rags from the dirty Chinese uniforms, I finally managed to stop the flow of blood from the stump. I cleaned the wound with some vodka. But the kid, lying in a fetal position at my feet, grew still as I struggled to get the sampan turned around to go back in the harbor.

He needed a doctor. But the tide proved too strong, and, after a while, weak from horror and the rush of adrenaline, I gave up and let the current take us out. I lay by the kid, holding him tight, trying to assure him everything was going to be alright. His breathing, while ragged, was steady. I closed my eyes, allowing the luxury of sleep to salve our wounds.

The empty vodka bottle rolling from side to side woke me hours later. I checked to see if the kid was still breathing. He was sleeping fitfully, but at least he was still alive. The heat from his body said fever was setting in. I untangled myself from him and sat up.

The sampan bobbed and slid gently up and down elephant-sized swells. The sun was hot on my neck, and I had a feeling the rolling bottle would be needed for the two of us, just in case it rained. I picked it up, and, staggering on my novice sea legs, made my way under the flap of the bimini and took inventory.

Crazily, five vodka bottles, filled with rain water from bimini run-off during the trip down the river, sat full in their wooden case, giving no hint as to how they had kept from shattering or spilling during the harbor bombing. The empty bottle in my hand made a full case of six bottles for water. The second case of vodka was also undamaged. One rice sack had been pierced by the strafing. It was the one under which the kid had been hiding, and I spent a long time picking up the grains carefully after throwing away what was left of the arm. We would need all our rice. The other two sacks, like the kid's other arm, were fine.

I set the sacks as high off the floor as I could to protect them against water sloshing in from the waves. The fifteen

LRRP ration packages were protected from the water by plastic packaging, so I left them on the floor. The case of *Nuoc Mam* sauce clinked in the front hull of the boat. The sauce was in small glass containers with corks. Two were shattered, and the rotten fish smell made me gag, but the rest were fine. I would use one bottle to store our daily ration of water from the vodka bottles.

The kid had stored a box of matches in with the *Nuoc Mam* bottles and some of the matches were soaked. I spread the wet ones carefully on top of the bimini, poured out one of the plastic packages of LRRP rations into the rice pot, and wrapped the dry matches inside the package as tightly as I could.

I kept one rifle, the rest I threw overboard after taking off the stocks and slings. Using what I could find in the boat, I made a small shade covering over the kid with two of the rifle stocks supporting a dirty uniform shirt spread like a tent. I couldn't put him forward under the bimini because it was too hot. I wanted him where I could watch him closely, and where I could rub him down with a cool wash cloth.

I felt the sleeping child's head. It was hotter. I wasn't sure if it was from the sun or from fever. Only time would tell which it was. There was no doctor in this house, but at least the boy had some shade now. I dipped a rag into the ocean and wiped his forehead.

The kid would be awake soon and need food and water. I scooped a pan of saltwater from the ocean and mixed it with three handfuls of rice, some *Nuoc Mam*, and the dry LRRP rations in the rice pot. I still had a half-sack of charcoal, probably two weeks' worth if I cooked a large amount of rice once a day. I would cook the LRRP rations with the rice once a week.

Since I would need the gasoline only for cooking, and not for the sampan, I dumped the motor overboard. I poured a small amount of gasoline on the charcoal and let it soak. When it had soaked enough, I took a match, lit the charcoal, put the rice mixture on the charcoal, and waited for it to boil.

An hour later, I heard the kid say something. I crawled over to him and helped him sit up against me. He was asking for his mom. I shook my head, and he turned away for a little while. Cradling him in my arms, I listened to him cry his pain out.

I got a little water down him and about three spoonfuls of the rice mixture. It was a good sign for two reasons: he hadn't lost the will to live, and he was strong enough to keep the food down. His breathing became regular as he fell asleep again leaning against me, head resting in the crook of my arm. His forehead felt cooler to me, and I hoped that meant he was stable for the moment. Sleep was the only medicine I could offer.

I waited until he was in a deep sleep before cauterizing his wound with a fiery rag lit from the charcoal. While the kid struggled from the pain of what I was doing to him, I thought of Jose and his story of the branding iron. Was it too much to hope for that the kid would live, so I could tell him the story about the old horseman?

If the kid forgave me.

Once the little one's breathing became regular again, I looked out from the boat. A desert surrounded me once more. It was deep green and its hills rolled; a quiet desert where one could see for miles. The sunset reminded me of the glorious ones Jose and I had watched from the little house at Barrel Springs.

I looked at my little home and my injured child. I knew water was valuable, but I shed some tears for the child. So much pain visited on such a small package. In one week he had lost a father, a mother, and an arm. If there was a God, he was not gentle and loving on this boat. And he was a hard-ass to the kid.

I checked the pan where the rice had boiled and set it off the fire, mixing some hot ashes with seat water to make a crude poultice for the blackened arm. The rest of the ashes I dumped in the ocean, listening to them hiss. There was a beautiful pink and yellow evening light above me, and the boat floated gently onward, perhaps to some destination far away from war. With our stock of food and water, I figured we had about two weeks to survive before someone found us.

During the next three days, the kid slipped in and out of consciousness. Sometimes, he would ask for his mother, and I would have to tell him all over again that she was gone. Other times, he would take my hand with his good one and make me rub his back. He liked that.

On the good nights we would lie there in the boat, looking at the stars. He would point to one, and I would give it a name. He would try to repeat it. When he grew tired, I would say a little prayer as he drifted off to sleep. Praying was not one of my talents, so I did my best:

When you wish upon a star,
Makes no difference who you are...

I couldn't remember the rest, so I repeated it over and over, and the chant helped to calm the fear in my heart.

I couldn't quit holding him. Even when I saw land approaching on the horizon, I would not release the small body. Gradually, over two days, he moved less and less. Finally, he lay still in my arms.

I was determined to punish myself in the worst way. Starving or dying on the ocean seemed in order. Using a rifle stock as a crude oar, I deliberately avoided ships and islands.

I sailed in circles until nightfall, my sampan too small for the large freighters that passed by to notice. At night, I paddled or drifted quietly by the shores of islands, close enough to see tourists walking along the beach, close enough to see the light from the rooms of the beach hotels. I didn't care if they were Communist hotels or Filipino hotels. These islands were to be avoided if my punishment was to be complete.

After passing the islands, and once more out in the open sea, I dropped my little one into the silent waters. I wrapped him in some of the Chinese soldiers' clothes, not sure why, maybe to keep him warm on his long, wet journey.

I hung on to his hand as long as I could; maybe I was holding on to the damaged child in me, or maybe I held all the damaged children in the world through that one little hand in mine. Either way, I didn't want to let go. But sleep overcame me and when I awoke, he was gone. I looked frantically for him, but he wasn't near the boat.

I would have gone crazy if it hadn't been for Jose bringing the kid back to the boat with him. The ocean is a big place, so Jose's finding me was a stroke of luck. I accepted their being there as normal; one day I was alone, the next, he stood at the bow of the boat talking to me, holding the kid's hand.

His voice began in mid-sentence: "...found him a few miles back, looking for you. I tried to call to you several times, but the waves drowned out my voice, Chapo."

"Aren't you dead?" I asked.

"Do we look dead?" The child gave a little laugh and hugged Jose with both arms, like he did me the first day we met. I smiled.

Jose brushed the kid's hair and laughed softly. "The ocean is peaceful, quiet. We'll use it to help us heal. Come up here beside us, Chapo, and listen to the universe hum in the wind. Watch these waves. When the music quits in the air, the harmony carries on in the ocean's roll. Look at the sky, Chapo, it burns grape-red from the volcano dust of South America."

I frowned. "Jose, that sounds too poetic for you."

He nodded and said, "Death makes you poetic about life and what it has to offer."

They came back each day. Usually, I would soak the rice in the sea water, pour one drop of *Nuoc Mam* sauce in for flavoring, take a drink of vodka and one of water from my daily ration of liquid, and wait for the sun to do what it could to soften the rice for me. Then, maybe, I'd eat.

If a wave didn't flip the rice.

If I remembered the rice was there.

If I remembered I was hungry.

"Chapo?"

I reached out for the kid. "Hey, I need someone to talk to. This boat trip ain't working out. I'm not dying like I'm supposed to."

Jose hit me on the side of the head with his hand. It was so hard it felt like the side of the boat. "Only cowards try to die. I didn't spend my time with you so you could do something stupid. Now, curl up and sleep."

I watched his lean brown hands take the tiller from me. The kid crawled up in his lap. It seemed natural, the two of them hitting it off so well.

"I didn't know you knew how to sail, Jose."

"I don't. But I know horses, and so do you. This ocean is just another horse to break. You're a little tired now, so I'll break it for you."

"Thanks, Jose," I said, stretching out on the floor of the boat, but not before wrapping my hands with bits of cloth.

Jose was curious. "Why do you do that?"

I examined my hands. "The mosquito bites have rotted into boils. And look at this one here on my thigh. It's made my foot swell. I wrap my hands with parts of the old uniforms the Chinese left behind to keep me from scratching the sores in my sleep."

"Weren't those men your enemies?" Jose asked looking straight ahead.

"Jose, I'm not sure anymore." I wrapped my hands tighter with the driest pieces of uniform to keep the salt water from seeping into the open sores.

It seemed crazy talking to an empty boat, but with Jose and the kid there, it was okay. "I don't think I can hate anymore."

Jose looked at me. "What about Hide Eberhard? You still hate him, don't you?"

"Oh no, you don't," I said reaching up for him from the floor of the boat. "Don't you go disappearing on me. I hate that I spent so much of my life hating people. And all the hate doesn't make me stronger."

"So?"

"Like now. I need to get up and try to survive one more day, but it might not be possible."

The kid whispered in Jose's ear. Jose turned and looked at me. "I thought you wanted to suffer as much as possible."

"I do. Or I did. But you're taking care of the kid now. I don't need to suffer anymore."

My voice cracked. "I'm dying, Jose: in the middle of the Pacific Ocean dressed in tattered black pajamas, thousands of miles from Texas, full of rice and smelling of *Nuoc Mam* sauce, with very little water and no vodka left. I'm dying."

He looked at me with age-old eyes. "What makes you weak is not trying."

"I'm just tired of fighting, Jose. Give me a break. Maybe the bull killed me and this is all a dream. Maybe those stitches on my scalp came from a careless seamstress working on my death shroud."

He laughed at my problem. "You expected me or the world to care about you? Well, don't. That's part of the price you pay to live. Scarring is part of the process. And now you feel sorry for yourself because you're here? Well, everybody has to be somewhere. You can't shape the music to your truth, Chapo. The truth must conform to the music."

He slapped me again.

"Stop it, Jose." I could feel my anger rising like a big fish from the deep.

He continued hitting me, his voice resonant and loud. "At least you're here. You could be where Jack and Ski are."

He spat at me. His voice grew louder. "I thought you were better than the other gringos, but I see now I was wrong. At least I killed the men who killed my mother."

He sneered at me. "You? You're going to lay down with a whimper and die in this ocean. You're not going to avenge your mother's death. You're going to let Eberhard get away with it. You're not even going to avenge my death."

He spat again, and his spit hit my face. The kid started spitting on me, too.

"You sonofabitch," I croaked, trying to rise from the bottom of the boat, trying to get out of my fetal position, "don't tell me I gave up on my Mama! And you two quit spitting on me!"

That's when I felt the rain. It was cold. I tried to call Jose, but could only manage a tiny, feeble rasping. I tilted my head back to try and scream again and felt the rain run down my throat. I sucked the hairs on my arm to get more of the moisture that clung to them. Finally, I felt my throat was ready.

"Jose," I screamed.

"Jose, Jose," came back the echo.

An echo in the ocean? That's when I saw the hull. Stupidly, like some petulant child repeatedly knocking at a door wanting to come in from the rain, the sampan was banging against the side of a huge ship. I could hear someone above me, saying something, but I was too tired to even raise my head.

I wasn't too tired to put the loop of rope that appeared in front of me under my arms, however. The rope tightened and I began to inch upward away from my sea home. As the sampan disappeared below me, I wondered if this was really happening. Then, I brushed against the barnacles on the side of the ship, and saw the blood flow from the cuts on my arm.

It was real.

I knew it was a Filipino freighter headed east towards Hawaii or San Diego. It had to be a Filipino freighter, dead in the water, working on engines. Who else would be just past the Philippines, headed into the Pacific? I twisted upwards, trying to see the name of the boat that saved my life. I bounced with my feet outward from the hull, craning my neck to see the giant letters on my right. The spelling was unreadable.

The hammer and sickle beside it were not.

Spelling Is Not My Long Suit

The captain of the ship wasn't so tough. Every time the brutal bastard hit me in the face, I could see him wince from the pain of his knuckles scraping my broken teeth. The two guys holding me seemed almost apologetic as they picked me up each time I fell from the blows. After all, what was Ahab's problem? Why did he have to beat me for information? Just because an emaciated, sore-ridden sailor in tattered black pajamas had been rescued from a sampan full of blood stains and empty Russian vodka bottles? Just because part of a child's finger had been found under a half-empty rice sack?

If I could have spoken Russian, I would have told him the whole damn story. Instead, silence seemed to be golden in my case. But even golden silence was cracking under his blows, along with my lips and teeth. He could've shown a thing or two to those damn Border Patrolmen who'd asked Jose and me for our papers.

Finally, I blurted out, "*¡Juan Bizcocho! ¡My nombre es Juan Bizcocho!*"

I feared if I said in English, "My name is John McBride," the whole crew might take turns hitting me. Most of them looked a lot tougher than the captain.

The beating stopped. The captain looked around vaguely for what to do next. The crew shifted around to allow an old man, skin browned from too much time at sea, to totter forward. From the stained shirt and gravy-colored apron around his waist, I assumed he was the ship's cook. The smell of onions that preceded him was another clue.

He bent down and peered hard at me with a wizened eye.

"*¿De donde eres?*"

"*De Ojos Calientes,*" I mumbled through swollen lips and broken teeth.

A smile creased his wrinkled face. "*¡Ah! ¡Un cubano! ¡Este hombre es cubano como yo! Yo conozco su pueblito.*"

That there should be a village in Cuba named Ojos Calientes just like Jose's village in Mexico was one of those little quirks in life that makes you wonder who's pulling the strings. Or maybe the old man heard something else. I couldn't articulate very well and he was old enough not to hear well.

I started to laugh maniacally. "Funny joke, Jose. Wrong time to pull it, but a funny joke."

The crew began to smile. Even the captain laughed and helped me to my feet. The old Cuban steadies me as I staggered to a standing position.

"My name isn't Jose. It's Ramon Perez. I am the ship's cook." I winced as he wiped my bleeding mouth with his greasy apron.

"Let me explain," he continued, "why you were beaten. Basically, the captain has had a bad day. First, we lost one of the engines, so we are stopped fifty miles from the Philippines while the crew overhauls the engine; second, he is under pressure to return quickly to Cuba to pick up more supplies for North Vietnam. The last bombing of the harbors created some critical shortages. But he finds your boat bumping against his ship, which potentially creates more setbacks, because he was afraid he would lose time if he had to take you back to Vietnam. So, you can understand his losing his temper with you."

Sure. It's common to beat strangers in the mouth when you first meet them in the middle of the ocean. I glanced at the captain. He quit smiling and said something in Russian to the old Cuban.

"He wants to know what happened to the rest of the men in the boat." Ramon was watching me intently.

"They died," I answered truthfully.

"How?" asked Ramon.

"From the American bombing at Nam Dinh."

Ramon translated for the captain, who nodded his head and spoke rapidly in reply.

"The captain said he lost a sister ship in the harbor. He asked if you saw what happened."

I nodded my head. "Was it the one carrying heavy weapons?"

The captain nodded "yes" after Ramon translated.

"The ship lost its hull and sank. Some of the men were rescued, I guess, because it was not sinking fast, but we had lost our engine by then and were drifting out to sea."

The captain turned away and stared over the port side.

"He had a brother on that ship," Ramon whispered.

If the brother was anything like this guy, I thought, the world is better rid of him. We waited quietly until the captain collected himself. He turned, barked some orders to Ramon, and left.

Ramon motioned for me to follow him. "You are to help me cook once you've regained your strength. It will take us about two to three weeks to reach Panama."

I panicked. "Panama? Why Panama?"

"Our embassy is there, of course. We'll turn you over to them, check out your story, send you home, let you spend a little time with your family, then they'll probably ship you back again to help advise the Vietnamese in their glorious cause."

There was nothing glorious about combat no matter whose side you fought on. Cuba in 'Nam? The world was indeed shrinking. But it made sense. South Korea, Thailand, Australia, and Turkey fought beside American troops in Vietnam, along with "observers" from countries who wished to remain neutral until the next war.

Ramon led me into the lower decks of the dilapidated ship to a kitchen that had seen better days. "The food on Russian ships is so bad, these guys prefer my cooking to theirs. So I cook black beans, rice, menudo, empanadas, Cuban tamales, soups, and stews…add some flavoring. They don't know any better. Compared with Russian food, anything with flavor is a step up."

He flipped down a cot held by a chain to the side of the ship. "Welcome to your home. We sleep, eat, and cook here for our fine Russian friends."

The way he said this made me look up. He was watching me intently. I had seen this look in Jose's eyes long ago.

He smiled at me. "Your accent is not Cuban. I knew that upstairs."

"Then why didn't you turn me in?"

"I don't like to speak Russian. I'll speak to a Mexican anytime over a Russian."

"They don't like our language?" I said, timidly.

Ramon gave a bitter laugh. "Things were better in the days of Hemingway." He looked around the rusty kitchen. "We traded sugar and gambling casinos for those communist assholes."

Ramon threw me a knife across the work table. "Enough talk! See if any of my uniforms fit you. There's a pair of sandals underneath the stove. Once you're dressed, peel the onions. We've got dinner to get ready."

So I dressed and peeled onions.

Until I fell asleep holding the knife in one hand and an onion in another.

Twenty-four hours later, Ramon kicked me awake.

It felt great.

For the next week, eight hours per day, I peeled onions. When I got tired of that, I sorted pebbles from the dried beans before Ramon cooked them in large vats on the ship's stoves. He added great quantities of freshly ground chili powder hoping, he said, to give the Russians bad bowels, but their cast-iron stomachs just begged for more.

Most of the time we worked quietly together, talking in Spanish. There was a lot about Ramon that reminded me of Jose, but the difference was that Ramon had long since given up hope. He was a cynic about the world, about communism, and about war. He was a man who watched out for himself long before he watched out for others. An opportunist, he had signed on as a cook for the Russians to keep from serving in the Cuban military.

"They send us everywhere to die," he lamented, "to Africa, to South America with Che, and now, to Vietnam. We are getting as bad as the Americans! They send their young to die all over the world."

Ramon spat into the vat of beans. "The revolution was supposed to cleanse Cuba of opportunists, not opportunity. Now what do we have? Now we die in foreign countries. For what? To give people hope that they can win what we did?

"What did you win, Ramon?"

He shrugged his shoulders. "Don't know. No one ever told me. But if shit was worth anything, the poor would not be allowed to have assholes."

"I know what you mean, Ramon."

He spat into the beans again. I made myself a mental note not to eat dinner that night.

The days passed. I judged time not by daylight, for I was rarely allowed to step on deck, but by what we were cooking. Breakfast was black beans and tea. Lunch was black beans, rice, and more tea. Dinner was occasionally salted meat, black beans, rice, tortillas, and still more tea. Ramon's Cuban specialties were reserved for national holidays.

The variety was dizzying.

Still, on the rare occasion Ramon and I got on deck, there were many things to see. The deck was mostly our own to explore. The crew, a dull lot with no love for the job, drank

heavily and made no attempt to hide it from us. They pretended
to be busy when the captain was around, but for the most part
did the least they could, drinking to dull the day-to-day monotony
of duty at sea.

The Pacific sun seemed to make them ill-tempered.
They spat at us and cursed us in Russian whenever we came
too close. They preferred the shade while Ramon and I walked
around the ship in the sun. We relished its warmth. Our brown
skins soaked in the reminder of whence we'd come.

"Juan, it won't be long until we see land." Ramon
breathed deeply. "Already, I can smell it. Look there, a frigate
bird. You remember those, don't you?"

Sure. Lots of those in West Texas. I smiled wanly at
Ramon, hoping I was looking at the right bird.

He laughed, enjoying my confusion.

"We'll see the coastline of Mexico first, follow it down to
the canal, take a day off at Panama City where we'll drop you off,
then through the canal to Colon."

Ramon rubbed his hands in anticipation. The wind blew
his hair into his eyes. "There is a cantina in Panama City called
'The Blue Room,' where you can find women who'll hold you
tight when you make love to them. Maybe I can take you there."

Mexico. Ramon had said, "Mexico."

I kept my voice bored, vague. "How soon until we see
land?"

Ramon sniffed the air. "Two, maybe three days. Can't
wait for the women, eh?"

He took a deeper breath. "I can smell their hair now."

I ignored Ramon's last comment. There would be time
to smell a woman's hair in the future, but I would be an old man
like Ramon before I smelled anything resembling a woman by
the time the Cuban embassy got finished with Juan Bizcocho.

If they allowed me to live.

The KGB would make the ship's captain look like a
cruise director.

There was a lifeboat next to where Ramon and I leaned
over the rail watching the foam from the ship's wake. There
seemed to be more rope than needed to lower it to the ocean. I
studied the chocks that held it in place.

"Time to cook, Juan." Ramon's voice startled me and I
jumped a little.

He eyed me. "Something wrong, Juan?"

"My family," I said weakly. "Your talking made me think of my family."

Ramon slapped me on the shoulder. "I can tell you haven't been to sea before. Come along. It won't be long until we get you some women. Then, you won't be so serious."

The next night, a storm hit. Like many lows that start in the Pacific, it was sudden and harsh. We had indications of its growing intensity from a gentle disturbance on the surface of the vat where the beans lay soaking to a larger roll of the whole ship, which caught us unaware.

"Juan!" I heard Ramon's shout for help as I was checking on the evening's rice.

I turned to see him trying to catch the large vat of cooked beans we had removed from the stove and placed on the large work table in preparation for dinner. I grabbed two towels next to me and ran to help. His face was twisted from the pain inflicted by the hot vat against his old arms. I took the vat from him and set it heavily on the floor, sloshing some of the contents.

As I set the vat down, Ramon was struggling to run cold water over his burns. Bits of blackened flesh hung from his forearms.

"Get me some help," he shouted.

I sprinted up the two flights to the deck and struggled to open the outer hatch. As I stepped out the door, a huge blast of wind with peppering rain hit my face. The sky was prematurely dark and the deck was deserted. I could see movement at the far end of the ship, and started for the lights I could see in the captain's watchtower.

Huge waves crashed onto the ship and I understood why the deck was empty. Somebody could be swept to their death from the force of the breaking seas that spilled over the ship. An empty bottle floated eerily by, missing all the hard objects that could have broken it, and then calmly caught the next huge wave out to sea, still intact. A lifeboat banged against its poles as if protesting the wind. I clung to the rope of the boat, working up my courage to sprint across the deck to the tower to tell them of Ramon's injuries.

I looked at the rope.

Another wave crashed in front of me, sweeping some crate out to a lonely voyage in a large sea, joining the bottle.

Mexico. Freedom.

No. Ramon needed help.

Reaching the steps to the pilothouse, I found my way up through the wind and water. The door tore from my hand as I opened it. The watch on duty, a group of four men, looked at me, astonished anyone would be stupid enough to be on deck in this weather.

"I need help," I said, "Ramon's been burned."

They stared at me. In my panic, I had blurted out the words in English.

"*¡Un accidente en la cocina! ¡Ramon necesita ayuda!*" I shouted, my voice fading as I realized they hadn't understood a thing I had said in Spanish, either. They were still shocked at my perfect English.

I slammed the door shut and sprinted back down the steps, fancying I heard a shot ring off the steel hull. It might have been some piece of metal banging against the side, but I wasn't waiting to find out.

I had to do it now. I was in the boat, clawing at the winch chocks that held it in place. When I managed to release them, the boat dropped quickly downward, smashing against an oncoming wave. As the wave swept the boat high, all the ropes snapped, and suddenly the ship was in front of me, then past me, and I was astern.

I could still see the lights on in the watchtower, and I suppressed the silly thought that the next wave would take me above the tower, and I'd be able to wave at the outraged crew as I drifted back down. I hoped they would tend to Ramon. He had saved me from the captain's beating, and I owed him that much.

The ship's lights faded into the distance and I was alone on an angry sea that cared nothing for my reasons for launching. Without food. Without water. Not knowing where I was. I glanced around the boat. No oars.

Two or three days, Ramon had said. Of course this information came from a man who grabbed scalding vats with his bare arms.

A bolt of lightning split the sky and waves rose around me.

Call Me Lost

"I bet there's no coconuts when I get to the top," I whisper in the cold mist, as I try to find a grip on the cliff before the next wave breaks. My hands slide against the cold stone; I ignore the cold's insistent bite. I reach for an outcropping just above me, but it's too slick and my hand slips. I grab again at the rock just before I slide out of reach, sticking this time like a fly on a wall. Inching upwards, my fingers crawl towards the top of this rocky table.

Twenty feet. Thirty.

Sixty feet.

I don't look down as my hands squash in some wet bird's dead body lying on the next ledge. My hands squeeze past the ooze and find a hard shelf. It would be so much easier just to let go. My chin rests next to the rotting beak while my hands search for holds above. I stare into the dead eye. It stares back.

I should have stayed on the ship.

Like all storms, mine, too, had blown over, leaving only passing squalls. That night, once or twice, I thought I saw the freighter returning, but it was only my imagination. Russian freighters do not backtrack for Cuban cooks.

The afternoon after the night's storm, frigate birds, at least I thought they were frigate birds, screamed a welcome to my small vessel as I bobbed towards what appeared to be an island. Other birds joined the frigate birds' cries, including vultures circling lazily overhead, their silence speaking volumes. I was determined to give them no satisfaction.

When I finally reached what appeared to be land, I discovered something Ramon had failed to mention: a reef that surrounds the land around these parts. I had tried to slow the boat's charge toward the reef, but with an offshore wind still lingering from the storm, and my inability to maneuver against the high-tide current bringing me inland, the boat smashed on the jagged coral, tearing a large hole in its bottom. The next wave took the boat past; unfortunately, its bottom stayed on the reef. I surfed the waves involuntarily until they deposited – smashed – me against the rocky face I now climbed.

As my hands reached for the top, I told them, "If you'll pull, I'll get the rest of us over."

They grabbed a tough clump of grass, fulfilling their job. Struggling over the jagged top, I knelt exhausted on an upward sloping field of sun-yellowed grass. Red flowers adorned the cactus dotting the filed in front of me. The cactus stretched their arms in supplication to a very dry sky. I smiled. They were the first living plants I'd seen in a month. Maybe two. I took a deep breath. It is a sweet smell that emanates from solid earth.

Looking about cautiously, knowing something bad was about to happen – again – to a McBride, I began hobbling towards the top of the grassy knoll in front of me. The ground was volcanic stone, and I winced as my tender feet complained of my losing Ramon's sandals, along with the rest of the clothes he'd given me as the waves tossed me towards the shore.

At the top of the knoll, naked, I observed I was on one of three islands. In front of the island, maybe fifty miles across the dark blue water was a large landmass. It looked dry and brown, with few trees. Mexico? Down the slope from where I stood, a quiet, light blue-green bay opened into deeper blue ocean. I reinterpreted the stance of the tall cactus: they held their arms up in surprise that I'd made it back to the Americas.

What were my options? I could go to the first American consulate I found and turn myself in. How could I explain what I was doing in Mexico without a passport, when I was supposed to be fighting in Vietnam?

My next option was to find a phone, or use the one in the first American consulate I stumbled across and call Vietnam. I tried to imagine my conversation with Special Forces Headquarters in Nha Trang:

"Will you accept a collect call from Mexico?"

Long pause: "Is that you, McBride? Are you drunk again in Saigon?"

"This is Johnny McBride in Mexico. Come on, guys, accept the call. I don't have any money."

Long pause: "Right. C'mon, McBride, the old man will be in anytime and jump dead in your ass. Now, tell me which Saigon whorehouse you're in…"

Me, in final desperation: "I floated down the Red River, past Nam Dinh harbor, and out into the South China Sea, somehow managing to miss Borneo and the Philippines…" my voice starting to falter at the impossibility of it all, "and…and I got picked up by a Russian ship, but I jumped ship and drifted to Mexico… See there was this storm…"

My voice trails off.

Loud laughter and, after a long pause: "Damn McBride, what a sense of humor. What happened next?"

I tell him about the woman and the kid.

More laughter: "Stop it, McBride, I can't take much more of this. Hey, Joczik, c'mere, listen to this. McBride is drunk in Saigon again. You're not going to believe his crap…"

Looking at the quiet bay stretching out below the cliff, I noticed for the first time a white sailboat floating there, like a tethered cloud hovering over the clear water.

I shut my eyes. I open them again. The boat is still there. Still nude, I start down. The closer I get to the boat, the worse my feet complain. I could care less about cactus thorns. I'm going home.

The boat's crew is on the beach somewhere. I find a bikini top first, then the bottom. I pick them up and carry both with me. I find some swim trunks up the beach and slip them on. They're a little loose. From there it's a simple matter to follow the footprints, chasing each other in the sand, to where they disappear. The sounds from the other side of the fallen palm tell me that someone is busy over there.

What should I say to them? In which language?

Their enthusiastic moans slow to soft murmurings, and I clear my throat. Two heads pop up, wide-eyed, staring at the stranger just the other side of the palm trunk, wearing someone's discarded bathing suit.

"Could I get a ride with you when you finish?" I ask in Spanish.

Two If By Land

Nervously, Bob takes the beer from my hand.

"Better? Let's find out some more about you." Bob begins to shout at me as if volume alone could overcome language barriers.

"This is where you found us – Tres Marias Islands." Bob points to a grouping of three islands on his navigation chart.

"We didn't mean to seem frightened of you," he smiles sheepishly, "we were in a restricted area, and we were afraid you were the authorities."

I follow his finger as he traces Tres Marias Islands, then upwards. "Here is Baja California. We're going to take you up through the Sea of Cortes to Topolobampo. We rented the boat there, and we've got to be back day after tomorrow."

He continues to shout as he shows me on the chart the route we are to follow. I nod my head slowly, reaching for another of the sandwiches his wife Patricia has prepared. I look around the cabin and then check out the tennis shorts and T-shirt that hang loose on my emaciated frame.

Bob continues, "Lucky for you Pat here's a nurse. I'm a nursing home administrator. We're on our vacation."

He laughs and gives his wife a knowing look. "Our first aid kit is pretty extensive."

Pat has done as much as she can for me. There are gauze patches all over my body, covering wounds treated with some kind of smelly salve. Even the beach thongs feel good on my bandaged feet.

Bob is still talking to me like I'm an idiot. He slows his speech down and raises his volume even louder.

"Are you from M-E-X-I-C-O or C-A-L-I-F-O-R-N-I-A?" he switches to spelling the words loudly, thinking perhaps I'll translate them better.

Pat's voice joins his. "WE ARE FROM SAN DIEGO. WHEN WE FINISH SAILING, WE ARE GOING TO TAKE THE PLANE HOME!"

My predicament is not good. I sigh deeply, shutting out Bob and Pat for the moment. His hands look soft. I close my fist to hide the calluses on mine. Their smooth, arrogant hands embarrass me. I've been too long on the other side.

Pat dabs something on my face. It stings and cools at the same time. "Maybe he doesn't speak English, Bob."

Bob looks at me. "Funny. I could swear he understood what I said."

He flips open *Spanish for the Tourist* and looks up the words.

"*¿DONde esTA USted?*" he screams.

I look at California on the chart. I look at Mexico on the chart. Vietnam is over for me. It is time to go home to the only place where I've ever felt welcomed. I point to Mexico.

Bob smiles. "We're making progress."

Flipping of pages.

"*¿Que ES su NOMbre?*" He makes it sound like, "*¿KAY IS su NUMber?*"

This one is easy. "*Juan Bizcocho.*"

Bob smiles at Pat. "Hey, at least we know he's Mexican. Now, let's try and see where he came from.

Bob points to the chart. "*¿Donde?*"

I put my hand on top of the chart, hesitate, then swing it to the left, off the chart in mid-air, just about where the Philippines would be. I smile at the two of them. They stare stupidly at my hand hovering above nothing.

Bob folds the chart up and says quietly, "*BasTANTE por la NOche.*"

Later, I hear them talking quietly in their cabin.

"What is he telling us – that he's floated over the Pacific?"

Bob sounds unconvinced. "What would a Mexican be doing in the Pacific? I think he's a drug smuggler who crashed on the islands. Anyway, let's turn him over to the authorities at Topolobampo and quit worrying about it. We'll be there by noon, day after tomorrow. Come here. Let's finish what he interrupted on the island."

Pat moans as I lay in the bunk, still eating what's left of the sandwiches.

"Day after tomorrow," I whisper to myself in the dark.

When I hear their breathing deepen, I wait another hour and get up. Bob has left his wallet by the charts. Moonlight spills from a porthole above the table and I count out two fifties, four twenties and three hundred pesos. If I'm to get back to Sofia and her children, I'll need the money.

I look at his maps. The money will have to get me over a range of mountains called the Sierra Madre Occidental, past a huge canyon called Barranca del Cobre, and over eleven hundred more miles to Ojos Calientes along the Texas border.

After the Pacific, what's ahead of me is a piece of cake.

Speaking of which, I grab as much food from the galley as I can fit in my tennis shorts, and wrap a plastic trash bag around the food to keep it dry.

I creep up on top and look for the dinghy. It floats behind in the Mexican moonlight, tied by a rope to the stern. I find a pair of wet deck shoes and add them to my food bag. Easing over the side, I follow the rope back to the dinghy and untie it. I wish Bob and Pat well. They were the first good thing to happen to me in a long time.

And I steal their money, shoes, food and dinghy to show my gratitude.

The McBride tradition lives on.

My plan is to ditch the dinghy on shore, then follow the coast north to a town or a railroad station. From there, I'll take the train to Chihuahua, find a bus to Ojinada, a little place with a bus station near the Texas border, and walk the last eighty miles through the desert to Sofia and the girls. It's a solid plan.

Home Is the Hunter

The sunrise revealed a beautiful beach stretching in both directions, but I was too busy to look at it for long. I hoped Pat and Bob wouldn't be charged too much for the loss of the dinghy, which was now sinking. I waited until the ocean claimed my second boat in as many days. Still wearing tennis shorts and T-shirt, I began walking north on a road that paralleled the beach, hoping eventually to find a railroad. I promised myself never to look at a boat again. And immediately break that promise.

I glanced at the Sea of Cortes and at that one beautiful white sailboat on the water, a painted ship upon a beautiful painted ocean. I continued walking, refreshed by the beauty of the blue sea, the sailboat, and the deep colors of the Baja California morning. Next time I glanced at the sailboat, however, it seemed closer.

Ship to shore radio. One minor detail I had overlooked.

On this particular white sailboat were an angry Bob and an angry Pat. There is a jeep coming down the road full of Mexican policemen. And I'm walking on that road wearing rather conspicuous white tennis shorts and a T-shirt, walking in deck shoes that don't fit, with pockets full of stolen money, carrying a bag full of stolen food.

I blend right in with the populace.

Looking wildly about, but remembering my escape and survival training – remain calm; do not bring attention to yourself, etc. – I stumble down the first embankment I can find and hide inside a bridge culvert.

The jeep roars by on the highway.

I hear a cough behind me. I'm captured.

Turning around slowly, hands in the air, I see three people covered in rags by the culvert, looking at me with concern: a woman with small baby, and a very thin, young man with a bad cough, whose hand shakes as he holds a very dull knife in front of him. They eye my clothes.

I'm a little overdressed for the culvert set.

I show him Bob's wallet. He pinches himself. I drop the food bag slowly, letting its contents spill onto the ground. He crosses himself. The woman springs on the food and takes it back to their side of the culvert, wolfing down some cheese and tearing a piece off for him.

I point to my shorts and T-shirt and then to his clothes. He shakes his head. I hold out Bob's three hundred pesos. Quickly, he hands me his torn brown peasant pants and dirty shirt. I point to my shoes. He shakes his head.

His wife, chewing hungrily on some bread, scurries over, gives me her sandals, which was made from discarded auto tires, and takes the white shoes. She's got big feet.

I hold up one of Bob's twenties. The man throws in a straw farmer's hat.

I climb out of the culvert and join a growing stream of people heading north. Another jeep roars up behind us, slows, then honks its way through. Pat and Bob sit in the back looking at us. They're trying to find tennis clothes, so they look at me and through me. I'm just another dirty peasant now. The jeep drives slowly past the crowd.

The longer I limped along with the others, the deeper I felt myself sinking into Mexico. I needed time to heal. Would Sofia allow me to stay? It didn't matter. I could stay in Ojos Calientes with the little money left until it was time to head north.

In the distance I heard a church bell. Was it Sunday? I thought about the family in the culvert. They reminded me of the family I had lost in Vietnam. I said a silent prayer. Each day for them was a struggle to survive, and that was the triumph of the poor. They understood both the terror and joy of living, the daily miracle of just staying alive in a violent world.

At the little village of La Cruz - at least that was what the sign said at the town's limits - I brought a train ticket for one hundred pesos for the thousand-mile journey to Chihuahua.

According to the station master, the trip would take two days and three nights. I watched the ocean fade from a wide expanse to a sliver of blue as the engine pulled us away from shore, sailing onto an inward ocean.

The train passed field after field of wheat and rice as it followed the Fuerte River into the Sierras. Gradually, the golden fields faded away and granite giants took their place.

There was an old woman watching me as I tore a piece of bread from a fresh loaf I had purchased at the train station. I tore a piece off and handed it to her. She smiled a toothless "thanks."

"That's for the meat," I said under my breath. She looked puzzled as she chewed the bread.

The next morning found the train in the Barranca del Cobre, a great scar along the belly of Mexico. I could look out the car's cracked window and see cars in front of mine climbing three different switchbacks as the train inched carefully upward. Above the train, at the top of the canyon, great flocks of doves unfurled like welcome home banners in the sunlit sky. Mule deer clattered down the rocks away from the noisy train, scattering flocks of goats trying to cross the tracks. Angry shepherds shook their fists at the train, just as Jose had done at the B-52s.

I smiled at the beauty of it all. The air broke crisp and fresh at the top of the ridges, and we all shivered in the cars. The discomfort only moved us all deeper into contact with the huge cliffs and deep canyons. Those tourists in the window cars at the head of the train saw the canyon. I not only saw it, but also smelled it through the cracks in my window. I fell asleep at midday and awoke in the night as the train rumbled past small isolated cooking fires surrounded by the huge nothingness of the Chihuahuan Desert.

Across from me, a beautiful woman patted a child wrapped in a saddle blanket and hummed a tune I could not hear. An old man rocked with the train, his body leaning this way and that through the curves, as if the body were awake while the spirit slept. One little girl tapped her foot against the wooden seats in time with the clicking of the train wheels. The lights shining in the tourist coaches in front of our car seemed like fireflies we were chasing.

The lonely whistle at midnight crossings announced my homecoming.

End of the Line

The train stopped in Chihuahua on a clear, hot morning. I limped off the car, waving good-bye to the little girl who kept train time with her foot the three days we traveled by rail. Watching her through the nights, I became confused as to who was really driving the train. If her foot had stopped once, I would have panicked that the train, too, would stop.

She waved back and disappeared into the large crowd with her family. The air around the station smelled of interior Mexico, unregulated, careless, and free. Diesel, wood smoke, and open sewage mixed with the general smells of living. Buses going nowhere caromed by, under the command of drivers in their usual state of mindless hurry, just missing the confused tourists and the scurrying families from the countryside. I recalled the bus ride with Jose the first time I ever visited Ojos Calientes.

At the ticket window I asked what time the train left for Ojinaga, the Mexican town just across the border from Presidio, Texas. Ojinaga was the last stop before the Texas border, and the nearest one to Ojos Calientes. The surly station master shrugged his shoulders and walked behind a partition in the back, extremely involved in a task that kept him from answering the public's silly questions. He never said a word to me. And he didn't come back.

After ten minutes of waiting, I was going to reach through the ticket window bars and shove his metal cash register onto the floor to get his attention. I checked my impulse, however, when I saw two *federales* at the end of the platform, looking at a flyer, and checking the people exiting the train against whatever it said. The station master was hurrying towards them.

Now, maybe they weren't looking for me, but I wasn't going to go up to them, take the flyer point to myself, and say, "Looking for me?"

The station master talked rapidly to them and pointed in my direction. Surely, the dinghy wasn't that important. It had to be something else.

They turned and stared hard at me.

Maybe the dinghy was that important.

I turned from the window and walked quickly from the station and out into the busy street. After a few quick attempts to make sense of the bus schedule posted on a faded green wooden bulletin board, I got on the first bus waiting in the front of the station, an old expatriate American school bus with **La e o Scho 1 Dist l t** barely visible on the side. I wondered if the Laredo schools even knew if it was gone. I walked to the back and sat down on a cracked vinyl seat next to a dirty window. On the street, a cart full of beer bottles rolled by, pulled by a sick donkey, and driven by an even sicker man, judging from the phlegm that he spat on the side of the bus as he rolled on. The driver got on the bus, chewing on a cookie.

With its motor blowing a cloud of black diesel smoke, the bus quit the train station just as the two *federales* came around the corner blowing their whistles. The driver said a couple of cuss words and lurched to a stop. One of the passengers, an old woman, crossed herself, and began to mutter under her breath. I turned my head, looking out the window, my heart doing rhythmic gymnastics.

What would happen to me now? First, a couple of years in a Mexican prison for the dinghy, then, a couple of more for desertion in an American prison. If I was really unlucky, a distinct possibility given my heritage, I would probably receive a severe beating, or be thrown in a jail cell with someone named Big Bubba or Pablo Grande. I was just not meant to get anywhere in my life without some kind of complication. Just once, I wished life would be different. The consistency of bad luck was growing tiresome.

The two officers stepped on the bus dressed in olive green uniforms, looking tough as they eyed us all. With their holsters hanging loose at their hips they looked like outlaws boarding a train in some early cowboy movie. One particularly ugly eye, set in a particularly ugly face fell on me, but I ignored it and stared out the window.

"*Papeles, por favor,*" they asked at each seat, as they walked slowly towards me. Both of them were huffing louder than the trains in the station, from having had to jog after the bus while blowing their whistles.

What kind of papers were they looking for? A pass to visit the city, maybe, or citizenship papers? I realized I knew nothing about official procedures in the country of my fondest memories. I had come into it by the back door at a very early age. Navarrete was not the kind of man who cottoned to paperwork, whether American or Mexican.

As they got to the seat directly in front of mine, I began to steel myself to leap from the seat when the first one got to me, shove his huffing three hundred pounds out of the way, knock down the other monster, a supple two-hundred-and-fifty, and hobble quickly out the door while dodging the fire from their pistols in the narrow aisle of the bus.

The odds were good I would make it.

As I began to stand, startling the taller of the two federales, a young man two seats in front of me suddenly bolted for the bus door. If the he old woman hadn't screamed, I don't think they would have known he bolted. But she did, and the huge bodies swiveled in the small aisle like large ships trying to maneuver into small slips. Their gun belts snagged everything as they turned, knocking packages and groceries to the floor. Blowing their whistles, they ran after him, the rear one just missing the young man with a thrown wooden baton as he leapt from the bus.

The bus driver just sat there eating that cookie, seemingly unaware of the drama swirling around him. And he still sat there, minutes afterwards, waiting for them to come back. Finally, two older people got up and left the bus to go to the bathroom back at the station. I decided to follow their example. The bus driver watched me lazily in the mirror as I stepped off the bus.

Once outside, I hailed a taxi and asked him to take me to the highway leading away from Chihuahua towards Ojinaga.

"*No hay problema; es el número dieciseis.*" And constantly, leaning on his horn, we cleared the station, leaving the bus still waiting for the return of the two *federales*.

The taxi driver had an evil grin, which grew larger when he left me alone outside Chihuahua on Mexican Highway 16, twenty sailboat dollars poorer, and facing the prospect of walking, on bad feet and without water, through three hundred miles of the Chihuahuan Desert. I tried to concentrate on what he was saying, but the heat radiating from the road was already making me uncomfortable.

He was rattling off the towns to the north along Highway 16, "*Aldama, entonces, El Morrin, Despues, Placer, Guadalupe, Grutas Coyame...*" The litany was accompanied by dire warning that it was "*muy peligroso,*" to walk along the highway in the heat of the day.

"For a few dollars more, I'll take you...," but he spoiled his sales pitch by grinning at me, a wolfish grin like that of the Chinese officer along the river back in what seemed ages ago.

Screw it. I was too weak to fight him off, and the further we got from town, the better his chances to rob me or even kill me. I began walking, not looking back. As the desert opened in front of me on both sides of the shimmering asphalt, I heard him start the car, hesitate, then turn around. Was he going back to town to get the federales?

I decided it would be best to seek some shade under the next bridge I found. Two miles later, thirsty and tired, and with the old lava wounds from the island already reopening on my feet, I found the bridge and the shade I was looking for. I shared it with two lizards, a sick jackrabbit, and two doves. They seemed to be sleeping, and I joined them.

ROAR!

Incoming.

I waited holding my breath in the dark, trying to remember where I was, why I was curled up into a defensive position waiting for a mortar attack, and what had disturbed my sleep. I shivered in the desert night. A stone skidded down the cement under the bridge as something scurried by, frightened by the same sound that woke me.

I crawled to the top of the bridge. A cattle truck idled just beyond. The smell of air brakes applied against tires still lingered in the cool night air. A truck door slammed and the driver walked in front of his rig, silhouetted in the headlights. He was relieving himself.

I waited fifteen minutes.

Normally, it's not a favorite activity of mine to watch someone pee in the middle of the night in the state of Chihuahua. But I was hungry, and thirsty, and needed a ride. Protocol be damned. I dusted myself off and started toward the truck.

Nobody needed that much relief.

He was standing in his headlights looking down the road, a tall, gaunt red-headed bearded giant, who looked like some biblical patriarch, and he was talking to the empty highway.

I walked up beside him, whistling.

"Evening," I said, staying just out of arm's reach.

He turned and looked at me, his eyes bright, pupils enlarged either from the truck headlights behind us, the diesel fumes, or something chemical running through his veins.

"*Buenas noches,*" I tried again in Spanish.

He turned, and looked wild-eyed back to the road.

"Damn train's taking forever to cross," he said In a strong Texas drawl. "Hell, if I ain't rolling, there's no money. Man's got to eat and pay taxes. That's what life's about, ain't it?"

I looked down Mexican Highway 16, illuminated by his headlights, our shadows stretching long into the Mexican night. There were no railroad tracks.

Not within thirty miles at least.

"Yep," I said, squatting slowly beside him, slipping back into the Texas drawl of my youth. "That's what life is about, I reckon."

"Damn! Why would they put together another engine in the middle like that? That is going to be a long one." He brushed back his wild red hair with shaky fingers and gave a high-pitched laugh. Behind him, a cow moaned in the trailer.

He looked down at me. I didn't dare look up. I just knew from his shadow he was staring hard at me. No sudden movements.

The shadow knows.

I watched his shadow watching mine in the headlights for a long time before he spoke. I could feel the precious sweat slip down my spine.

He cleared his throat, and began talking again in a loud whisper.

"They talk to me, you know, like when I'm taking them to slaughter?"

"Who?" I kept my voice level.

He popped another pill. The whisper changed to a quavering voice. "I try to explain it's just my job, but they don't listen."

"Who?" I asked again.

He was quiet for a moment, watching ghost railroad cars whip past.

"I don't eat at McDonald's anymore," he said louder into the night. "I can hear them screaming in back while they're cooking. They scream my name over and over. 'Eddy, Eddy.' When they cook 'em well-done, I hear them scream an awful long time."

"Who?" I felt like a desert owl.

His voice took on a preacher's edge. "Do you like meat?"

"Vegetarian." I kept my voice carefully modulated. "I'm a vegetarian."

Which was partially true. I hadn't eaten any meat in Chihuahua.

He changed the subject. "McDonald's sends me down here to pick up Mexican cows they buy cheap. I take the cows to Ojinaga. Meskins keep 'em quarantined for thirty days. The ones I took there thirty days ago, I get released from quarantine, and truck 'em on up to Dallas and Fort Worth. Then, I turn around, drive all the way back to Chihuahua, and start all over again.

"I haven't been off the road for three years, seven days a week, twelve hours a day, and I'm real tired."

His voice took on a shrill edge. "I think I have a wife. Can't remember. The cows began talking to me last year. Told me how they're killed in Fort Worth. Want to know how?"

I shook my head, salivating at the thought of a hamburger.

"Force feed 'em until they're so big, their stomachs almost pop. Then, a big hook pulls 'em, still kicking, up a belt until they're inside the slaughterhouse, where sharp knives strapped to machines strip off their skin for the leather – did I mention they're still alive? – then, something slices 'em open and cleans 'em out. Still kicking, they're moved down the line, hooves ground up for Jell-o, bones sucked out for dog meal, and the whole mass, what's left anyway, is dumped into a hamburger blender, while the heart is still beating."

He screamed at the night.

Why didn't I let those *federales* catch me when I had the chance?

He slapped my head, hard. "Did you know them fast food stores have more people working for them than the government?"

"McDonald's buys more beef from Mexico than the rest of the nation put together. They have more employees here and in the United States than both governments combined. I'm going to tell you something…"

I found down the urge to run. I needed a ride real bad.

He squatted beside me. I could smell his onion breath as he leaned close to my ear.

"McDonald's *is* the government. When they run out of cattle, they'll have me hauling old Mexicans back there. They got to feed us something. There ain't no flags no more, just giant golden arches everywhere. Even the Pentagon has golden arches on their sleeves."

He passed, whispering beside me. "They got 'the Bomb,' you know, for when there get to be more people than Big Macs. Making more things, selling more things, buying more things. We're coming to a corner we can't get out of."

He gave that little laugh again. "This must sound crazy to you, but you look like someone I can talk to. I get so lonely out here."

I nodded that I understood crazy. "Look, when the train stops, how about a ride? Since I'm a vegetarian, maybe the cows won't talk to you as much. At least we can keep each other company across the desert."

He stood. He was making little struggling sounds with his voice, like a dynamo with no lubrication as it burns itself out, whining at a high pitch just before it breaks down.

I waited for the blow to fall and braced myself.

His voice returned to calmness. "Yeah. Good idea. I'll drop you off this side of the border or wherever you want, as long as you ride most of the way with me. They don't let your kind into America, you know."

I felt goosebumps run wild over my body. Maybe this was that one crystal moment of pure luck handed to a chosen individual. A McBride was finally in the right place at the right time.

Two-hundred-and-ninety-five miles south of Ojinaga God smiled horribly down on me.

I stood up and spread my hands toward the cosmos.

I BELIEVE, BROTHERS AND SISTERS!

The truck driver put a huge oil-stained hand on my shoulder and squeezed.

"Here comes the caboose. The cows are quiet, and I've found me a buddy in the Chihuahuan Desert. Damn, this is my lucky night!"

Yes, it was. We both waved at the man in the little red car as it click-clacked by.

THROW AWAY THOSE CRUTCHES, AND RIDE, BROTHER, RIDE!

It Doesn't Take Brains to Live Simple

By the time Eddy unloaded his cattle in Ojinaga, even I was listening to what the cows were saying. He ran around the men in the Mexican stockyards gesturing wildly, but they ignored him, having heard his dire warnings many times before. Warnings don't fill Mexican children's bellies, and families still need money to exist. Wild red-bearded prophets were clearly ignored here in the desert as well as at points north. The stock handlers drove the cattle away from the raving driver into a holding pen, leaving him defeated and alone in the swirling dirt of an empty corral.

I hopped off the fence, from where I had watched it all, and tried to console him.

"It's okay. They didn't listen to John the Baptist either, when he warned them."

The truck driver stared blankly at me. "Does he work for McDonald's?"

I turned away and hobbled along the Rio Grande, keeping it on my right. I knew if I followed it long enough, it would take me home to Sofia and the girls.

Mesquite branches make wonderful crutches for about ten steps. Then, their brittle thinness pops, and down you go. Fortunately, there's a mesquite bush every nine steps, so it's not that hard to find a new crutch. It just takes longer to walk from Ojinaga to Ojos Calientes, that's all. And you're still in the same desert, with the same sun. There are no buses along the river road, and the Rio Grande still flows wide, brown, and shallow, like it did the time Jose and I crossed it five years ago.

As I walked and fell, I had time to start feeling the country again.

Literally.

I heard the twittering of the Mexican bats in the evening as they twisted out of some small cave in the canyons, hungry smoke sweeping across an insect field. I saw bullbats, dark birds with white underwings, dive along with their namesakes, only their size telling of their true heritage. The Mexican bat worked as hard as his countrymen for his dinner.

A coyote stopped, shocked at the crippled figure walking alone.

"That hunting thing with the mesquite crutch is definitely going to starve," it said, trotting insolently along the road just in front of me.

The air smelled dry and hot, not like the morning air had smelled on my train trip through the high mountains. Here, it smelled of primordial beginnings and constant endings.

To get my thoughts off tomorrow's simmering heat, I drank in the beauty of the sweeping tail of the coyote as the animal slipped into the next arroyo. The moon came up and tracks showed where the coyote had turned to hunt in the dry river bed. I struggled along alone, my feet kicking moon dust into the night.

One foot in front of the one left behind. It was a mantra played over and over in my mind. Had I slept? Did I sleep? I don't know. I just knew, when I finally stopped, leaning on the crutch in the mid-morning sun of the next day, or the next, I was staring at two girls, no longer eight and ten, but in their teens, standing in front of an old adobe home framed by sandstone cliffs that overlooked two cottonwoods.

Behind the cottonwoods, curious horses looked over the corral fence. One of them, black and much larger than the others, flicked its ears back and forth. The second summer I spent with Jose, he taught me that the ears gave an indication of the horse's intelligence. I had been a junior in high school, then.

Now, six years and a lifetime later, Oso raised his head and called to an old, very old, ex-soldier of twenty-four. My feet began to shuffle forward even if I could not. There were no more tears to relieve the lump building deep within. Just memories. It was the only baggage I carried.

The two girls turned and ran inside. Sofia came out with the girls, staring at me. I tried to straighten away from the crutch, ashamed that I showed so poorly to the three fine women who stood waiting. I heard a small cry escape from Sofia and she took two hesitant steps toward me.

One more.

She broke into a run and suddenly, I was against her blouse, my head buried in her shoulder

"*Chapo, Chapo,*" she said, "*no estas muerto.*" She said it like a prayer.

"I would like some of your beans," I managed to say before collapsing.

Once again, I dreamed of heaven, but instead of the manicured hand of a beautiful woman stroking my forehead, I dreamed of a roof over my head, a hot, tasty meal, and a bed. And when I awoke, I was in heaven. Sofia sat at the edge of the bed, a plate of beans and tortillas in her lap. I turned and tried to look out the window, but it was already twilight. A small bug made his getaway over the adobe wall. I could feel the heat in the adobe still radiating from the day I had missed.

"Looks like I've slept the day away," I said, eyeing the plate of food.

Sofia spooned some beans into the tortilla, folded it, and handed it to me.

"Two days," she corrected.

I chewed the beans slowly, relishing their fine taste, feeling the flavor of the fresh green chilies explode in my mouth. The house was still simple, but the furniture seemed new, and there were new curtains on the two windows overlooking the corral. A fresh hot breeze lifted one of the curtains.

"Did you get my paychecks?"

Sofia nodded, watching me eat.

When I finished, she frowned. "Chapo, will we have to give the rest of the money back?"

I sopped the bean juice with the last half of the tortilla.

"What money are you talking about?"

"A few months ago, a letter came and told us you had died. Inside was a large check. 'GI Life Insurance,' it said. Inside was a letter saying you were dead in Vietnam.

The empty plate in her hand trembled.

"I wrote them back and asked them if they would take back the money so your body could be sent to us, and...," her voice faltered, "they said, the body was not available."

She got up, took the plate into the little kitchen, and came back with the check.

"Here." She was smiling. "We must send this back, now that I have the body, and it is in my bed eating more beans than I can cook."

The check was for twenty-five thousand dollars, basic for an enlisted man's life. Standard insurance companies would not insure soldiers. After all, their job was to die. That throws a lot of life insurance actuaries out of business.

I put the check back in her hand and folded her fingers around it.

"Keep it. That mad is dead and must stay dead. If we send it back, questions may be raised. I want to get well and live here for awhile. Let me break horses for you, teach the girls what Jose taught me, and work the land if the offer is still good."

Sofia stared at the check. "There is some land next to this little ranch of ours for sale. With the money, we could raise more horses, breed them, maybe even race them in El Paso or New Mexico."

She leaned onto the bed and hugged me. A little too long. I assumed this was Jose's old bed. It kinda gave me the creeps, lying in Jose's bed, his widow hugging me. My feet still hurt. I thought of all the excuses I could think of, but none were helping me out of this situation.

A woman bobbed in my mind.

I fought my way to the top of the water. Sofia stood up. I could see the hurt in her eyes.

"No, Sofia. Just give me some time. Some things happened over there, terrible things, and it's hard to pretend we're not different when we know we are. I need my time to sort what's happened. Get stronger. Up here," I tapped my head, "as well as the rest of me."

She took down her hair. It spilled over one shoulder like an auburn waterfall.

"How old are you, Juanito?"

"I was eighteen when I left. It's been six years, I think…"

She traced my lips with her fingers. "And I am forty-three. I've had no man since Jose. None of the villagers will do, and they know it."

She bent down and brushed my mouth with hers.

"I want to see desire one more time in a man's eyes," she whispered.

I watched her straighten, and walk to the window, where she leaned on its sill, smiling at me. The sun shined through the window, making her blouse transparent.

Even with torn feet, a body wracked by months of hardship, and memories that would haunt me for the rest of my life; even with all that, I had a feeling she just might.

That Silence of Rivers

The feet had healed, and I began to leave the war in the dust of the corrals, breaking up the horror under the hooves of horses. Sofia bought more land and as our property grew, strangely enough, the love between us did, too. There was talk in the village, but as long as we kept to our jobs in the daytime, Sofia with ranch business and me with the horses, they didn't seem to mind what we did at night.

The daughters learned their father's horsemanship through me. It felt good passing on Jose's legacy to his real heirs. He would have been proud of their skills.

As they grew older, Sofia and I watched them become women, court with young men from other ranches in the area, each choosing the man they wished to make a life with: Blanca with a young rancher named Hector Garcia from the village above us, Cajoncitos; Elena with a cowboy named Serapio Guerrero from Lomas de Arena, the village below us. Serapio was dirt poor but a good ranchhand. All they needed was a ranch. Sofia and I helped them buy a small one bordering the Rio Grande. It wasn't much bigger than Tudisishn, and I worried they wouldn't do well.

"They're poor, work night and day, and probably will starve. They couldn't be happier," said Sofia.

The weddings were performed, a year apart, in a plain white stucco chapel near El Porvenir, some ninety miles northwest of Ojos Calientes, which was the nearest chapel. The mayor of the town, a balding, sweaty man, performed the services since no priest came to the remote villages anymore. Still, some kind of God was there, and Sofia did cry as all mothers should at their daughters' weddings.

Each year, I swore to kill Hide. But each year, there were more horses to break, more fences to men, more feed to get in. Besides, Time would kill him for me. I was at peace.

With Serapio's and Hector's help and Oso's bloodlines, we began to raise and train excellent quarter horses to race and sell. El Paso had a fine race track, called Sunland, as did Ruidoso and Raton, New Mexico. Over the next fifteen years, our horses won more than they lost. We bought the best horse trailers and trucks, keeping them at Hector's or Serapio's ranches. It wasn't good to draw attention to our place since I was still a man without a country or papers. Sofia enjoyed going to the races with her daughters and their husbands, but I always stayed behind.

"The war is over, Juanito. Come with us to see your babies race," she pleaded.

I shook my head as I helped load the horses for their trip north.

"It's too dangerous. I haven't any papers, and it might jeopardize our horses and our winnings."

Sofia smiled, we kissed, and I waved good-bye to them as they drove away. To keep from being too lonely during their absence, I would saddle a young horse and lead Oso for some exercise. I would ride until all three of us worked up a good sweat. I'd let them drink their fill from the river and then, we'd return.

This time had been no different. Sofia and her daughters were off to another race, and things had slowed to a pace Oso and I could handle on the ranch by ourselves.

I'd look after the three ranches while they were gone, putter around the corrals or check a fence line or two. In the late afternoons, Oso and I would keep our little ritual of ending the day with a long walk. He was too old now to take into the mountains or the rougher pastures. Instead, we'd follow the road that led from the village along the Rio Grande.

When we'd return, I'd unsaddle the two horses, watch them roll the sweat off in the corral, then listen to them eat their evening feed of hay and oats. The smell of the horses, the corral, and the feed would mix in my mind and acted as a time machine, taking me back to Jose and Barrel Springs.

Afterwards, as I sat on the porch, sipping a glass of wine, I watched the evening sun glow off the cliffs, then dim for the night. It was quite a show, and it was free. Perfection was not a word I bandied about, but this was as close as it would come.

Oso died after one such ride. Something about his walk back from the river road bothered me but I chalked it up to old age and after watching him eat, went up to the porch. Later that night I heard labored breathing in the corral. Slipping on my boots, I hurried to the fence and climbed over. Oso lay in the dirt, his feel folded under him. The breathing was from his massive struggle to get back on his feet. They just refused to obey the old horse's will.

I ran to the village to get help to try and get Oso back on his feet but by the time we returned, Oso was dead. At the first light of day, two villagers and myself on horseback tied a rope to the stilled hooves and pulled Oso into the pasture. I wanted him buried, not torn by the coyotes and the scavengers. The villagers thought I was crazy, of course, but it's surprising what the promise of good money will do to the work ethic.

After burying him, we scoured the pastures for milk week but found no great patches, just small complete clumps of the green squash-looking plant along the arroyos where it always grew. Oso's symptoms indicated he may have grazed on the plant which can kill a horse or a cow in hours if left unmedicated. There were no horse hooves in the ground around the plants we did find so his death was probably due to his advanced age. We thought that until the paint died two days later after Sofia's return. The symptoms were the same.

After Sofia got back and learned the news, we quickly quarantined all the horses on all three ranches but there were no further deaths.

A month later, Hector and Serapio began losing their horses in similar ways, so we moved their stock to our ranch and the deaths stopped. A veterinarian from Juarez came down and shook his head at the mystery after charging us quite a bit of money to watch him shake his head and shrug his shoulders.

"The only thing different is your horses drink from the springs and the others from the river."

Shortly after his visit, the village sent a delegation. Sofia and I were sitting on the porch and motioned for them to sit down. We offered them some wine but most declined.

There was concern, they said, with some sickness in the village that they didn't understand.

"The river is no good anymore," said one old man, "the taste is different."

"What kind of sickness?" I asked.

"The older ones shake and have shortness of breath."

"Have you boiled the water?" I asked.

"We do that already, to drink," said one of the women as she held up the hand of her daughter, "but we bathe in the river and wash our clothes in it and now, look what it has done."

The sores looked like giant ringworms had infected the hands and arms.

"It's the young who get the sores. The old ones shake." The woman was joined by her husband.

"We would like to use your springs to drink."

We gave them permission to use the spring for drinking water, and after they left, Sofia and I discussed the river and what needed to be done.

"Hector and Serapio need to have wells drilled on the ranch. They can't use the water from the Rio Grande. That's what is killing the horses and..." Sofia touched my arm, frowning.

"What?"

"Blanca is pregnant."

I smiled. "That's wonderful!"

She shook her head. "Is it?"

"Of course it is! You and I are going to be grandparents."

"They drink from the same river as the villagers."

She stood, walked to the edge of the porch, and leaned against one of the wooden posts supporting the tin roof. She stared down the hill to the river.

"Listen," she said.

I didn't hear anything and told her so.

"Jose and I used to listen to the frogs sing their love songs. They don't sing anymore."

There were no sounds. Looking back on my last trip with Oso, I tried to remember if I had seen or heard any frogs plot into the river when Oso stepped to the edge of the water to lower his nozzle for a drink.

"We'll dig some wells on the two ranches and in our village. Everything should be okay, then." I tried to sound confident, but I didn't feel that way.

The wells were dug, clean water was available once again, and things returned to normal. Like most humans, bad news is forgotten as the tediousness of everyday life eats away our time. Besides, Sofia and I had something to look forward to.

Blanca was about to give birth.

Jose's first love may have been horses, but he had also started a dynasty of fine women: smart, tough, and beautiful. Maybe he understood bloodlines so well that he picked Sofia to complement his own qualities. Who could say?

Sofia and I rode horseback to the village to be with Blanca when her time came. Feeling Oso's colt under my saddle made me feel close to Jose. Maybe the colt wasn't as quick as Oso, but his strength and intelligence made up the difference.

Sofia's mare also reflected Oso's lineage in size and intelligence, and, added to that was the swiftness of a purebred Arabian. When we rode into Cajoncitos, we turned heads, like a couple in a fine sports car would have elsewhere. Sofia enjoyed the recognition. It was a small vanity, and I easily forgave her for it.

The midwife, an old crone of dubious character but tremendous knowledge, had already chased Hector outside while she, Sofia, our other daughter Elena, and two village women tended to the birth. I joined him by his old blue pickup, which still had a horse trailer hitched to it. In my pocket was our gift to the baby, a couple hundred dollars Sofia and I had managed to put together.

"When I got home from riding the fences, she was in pain," he said to me with a tinge of guilt.

I nodded, feeling strangely guilty myself. Maybe all men feel guilty during these times.

An hour later, a smiling Sofia came out announcing it was a girl, and motioning Hector to come back inside. To give Hector time to be alone with Blanca and his daughter, Sofia and I waited on the front porch where it was cooler. Elena joined us there.

When at last we tentatively entered their bedroom, Blanca and her husband were staring at the baby, who was wrapped in a hand-woven blanket provided by the midwife. The old woman, a worried look on her face, was bent over the baby, waving her fingers in front of its eyes. She clapped her hands hard above the baby. My granddaughter did nothing except lie there, beautiful and peaceful. She seemed like a stiff, porcelain doll. Not a muscle moved beneath the soft skin. The eyes stared blankly at nothing.

The old one took us aside. "Something is not right with the baby. Maybe blind. Maybe deaf. Maybe it has the river sickness."

"River sickness?" I asked.

The old woman shrugged, wiping her hands on her bloody apron. "Your baby is one of the quiet ones. They see nothing, hear nothing, speak nothing. They don't even eat. Life does not interest them. I've seen two like her this year alone."

Sofia gripped my hand. "What needs to be done?"

"Cure the river," was the old woman's simple answer.

The midwife looked back at Blanca.

"She's strong," she said softly. "There will be more. You must take the little one to the hospital in Juarez. Maybe there the doctors will know what to do. I can do no more here."

She started to turn back to the young couple, holding each other on the bed, staring silently at their new baby, then hesitated.

"Take Hector with you. He'll just worry us and his wife if he stays," she said. "Your wife must stay. She will be needed here to ease her daughter's sadness. Elena will go along and help with the baby."

"What do you think causes the river sickness?" I asked as Sofia went to join her daughter, leaving me alone with the old woman. I was thinking about the silence of frogs.

The crone waved her old, thin hands. "*No se.* Things are struggling there in the river like this baby struggles for its life here on land."

The midwife spat, and said with bitterness, "Where are the priests when you really need them?" She took the baby from the bed and handed it to me. As I walked out of the room, I could hear the woman crying softly.

Hector was grateful to have something to do, and he drove the pickup the hundred miles to Juarez. The baby in Elena's arms, my granddaughter, never made a sound. The only way I knew she still lived was by putting my hand on her tiny chest and feeling it go up and down. I had not given Hector and Blanca their baby's gift. I had a feeling it would be needed at the hospital in Juarez.

If you have no insurance, money talks, so we didn't have long to wait. A young doctor, Dr. Villalobos, after examining the baby and running some diagnostic mumbo-jumbo on her blood and urine, patiently explained to us what was wrong with the baby.

Seated behind the large desk in his office, he read from a printout: "There is only a brain stem where the brain should be." He separated the three-page foldout and stapled it to the child's folder. "There is enough for basic functions, but not for higher levels of activity."

Hector nodded slowly, twisting his straw cowboy hat over and over in his hands.

"There is no brain," he whispered.

I thought of the beautiful still child we had brought to the hospital.

"Like a flower with no petals."

The doctor nodded. "We call it anencephaly."

"What can be done?" Elena asked.

Dr. Villalobos walked us out of his office. "Not much. There's nothing to do, nothing to be done. We wait."

"There has to be something, for God's sake," Hector sounded angry, "she just can't die like that."

He looked at Hector. "For God's sake it is better she die."

Hector leaned against the light green wall in the antiseptic corridor and Elena stayed with him. I followed the doctor back toward the baby. I told him about the sicknesses in our village, the death of the horses and frogs.

Dr. Villalobos looked at the chart and made some notations. I watched each note carefully, hoping it was the one to bring Blanca's daughter back to normal.

"Your grandchild is not the first," he said without looking up from his chart. "I've treated two just like her this year alone."

"Have you had a lot of these births?"

"Three – before this year."

"You had three last year?"

"Our records indicate three in the history of the hospital. And it's forty years old."

"Then something that entered the river two or three years ago is causing this."

He gave a wry frown. "No. That began some years ago when your daughter was still young. Let me show you something about your granddaughter."

He handed me the chart. "Do you see here, the urine analysis of the child? It contains heavy metals, dioxin, and human fecal material. How did it get there? How can a child barely a day old and certainly not capable of breast feeding have these things in its blood?"

"It can't," I answered.

"Precisely. They reached the baby through the mother."

"From where?"

"*Maquiladoras* and their *maquilas*."

The word was unfamiliar to me. "Which means?"

"Maquiladoros are the vultures that follow the industries that relocate just on our side of the border from the U.S. hungry for cheap labor. They are the waste dumpers. Since no one enforces laws here, no one even knows what is being dumped in the river. No one except our bodies. They tell us, it is not good."

He took back the medical records. "So I keep records, file protests, and nothing happens. God will decide about the baby. We'll watch it for a few days, then send it home when it dies."

The doctor looked at me with sad eyes, strange in the face of one so young. They were the eyes of a soldier, too long in combat.

We checked in to the Camino Real Hotel near Benito Juarez Park to wait until the hospital called. When the bellboy left, Hector and I stood in the middle of our room, feeling strange in the unfamiliar plushness of dark velvet upholstery and varnished wood. It was not the best of décor for our mood.

The second day, to get Hector's mind off his little one, Elena and I took him to the open market. There, Elena bought us three grape-flavored snow cones, which the vendor wrapped in old newspapers to keep the sticky syrup off our hands.

We sucked on the cones as we walked along the stalls in the giant mercado. There were birds from the Yucatan, handmade saddles, onyx chess sets, and even silver hubcaps. I was trying to find something to say that would help Hector, when I glanced at the grape-stained paper that surrounded my snow cone. My heart skipped a beat.

Hector and Elena wandered out in front of me as I unwrapped the paper and read the article that had caught my eye. It was an old paper, from three months ago, according to the date at the top, and I had to be careful not to tear the wettest area. The paper was the *El Paso Times*, and, if it hadn't been for the content of the article, I would have laughed out loud at how strange the language seemed to me. It was the first newspaper I had read since Vietnam.

I spread the paper out on the rough concrete floor, oblivious to the tourists and the customers who had to walk around me. Even the vendors stopped their selling to stare.

Right in the middle of the grape juice stain from the snow cone was the following:

El Paso Cements Future Water Supply

El Paso Water Commissioners announced Tuesday that the final piece of property sought in Water Project/21st Century was purchased yesterday when long-time West Texas rancher, Mac McBride, signed the contract with the city to transfer the water and property rights of the McBride Ranch to the City of El Paso. This purchase represents the final link of the municipal water pipeline to be built from El Paso into the Sierra Blanca Aquifer, just west of Van Horn. The transfer of the ranch is challenged by the Eberhard Effluent Corporation and the Van Horn Ranchers Association. Feelings ran high at the town...

I unwrapped the cone in a futile attempt to find the rest of the story, while ignoring the stares of the people around me. I read the article again. Hide Eberhard, if he was still alive, was trying to prevent a McBride from leaving the area. The irony didn't escape me. Did he think there could possibly be worse neighbors than the McBrides? The thought made me shudder. But fighting to keep Mac from selling the ranch? Was Eberhard against the sale? Or was he against the loss of the water rights? Why should he care about where Buffalo Shit's water went?

And why was Mac selling the ranch? The old man was probably dead from drinking too much beer by now, but Mac wouldn't sell the ranch, would he? Why should he, with the old man gone – if he was gone? But if he wasn't, why would he give Mac the rights to sell the ranch? Dad never trusted either one of us, even as kids. But our land! It was the only thing that gave meaning to the McBrides. We all knew this down to our very depths. And that's *way* down in a McBride. We didn't want to fall any further.

I was angry with myself. There was no reason why I should care. I hadn't thought about my family for twenty years. Knowing them, they probably hadn't thought about me either. I thought about the Chamizal Bridge just a few blocks from the Camino Real Hotel. I could walk the distance, cross over into El Paso, and be at the ranch within hours. A McBride would never sell the ranch to an Eberhard. That was as basic as our blood.

My hatred for Hide clouded my judgment. I knew my place was with Sofia and Blanca. I knew I shouldn't leave Hector and Elena to face the death of the child alone, or to be the ones to tell Blanca her child was gone. I knew all these things. Still, I had to find some answers to questions that had been asked so long ago and the ones confusing me now. I just couldn't let it rest.

I caught up with Elena and Hector, who were watching a puppeteer entertain tourists.

"I'm going to the United States for awhile."

Elena stared at me, uncomprehending. "What about the baby?"

"You heard the doctor. There's nothing to be done. Tell Sofia where I've gone."

"Will you come back?" Hector asked.

"Sure I will." I hoped I sounded more confident than I felt. "You and Serapio can run all three ranches. Blanca can move into our house with Sofia until she recovers."

I shook his hand and hugged Elena.

"How will you get into the United States? You have to have papers," Hector reminded me.

I counted out almost all the money we had brought for the baby as a gift from proud grandparents, and handed it to him. He put the money clumsily in the pockets of his pants.

"How are you going to get in?" Hector repeated.

"With a haircut," I replied.

They both looked at me. I went to find a barbershop.

After the haircut I sat at the Mexican end of the bridge, waiting for my chance. Finally, some drunken soldiers in civilian clothes appeared, staggering towards the bridge. I fell in behind them. I knew they were soldiers, because the shaved sides of their heads gave them away every time. Just like mine would me, I hoped.

The official on the Mexican side didn't check us, but the walkway across the bridge led into a glass-partitioned U.S. Customs checkpoint, where all passengers of buses coming from Mexico disembarked and joined those of us crossing on foot.

We all formed a line that wove back and forth between iron railings. It was like those lines you see at an amusement park.

My first problem was that the solders weren't American. They were Germans, drunken Germans, friendly drunken Germans. Apparently, they were in an exchange pilot-training program at Fort Bliss, the army base in El Paso.

One kept draping himself over me and talking loudly in German. I decided to play along, laughing when he laughed, frowning when he frowned.

It was a heck of a conversation.

As we approached the customs inspector, one of the Germans took out six passports and handed them to the inspector.

The inspector counted us.

Seven.

So, we lined up, and he matched pictures with faces.

"And who are you?" he asked me.

Well, it was time to tell the truth – or at least some of it.

"I'm an American. Sergeant John McBride, assigned liaison with this bunch while they partied in Juarez." I winked at the officer and turned to the Germans.

"Boy, did you guys give me hell trying to round you up!" I said loudly to the Germans. They stared blankly at me, then burst out laughing at this new stranger.

I gave a what-can-you-do-with-foreigners shrug to the customs man. He glanced at my haircut and waved us through.

It was that easy to go home.

Home

Four hours later, I arrived at the still stinking Tudisishn. The Greyhound driver seemed reluctant to let me off in the middle of nowhere.

"You sure about this?" he asked.

"I'm sure."

"There's no one here." He sounded worried, peering out into the darkness.

"Let the bastard out," growled a sleepy voice behind us.

I stepped down from the bus and watched the taillights fade towards Valentine and Marfa. There was a U.S. Highway 90 sign at the cattle guard leading down the road the Eberhards built across our property long ago. A sign nearby said, "Eberhard Effluent Corporation Headquarters 25 miles."

I looked at the sign closely in the dark. It was new. The old one used to say Eberhard Oil Company Headquarters 25 miles.

I walked across the cattleguard and down the dirt road that twenty years ago had taken me to a rodeo and Hide Eberhard. A road that had taken me from my damaged family. The house waited like a period at the end of a dusty sentence.

I guess the regret in my heart was for having never absolved my father of my mother's murder. The anger that had been growing there since Juarez was over my brother's selling the ranch. It had nothing to do with money. The only tenacity we McBrides had ever shown, our only common bond as a family, was to cling to this little island in enemy territory. Had it all been a waste of time? If we were going to sell out like that, why had we ever stayed?

When I approached the house, I saw a flickering light in my Dad's room. Closer still, I realized it was a candle, and I wondered why the lights were out. Inside someone coughed. I stopped midroad, then crept to the side of the house. It hadn't changed all that much, from what I could see.

Two figures stood in the dark on the porch. One of them seemed to be stroking the other. I squatted, squinting, looking away out of the corner of my eyes, the way special forces had taught me to see in the dark indirectly. It was a good way to look at my old home. One of the figures turned and went inside; the other swung back and forth on the porch. Had Mac or Dad finally followed their natural urges to seek revenge on Hide and hung him? If so, I'd know everything was almost back to normal and could catch the next bus back to Sofia. No, I still needed to know why they sold the ranch.

I crept closer to see who had been hung. The antlers gave it away. It was a deer carcass, swaying by its antlers, which had been tied to one of the timbers of the adobe porch. I thought about what month it was: August, maybe; September at the latest.

Deer season starts in December. At least, we still hunted out of season.

Something hungry grabbed a chunk from the deer and scurried away when it heard me open the yard gate. It was fast, probably a kit fox. Then a coyote ran past me after it. My eyes clouded over. There were a lot of sad memories here. I peered through the darkness. I could vaguely see the form of the steel tank where Mama had died.

You can't go home again. That's wrong. You can't get rid of home. You take home with you wherever you go, anywhere in the world. You're tied to the family's spot forever. It's like a knot that can't be untied, wrapped around your life.

I crept along the porch and looked through the window where the candle burned. Lying propped up on some pillows, an old gray-bearded, balding man wheezed in his sleep. In his right hand, between two yellow-stained fingers, were the dead remains of a rolled smoke. Death's pallor had so completely erased the brutal vitality I had always associated with him that it took me a moment to register this was my father.

The room itself was a dirty sallow color in the glow of the candle. His boots were in the corner, with a pair of jeans thrown over them. Part of the adobe wall revealed the darkness outside. It wasn't a big hole, but it said a lot about a lack of will to repair. Near the door that led to the hallway, next to one of the kitchen chairs, was a twelve-gauge shotgun. It looked cleaned and well oiled. I knew that it was loaded.

A bug crawled up the far wall. It was the only thing not dying in that room. The smell of urine and flatulence wafted out the window to my nostrils. To the house's familiar bouquet of tobacco, smoke, old cooking grease, and bad plumbing, death now added its own fetidness.

I heard footsteps in the hallway and leaned back into the darkness.

The door opened slowly. Someone entered, holding a brown tray. That someone was my brother, older, and from the look of him, a whole lot less carefree.

Mac walked to the bed, set the tray down on the side table missing a drawer – if it ever had one – and shook him awake.

"Here's your goddamn food."

Dad took the bowl from him and began eating. "Deer stew again? Can't you be original just once?"

"Is the stew too hot?" Mac, concerned?

"Hell, yes," Dad said, eating quickly, eyeing Mac.

"Good."

It warmed my heart to see my family still cared for each other.

I debated whether to walk in and announce my presence. I glanced at the shotgun. Maybe tomorrow would be better. On the porch, there were two broken chairs and a bent lounger missing some of its bottom straps. I waited until the candle went out, heard my Dad's labored breathing, and the house growing still before stretching out in the lounger. It wasn't much of a bed but it beat the hell out of the cramped bus seats. It didn't take long to fall asleep.

I smelled coffee, opened one eye, and tried to shift my weight on the ripped seat of the lounger. Why was Sofia up before me? Then, I remembered where I was and opened up the other eye. A coffee cup sat on the floor next to the lounger. A shotgun barrel was next to the cup.

I was wide awake. My eyes followed the barrel up to Mac, sitting in one of the broken chairs.

We looked at each other for an eternity.

"Drink that cup if you're alive." The barrel clinged the chipped coffee cup.

It was an easy enough request.

"How come you ain't dead? The army told us you was."

Not taking my eyes off Mac, I picked up the coffee and took a sip. Except where the sun had carved crevices in his face, the mark of all true West Texans, he was still recognizable as my brother. The stomach stuck out over the belt a little further, the hair receded back to a new low-water mark on the scalp, but the calloused hands spoke of years of ranching. Come to think of it, he resembled Dad the day he fell off the windmill.

"What brought you back?"

"Read you sold the ranch."

"Why should you care?" Mac stroked the wooden stock of the shotgun lovingly. "You gave up that right when you left."

"I wanted to know why you sold it. That's all. I'd like to know what could drive a McBride to sell his only legacy."

Mac gave a bitter laugh. "You went away. You left me here with that old son of a bitch for twenty years and now you want questions answered? You're lucky I don't shoot you."

I jerked the shotgun from his hands as I leaped to my feet. The bent chair fell over, spilling Mac into the yard. I popped open the gun and saw there were no shells in either chamber.

"And you're lucky the gun wasn't loaded," I said tossing it back to him.

"Damn. I knew I forgot something."

Mac sat there in the dirt, holding the shotgun. "I didn't see the ranch."

"Paper said you did."

"Paper said you were dead, too." He had a point. Newspapers are often wrong. "We've signed a contract, upon Dad's death, to agree to sell. They have first option on the ranch."

"Why are Hide and Van Horn fighting it?"

Mac looked puzzled as he got to his feet. "I can understand Van Horn's anger. Hell, once El Paso taps into the aquifer under the ranch, them and Sierra Blanca and Valentine, and probably Marfa are history. There'll be no water for them."

"What aquifer? What are you talking about?"

Mac looked at me and sat the shotgun down as he picked up the chair and sat gingerly back on it, testing its bent legs.

Satisfied, he continued, "That's right, you don't know about that, do you? Well, after Hide's oil wells were capped, he didn't..."

"They go dry?"

"The companies quit buying from him. They made more money shipping the oil from them Arabs or Eskimos or wherever the damn stuff comes from. It's too cheap here in the interior of the country. So, they just capped the wells and will wait until the whole world goes dry, then open 'em back up and make a bigger killing.

"Well, that left old Hide holding his cajones. 'Course our road-rent money dried up along with his oil money. So he sent out some geologists hoping to find some gas deposits he could sell to the El Paso Gas Company. The geologists didn't find any gas in their experimental drilling but they found something else."

"And that was?"

"Where Buffalo Shit."

"Mac, everybody around here knew about this place."

"Yeah, the smell kept them from investigating further. But these geologists didn't know nothing about that. What they found was the second largest underground water aquifer in the United States. And guess where the shortest distance is to that aquifer?"

"Where Buffalo Shit?"

"Ironic, ain't it?" Mac smiled. "There's all kind of deep rock between the aquifer and the surface except right here. All they got to do is poke a little hole and suck on the straw."

"How much water is there?"

"Enough to give El Paso and Juarez twenty more years of water to feed a couple of million people."

"Why doesn't Van Horn sue?"

"Here's the beauty of it. They don't have enough tax money to hire a lawyer to investigate whether or not they can sue."

"Won't Texas do anything to help?"

Mac looked at me hard. "You sure got stupid over the years. Where are the most voters, El Paso or Van Horn?"

"But that still doesn't explain why Hide is against it."

Mac frowned again. "I can't figure it out. You'd think he'd be glad to see the McBrides leave. Hell, it's been a goal of the Colbys and the Eberhards to squash us. Now that we're doing it voluntarily, you'd think he'd be happy. 'Course it could have something to do with his operation at the end of the road."

I thought about the sign at the cattleguard. "Yeah, what's an Effluent Corporation?"

"Maybe you ought to ask Dad that. It's what is probably killing him, gave him the cancer."

"So what is it?"

"Ask Dad first and then I'll show you. It's easier than trying to explain it."

"Wouldn't Dad probably die from shock seeing me?"

"Hopefully," he said as he motioned me to follow him inside.

"I noticed the lights were out last night," I said as I followed him through the front door.

"Hide's had the power cut to try and force me to reconsider selling."

"Why don't you tell the cops?"

Mac stopped and looked back at me. "You been that stupid since the accident with the bull when you was a kid or is this something that's come on just lately?"

"A combination of both, probably. So, he owns the cops. I have forgotten a lot of things, Mac."

He walked back to the front door and looked through the screen. I joined him.

"How do you like my new truck?" Mac pointed to a new red power wagon, glittering in the sun.

It seemed to me to glitter too much. "What happened to its windows?"

"When I went to Van Horn to try and get the electricity back on, someone smashed all the windows. They're pretty upset with my agreeing to sell the ranch. Besides, the power company and I owed back payments."

"Do you?"

"Can't phone to find out. Hide had our phone changed to a 'party' line. Guess who the other 'party' is?"

"Hide?"

Mac nodded.

"You could always write them."

"If the people in the post office would let my letters go through. Hide has the whole town working against us."

"Just like old times, I guess."

"Screw 'em," Mac said. "Let them take a bath with the dirt from their pipes where the water used to be."

"How does Dad feel about all of this?"

"He doesn't want to sell, either."

"Dad agrees with Hide?"

"Not exactly. He wants to bottle the water and sell it in grocery stores all over the nation as McBrides's Pure Spring Water."

The thought of our water being drunk by a thirsty nation was too horrible to contemplate.

I followed him into the room. The smell hit me hard. Dad was lying half-in and half-out of the bed. He had been reaching for his pouch of tobacco. My brother picked him up and propped him back on the pillows.

"Dad?"

I watched Dad's eyes look over Mac's shoulder and stop on my face. I walked closer so he could see me better. His eyes slid over me and looked aimlessly about the room.

"He doesn't recognize me."

"He has his good days when he's mostly aware of things. Hang around. He'll get better."

"You mean as bad as he used to be?"

"Yeah."

Mac went and got a washcloth from the bathroom. I looked in and saw the top of the commode's tank was still missing. There was a gleaming Dodge Power Wagon out front, and we still didn't have the top to the commode.

Mac began giving Dad a sponge bath.

He dipped the rag back into the water and squeezed off the excess. Dad still stared at the wall while Mac worked on him.

I left them and walked into the kitchen. There was a piece of broiled venison in a pan, and I cut a piece off and ate it while looking out the window. Nothing but sand and scrub brush, and a greenish haze off in the distance.

Mac walked in and I asked him what the haze was.

"You'll see."

We walked out to the new truck.

"Careful of the broken glass," Mac said, waving me inside.

We drove twenty miles down the road toward the green haze. Mac suddenly whipped the truck off the road and parked it at the base of a small hill.

"Come on. We'll climb from here." He scrambled up the hill.

At its top, I saw the future. In front of us was the Eberhard fence. A metal sign warning of toxic waste flapped uselessly in the wind. Beyond the fence was a mossy, green layer of something that stretched as far as I could see. In the middle, bisecting the soft, furry green expanse, was a dark line of railroad tracks. Not even grandfather could have cut the fence that stood between us and the green. The smell reminded me of something, but I couldn't quite place it.

"What the hell am I looking at, Mac?"

He gave a maniacal laugh. "That's exactly what I said the first time I saw that green haze from the window in the kitchen."

"Well, what is it?"

"Just wait. Watch."

A whistle blew, and soon a large gray locomotive, its engine groaning from the strain, came into view, backing thirty tanker cars down the railroad spur into the middle of the green. A bell sounded and little figures, in color-coded jump suits, ran forward along the tracks and slid large hoses from underneath the tanker cars, connecting them to brass hose couplings on either side of the tanks.

I watch as the hoses twist full and ejaculate a brighter green liquid over the Eberhard rangeland.

"More will come," said Mac. "Hide is just getting started."

"What am I looking at?"

"Liquid shit."

"Yeah, I figured that, but what exactly is it?"

"I told you. Shit."

"I don't understand."

Mac sat down on a rocky outcropping, his back to the spraying tanks. "Hide has leased his ranch to the Dallas, Fort Worth, and Houston Metropolitan Sewer Districts. New York is coming on line any day now, and Chicago and Boston will soon follow."

"You mean…"

"Yep. That's treated human waste they're blowing out of those hoses; that sludge stuff that's left after everything is treated. Hide can make more money letting them spread it on the land than selling horses or cattle."

"Is this legal?" I protested.

"Why do you think I agreed to sell the ranch?" Mac whispered, his back to the scene I watched with morbid fascination.

"I tried to stop it, but when a lawyer told me that the Texas Land Commission had approved Hide's little venture, I knew I couldn't fight the whole state."

He threw a rock at a lizard. "So I bought a new truck instead."

The resignation in his voice was something I hadn't heard before.

"What do they do with this stuff?" I asked, changing the subject. "They just leave it there for the wind to blow away?"

Mac didn't even turn around. I guess he had the scene memorized. "See that building in the middle of all those ponds?"

I saw the large warehouse of a building, complete with huge doors opening into a dark interior. Men in orange overalls scurried about. Two bells rang and a strange yellow machine looking like a low-slung wheat-thresher, with a conveyer following behind like an obedient dog on a leash, moved slowly from the building.

The conveyor was followed by several dump trucks and as the thresher drove over the driest green, it scooped the green powder hungrily onto the conveyor and into the trucks. As each truck filled, it drove back into the darkness of the building up a ramp and through the large doors into the center.

The train whistled and a group of orange overalls guided it onto a siding where the tanker cars were unhooked and the engine guided onto a separate track where flatbedded cars were stacked with what looked like full cement bags. Once it was coupled with the flatbed cars, it rumbled back the way it came.

"It's fertilizer," Mac said in a flat voice.

"The whole world is Hide's market. Those men down there work for a Japanese company. They were brought in as partners by Hide."

I sat down next to Mac, stunned. I didn't think anybody, even Hide, was capable of turning perfectly good land into a place worse than the two of us grew up on.

It looks like I was wrong again.

"Mac, I did I tell you how Jose Navarrete died?"

He looked at me. "While you're at it, why don't you tell me how you died. At least, why the paper said you did."

So I told the whole story. Then, we walked back to the truck. As we walked, I followed the fence with my eyes and saw that the road ended at a guard house with two guards, their chairs propped in the shade under the roof of the house. "Mac," I asked, "why does Hide need a guard house?"

He shrugged his shoulders. "Afraid somebody will try and steal his shit, I guess."

As Mac drove us back to the house, I thought about the deadly skirmish between the Apaches and the Ft. Davis army patrol on the little hill behind our house. Was Hide's operation the end result of all that fighting and death? Was this why Americans, native and adopted, spilled their blood on this land? Fought and died in foreign places in Freedom's name? All that death so some corporation could spread a green fungus over the land?

Was this the hope of Democracy?

Dad was calling when we got back. Mac went in first and I could hear them arguing about something. I took a step into the room. Dad stopped in mid-sentence.

"What the hell you doing here?" he said. "Give me the shotgun over there, Mac. I'll see if he's alive or not, by God!"

"It's me, Johnny." I took another step.

"I may be dying, but you damn sure don't have to introduce yourself to me. I know a cowardly son when I see him. Couldn't take it, had to run away and be a big shot!"

He looked me up and down. "Don't look like you got too far in that direction, either."

He turned his attention back to Mac who was dipping the dirty washcloth into a fresh bowl of water.

"Give me that damn washcloth, you traitor!" Dad glanced back at me. "What do you think about your brother? Sold the ranch right out from under his old man. Well, I ain't signing no Power-of-Attorney until I'm dead. And that won't happen for awhile, neither. If I can get my hands on that shotgun over there, you might just go before me!"

Mac shook his head and threw the washcloth to me. "He's back to his old self today. Too bad."

"Where you going, Mac?" I asked.

"To see if I could find some shells for the shotgun. There's gotta be some somewhere."

"Better hurry with that washcloth, Johnny," Dad said, eyeing Mac's exit, "might not need it if he finds any shells. Of course, he won't."

"Why not?" I asked, washing off the sickly sweat off his forehead.

"Because I hid them," he cackled. "Now, how come you showed up? Don't think I'm going to leave you anything when I die. You gave that up when you left."

"The last thing I wanted was this place," I squeezed the rag in the bowl, and turned to clean up his front. "But you ought to leave it to Mac."

"Not if he's going to sell it. Did he bring you back to help him?" He paused, thinking about it. "Naw, he thought you was dead just like me."

He jerked the rag from my hands. "Goddamn pervert! I'll do it myself."

As I watched him struggle to clean himself, I drew the old kitchen chair beside the bed and waited there until he was finished. He threw the rag to me. I caught it and put it in the bowl.

"He wants to sell it to stop Hide," I explained.

"If he kept it, he could be as rich as Hide," Dad countered.

"McBride Bottling Company? Who's going to loan Mac the money to get started? Van Horn Bank? Bank of El Paso?"

Dad closed his eyes and gritted his teeth. "To get this close to money and lose out. Hell, that's what is killing me quicker than this cancer."

I looked at Dad. "Hide killed Momma, Dad."

His eyes opened quickly. "How you know that?"

I told him about my therapy session with the Chinese soldier in North Vietnam. He didn't say anything after I finished, and I thought he had drifted off to sleep. I got up to leave.

As I reached the door, Dad's voice stopped me. "I thought it might have been Hide if it wasn't a suicide, but I couldn't figure out why he'd do it. Even with what you've told me I still can't see why. Remember that wedding veil you thought you was holding?"

I nodded. "Every night in my dreams."

"You weren't holding it. It was tied around your hands. I untied you. You were hysterical so that's why you thought you were holding it."

"Why didn't you tell the cops?"

"Two reasons. I didn't want them thinking she was going to take her kids with her if it was suicide; and if it wasn't, I didn't want them or you kids thinking I tried to kill you. It'd look too bad for me at the trial."

Mac's voice behind me made me jump. "Hide killed Mama?"

Mac handed me a bowl of venison stew, and carried the other one over to Dad.

"So what are we going to do about it?" he asked.

Dad gave an evil grin. "Get even."

Mac glanced back at me. "Does that mean you'll sign the Power-of-Attorney so we can sell the ranch?"

The old man waved his son off. "Hell, I'll sign that later. Besides, I might not live long enough to watch him dry up and blow away like that manure pile he's got at the end of our road. No, what I've got in mind is much better and Johnny here is our ace in the hole."

Dad looking lovingly at me. That scared me worse than when he used to beat me.

New Smells

If there was something to be said for our family, it was that we always had enough intelligence to know our fate, just not enough intelligence to do anything about it. But, among the three of us, we came up with a plan based on Dad's idea.

He added a little twist by telling me, "Tie up your brother and gag him. Make it look good. Hurry! I hear Hide's car coming."

I finished tying Mac up and dumping him next to the shit-stained rags. He said something about his position, but I couldn't understand him through the gag.

"Now get the shotgun and stand in the next room."

I followed Dad's instructions just as the front door opened.

"Back here, Hide," Dad called out weakly.

"This better not be a damn trick, McBride. I got my 9mm with me."

"Hell, I can't even get out of bed, Hide."

"Your son's truck is out front. Thought you said he was in town. Where the hell is he?"

"Got him tied up in the room with me."

Hide peeked around the corner of Dad's room, stepped in and smiled. He put the handgun back in its holster.

"Well, what do we have here?" He walked over to Mac's prostrate form. He glanced at Dad propped on the pillow.

"How were you able to do that?"

"Simple," Dad growled, he came in drinking a beer, trying to bully me in to signing that Power-of-Attorney. That's it on the floor over there by the door. I let him bully me for awhile, then gave in and told him to go get a pen so I could sign.

"While he was gone, I slipped a bunch of these cancer pain pills into his beer and waited. When he came back I stalled while he drank the rest of the beer. The rest was easy."

Hide walked over to the Power-of-Attorney papers on the floor, picked them up and began to leisurely tear them up, letting the papers sprinkle on to Mac.

"So you called to give the Power-of-Attorney to me to keep your own son from killing you." Hide laughed out loud. "Damn! That's rich. It's a crazy damn world!"

"It's a weird one, too, Hide," I said as I stepped out of the bathroom with the shotgun aimed at Hide. Dad had told me where he hid the shells.

I studied Hide as I lifted his pistol from his belt. There was something tired in his eyes. The red blotches on his cheeks and nose said he drank more than he used to. His hands shook. I couldn't tell if the shaking was from some nerve disease or the shock of seeing me.

"You can't be here. Your name is on the Wall!"

That confused me. "I didn't write my name on any wall."

"He means the wall that lists all the dead soldiers of Vietnam," said Dad, pulling the covers from his sick body and struggling to stand up.

"They built a monument to us?" There was a strange feeling inside me.

"Not exactly. Other veterans paid to have it built. The government donated the land."

"They shouldn't build monuments to losers," Hide sneered.

I shoved the shotgun under his chin, driving him back against our adobe wall.

"Why don't you untie your brother? He looks a little uncomfortable. I'll take care of Hide." Dad took the shotgun from me.

"Best be careful there, Hide. I'm pretty weak. About all the strength I got left is to pull these triggers if you even fart. So don't move."

The first thing Mac said when I took off the gag was, "Thanks for throwing me into Dad's shit rags."

"I didn't throw you, that's where you fell."

"Yeah?"

"Yeah."

"Will you two quit arguing and tie up this old bastard?" Dad's voice was again as strong as it used to be. We obeyed quickly.

"My family knows where I am, McBride. Don't do something stupid."

Mac kicked Hide hard.

"Dad can do anything stupid he wants to, you old bastard."

Dad and I looked at Mac.

"What did I say? What?"

Dad handed me the shotgun and staggered back to the bed. "You boys take him outside and put him in his car."

We looked at each other.

"What for?" I asked.

"He can't drive tied up," Mac added.

Dad struggled to put on his boots. He's not going to drive. I'm going to do it for him."

"You're too weak," Mac blurted out, "you'll have a wreck before you get to town."

"Wouldn't mind that," the old man growled, putting the other boot on.

"Why you taking him to town?" I asked, holding Hide to take him outside to his car.

Dad rolled himself a smoke. His hand didn't shake. "He's going to stand trial for killing your mother."

"He owns the town, nobody will convict him!" Mac sounded a little frustrated towards Dad.

"Hell, they won't even arrest him, the way they feel towards Mac for making the deal with El Paso," I added.

"Won't be no deal. Not going to sell the water." Dad lit his cigarette and looked calmly at my brother.

"Not going to sell the water if they'll convict Hide. That's the deal I'll make."

"And that's a chance I'll gamble on! Keys are in my right hand pocket, McBride," said Hide, smiling broadly.

"Just one thing," said Dad, blowing out a ring of smoke, "why did you kill the boys' mother?"

"Why should I tell you?"

"I'm all that stands between my boys and you. The way I see it, Johnny here could drive you down the road, kill you and nobody could do anything about it."

Sweat ran down Hide's forehead. "How do you figure, McBride?"

"He's dead. Name's on the Wall. Said so yourself. How they going to arrest a dead man?"

If we had had a clock, you could have heard it tick in the silence that followed.

Hide thought for a moment. "Okay. I'll tell you, but you have to give me your word you won't kill me. You'll turn me over to the sheriff."

Dad shook one of Hide's tied hands. "I'll see you get justice." Then, "It's a deal."

"You treated her poorly, McBride. Underneath all that dirt, she was a pretty woman. Ignorant, but pretty. I stopped by a lot when the kids were in school and you were off working. But we weren't careful enough. She got pregnant. You're lucky she didn't leave sooner, the way you treated her."

He hesitated, remembering.

"She was going to tell Barbara Anne. I couldn't have that. So I agreed to marry her, and told her I'd get a quickie Mexican divorce in Juarez. Even had papers drawn up making it look authentic. Money buys a lot of things in Juarez.

"When I drove up you were off on a buying trip, McBride. I showed her the papers. The crazy woman made me wait; said she had a surprise for me. I didn't know she'd put on her wedding dress."

Hide glared at Mac and me. "It was easy getting her into the tank, but I didn't know you two would come running up out of the pasture. You were supposed to be in school."

"Why didn't you kill us, too?" Mac asked.

"They'd know it wasn't your old man, if you two were dead along with your mother. He'd beat the two of us, but a McBride would never kill his own sons. With just her dead, suspicion naturally fell on him."

"If Mom was pregnant wouldn't that show up when they got her ready for burial?" Mac asked.

Hide looked at him. "They'd just think it was your dad's."

"Weren't you afraid we'd identify you?" Mac asked quietly.

Hide curled his lip. "Who would believe a McBride? Besides I had plenty of workers who would swear I was with them at the time."

"Yeah, they'd swear," I said to no one in particular, "or else it would be back to Mexico."

Dad cleared his throat. "Place him in the back seat, boys. Time for me to take him to town."

Mac held open the door and motioned Hide to get in. With his hands tied in front, Hide bent his large frame and sat in the backseat behind the driver's seat.

I wiped the sweat off Dad's head, aware of his sickly color out in daylight.

"You going to make it?" I asked.

Dad's breath came out in short, raspy bursts. "You going to cry if I don't?"

266

He looked around as Mac shut the car door on Hide, then back to me, "Boys, it's come full circle. I used to wipe your asses, now I have to fight it to keep you from wiping mine. That ain't no way to live. I swear it ain't. It's bad enough living here, but living here poorly..."

He started to get in, hesitated, and motioned Mac to open Hide's door again.

"Not good enough, Hide. Almost had me but not good enough."

Hide laughed nervously. "What do you mean, McBride? I agreed to go in with you. What more do you want?"

"Truth," Dad said simply, "the truth why you want to keep the water rights to my ranch. You've got enough water at Needle Park to support what little livestock you got left; so why fight Mac on his sale of this place to El Paso? You don't care about what Van Horn drinks or if any other rancher around here has water or not. You've got your own source. So why fight it?"

His hand smacked Hide across the mouth. Mac and I both rubbed our chins at the same time. Old memories die hard.

"What the hell you doing, you crazy old man!"

Dad slapped him again, then leaned against the car door, breathing hard from the effort.

Blood trickled from Hide's mouth. Hide kicked at Dad. Dad slammed the door hard on his shin.

Hide howled.

He was slow putting his leg back inside. Dad slammed the door again.

"Let me try it," Mac offered.

"Stay out of this," Dad growled.

Hide glared at Dad. "You want to know something, McBride? You're too stupid to realize what potential this country has."

We looked around at the prickly pear cactus and mesquite bushes, the sand, and dry arroyos. He was right. None of us could see any potential.

"There ain't nothing here, Hide. Never will be. There's not enough water!"

There were small bloody bubbles at the corner of Dad's mouth. He wiped with the back of his hand.

"But there's enough land!" Hide spat back through bloodied lips.

"For what?" I asked, afraid to know.

Hide shook his head. "If you can't see it, be damned if I'll tell you."

Dad put the shotgun between Hide's legs. "Tell me."

Hide licked his damaged lips nervously. "Uh, the effluent dump at the end of the road gave me the idea. Why stop there? The country has all kinds of things it can't dump near cities."

"Such as?" Dad poked him with the shotgun as an incentive.

"Nuclear waste, used x-rays, AIDS needles, sheets, rags. Hell, McBride, the potential is enormous."

"If that got into the aquifer, it could kill everybody around here over time." Mac had finally said something intelligent.

Hide laughed, then groaned as he massaged his shin with his tied hands. "And how many people is that? Eight hundred? A thousand? What's that to the population of one major city?"

"Van Horn will lock him up for good when they hear about this," Dad said as he got into the front seat.

"What do you want me to do with his pistol?" asked my brother.

"Throw it in the front seat. I'll sell it in town and buy some groceries if we make it. Now, out of the way. It's time Hide got what's coming to him."

He powered down the driver's side window. "That's nice. Your new power wagon have these, Mac?"

"When I had windows it did," said Mac, glumly.

Dad gave a crazy grin as he backed the car and swung away from the old ranch house.

"I always wanted to drive a Cadillac!" he said as he pointed it towards the highway. We watched the blue caddy drive off, gaining speed when suddenly the brake lights came on. We could see something going on in the car but by then it was too far away to see exactly what was happening.

Mac and I sprinted to the car, and I was ashamed to say he beat me to it. Dad was slumped over in the front seat, Hide slumped in the back. Blood trickled from Dad's mouth.

"What the hell..." Mac jerked open Dad's door. As he reached for the prone body, Hide sat up in the back seat and put his gun against Mac's head.

I skidded to a halt.

"Get on it, Mac," Hide commanded. "Johnny, you stay back. I just need one McBride at a time."

Mac turned Dad's head and looked at him.

"That's right, McBride, I choked him. Cops always put the cuffed hands behind the person, not in front. Jesus, I can't believe how stupid you are!"

"Johnny?" Hide kept the gun against Mac's head. "You back off."

I complied.

"Now, sit down in the driver's seat, Mac. Johnny, if you make a move before I tell you to, I'll kill him."

I stayed still.

"Now, Mac, start the car. Your old man let it die when he was choking on something." Hide laughed at his own joke.

I watched Mac settle in the driver's seat, start the car again and put both hands on the wheel. His face was tight. I could see his jaw muscles working. His knuckles strained as he gripped the wheel. He glanced at me, eyes glistening, and shook his head slowly.

"That's right, Johnny, ain't nothin' you can do." Hide smiled at me from the back seat. "Your brother and me are going to drive back to my ranch, have ourselves a little talk until he signs the Power-of-Attorney I brought for your old man to sign. After all, this all belongs to Mac now."

Mac began to drive off slowly. I watched Hide settle into the back seat. I knew if they got to Hide's ranch, I never would see Mac again.

Turning, I sprinted towards the new power wagon. As I got there, I saw Mac turn on the highway towards Needle Peak, Hide's headquarters. I searched frantically inside the truck trying to find the keys.

Mac had them with him.

I slammed my hand down on the steering wheel. That's when I heard the Cadillac's tires scream. I turned in time to see it whip off the road, taking a couple of fence posts with it and road back towards our dirt road at a dangerous speed. Of course, Mac always drove that way.

I smiled and stepped from the truck, waving at Mac. Vaguely, I wondered how he'd got the gun from Hide.

He didn't. The Cadillac shot by me still picking up speed, its tires churning up the gravel in the road. Mac's hand appeared out the front window and his keys came sailing across landing on the dirt road behind me.

Hide was in the back seat, waving the pistol, but too afraid to shoot him because the speed would kill them both. I saw him try to hit Mac over the head with it, but a bump slammed

Hide's back into the plush leather. At least he had a comfortable landing.

Mac couldn't stop. Hide would kill him for sure. I grabbed the keys, jumped in the truck and followed the Cadillac's dust plume. I thought maybe I had a chance to stop him but the caddy was just too fast.

The guards, seeing Hide's Cadillac, left the chairs and stood officially waiting for him to drive up. Mac shot through without even waving. The car skidded past two full fertilizer trucks, taking their place on the loading ramp. Mac must have been doing at least a hundred when the caddy reached the top of the dock.

For a moment the car hung in midair, framed by the warehouse doors, looking like a hawk searching for a rabbit. Hide was slamming the gun down hard on Mac's skull, but I knew how hard that was. He was lucky the pistol didn't break.

The thought of a gasoline explosion mixing with about twenty tons of highly explosive fertilizer dust made me slam on the brakes and try to get the truck turned around before the blast hit me. For a moment I did feel sorry for the workers at the plant. Then, I thought: anybody stupid enough to dedicate their lives to spreading shit wouldn't be missed that much.

The shock wave bounced the truck and I fought to keep it on the road. In the rearview mirror I saw the effects of a Cadillac enema as a giant black fireball spilled upwards into the sky. All that power suddenly released, cracking the cheeks and blowing the wind. I had to smile through something wet as it dripped past my nose. Tears for *my* family? It was indeed a strange new world.

I parked Mac's truck at the house and threw the keys as far as I could. A horse snickered nervously in the corral where long ago, Mac had tied me to a bull. I saddled the horse, a small mouse-colored mare, and led her over to the broken fence around the front yard. I went inside for the last time, looking around to see if there was anything worth taking. Only one thing caught my eye. The rest could go up in smoke like the effluent plant that burned in the distance. I started a fire in the kitchen, made sure it had a good start, then walked back outside and stepped into the saddle.

As we left the burning house, I could hear sirens in the distance. I broke the mare into a gentle lope as we rode across the pasture. Police cars and one ineffectual fire truck drove past us on the way to our ranch road. The truck could at least put out the fire at our house, and I stopped to see if they would. All of them drove past the burning adobe house, their eyes on the huge smoke column in front of them.

I patted the horse's neck. "It figures."

Touching her sides with my boot heels, we loped towards the fence in the distance. I didn't need to worry about a gate. My Great-Grandad's old wire cutter that I carried on the saddle was quite capable of making a new one.

What Happened in Van Horn

I almost made it past Van Horn. The cops were all occupied at the burning plant, and too busy to take time to notice a lone horseback rider trying to get to Mexico.

The *chotas*. I'd forgotten about *la migra*. They were waiting west of Van Horn just like they always did. I was so busy looking over my shoulder to see if I was being followed I didn't notice my mare's ears flicking at something ahead until it was too late.

"*¿Tienes paples?*" A small but intense man with a gun drawn stepped from behind a bush.

I shook my head. He talked into a hand-held radio, watching me as I sat on the saddle watching him. Soon, a light green jeep arrived and I was placed in back. They took me to the old Border Patrol checkpoint outside Van Horn. It still looked the same, but the pens were bigger, the crowds of immigrants larger. I mingled with the crowd inside the holding pen hoping the bus would arrive to take me to Juarez and safety.

The Van Horn policy and the Texas Highway Patrol got there first. They examined the mare and found the wirecutters.

"These belonged to McBride, all right," said one cop handing them to a tall, lean Highway patrolman. He turned and looked at all of us in the pen.

"Where is he?" he asked the Border Patrolman who brought me in.

In no time flat, I sat in the small conference room in the low ranch-style Culberson County courthouse as a Jimmy Goode lookalike squinted hard at me and asked me in Spanish if I knew anything about the fire out there on Eberhard land.

"No."

"You came from that direction, riding a horse shortly after the incident occurred. What interests us is who you are and what you were doing out there."

His eyes narrowed. "Have I ever run you in for anything, getting drunk on Saturday, speeding, anything like that? What is your name?

"Juan Bizcocho, boss. I don't have no papers, but Mr. McBride hired me to work at his ranch."

"A wetback, huh? What did he pay you with?" The sheriff leaned closer.

"I'd only been there a week," I answered.

A deputy walked in and handed him a sheet of paper. He looked from paper to the deputy.

"Are you sure?"

The deputy nodded.

"Three men? In Hide's Cadillac? Doesn't make sense."

He looked back at me. "And we got this piece of the puzzle that fell off the game board. Hell, he might be a terrorist."

I stared at the dirty carpet in the room and kept silent. I was terrified, but no terrorist.

The sheriff's voice grew quiet and deadly. "Stand up, Bizcocho, let me have a good look at you. You speak English?"

I shook my head.

"Turn around and face the wall," he said in English. When I didn't move, he repeated the command in Spanish.

After turning, I studied the wall in front of me for the longest time, trying to ignore the silence behind me.

There was a sound of a slowly unholstering pistol.

"Now, Bizcocho," he said in English, "I'm going to shoot you if you don't turn around."

The sweat formed on my forehead. I studied the wall harder.

The hammer on the pistol made a clicking sound as it locked into the firing position.

"Sir, you're not really going to shoot him, are you?" The deputy sounded scared.

Not half as scared as I was.

"Prisoners try to escape all the time," said the sheriff in English.

I closed my eyes, feeling him take aim at my back. I heard the door open. The sheriff said, "Can't you see I'm busy with a prisoner?"

A voice said, "It's Mrs. Taylor. She's outside wanting to know about Hide."

"Tell her to check with the fire department. We haven't any confirmation yet. We don't know if Hide's in that Cadillac or not. No, wait a minute, I've got an idea. Tell her to come in here."

I started to turn.

"Stay facing the wall, Bizcocho," he said in Spanish, and I turned back to the wall.

I could hear him holster his pistol, but I was sweating even more. Why would he want this Taylor woman? There was a beetle crawling on the floor along the wall. At the moment it was enjoying a lot more freedom than I was.

"What word do you have about Dad?" Her voice was deeper than I remembered.

"We got somebody here that might have had something to do with all this mess. Maybe you can identify him. Is the Senator with you?"

"No. He's flying in to El Paso from Washington tonight. You think this man had something to do with my father's car?"

The sheriff stepped near me. "Turn around, Bizcocho, or whoever you are."

Slowly I turned to face Sarah. They say the first time you fall in love, it's with that person. After that, you just fall in love with the feeling of falling in love. That was the difference between how I felt about Sofia and my feelings for the woman in front of me. Sarah was more beautiful than I remembered. There was so much of her mother's beauty radiating from her, I could feel the shock upsetting my balance.

We stared into each other's eyes, and I saw the color slowly drain from her face. It was obvious that her life included expensive buying trips to large cities. Apparently, a lot of crap can buy a lot of clothes.

Her hair curled over one eye and spiraled downward in gentle twists along her neck. She placed well-manicured fingers over her heart, and I wondered if it was just good acting, or if she too was feeling something from long ago. I tried to brush the dirt off my shirt, but immediately stopped, because the gesture was so foolish.

"Well?" The sheriff's voice sounded far away. "Do you know him?"

A tear glistened at the corner of her eye, but her voice never quavered or broke. Breeding always shows under pressure.

"He's a Mexican that quit Dad and went to work for the McBrides. He didn't have any papers, so he's not going to tell you much. About every three months or so, the Border Patrol comes and gets him and takes him back to Juarez. Somehow, he always manages to come back."

She turned and looked at the sheriff. "He's harmless. Let him go."

She looked back at me and smiled, and, once again, we were children looking into a canyon, learning the secrets of the desert.

"I'm sure about his identity, sheriff. If you could wait a moment outside, maybe he will tell me if he knows anything about Daddy."

The sheriff hesitated. "You sure you'll be okay?"

"I'm sure." They left the room.

"Hide is dead," I told her. It was all I had to give her.

Her hand touched mine. "My father never loved anything but money and his reputation. Ever since Jose's death, I've hated him every moment of my life. Once, I said if you saved that antelope, I would love you forever. I never forgot my promise."

I looked at the manicured nails and the soft hands. Lifting my eyes to hers, I looked deep within, trying to find the time machine that could take us back. Placing a finger on my lips, she bent forward and whispered, "Go find happiness for both our sakes, Johnny."

She turned quickly and walked out the door. I followed her with my eyes until she turned the corner and left my life forever.

"Good-bye, Sarah," I whispered.

I wished her and Senator Taylor all the happiness in the world.

"Get him some coffee or something," said the sheriff, coming back in with his deputy. "Get his fingerprints, and keep him here until we've got the okay to release him to the Border Patrol. They'll be here sometime later tonight."

"What about the horse?" I asked in Spanish.

The sheriff stopped at the door. "What about it?"

"He belongs to Senora Taylor."

"Hell, she's already left. Where is the horse, anyway?"

"It's tied to one of the patrol cars out back," said one of the deputies.

The sheriff nodded towards me. "I'll try to catch her before she leaves town. See that the animal gets some water. He rode it awfully hard."

After getting my fingerprints, the deputy shut the door and went off to see about the horse. For the first time I was alone. How was I going to get back to Mexico? If my fingerprints came back before the Border Patrol arrived, there would be a whole new set of problems to deal with.

Like where I had been for the past twenty years?

Like why wasn't I dead?

Like what was I doing back in the United States?

A fireman stuck his head in the door. "Excuse me. I thought the sheriff was in here."

It was crazy, but it was the only chance I had.

"He was a minute ago," I said in English, "but I don't know where he went. You been fighting that fire I heard about?"

He frowned at me. "Hell of a fire. Those guys did a job ruining that factory. It's going to be a while before it reopens."

He walked on in and laid his firecoat, still wet, on the chair.

"Better watch that," I said, picking the coat back up, "you know how cops like to keep their furniture clean. Say, this thing is heavy."

"Heavy enough to keep your clothes from burning off fighting fires like we did today."

"Mind if I try it on? Always wanted to see how these things work."

"Sure. You from around here?"

I smiled back. "No, Jeff Davis county. Cowboy a little over there. Say, you didn't happen to see my horse outside, did you? Damn thing was stolen by some Meskin. Sheriff here called me to say he'd found it near Van Horn and was bringing it in."

"Yeah! Parked right next to it. Some copy was havin' a hell of a time trying to give him water from a hose. I told him you couldn't give a horse water that way. C'mon with me. Show you where it is."

And just like that I walked out of the courthouse, raincoat and all. Of course, I kept the fireman between me and the few police officers standing around the station. To them, two volunteer firemen were leaving the building, looking for the sheriff. It was early evening.

The horse was nervous and dripping water. I spoke to her and calmed her down. The fireman watched me.

"That's her all right. Here's your coat back."

"Do me a favor, will you? Tell the sheriff to call the fire house. We got three bodies coming in for him. They're pretty burnt, but we're pretty sure who they are. I need to be there when they come in."

"You go on. I'll tell him."

"Thanks. Glad you got the horse back. Just can't trust Meskins. Sneaky as hell, ya know."

"Yeah, I know."

I led the mare quietly away from the Van Horn courthouse. It still wasn't too unusual to see a saddled horse being led by an old cowboy around Van Horn. Thinking about it made me smile. Van Horn was probably the last place in Texas where it wouldn't be unusual. The little town was that far behind.

The town's lights shone behind me as I found a large arroyo to lead my pony down inside. It ran south as all arroyos do, emptying eventually into the Rio Grande if the hungry earth didn't absorb the water first. When I was far enough away from town, I swung into the saddle, topped out of the arroyo and rode towards the Eagle Mountains. There was a canyon there where the horse and I could hide from any Border Patrol airplanes during the day. The land was too harsh for even a jeep to follow, just the human spirit.

Leaving the horse tied to a century plant in the dark, I climbed towards the ledge where Jose had shared a secret with me. I would wait until morning to see if everything was okay. It was dangerous enough climbing around in the Eagles in the middle of the night. It was downright foolish to stick a hand into a crevice looking for a saddle or big bottle with a floating head. Finding a ledge, not sure if it was the right one or not in the dark, I stretched out and soon fell asleep dreaming of two kids playing in an old *tinaja*.

The sound of thunder shook me awake the next morning. For a moment, my heart in my throat, I thought someone was shooting at me. Then, I saw the thunderhead sweeping with the rain beneath it across the valley towards the still-smoking plant, cleansing everything before it. A cool wind blew up the canyon to where I sat. The pink and light hues at the top of the thunderhead reflected the morning light, the cloud darker and more ominous the closer it got to earth. I strained to see my old ranch house but, as usual, it was covered with swirling dust from the approaching storm.

I thought of my life. I turned and looked in the crevice. There was a leather saddle, weather-worn from the years of being exposed to the elements of nature, storms like the one across the valley. Jose's face was in that saddle. There was even a small scruffy reflection of all the McBrides. Surprisingly, the bottle was still there, too. The angry head of Doroteo still looked northward.

I brought the tequila bottle out from the crevice and blew the dust off its cap.

Breakfast.

As I sipped the bitter, burning liquid, watching the storm in full fury and sound in front of me, I thought about the blows nature struck time and again against the earth. I thought about man's feeble attempt to control and manipulate the land and others, all in a futile gesture trying to make sense of something too large to understand.

War, Hide's ranch, murder, love, betrayal: all just words trying to drown out the laughter from the million-year-old mountains looking down on the fools.

The Apaches and Jose had it right.

Hide just didn't pay attention.

The little mare scratched the ground impatiently down below me. I put the bottle back in the crevice and walked down to her. She would be hungry by now, and I needed to find her some grass before evening came again. We had a long way to ride.

The morning sun shone brightly on the century plant where I had tied the mare the night before. I had never seen such beautiful flowers. The plant blooms, according to legend, once every hundred year years. Feeling incredibly lucky, I stared at the white cluster of flowers at the top of the stalk, a desert magnolia standing in stark beautiful defiance to the dry, brown desert floor which waited for the inevitable fall of the flower's petals.

Can any of us do any better than that?

Adios.

Made in the USA
Monee, IL
16 July 2022